He gave her a quick kiss before gently sliding her shirt over her head. An intimate glow of pleasure warmed her, sending a flush that began between her breasts and rose high along the dusky column of her throat. AJ's fingered her cheek. She closed her eyes, savoring his touch.

He kissed her once more, teasing her, pulling away before she wanted him to, and the spiked flush of cinnamon surged through her veins again. Marlea pulled back the shower curtain and stepped inside. "Are you coming with me or do I have to do this alone?"

AJ's eyes lingered longingly on the lushness of her naked flesh beneath the silvery fall of water. "No sooner said than done." His voice was husky, but his movements were sure as he swiftly stripped away his shirt and shorts to join her.

Bracing his hands on the shower wall above her, he shared the fall of water. Turning slowly, Marlea let warmly persistent water drum along the curve of her spine. When his hands moved over her naked back, the shiver of unrelieved anticipation left her blinking.

Behind the embroidered curtain of the shower enclosure, warm water and scented soap stroked the smooth silk of Marlea's skin, bringing her against AJ's rougher maleness. His gasp at the exquisitely tender sense of her hand against the tight flatness of his male nipples touched her with more anticipation. Marlea knew she would never regret what she was committed to giving.

DREAM RUNNER

GAIL McFARLAND

Genesis Press, Inc.

INDIGO

An imprint of Genesis Press, Inc.
Publishing Company

Genesis Press, Inc.
P.O. Box 101
Columbus, MS 39703

Copyright © 2008 by Gail McFarland

ISBN: 13 DIGIT : 978-1-58571-317-2
ISBN: 10 DIGIT : 1-58571-317-1
Manufactured in the United States of America

First Edition

Visit us at www.genesis-press.com
or call at 1-888-Indigo-1-4-0

DEDICATION

For my Mother, who loved me always,
For my Father who loves me because I am his,
For all Tarblooders, past and present,
For my extended family who always knew this was
    coming,
And for the friends who love and stand with me when
    there is no one else.
I love you all.
Thank you for all you've given me.

Seduce my mind and you can have my body,
Find my soul and I'm yours forever.

~Anonymous~

PROLOGUE

Los Angeles, 1984

Marlea Kellogg was eight going on nine years old the sunny afternoon she and her mother climbed off the cross-town bus to stand outside the Olympic Stadium in Los Angeles.

Cyndra Kellogg had already explained why they wouldn't be going in—tickets cost too much for a single mother raising two growing kids in Watts, *and I could be puttin' that money into shoes* . . . But standing outside was free. A kid should be able to dream, and just the idea of being close . . . so close to the best athletes in the world was exciting for both of them. Cyndra held onto the damp hand Marlea slipped beneath her palm.

Marlea was fairly dancing, and hadn't been able to keep still since she had talked Cyndra into bringing her here. "This is the Olympic Stadium," the girl breathed. "Valerie Brisco-Hooks is going to be in there. So is Evelyn Ashford. You know she can run the hundred in under eleven seconds? That girl is for sure fast."

"Fast," Cyndra agreed, trying to remember a time when she got that excited over anything. How many life-times ago was that?

"Yeah, fast," Marlea echoed, bouncing from foot to foot, watching people with tickets heading for the stadium. "I wish we could go, but I know . . ." Twisting to watch the lucky ticketed ones line up for entry, she sighed a little. "You know, tonight is just the opening ceremony, but later on, when they get ready to run . . . watch out! That lady from Jamaica? The one they've been talking about so much, Merlene Ottey-Page? Humph! They say she's so fast, but she ain't gonna see nothin' but dust when my team takes the track."

An' she oughta know, Cyndra thought. Marlea collected sports magazines and cut up the sports pages for her scrapbook the way other young girls collected fashion magazines and make-up tips. The girl was in love with the track and field women, called them 'fly sisters,' but loved them because they had goals and did so much more than just look good. With their strong bodies, fast feet, and focused eyes, they were different from the few singers and actresses that she had pinned to her bedroom walls— different even from Janet Jackson. These runners were the young sisters who defined womanhood for Marlea. They were about more than just rump shakin' and glamorous clothes. Janet Jackson, Natalie Cole, Whitney Houston? Marlea would tell you right fast, none of them could compete in a run for the gold.

"One day, I will, though," Marlea was always quick to promise herself, and anybody else who would listen. "One day."

Determined little thing, Cyndra noted, looking sideways at Marlea. She was a tall and slender young woman-in-training. *Almost nine and already dang near as tall as me. No hips or butt to speak of, though. Thank goodness.*

She's a good girl, but I don't know what I'd do if she was like one of those fast little womanish things down the block from us. Or like her mother . . .

Cyndra refused to let the thought go any further. She had already spent years banning such thoughts from her mind: down that road lay bitter tears and madness. Down that road lay the story of a pretty baby sister and a charismatic wild man. It was the story of a man who had enough music in him to make a good girl turn away from a grandmother's powerful teachings. A man who had enough will to knock up a pretty girl, but not enough to stay out of petty card games that he couldn't win. Cyndra sighed, and tried not to remember, but she did. She remembered honey-skinned Marlon Carlyle with his curly eyelashes and sweet Cupid's bow lips; too good-looking, and no good for any woman around him. Certainly, he was no good for Leah, never married her, but Leah swore she would die without him. As it was, Leah died because of him.

An' she left me Marlea for my own, made me a mother even as my own son was being born. Not that it mattered; Cyndra loved her niece every bit as much as she did her own son, Joshua. She called Marlea her daughter for the girl's entire life, and she meant it every time. When she bought shoes or toys for Josh, she bought them for Marlea, too. A single parent, Cyndra never made a difference between the two children. She couldn't.

I look in Marlea's face and see my sister. She's the spittin' image of her mother, with those big ol' sparkly eyes and dimples. Thank God, she hasn't got her mother's ways. A boy don't mean nothin' to her. All she wants to do is run and run, and run faster still. Thankful for the child's tomboy bent, Cyndra enjoyed the sight of the coltish legs revealed by Marlea's denim shorts. Long brown legs and that need to run seemed to define the girl's body and her life. *Seems like she's been runnin' from day one. Guess it's a good thing though; it keeps her out of trouble.*

Marlea slipped her arm around her mother's waist, and leaned against her shoulder. "They say American women don't take the 400, but they're wrong."

Cyndra leaned her head against the girl's, enjoying the closeness. "Who is 'they'?"

"'They' is people who don't know me . . . And if I keep on runnin', keep on trainin', then Coach says I can do anything, go anywhere." Marlea looked at her mother, eyes wide with the innocence of youth. "An' I can show them that American women really can run the 400. Maybe I could start with a PAC10 school in college. You think I could maybe get a scholarship? For running? Maybe go to college?"

"College? I never thought about college." *I guess I was too busy tryin' to feed y'all.* "What would you study in college, Marlea?"

"I would be a teacher, maybe work with the special kids. You know, the ones who don't always get enough attention. The kind of kids who need me."

"I can see you now," Cyndra smiled. "You would make a good teacher."

Marlea's eyes went across the parking lot that separated them from the stadium. "Yeah, Ma. After college, maybe the Olympics?"

"Maybe." Her mother smiled and stuffed work-roughened fingers into the pockets of her white work uniform. *Do they give girls running scholarships? I ain't never heard of one, but if they do . . .* Cyndra's breast swelled with pride. *Wouldn't that be something? Just the best thing? My Running Baby in college. Get a good education and have a real career! Would never have to worry about mopping no floors and cleanin' up other folks' nastiness. Have her own money, make her own way. No leftover, second-hand nothin' for my baby. No more.* "Maybe . . ."

"Run in the Olympics. Run. That's what I'm gonna do."

CHAPTER 1

St. Louis, Missouri:

In the "zone," Marlea Kellogg closed her eyes and let the breath settle through her body. Exhaling slowly, she counted eight beats, then sucked in another big breath and let it course through her long, lean frame. She visualized herself heading for lane four and bending to the blocks, concentrating on what it would feel like to release the power and run, to feel the slap and push of her feet against the track.

Palms flat against the cool tile wall of the field house, her eyes moved behind her closed lids, tracking, seeing herself flashing past the others. Though her feet were still, Marlea could almost feel her body crashing the finish line, and she blew out hard when she imagined the kind of exhilaration that only a win could bring.

"Yeah," she whispered, sliding her hands over her sleek head. Ponytail intact, she almost laughed out loud. "Libby was right; this mind/body thing has got me so revved up, I can outrun anything and anybody on the track."

She had proven that in the trials. Moving as though she was the only one on the track, Marlea Kellogg kicked it. She had blown past the two girls from Cal State as if they were standing still, never mind that they were from her alma mater. Marlea had done what she had to do, showing them the way it was supposed to be done. Her time on the 400-meter run was an effortless 49.75 seconds. Libby, restricted to trackside with the other coaches and trainers, had gone wild. Six years as Marlea's coach, and she had never seen her protégé come so close to a record time.

"It was a fluke," Marlea said, when Libby finally reached her side. "I've always loved the 400, and this time it just loved me back."

"Shut your mouth, girl! Be humble with somebody who doesn't know you. Honey, you ran the hell out of that track and you know it as well as I do. And you can do it again if you just get your head right."

So Marlea took another deep breath and concentrated on the sound of her heartbeat and the rush of her blood. Opening her eyes, slowly grounding herself, she knew Libby was right. This run, this race, they belonged to her, and nothing about them could be called fluke. Marlea bent into a lunge, felt the balance, shifted her legs, and knew the truth. "This is my destiny."

Raising her arms high over her head when she stood, continuing to stretch as she walked the path back to the track, Marlea struggled to keep her feet on the ground. "This time is gonna be different."

"Talking to yourself?" Libby Belcher spotted Marlea the second she stepped onto the cinder path leading to the track and pushed past other runners to get closer. "All I've got to say is, go on out there and do what you came here to do: run."

Above her head, the tinny loud speaker blared, "400-meter contestants to the staging area, please. 400-meter contestants, please." And Marlea knew it was time to move forward. She felt the edge of her red spandex top separating from her brief shorts and tugged it down. A moment of panic made her drop her hand to check for her hip number. It was there; her fingers found it right where it was supposed to be. No panic, no fear, she reminded herself. "Time to run."

Libby raised both hands in victory. "Do your thing, girl."

"No doubt," Marlea winked. It would have been a privilege to have run in the first heat, but she knew those were for elite runners, runners with higher lifetime marks, but that was okay. She had run in the second heat, and that was okay, too, because her time put her in the finals, easy. *They have to face me now. Now they have to run my race, my way.*

Eyes sweeping the stands, Marlea saw the crowd as one great blur, and loved the busy low roar it made. She heard the final call for the 400-meter run and her blood stirred. Orgasmic anticipation trembled through her, and she looked around to see if anyone had noticed. Not that it mattered; she knew with undeniable certainty what the outcome of this race would be.

Runners, take your mark . . .

Shaking off anything that had nothing to do with the run, she approached the start. Coiling her body, she folded low to fit herself into position. Pressing her heel against the block, she silently called on Jesus and dropped her head.

Get set . . .

Breathe . . . find the rhythm.

. . . go!

The sound of the gunshot was almost a cliché, but Marlea was more than ready for it as her body broke free. Long legs working with hydraulic precision, her feet found their flawless path. Never good at shorter distances, Marlea had no time to worry about it. Knowing that she had enough distance to build, she felt the speed pump through her muscled thighs as she passed someone at 100 meters. Passing the fast-talking Jamaican woman at 200 meters, all Marlea could hear was her own breathing. Rising on the wind, flying the only way a woman can without wings, she barely saw the competition, scarcely felt the break of the ribbon across her chest, and almost cried when she realized her 400-meter dance was done.

Her feet, trained for more years than she could count, continued to run, carrying her another 25 meters before the adrenaline began a slow ebb through her hot-fired body. Her breath pulled tight through her nose and rushed out past her open lips. Her mouth was dry and her lips parched, but her legs felt like she could run for an eternity. As it turned out, that wasn't necessary.

"You did it! You did it!" Libby Belcher screamed, running toward Marlea. Six years together and every win still made the trainer spastic. Libby's short, dark hair stood on end, and her arms flailed the air in delight as she ran toward the fence separating the stands from the track.

Marlea, high on adrenaline, couldn't hear Libby. The sound of the crowd and the slap of her slowing feet filled her ears. Breast rising fast, eyes on the time clock, she feared the seconds might not be enough, might not buy the dream she had wanted for so very long. What was taking them so long to . . .

In lane four . . . Marlea Kellogg . . .

Her knees turned buttery, and her head ached with the effort of trying to hear.

. . . track record . . . time of . . .

"What time?"

. . . 48:52 . . .

"You made it!" The Jamaican runner slapped her back, and Marlea remembered to breathe. Libby finally made it to Marlea's side just as the roar of the crowd confirmed what the runner cherished with her own eyes as her time was posted.

"I qualify," Marlea whispered. "Team trials, and then the Olympics. I qualify." Her eyes closed on the tears she had promised herself she would never shed. She had made that promise back when the "cute" girls teased her for racing boys, and foolishly beating them. And she had promised the tears would never fall back when her back and legs were sore from pounding out the miles, and she still had to make it in to her job at McDonald's, a job that she had to keep to pay for her running shoes.

"I qualify." *I'm finally good enough*, she didn't say, not daring to give voice to the hope that dared to creep around the disappointment she had learned to live with back when she was beaten out of a spot on the 1996 team in Barcelona. Gwen Torrance had blown by her like a force of nature. Marlea had bitten down hard on the hurt back in 2000 when she shortened her distance to 100 meters. The shorter run was nothing like her beloved 400, and all she ever saw of glorious Gail Devers was the back of the girl's head hurdling toward 100 meter glory—and she missed the U.S. team again.

After failing to make the team in Sacramento, she had watched Marion Jones's bright smile televised live from Australia and tried to smile back. Swallowing the bitter taste of ashes, she ignored Jones's flashy speed suit and accumulated medals from 2004. Knowing it was time to get on with her life, Marlea told herself that running didn't matter, but her heart had been promised Olympic gold, and her soul wouldn't rest without it.

When Libby and Hal Belcher decided to move to Atlanta to be close to aging parents, Marlea packed up her special ed degree and followed, as there was nothing left to hold her in Los Angeles. Not a bad move, all things considered. She settled in Marietta, just north of the city, and found a place on the staff of the Runyon Day School. Small and private, Runyon gave her a chance to work with the children she loved, and time to run.

At Runyon, Marlea met the kind of children she longed to teach. Diagnosed autistic, dyslexic, troubled, and otherwise learning disabled, they were children of wealth, privilege, and circumstance. They came from old aristocratic and new money families, and they were of diverse racial backgrounds. But they shared one thing: they all loved their teacher. In part, that love might have come from the fact that she expected the best from each of them and went out of her way to draw out their best efforts.

Her kids were especially proud of her running. There had never been a teacher quite like Marlea at Runyon. Her students thought she was a superhero, kind of like Wonder Woman or something. In each of her races, she had worn something they made for her, and she had won every time. Those gifts were the closest things to good luck charms Marlea Kellogg had ever owned. Today, she wore a band of bright braided thread around her right ankle, a gift from the kids.

And now she had a special gift for them. "I qualify," she said again, just loving the sound of the words.

"Not quite," her coach said. "You're only a couple of points short. A good local race and you're in. This is your year, babe. There's no denying you. Just hit a solid 10K, pick up the points you need, and you're good to go."

"The Peachtree," Marlea said without hesitation. She had already spent a lot of her off time working with her kids and their families on 2, 5, and 10K runs during the school year. Her children, labeled and sometimes limited by their learning disabilities, loved to run. And having them run with her sometimes gave her an advantage in the classroom. A 10K was a longer distance than she preferred to run, but Marlea knew it was absolutely doable.

"If I gotta run one more, then that's a good one." She stopped there. No need telling Libby that she would run through hell in gasoline drawers if it would help get that Olympic gold. One final race to run to qualify for the

Olympic Trials and it's the Peachtree Road Race—a piece of cake. Fourth of July in Atlanta would be one hot piece of cake.

~~~

Wind sprints were the most irritating thing in the world but . . . if they kept a brother fast enough to stay in the NFL, then he would run wind sprints until he couldn't move. A running back, AJ Yarborough knew he had outlasted a lot of the best, but he also knew that a knee, blown two years earlier, still took some pampering.

"I take care of you, and you take care of me," he bargained with his right knee. "It takes two, you know." The knee didn't make an audible reply, but AJ felt it twinge, and slowed to a jog. "No need overdoin' it," he cautioned himself. Four months out of surgery and a contract up for review—this was no time to jam up your knee, especially with new kids out there every year making it harder and harder to compete, particularly when you looked at players like LaDainian Tomlinson, Larry Johnson, and Shaun Alexander.

"The new guys are all so damned young, and not in a refreshing way like the guys who came along with me." True enough, most of those who started with him were done; except for the rare ones like Ahman Green or Warrick Dunn, most of them were retired warhorses. But these young ones, they were fire-eaters. The boys weren't just young and fast, they were smart, and learning more every time out. They were the competition, the contenders.

They were the future.

The future. "Humph, that used to sound like, 'once upon a time' to me. Now it sounds like a deadline." Truth be told, coming back from injury, it sounded like the end of a lifelong passion. At thirty-four, AJ knew the career wouldn't last forever—but that didn't stop him from wishing and hoping for the best. So he ran harder. Liking the solid sound of his feet against the road, he sniffed cool air and ignored the tiny electrical jolt in his knee. "Doc said I'd feel a little somethin' there," he recalled. "Least I know that my knee is working now."

The click in his knee paced his run and made him analyze his whole body. Taking inventory as he ran, he was pretty sure that everything seemed to work right, but he could practically *hear* his knee. The surgical reminder sounded almost mechanical to AJ's ear. "A machine," he complimented himself, looking for the silver lining and enjoying the free flow of his healthy body as he ran. "This man is a machine."

Following the rolling hills of his southwest Atlanta property, that was easy enough to say, but he sure hadn't felt like a machine during that last game. That was the one where he had been close enough to taste the rushing record. Instead, he had taken the hit—a hard one, right at the knees. It sent him airborne and he had to be helped from the field in anguish.

Still running, he heard the steps of another runner. The pace had a distinctive rhythm, one foot slightly lagging. A hard-breathing man from the sound of it, probably his on-again, off-again house guest. He turned to see who it was. Sure enough, Dench Traylor slugged along, steadily pickin' 'em up and puttin' 'em down. Struggling, the man pulled even with AJ when the bigger man slowed to accommodate him. Puffing, he put out a hand, entreating.

AJ was surprised. Dench had always hated running and he had never made any secret of his dislike for recreational running—not even during their days of scholarship-enforced athletics. Traylor, now a Miami assistant special-team coach, wasn't in bad shape, just not NFL prime. "You running today?"

"Tryin'," Dench puffed.

The player slowed, then stopped. "You might as well know it now, Rissa's not out here with me," he teased. Marissa Yarborough was about the only person in the world that Dench would willingly run behind.

"This is not about your sister, man."

AJ grinned when Dench stopped and sucked wind. AJ circled him, letting his cooling muscles wind themselves down. Dench Traylor shook his lowered head and held out a white envelope. "Whatcha got?" AJ grinned, slitting the envelope's flap with a long thick finger.

"Read it."

Pulling the typewritten sheet from the envelope, AJ was confused by the stiff formal paper. Didn't that make whatever was written official? The letterhead sheet featured his team logo, and for a blank half second, he wondered why anyone from the Miami-based team would be sending him mail. Baffled, he shook the letter completely open and read it. He had to read it twice to make sure of the contents. "They're letting me go? Just like that?" He read it again. "Just like that?"

"Dude," Dench said.

"What's that supposed to mean?" AJ was hard pressed to know whether it was a comment or a criticism. He crushed the letter in his meaty hand and glared at the assistant coach.

Finally able to breathe, Dench stood straighter and stared at the ground. "I thought you ought to know," he said.

Ought to know that his career was over? Know that his numbers were as high as they were ever going to go? That he would never earn a Super Bowl ring to call his own?

Eyes on the sky, it took AJ long seconds to reply. "Yeah, but I thought that when it got to be this time . . ." *What? They would throw me some kind of special big hints? An "over the hill" party? What?* That last play of his last game unwound itself in his head again. The memory was so vivid, he almost felt the searing rip hack its way through his knee when he went down. He could hear the muted voices, as if they thought he couldn't hear . . .

He's had a long run . . .
Could be career ending . . .
More than a setback . . .
What if this time . . .

What could anybody say that would make it any easier? He could go back to his agent, get her to find another team. That was the beauty of hiring your kid sister as your agent. She could ask for some kind of waiver that would give him . . . *a Super Bowl ring? That rushing record I've run my whole life for? Or maybe I should just shut my eyes on the game, the only thing in life that has truly given me pleasure, and move on. Suck it up.*

"I didn't want this to come as any more of a shock than it already is. They won't make the announcement for another couple of weeks, but I wanted you to be ready when it came out." Dench watched AJ circle him, and knew the thoughts that must be running through his mind. He had come so close over the years. Been traded twice, always up, but traded all the same. Every team promised but none fully delivered. AJ was always left hungry.

"I always knew this wouldn't last forever . . ." Even as he said it, AJ couldn't stop himself. A lot of what he thought tended to spill from his lips. It was a bad habit, talking to himself, but it was one he had never been quite able to shake.

Dench crossed his arms over his solid barrel of a chest. "We've been together a long time, man. I know the hurt you're feelin', but this doesn't have to be the end. You've still got power. You can still run."

"An' I'm a thirty-four year old runner in a game played like war by twenty-two year olds. Lasting 'til you reach thirty is a good stretch for a runner. The irony is not lost on me."

"But it's not the only thing you know. You've got other things going for you," Dench suggested. Antoine Jacob Yarborough Jr. was a smart man, smart in a lot of ways. Not a lot of the men gifted enough to play in the

NFL had his kind of savvy—even if he did talk to himself. AJ might truly hate his given name, but he was smart enough to have finished the education degree as he had promised his folks. He had gone on to complete the master's degree that got him into physical therapy school during the off-seasons. It's not like he'll ever be hurtin' for money, his friend thought, realizing where the real pain would always come from.

"So, ah, AJ? You got any plans?"

"Not yet," the now ex-player said, pacing. "Maybe I'll go ahead and set up a PT practice on my own. The Lord knows I'll sure have time for it now." Stopping midstep, he looked back the way he had come, then turned and stared out at the road ahead of him. His eyes narrowed, and he wiped his big hands against his sweatpants. "Besides that, I don't know, but I gotta go forward. Got to."

"How you gonna do that, AJ?"

The player began a steady jog up the road. "Only way I know how." He picked up speed, forcing the other man to run harder. "I'm gonna run."

CHAPTER 2

July 4th, Peachtree Road Race

Standing in the middle of Peachtree Street, Marlea glanced over at the Westin Hotel, then back over her shoulder. For as far as she could see, past the stretch of Lenox Mall and down the hill, there were wall-to-wall people, six lanes of die-hard runners decked out in holiday-themed running gear. Lots of red, white, and blue, with more than a sprinkling of Uncle Sam or Lady Liberty outfits. *Good thing the weather's cool this morning,* she thought, watching the runners line up around and mostly behind her.

Spectators had been stopped and rerouted a mile back. From where Marlea stood, she could see the seeded runners, those with highly competitive amateur time records in the time group behind hers. *You'll be in the first group,* Libby had fussed. *Even though you're running with the elite runners, I don't want you taking any chances. Don't push any harder than you have to, a six-minute mile is good enough to get you in—anything else is gravy.*

Libby's words were like music to her ears, and Marlea's face changed, lit by her inner smile. *Elite runner, that's what they call the people this far up in the crowd. That's what I am, and though this race is outside my usual class, I'm going to prove it.* Libby caught the smile. *Just don't get hurt out there, you don't have to prove anything. And keep your feet dry,* she had added as an afterthought.

"Right, right, right," Marlea had agreed to get the trainer to move on. "Everything's going to be great. I'll see you in the park."

Not convinced, Libby reached for Marlea's race number and flipped it over. "You didn't fill it in. You left all the emergency information blank. What were you thinking?"

"That I'm a healthy, capable adult?"

"Here." Libby pushed a black ink pen into Marlea's hand. "I don't believe you, 55,000 people out there, and you want to take a chance like that . . ." The coach's voice was as dry as her expression. "Be sure to put my name and home and cellphone numbers on there. Just in case . . . just in case."

"Just in case," Marlea mimicked, dutifully writing. Finished, she accepted safety pins from Libby and pinned the number to her shirt. "Satisfied?"

"Very." Libby sucked water from the bottle draped over her shoulder, and looked around. "This is a sharp group," she noted, watching the runners headed for the starting lineup. "I think I know him from the Colorado training center," she said, pointing, then waving, at a tall blonde runner who noticed her and waved back.

"I want you to go out there and do what you came to do, Marlea, but have some fun, too. Don't think of this as work."

"Running is never work for me, but don't you need to head for the train if you're going to make it back to Piedmont Park in time to catch my finish?"

"Oh, you're going to run that fast?" Libby raised a brow and tipped her head when Marlea stopped and crossed her arms. "I'm just saying. You might meet somebody nice during the run—if you let yourself. Somebody you might want to get to know better. It happens."

"It happens," Libby repeated.

Sure, it could happen—in my dreams, Marlea thought, ignoring the smile from the lean, dark man wearing number seven as she bent to stretch her hamstrings. He offered a brief two-fingered salute, but she pretended not to see. She heard Libby's voice again.

"Here I am ignoring him—as if he's about to ask me for a date or something." And if he did, then what? Marlea shook her head and changed legs, knowing she would laugh the invitation off. Not because he wasn't handsome, because he was; and certainly not because he wouldn't be able to understand her physical discipline, because his number seven said he himself was disciplined.

Olympic gold and men don't mix. Marlea still had a laugh from time to time when she remembered the first time that she had heard that line, though her mother had been talking about a boy and not a grown man. It had been years ago, while she was still in high school. A thoroughly pissed-off Cyndra caught Marlea kissing an excited and happily adventurous Robert Jennings in the back hallway of the old house on Grand. Both teens had been thoroughly embarrassed. Robert got sent home and threatened with a report to his parents. Sixteen-year old Marlea's suffering hadn't been nearly so brief.

A boy can experiment in a lot of ways a girl can't, Cyndra had lectured, shaking a stern finger under the girl's nose. *A boy having sex will never get pregnant. It's always a girl's baby and a boy's maybe. You are not a boy, and you are going to have to make them respect you, in every way, if you want anything out of this life. So let me tell you something, little girl. You go on experimentin', an' if you bring home a baby, girl, you are going to have to raise it. Your runnin' days will be over for the next eighteen years. Eighteen years. Do you hear me? Eighteen years!*

Loud and clear, Marlea recalled. *Relationships are never easy, and everybody isn't blessed to fall in love with a Bob Kersee. What I want takes sacrifice, and I know it. World-class runners have to make a plan and then stick to it, and that's what I've done. I get gold, then I'll get a man.* She looked around at the two Kenyan women stretching on either side of her. They looked as determined as she felt.

Loudspeakers blared, and runners shifted like cattle at the start of a roundup when volunteers toting flags and barriers moved her group forward. Marlea moved, too, stopping where the line held across the street. Funny how the start of almost any race set her pulse pounding. She closed her eyes and visualized the finish line, saw herself crossing the line ahead of the pack. And then the gun sounded.

AJ Yarborough felt more than saw the start of the Peachtree Road Race. Swept along by the wave of runners, his run began with shambling steps, almost a hobble. Morning air, cool for Atlanta, took on a sudden humidity, almost as though it resented being moved by so many bodies. In the distance, behind him, he could hear a steadily growing roar of other runners.

Local TV and radio stations were out in force. A reporter, complete with remote microphone, jogged at the edge of the crowd. Runners, intent on getting to Piedmont Park and that coveted tee shirt, smiled and stepped around the reporter. AJ pulled his Braves cap lower over his eyes and headed for the center of the street. "No need getting noticed and winding up in a conversation I don't want to have."

Still not ready to discuss his release from the team, he wasn't sure of what he might say if asked about it. "Besides," he muttered, "football was good to me, and this ain't the place to share that." Enjoying the light jog, he kept his head low as the crowd pace picked up. He could afford to start out slow, knowing that he had a little over six miles to pick it up.

Overhead, a pair of Black Hawk helicopters maneuvered in salute to the racers, and a small airplane pulled an Atlanta Braves banner across white clouds in a china blue sky. It was immeasurably different from every other kind of race he had ever run. "Like being out for a run with 50,000 of my closest friends."

The first four or five minutes of the run allowed the runners to shift and find their own places along the width of Peachtree Street, and AJ wondered how many people were behind him. "If I'm wearing number 107, wonder what number the last person in this crowd has?"

"Don't even think about it," the long-legged redhead in a cutoff 1999 Peachtree tee shirt said, winking an emerald green eye. She shook back the curling mop of shimmering hair and grinned. "I know you," she said, "you're that football player, aren't you? Yeah, you are." She jogged faster, matching AJ's steps. "I belong to the Atlanta Track Club, and nobody told me you were going to be running this year. Is this your first time with us?"

"Yeah." Uncomfortable with the attention, AJ almost wished he had taken Dench's advice and skipped the race. The baseball cap wasn't a very effective disguise when your face had been on the evening sports shows for the past week. His feet moved faster.

"You tryin' to outrun me, big fella?" The redhead's laugh was a lilting giggle. "You might want to know I hold the club record for women in this race."

"That's, uh, nice." AJ was sincerely grateful for the dark-haired woman who pushed through the crowd to intercept his self-appointed buddy. Clearly angered by the intervention, the redhead stopped running, forcing traffic to flow around her and the dark-haired woman.

The narrow escape made AJ shake his head. "Point is, if I want a woman, I want to find her. I want to just happen up on her, spend time with her, know that we share some things in common. Not just have her drop out of the sky and try to take over. That one back there, she was too aggressive for my taste. Man, and I've seen aggressive."

Bianca Coltrane came immediately to mind. "Now, that was an aggressive woman." At the start of it, Bianca wasn't all that different from the redhead. She, too, claimed legs that went all the way up to her ears and had a clear, chiming laugh. Like the redhead, Bianca was more than pretty; she was beautiful, and she knew how to make the most of it—and AJ had been more tempted by her than he had ever been by any woman before or since.

But Bianca's exotic sexual tastes and limitless wanton hungers were beyond anything AJ had anticipated, and what might have been died before it was truly born. Not that she had been less than exuberant and imaginative in her efforts. "If I tried to keep track of her tricks, I'd run out of fingers and toes for counting," AJ muttered, his thoughts riddled with her last kisses.

They had parted at a cabstand outside JFK a year ago. She was twirling her paisley silk umbrella and he was leaning on a cane. She said something about life moving on, and AJ kept hearing echoed conversations—echoes of conversations with several, now former, teammates.

AJ recalled the words, the speculation on who and what Bianca had done. Personally unwilling to think the worst, he had bowed out of a lot of the conversations, but not before he learned that she kept a list and rated men on their performances. When he had asked her about it, she had unwrapped her white silk blouse, stretched it wide, flashing him. "What would be the problem?" she had smiled.

And AJ knew it was over—if it had ever been anything more than mindless, release-driven sex. The thought that his name, among others, might be on such a list was unbearable. "And those dudes didn't seem to have any problem with it."

Breaking up with Bianca was a kind of oxymoron. To break up with someone, you kind of had to be going with her, you had to have a specifically singular relationship with that person, didn't you? And if your woman was trying to set world records as a sexual athlete, what happened to that "singular" relationship? For AJ Yarborough, the answer was nothing—not even a birthday or Christmas card.

On Peachtree Street, AJ kept running past spectators shouting encouragement and holding signs. His speed was faster, and the sun was stronger and climbing quickly. Passing a water station, he accepted a cup from a boy of about twelve and winked when the boy gave him a thumbs up. He tossed the water down in a single gulp and returned the gesture.

From the corner of his eye, he thought he saw the redhead and picked up his pace. "Chicks like that—the reason I don't do Buckhead." It was a known party district, and AJ made it a rule to give Buckhead a wide berth for anything outside of restaurants and shopping. *Don't go lookin' for trouble and you won't find it,* his father liked to say. It was one of the few things about which he agreed with Antoine Jacob Yarborough, Senior.

Funny about Bianca, though. Nothing ever came of their time together, brief as it had been, but she always had a kind of hold on him. "Maybe it was because she came along around the same time my knees started to go," he speculated. Or maybe it was because when he had looked into her oval face with its beautifully matched features, he had wondered what their children would look like. Listening to her voice, soft in conversation or husky with passion, he had wondered what her 'mommy' voice would sound like to a child with a skinned knee.

He had shared the questions with Dench and looked sheepish when he laughed. "Man," Traylor said laughing, "you sound like your biological clock is ticking. I think you just need to get laid."

"I took his advice, and it ain't workin' yet." AJ smiled when he thought of the last woman he had slept with. Dark-haired and dark-skinned, she possessed the kind of curves that could only have been carved by the hand of a gracious god. She was elegant to the point of appearing almost feline in her grace. "She was also dumb as a rock." His smile widened when he thought of the conversations the beautiful woman was at an absolute loss to follow. "Dench ain't never settin' me up again. And I told him so, too."

Dench Traylor had sat across the table in AJ's broad-windowed breakfast room and laughed the morning after, swearing that the hunt wasn't always about capture. Sometimes, he insisted, it was just about the hunt. "I'm not just about the hunt," AJ had told him. "It's sure not that I don't like women; it's that I want to fall ass over teakettle for the right one and have her be a part of my life forever."

Dench just laughed. But the thing of it was that AJ knew and believed in his heart that every woman passing through his life had left something behind. Every one of them had left him knowing just a little more of what he did and didn't want. They left him knowing just a little bit more of who he was, what kind of man he really was.

Looking down, at his feet moving along Peachtree Street, he knew that every lover in his past had been a way station to completion—a stop on the way to where he knew he was meant to be.

"That sounds damned self-involved, if I do say so myself." He cast a fleeting look over his shoulder. The carpet of running, jogging, walking humans seemed to stretch for miles behind him. "Many folks as there are out here, wouldn't it be nice to just run up on the right one?"

Peachtree Street had always seemed like a series of curves to Marlea, but the climb to mile four of the race route was known as "Cardiac Hill" and, even in training, it was a challenge. Her face tightened and her arms pumped when she heard the timer beep on the monitor she wore on her left wrist. "I slow down, and I drop my time," she reminded herself, inhaling deeply. Lifting her head, she looked past the bulk of Piedmont Hospital, fixed her eyes on a cloud, and pushed to the top of the hill.

"Don't worry," a woman screamed, waving her flag frantically, "mile four is downhill!"

Thank you, Lord! Marlea exalted and ran on.

"In and out of this city all my life and it's never felt this hot." AJ slipped the cap from his head and swiped the back of his hand across his forehead. He jammed the cap back on as he noted the peach-shaped marker for mile five. Another hill. He almost cursed. A steep half-mile climb and a sharp half-mile descent had him sweating just almost as hard as he had when he was part of the back line. It felt good.

"Almost there," a white-haired man in a Peachtree volunteer tee shirt called out, urging the racers forward. "Almost there."

Almost there, and ahead of him, the crowd of runners had thinned considerably. No more than twenty people moved to speeds and rhythms of their own determination. Chancing a glance over his shoulder, AJ saw that like those ahead of him, he had far outdistanced the pack. These frontrunners, he realized, were the ones who had set the pace for the Peachtree. These were the class of the bunch. "And I'm up here with 'em."

Not thinking, he picked up his pace and grinned at the man next to him, who struggled to stay even. Seeing challenge in the man's eye, AJ pushed a little more. When the man fell steps behind, AJ cranked it up another notch and passed two women. "Well, this ain't too shabby for a brother with a bunged-up knee." No, it wasn't too shabby for a brother who held state records in high school and national speed records in college. The speed was part of what took him to the pros—a big part. AJ sucked air, shifted his run into higher gear, and relived his glory days. Then he couldn't help himself. He went for broke. "Wouldn't it be somethin' if . . ."

Marlea could almost feel the push of time against her hot skin as she made the turn, passing a man with gritted teeth, and a woman who screamed, "Noooo!" at her back. "Been there, done that, and never again," Marlea swore, tightening her resolve and leveling her gaze on the Nike-shirted back in front of her. A tiny piece of her heart bent for the screaming woman. She recognized the agony that came with seeing a rival runner pass you without so much as a backward glance. Her monitor sounded again as her feet pounded the path through Piedmont Park. Shielded by ancient oak trees, Marlea could see the finish line. The monitor beeped again, *five seconds ahead of the mark . . .*

"Damn," AJ said, his breath low and hoarse, "this was easier than I thought." He passed another man, and sited on the woman just ahead. Her head was high, her shoulders level, her hips tight. She had a nice long stride, the rhythm setting her ponytail swinging, and she seemed determined to finish fast. Her kick was high, and AJ felt his knee twinge when he tried to match it, but he did. Drawing even with her and pushing hard, he chanced a glance, then grimaced when his knee folded beneath his weight.

What the . . . Marlea had no words for what was happening. Pain in her foot and ankle, and the sudden slide of the whole world. Gravel bit into her knees and her palms as the ground rushed toward her. Something hard and heavy and . . . *manly?* crashed into her body, flattening her on the ground. She could hear cheers, cries of "aww," and a sonorous beeping that she finally recognized as her chronometer.

The time: My time!

Dazed, Marlea shook her head at the race volunteers who rushed toward her with outstretched hands. Waving them off, digging the toes of her shoes into the gravel, Marlea nearly gained her feet when the . . . *was that a man?* moved beneath her foot. Her eyes widened when they met his, and he wrenched his big body to one knee.

Feeling trapped in time, Marlea couldn't stop the disaster she saw coming and he crashed against her shins, bringing her down again.

The chronograph still sounded against her wrist and Marlea realized she had lost all track of time. Planting her hands against the ground, pushing herself up, she finally managed to untangle her body from the man's. Stepping over him, she sprinted for the finish line, eyes searching for the time clock. Unable to find it, she circled back toward the finish line. "Time?" she asked the nearest volunteer. "Where can I find my time?"

"Over there." The volunteer waved an arm in the general direction of the official podium. Marlea ran toward the high wooden bandstand in the center of the vast green space.

"Are you all right?"

"Fine." On his feet, AJ dusted his hands against his shorts and shook his head. "See? That's how we got cut," he scolded his knees. When they didn't respond, he stood straighter and looked down at the medical volunteer staring anxiously up at him.

"I'm okay," he told the short, white-shirted man. The hand he passed over his head told him he had lost his cap somewhere in his tumble with that long-legged runner. "Wonder where it went?" he mumbled, looking at the path around him. He saw the cap, muddy and obviously beyond repair, flop beneath the feet of a running quartet. "Poor hat."

"You took quite a tumble," the volunteer insisted, his blue eyes intense and bulging behind thick prescription lenses. "Why don't you . . . Hey, I know you! You're that guy . . . the football player . . . the one on TV who . . . I swear, I been watchin' you since before you took the Heisman trophy back in '92. An' that last game against New York, when you rushed for . . . Are you sure I can't help you?"

The man raised his bushy black brows, and AJ raised a hand. "Really, I'm fine. Can you tell me which way the lady went? The lady I, uh, inadvertently tripped."

Awed, the little man grinned sloppily and hunched his shoulders. AJ left him on his own.

Crossing the finish line, AJ raised his hand to greet clapping spectators, glad that they were happy to applaud any human body finishing the run. One little guy, about six years old, ran along the sidelines giving high fives to every runner he could reach. When AJ held his palm out, the kid slapped and grinned. Something about the boy's smile with its missing teeth made him feel better. Maybe the woman would smile, too, when he found her.

Still at a slow jog, he tried to remember what she looked like, but it wasn't easy. He had a distinct impression that she was tall and pretty, long, dark hair pulled back in a ponytail. She was wearing pretty much standard running gear: a white Nike shirt and bright shorts. "And she was serious about her running."

For the first time since the race started, Marlea was having trouble breathing. Instead of her usual rhythmic exhalation, she was panting. Anxiety, she decided, fingering drops of sweat from her face. Sighting the official time station, Marlea angled her run in that direction. Somewhere in the back of her mind, she could hear

Libby's voice: *Relax. Calm down. If this is meant for you, it's yours.* All those platitudes—what the hell did Libby know, anyway?

AJ finally spotted her running across the open green field toward the time officials. "Least I can do is own up to what I did and apologize," he figured, jogging toward her. "If I'm lucky, maybe she'll let me buy her dinner to make up for it."

"Excuse me." The end of the stage was so high that Marlea had to stand on her toes to see over it. Her fingers tapped the splintered edge. "Excuse me."

"Yes, dear?" Middle-aged with weathered skin and fading blonde curls, the woman in the light green red-lettered shirt pressed her clipboard to her thighs and peered down at Marlea. "How can I help you?"

"I . . ." Marlea pressed her lips together and tried not to think of the time she had lost while tangled up with a no-name spoiler. "My name is Marlea Kellogg. I'm a runner. I'm . . . I was in . . . Is there any way to get my time? I need to know."

"Sure, honey," the woman drawled. Taking her time, she adjusted her white sun visor and shifted her clipboard to a better angle. Squinting, she traced her finger down the list of times. "Kellogg?" she asked. Marlea nodded. "Kellogg? Kellogg? Ah, here it is . . . time is 40:11."

"No," Marlea said, disbelieving. "No, not 40:11. I was on track for less than thirty minutes for the whole race." Her shoulders dropped, and she closed her eyes. "I need thirty-six or less to qualify. Can you check again? That can't be right."

The woman knelt and looked into Marlea's eyes. "You were seeded, right?" Marlea nodded. "Let me see your number." Marlea held it up and watched as the woman ran her fingers over it. "Your time registered because of the microchip. It's right here," she ran her thumb over a thin bump beneath the paper. "Unless you can prove some sort of computer malfunction, I'm afraid we're going to have to go with the time your chip registered." Her eyes touched Marlea's. "I'm sorry, Ms. Kellogg. I'm very sorry."

"Sorry," Marlea echoed, reaching for her race number. "Thank you for checking."

"Your time still puts you high in the standings."

"Thank you." Numb and not caring where her feet carried her, Marlea moved away from the stand. Wending her way between triumphant race finishers, she didn't want to hear where she had placed among the runners. She knew it wasn't first.

"Excuse me, miss; I don't know your name . . ." The man's hand was light but firm on her bare shoulder, and Marlea hesitated. "I want to apologize for what happened out there . . . I wanted to, uh, say . . ."

She turned slowly, and her mouth dropped. "What? You want my DNA now? What do you think you have to say to me that's going to make your clumsiness go away? Where the hell did you come from, anyway? You had no business hauling your big . . ."

"Whoa!" AJ held up both hands, his conciliatory smile dangling loosely from his lips. "Wait a minute. Don't you think you're overreacting?"

"To what? Your clumsiness or your stupidity?" Marlea swung her fist, narrowly missing him. "Do you even know what you just cost me? No! No, there's no way you could. I've worked all my life to get to Olympic gold, and all I needed was to finish the Peachtree, and then you and your big ol' Bozo feet come along. You had no business . . ."

"Ma'am, I'm just tryin' to be courteous here. I said I was sorry. What happened between us was an accident, pure and simple . . ."

"Simple?" she flared, stepping closer.

"Well, yes. It's actually funny, if you let yourself think of it that way. Kind of like what happened to Mary Decker and Zola Budd in the 800 meters. You remember? In the Olympics, back in . . ."

"1984. Yeah, and Mary's career is over, too!" Marlea swung again, then kicked at him when he blocked her punch.

"I really am sorry; will you let me at least offer to buy you dinner? To make up for . . ."

"What you've done to my life? No, I don't think so." Marlea snatched her hand from the big man's grasp and turned her back to him. Her steps went from a march to a jog, to a flat-out run across the park. Running down Tenth Street, she heard and ignored the questions about the mystery design on the treasured tee shirt. She ignored calls from the people running for fun. She was too busy trying to outrun her rage.

Nearly blinded by tears, Marlea managed to find her way back to the lot where she and Libby had parked her silver Accord. Dropping to her scraped knee, Marlea snatched and pulled at her shoe, finally fumbling her car key free of her knotted shoelace. Still kneeling, she jammed the key into the door, then pulled herself upright when it opened. Falling behind the wheel, she realized she was still wearing her race number.

"Libby said I would need this in case of an accident. Well, I guess I had an accident." Without closing her eyes, Marlea could still see him—the accident. *I'll never forget him. I could pick him out of a lineup if I had to.* Caramel skin, closely barbered dark hair and a neat mustache over a nice . . . no, nothing about him was nice, the big, sweaty oaf!

Even features and broad shoulders, and feet the size of Texas! He was tall, but Marlea still wished she had connected on at least one of those swings she had thrown at him. *Probably would have broken my hand, but at least I would have had some satisfaction. As it is . . . I have nothing.*

Lips pushed together, she pictured him again. Tall, probably more than six feet, because he had towered over her five feet and eight inches, he had barreled into her, knocking her flat. He was heavy, too. Heavy, but not fat, she suddenly remembered that. When her body was tangled with his, he seemed all broad shoulders and long, strong-muscled legs.

Yeah, tangled is a good word for it. Every time I tried to free myself from him, some part of his body was pressed all up against me. Not only did he screw up my time, but I'll probably be black and blue tomorrow. Her finger poked at the scrape on her thigh. It was bleeding now, blood running down her leg, and she remembered shouting something about his taking her DNA. *Guess he got that, too,* she thought bitterly.

Her shoulders heaved, and all the hurt Marlea Kellogg had ever denied rose to the surface, and she slashed at the tears that finally fell from her eyes. Disowning the grief, she turned the key in the ignition and steered her car from the parking slot.

"I should have known better. It was going too well. Nothing is ever that easy." The car slid neatly into traffic as Marlea made the turn that would take her to the highway. Her cellphone chimed, startling her. Her eyes danced between the traffic framed in her windshield and the narrow flip phone. It was Libby; she knew it without answering or looking at the phone.

Marlea swore, her voice low, though she felt like screaming. "I don't need this. She's looking for me in the park. By now, she knows what happened, and she's going to tell me that she told me so. I swear I don't need this." Her right hand swept the phone from the car seat, sending it skittering across the floor on the passenger side. Breathing heavily, tears still sliding down her face, Marlea watched the battery snap free of the phone—no more ringing. "Good enough."

Wrenching the steering wheel, she turned off Fourteenth Street onto the entry ramp for I-75 and her apartment. "At least if I go home, I can lock my door and turn off the phone and just . . ." *Do what? Go home and forget that I've spent my whole life running and reaching for a dream I'll never realize now?* Holiday traffic was light but fast, and Marlea pressed her foot to the accelerator.

Looking for distraction, she pressed the button for her radio, letting song rise against the hum of the highway. . . . *I'll always love my mama* . . . Some old-school group named The Intruders singing some old-school song, something so old that the recording was scratchy over the airwaves. Marlea wanted nothing more than to dismiss it, but the words hit home and tore at her heart.

Marlea felt something break in her chest and knew it was her heart. *Mama.* It had to have been that one word. "I promised her." Marlea sucked back a salty tear, remembering the day she and Cyndra stood outside the stadium in LA. *I promised her, and this was my last chance to keep the promise. After this, I'll be too old to even train for the next Olympic trials.* Always coming up short, and now, knowing that there would be no other races before the August deadline, all Marlea could smell was the stench of failure.

"So what next?" Marlea slammed both hands against the steering wheel, and the Accord rocked against the asphalt. "What else can go wrong?"

CHAPTER 3

Hungover, running late, and suffering still fermenting anger, Parker Reynolds paused in the marble and gold-appointed foyer of his home. The place was palatial and had been featured in four different architectural and design magazines. The furnishings were the best his mother's pet designer could find, all carefully chosen to reflect his taste and temperament. It was his home. Pursing his lips, he narrowed his eyes and corrected himself. The place used to feel like home—until *she* came along.

"I don't know what I was thinking," he fumed, wishing for a drink and knowing that he would be calling Mark Teasley first thing tomorrow to sort the whole mess out. The problem with making that call was simply that Teasley, like any good attorney, had already warned him about her. "Parker, you've got to put some thought into the women you invite into your life."

"Pity is, hindsight is twenty-twenty," Parker muttered, debating the possible harm of going back for a bit of 'the hair of the dog.' Not really a good choice, he realized, knowing the possibility of his having to work before the day was out. Trauma surgery was problematic enough without alcohol thrumming through his veins.

"Okay, so that leaves the Bloody Mary out." Jamming a long slender hand into the pocket of his khaki slacks,

Parker found coins but no keys, and that did nothing for his disposition. "If I had known then what I know now, there is no way I would have let her into my life—or my bed, for that matter," he huffed, looking around. Turning in circles beneath the gilded chandelier was getting him nowhere, and he was already running late for rounds.

"I give up." He glanced at the shallow Wedgwood dish resting on the marble-topped commode. Still no keys. "Can't imagine where they got to." Time was growing short as he reached for the neatly secreted wall panel and keyed the intercom. "Steven, I'll need keys and the car. The Corniche, please."

"Yes, sir. Right away."

Wishing that more people in his life had Steven's capacity for obedience, Parker checked the time again. He wasn't scheduled to be on call for more than an hour, but it never paid to count on things running smoothly. He loved what he did, but he hated having to rush because the same unforeseen glitches that made the kind of life-saving, in-the-nick-of-time surgery he practiced so exciting and intellectually rewarding also made it nerve-wracking.

"God, I wish I hadn't made this change with Fortnam. He and that little wife of his have an unscheduled getaway, so I'm the elected good guy. They get beaches and I get stuck covering for him. And after the night I've had." Pushing a manicured hand through the thick, black waves of his silver-touched hair, Parker's put-upon sigh mourned his passing youth. He could remember when the broad expanse of his mocha-colored face had been tight and wrinkle-free. Now two-and-a-half deep furrows etched his brow, and a matching pair bracketed his thin-lipped mouth.

Worry has been known to cause premature aging, he thought, vainly ignoring his forty-five years. *Who am I fooling? I didn't look like this before Desireé ravaged my life.*

Crossing the foyer, Parker wished for the icy wash of a vodka Gimlet. Steven was taking his time pulling the Rolls convertible around to the door. *As he ought to*, Parker thought. Driving the car was like good sex: bold, aggressive, and satisfying. Nobody could blame Steven for being careful and enjoying the chore. While he got to drive the other cars regularly, driving the Corniche was a rare treat.

Even I don't drive it that often. Thinking about his dream car, Parker smiled, anticipating. Just hearing the engine purr and holding the keys was a kind of foreplay he would never tire of.

The Corniche was a quarter of a million dollars worth of superior engineering and perfect design. If Parker Reynolds could ever be accused of loving an object, it would be the Rolls-Royce Corniche. Thinking of the afternoon he had barely saved his car from one of Desireé's afternoon drives, the good doctor shuddered. Her drives often transported her to clubs and neighborhoods that he would never willingly venture into.

"What the hell was I thinking?" Her name and the memory of her brought a sour taste to his mouth, especially when he thought of the odd knock at his door last evening.

"I should have known better—opening the door myself." Any other time, Anne, his personal assistant, would have answered the door, but no . . .

Parker thumbed the heavy brass knob and pulled the curved handle of his front door. He stepped into the already hot simmering blue of an Atlanta summer morning. Stopping at the top of the curving red-brick stairs, he looked for Steven, exhaling noisily when he didn't see him.

Pushing at the fold in the sleeve of his oxford cloth shirt, he checked his watch and sighed again. "I pay Anne well to serve as my personal assistant, and *I* answered the door to a process server." The little man had looked more like a helper for his lawn service than like someone with legal contacts. Parker hadn't really thought much of it when the man asked his name and then shoved the large envelope into his hands.

"I always thought they had to say something, give you some kind of warning." But the little guy in the Braves cap and tee shirt had said nothing after asking if Parker was Parker. "He didn't even say 'good night.' "

Not that good manners would have made much of a difference. Retreating to the air-conditioned comfort of his home, Parker had opened the envelope and extracted the contents. Legal papers? He remembered thinking of it exactly like that: *legal papers?*

Who in the world would be sending me legal papers?

He remembered Anne calling to him from the office at the end of the foyer. Straightening the papers and reading words that only Desireé's arrogance could have conjured, Parker exploded.

"How dare she," he had thundered, bringing Anne on the run.

"Who?" Anne had asked. "*What?*"

Rage made breathing hard, and Parker felt his chest tighten. Peppering him with questions, Anne led him to a chair. He felt his hazel eyes bulge and his chest constrict, leaving him virtually immobile. He couldn't even manage to loosen his grip on the papers, and when he tried to focus on the hand-delivered documents, the palsy nearly defeated him.

Anne had pushed a glass into his hand. Parker sucked at the vodka over cracked ice, but the liquor failed to anesthetize the jolt he had suffered. It was bad enough to have spent all that time arguing with Desireé over what she saw as her due: then she got it into her head that she was owed palimony.

"She couldn't even spell the word before she met me, and after all the stress and embarrassment I had to endure to get her out of my home . . . But to send that little man to my door . . ." Parker nearly gagged. "Desireé knew that what we had was temporary. She had to, how could it have been anything else? Now, to be accused of having had a common-law marriage with her is disgusting."

The low and regal growl of the approaching Corniche caught his ear. Parker descended the stairs and stood waiting like a child on Christmas morn by the time Steven climbed from behind the wheel.

"Beautiful car, sir." Thick-bodied, with a glossy mustache that nearly outshone his bald brown pate, Steven trailed a lusting hand along the door panel. "Looks like a beautiful day, sir."

"Yes, Steven, it is." The fact that the houseman had taken the time to open the Rolls' top was not lost on Parker. Steven's ability to anticipate his needs and desires was one of the things that made him so good at what he did. Accepting his car, Parker felt a bit like a medieval knight accepting his charger.

Behind the wheel, gunning the engine, Parker pulled on Armani sunglasses and settled into the leather seat. He let the engine's liquid vibration lull him, then raised a hand to Steven and shifted gears.

Any other day, sitting in his car under a blue sky, feeling the soothing rush of sweet passing southern air would have been enough to appease him, but not today. Today, all Parker could think of was the night before.

"How did she even manage to come up with a scheme like this? Suing me for divorce. Divorce! As if I would stoop to marrying her! And to demand a settlement . . . She was little more than a whore, a concubine, and she wants to demand a wife's rights? She's a stupid little fool." The Corniche seemed to murmur assent when his foot pressed harder on the accelerator. Parker tried to ignore the headache building behind his eyes.

"Who in the world would put her up to something like this? I know she didn't do it all on her own. Hell, how she could even manage to rouse her one or two lonely brain cells long enough to get a decent attorney on the case is beyond me." After a night of drinking, Parker's vodka slogged-brain refused to help him out. "This is plainly some kind of trumped-up effort to milk me of money. Anyone can see she's a gold digger. People like me simply do not marry people like her."

Still, she had managed to put this little plan into action. How? "Probably came up with it with the help of a few of her less-kinky friends. Good thing for Desireé that they don't look down their noses at her the way she looks down hers at them."

Elbow parked against the window frame, Parker shielded his eyes with his hand and tried to focus. "If I'd known this little affair with her was going to turn out like this, I would have thought twice before paying to pare that nose down; that and the tits and ass I paid for, too." He blew out hard and tried not to feel like a complete fool. Truth be told, he had paid almost as much for her body as he had paid for his medical degree.

"And she still wants more!" For a one-trick pony, Desireé had more nerve than a brass-assed monkey. She was determined to get all she could, and the damned papers she had had him served with made it clear—she could get a lot. "Too bad I fell for her one trick," the doctor complained, remembering the things that girl could do with toys. His knees still grew weak when he thought of her singular array of talent.

It had started with a cocktail party dare. It was a boring party, featuring musty-tasting cheese and expensive but muffled wine and liquor, the kind of stuff you ate and drank to get along with stuffy, expensive people. Then along came Desireé. At first glance, she was a bit too much: too exposed, too loud, and far too brassy in her low-cut Versace knock-off.

"My name is Desireé Johnson. That's *Desireé*, with a accent over the e. It's French for desire." She extended limp fingers. "What's yours?"

"Reynolds. Parker Reynolds," he said, still holding the fingers.

"Um," she hummed, surveying the crowd over his shoulder. Spotting no one more interesting, she turned her attention back to him. "Um. Parker Reynolds. That kind of name sort of goes with this kind of a crowd." She wiggled her fingers, and he released them. "So Parker Reynolds, what are you going to do to make me smile?"

It was easy to see that she would never reach the point of being charming, but she was entertaining in a cheap and loose sort of way. Bored as he was, what Parker Reynolds thought he needed most right then was to be entertained, and something in him decided that it might be entertaining to make her smile. Clearly available, Desireé Johnson had an agenda of her own. Latching onto his arm, she quickly managed to separate him from the cocktail crowd—not that he needed much persuasion when she angled her décolletage at him.

"This party is a real drag, huh?" she said with her lips close to his ear.

"A simple social obligation," he murmured, looking into her face and wondering what lurked beneath the heavy, inexpertly applied makeup. Not much, he decided, tossing down the last of his drink. Without shifting his gaze, he managed to hand off the empty glass and collect a fresh drink from a passing waiter. His new drink was one of the fussy wines Teasley was so fond of, and Parker wanted to ditch it, but then he would have had to take his eyes off of Desireé.

The longer he looked at her, the more fascinating she became. What possessed a woman to dress herself in violently purple polyester and then climb up on a pair of four-inch heels? How in the world had she managed to paint her eyes, her mouth, and her cheeks so creatively? Could it be that she lived in a house with no mirrors?

His questions ended when she reached for him. His immediate urge was to avoid the inch-long nails, but the fascination held him in place. Her thumb and forefinger closed on his ear, pulling him into the vortex of her persona. "I've got a little joke for you," she whispered. "Want to hear it?"

Silly question; of course he did.

Her lips were thick and lush, liquid with gloss, and Dr. Parker Reynolds could hardly wait to hear what she would say.

"What's long and hard and filled with see-men?" She tipped her head to look deep into his eyes, letting the last word drag across her lips while Parker struggled to think of an answer. "Don't you know?"

"A, uh . . . A . . ." Parker couldn't bring himself to say the obvious word out loud.

"See?" Desireé drawled. "You're nasty. I knew you were a nasty boy; I could tell by lookin' at you. The answer is a submarine."

"A . . . submarine, of course."

"You didn't get it." Her laughter was soft and breathy, scented with the warm fruit of wine. The long-nailed hand she used to hold Parker's lapel was tight, and she was closer to him than his shadow.

"I get it. Seamen, not semen."

"Stupid, juvenile sense of humor," Parker whined, remembering the encounter in far too much detail. Reaching for the preset button on the Rolls dash, Reynolds tried to fill the air around him with music. Johnny Mathis sang "Chances Are," and Reynolds wondered why he had continued with the woman. "Maybe I just knew her for what she was and wanted to see if it was real." He snorted a sound that might have been mistaken for laughter. It was funny, Reynolds recalled. When she made her pitch, he hadn't seen it coming.

"What would you most like to do with me," she had asked, moving even closer in the crowded room, and seeming to tow him with her to a place along the Dutch blue wall. It was as if she had taken most of the air with her, but he swallowed hard and dared to dream.

Afraid to hesitate, he told her in the crudest terms possible. He wasn't entirely sure, but he might have stuttered on the letter 'f', it coming at the beginning of the word the way it did. And he wasn't completely sure of the word that began with a 'c', but he was pretty sure that he had used it in context.

"Is that a medical term?" Desireé was completely unimpressed.

"Not really." Parker felt himself floundering. "It was more on the order of an offer for a complete physical."

"You have no imagination," she suggested.

"Well, look here, how about this? It's a little trick I picked up in Spain while traveling with my parents." He plucked the maraschino cherry from her glass and popped it into his mouth. It took six minutes and a raised hand for him to work the stem on the tip of his broad tongue.

Desireé's raised brow was a study in derision. "You should practice more. Besides, lots of people can tie cherry stems into knots with their tongues."

"I suppose you could do better?" he challenged, folding the stem into a paper napkin.

"Absolutely. Time me." She not only did the same trick, she did it better, beating his time by more than five minutes. "I can do other things, too."

"Like what?" Intrigued, Parker fell into the oily, lip-sticked smile and followed her like a happy puppy. Towing him by his tie, she backed against what he first thought was a wall, but soon discovered was a closet under the staircase. Small and dark, the closet had apparently been forgotten by Teasley, because it housed only a small stack of sealed boxes. The boxes meant nothing to Desireé, who slipped to her knees in the dark and found Parker's zipper with no trouble at all.

Parker inched lower in his leather seat, remembering. Between his legs, an uncomfortable bulging swell testified to the memory of Desireé's skill and dedication to task. "The way she sucked, the girl could have changed her last name to Hoover," he sighed, trying to keep his eyes on the road.

Hard as it was to admit, Parker had been damned near giddy when she finally let him out of that hot little closet beneath the stairs. Carefully creeping from the closet, Parker felt an embarrassed exhilaration he hadn't known in years. People said sex in public places, places where the threat of discovery was heavy—well, they said it was exciting . . . and so it was. Standing again amid the guests with their good clothes, fine wine, and finer jewelry, he had wanted to do a little happy dance, but knew it would have been inappropriate. He watched Desireé correct the line of her fading lipstick with a daintily crooked finger. Around him, no one seemed concerned.

"Well, that was special." Desireé had finished with her lipstick and was working at her nails.

"Yes," Parker agreed, basking in what was left of his glow. "That was very special, indeed."

"I was kidding." Desireé's dark eyes rolled slowly over the doctor's face. "That was what you call *sarcasm*. What we just did in there was a little, um, a little icebreaker. S'just somethin' to make this dead-assed party a little more tolerable. If we were somewhere private, I would show you something else, something I promise you would enjoy."

"Like what?" Parker knew his tongue was hanging out.

"See that lady over there? The one with the cigarette, blowin' the smoke rings? Well, I happen to know that if you put a cigarette in the right place . . ."

"Really? You can do that?"

Desireé's breath sizzled past her teeth and across her lips when she laughed at his naiveté. "Are you sure you're a doctor? I woulda thought you would have known that a well-educated body can do a lot of things."

45

"Educated?"

Crossing her arms creased the purple bodice of her dress and pushed her breasts into prominence. She nodded, and Parker had the distinct impression that she really did know what she was talking about. Raising his thick black brows, Parker held his breath, then made his decision. "Got any plans for tonight?"

"Uh-huh." She slipped her arm through his. "I'm going with you."

"And fool that I was, I brought her home with me." Reynolds cursed himself. "If I hadn't been so greedy when she showed me what she could do in a bathtub . . ." Yeah, that greed had moved her right into his sprawling home in the exclusive Roswell Vinings enclave.

Traffic was light, so Parker barely slowed the Corniche as he turned the corner, Desireé still on his mind. His stomach lifted and rolled, greasy with frustration. A man could watch a woman with Desireé's particular brand of dexterity juggle billiard balls for only so long before she had to get dressed—and speak. Fully clothed and totally self-involved, Desireé left a lot to be desired. A woman with all the personality of an avocado, she had the nerve to be a snob on top of it. Nothing was ever enough, and beyond the realm of sexual acrobatics, her limited forté consisted of shopping.

Parker gripped the steering wheel tighter and wished for a drink. "But the heifer didn't have good taste," he recalled, "not even in groceries. Thank heavens she preferred to shop solely for herself."

After she moved into his home, Parker quickly learned that nothing was ever enough for Desireé. Initially intrigued by the toys, gadgets, and fripperies that money can buy, she had been compliant and easy to please—at first. As time passed, Desireé discovered her personal trump card: embarrassment. The woman was a bottomless and all-consuming pit of crude behavior. She would publicly pout and bitch and moan to get her way—anything to get on his last nerve, and bounce. He had tried to drown the whining and complaints in a glass of vodka. Over time, one glass became two, and two became five, and the glasses got bigger and bigger. Hell, by the time he finally got her out of the house, the damned glass was practically a vat.

And after getting the trumped-up divorce papers, Parker plunged deep into that vat again. "She can just use the body I paid for to reel in another sucker, for all I care. She's got all she's getting from me."

Even as he said the words, he knew that putting her out of his life was easier said than done. *Common as table salt*, his mother had once called her, and she was right. But common, selfish, and greedy as she was, Desireé had one redeeming trait: she loved him.

Being claimed by a woman determined to love him, and make him a better man, was a novelty. Nobody had ever wanted Parker the way Desireé did, and Parker wasn't sure that was a good thing—but it was certainly addictive. The look on her face when he called her name, having her there when he came home from a rough shift at the hospital, the welcome of her early morning touch;

all of this had become precious to him. But enough was enough, and he could live without her.

Determined to wean himself, Parker passed his hand across his face and decided that if he couldn't have vodka, he could at least get some coffee. *Coffee and maybe some food ought to help.* Flicking his turn signal, he made a right turn. "Can't imagine what the holiday crew might dredge up in the hospital cafeteria." He made an illegal turn and headed for the ramp going north on I-75. "Better not take the chance."

The American Café would be open. They never closed, not even on Christmas, and they served breakfast all day. Almost no traffic on the road; the trip there and down to the hospital would take next to no time.

Dr. Parker Reynolds hit the accelerator hard, and his ire returned in force when Desireé Johnson invaded his thoughts again. "How dare she?" he hissed, barely seeing the silver Honda Accord. The woman in the Accord was pushing the little silver bullet for all it was worth when he sideswiped it, sending it careening across the road.

The howl of creasing metal made him blink. The Corniche's heavily armored body barely swayed. The Accord didn't have that luxury. Horrified, he watched as reality slowly fell like a heavy cloak. Everything seemed to be happening in slow motion. He could see the shock and terror on the woman's face.

He saw the passenger-side wheels leave the road, saw her hands rise into the air. He saw her pretty brown face when her mouth stretched wide, first showing white teeth, then the raw pink of her scream. The Accord

seemed bent on destruction, lifting higher and pirouet-
ting across the far lane and into the center wall.

Parker's foot went to the brake and the Corniche
slowed. Stunned, he sat in the center of the empty
highway, looking back at the twisted mass of metal
wedged against the highway's dividing wall. Panicked, he
looked over at the other side of the wall and was amazed
to see no oncoming traffic. There was nothing in his
rearview mirror, either.

"Easy," he cautioned himself, "easy." Reaching for the
ignition, Parker Reynolds had an idea. Swallowing hard,
he turned the wheel lightly and steered the Corniche a
quarter mile farther down I-75 to the nearest exit. He
found the off-ramp and tried to control his breathing.

"Easy . . ." He checked the rearview mirror again—
nothing behind him. He made a left turn and found the
return ramp. "All I have to do is make a circle."

Eight minutes later, Dr. Parker Reynolds eased the
Corniche to a stop behind the smoldering, twisted
remains of the Accord. He took out his cellphone and hit
911 as he ran toward the car. "Hello," he shouted,
praying that the woman was still alive. "Hello!" And
where the hell was the 911 operator? Parker was still
clutching the phone when he heard the woman moan.

CHAPTER 4

"I don't know what I was thinking when I let Yvonne schedule me to work today."

Connie Charles was glad to refresh her memory. "You were thinking about the overtime—same as I was."

"Maybe, but this is way more than I bargained for." Holding her breath, Jeanette Washington turned still-wet clothes with gloved hands. "I can't believe we've been stuck with this again. First a shooting, now this car accident. And we're the ones who have to figure out who she is."

"Somebody has got to do it, and this time it's us. That's life in the ER. I hate working the ER, especially on holidays." Connie refused to look up from the running shoe she held. "Did you hear how bad it was?"

"Yeah, the team that brought her in had her on life support. Said they had to cut her from the wreckage, poor thing."

"Yeah, and to think Dr. Reynolds just happened to drive up and find her."

"Uh-huh. And bless his heart, he's still hanging in there with her. He's doing the surgery and everything. Do you think it was a drunk?"

"No." Connie angled her head toward her shoulder, letting her blue surgical cap catch the sudden drops of water on her forehead. "You ask me, I think it was some kind of evil, hateful bastard. Who else woulda left that girl out there like that?"

"I don't know, but I heard the car was totaled. It was so messed up, they couldn't even read the license tag. Now here she is, anonymous and in surgery. That really is a shame." Jeanette's eyes widened. "She was wearing running clothes, and look, this thing was balled up in them." She carefully pulled a thin, wrinkled sheet away from the thin fabric of the shirt.

"Lord, Jeanette," Connie said pointing to the running shoe. "That's one of those numbers you get when you run in a race. Today is the Fourth of July, the day they run the Peachtree Road Race. They ran it this morning. Do you think . . . Is that her number from the Peachtree? Do you think she filled it out?"

"Girl, I don't know." She turned the slick sheet, smoothing it out. "Looks like some writing. Let me try washing it."

Connie grabbed a bottle of saline and squirted the sheet. She waited a beat, then squirted again. Then Jeanette aimed a thin stream of water across the top of it. Connie flattened the sheet against the stainless steel countertop. Letters began to appear. "Praise Jesus. She did it, Jeanette. She filled it out."

"Can you read the name? A phone number? Anything?"

"Mary . . . no, I think it says Marilyn . . . or Marlene . . ."

"*Marlea,*" Jeanette whispered. "It says Marlea, and there's a phone number here, too."

"I'm glad we've got a contact for her, but I don't want to be the one to make the call. I did the hit and run," Connie reminded her colleague.

"Spare me." Jeanette said. Connie really did hate the ER. "I'll do it. I'll call." She squinted at the name on the back of the wet race form. "I'll call about Marlea."

———

"I got a call," Libby Belcher panted across the counter at the nursing station. Her hair stood up in sharp black spikes, and the panic in her blue eyes nearly matched the alarm in her high-pitched voice. The parchment-skinned nurse on the other side of the desk thought she looked as if she had stuck her finger into an electrical socket. Libby moistened her lips, swallowed hard, and shoved her cellphone toward the nurse. "I'm a coach. One of the runners, a friend of mine, she had an accident. I got a call that she was brought here."

The nurse's nametag read P. Bridgewater. A Grady veteran, P. Bridgewater was used to the frustration and anguish of those left to pick up the pieces when someone they cared about was in medical distress. Nurse Bridgewater's fingers clicked over a hidden keyboard, then she looked at Libby. "You can put that away now," she nodded toward the cellphone. "What's her name?"

"Marlea. Kellogg—like the cereal." Libby tucked the phone into the pocket of her shorts.

"Yes, she's here, but you won't be able to see her for a bit. She's still in surgery."

Oh, Lord no she didn't just say surgery! Libby gripped the edge of the counter and tried not to think of the worst that could happen. "They told me that she was in an accident. What happened? What's her condition?"

P. Bridgewater clicked more hidden keys, then hummed along a deep breath and ignored the questions.

Libby's wild eyes grew wilder. "You're not going to tell me? Is she dead?"

The nurse looked up, suddenly more human. "No, she's in critical condition, but definitely alive. Just follow that blue line and take the elevators up." She pointed to the colorfully lined floor.

Releasing the counter, Libby slowly backed away. "Surgery."

Oh, Marlea! What now? It wasn't easy, but Libby found the elevators and managed to follow the directions to the waiting area. Sitting across from the surgical suite, she phoned Hal to tell him where she was and that she wouldn't be home for a while—and that she loved him. Then she sat with the phone folded between her hands.

"Hi."

The soft voice roused Libby, bringing her back to the here and now. Without thinking, she smiled up into the gentle brown eyes of the thick-bodied woman studying her from the doorway.

"You Libby?" She waited for Libby's slow nod, then came closer, hand extended. If the woman had said that her name was Tootsie Roll, it wouldn't have surprised a living soul. Round and brown, she wore rubber-soled white shoes and floral scrubs. *Nurse,* Libby realized. "How do you know my name?"

"No mystery," the woman smiled. "I'm Jeanette Washington, the one who called you. I've been kind of watching for you." Libby nodded, then looked at the double doors across the hall. "I know, the waiting is always hard. You mind if I sit here with you for a minute?" Libby's lips trembled, and Jeanette sat.

"You two been friends long?" Libby's lips parted and closed. A fat tear shimmered at the corner of one eye, and the nurse gave her hand a gentle pat. "It's good to have friends who love you."

So very, very true, Libby thought.

"Does she have any other family here in Atlanta?"

"No family at all, unless you count me and her students. She's a teacher. Her mother and her . . . brother, they're both dead."

"I see."

"I'm pretty much all she's got."

"No husband? No boyfriend?"

"Boyfriend? Not Marlea. She's a dedicated runner, and as far as she's concerned, men and training don't mix. She's got no children of her own, no pets, not even a plant. She's a runner."

"Runner." A frown creased Jeanette's brown face and her eyes dropped.

Libby's stomach quivered and she was suddenly cold. "Yes, she's a runner. She's aiming for the Olympic team. She stands a good chance of making it, too." The nurse nodded. Libby leaned forward, seeking the other woman's still-averted eyes. "What is it?"

"I'm not a doctor," Jeanette said too quickly. "Dr. Reynolds is working with your friend, and he is wonderful. Trauma surgery is his specialty. Your friend couldn't be in better hands."

Libby's stomach lifted and fell again. "Trauma. That means life-threatening, doesn't it?"

"I'm not a doctor."

"But you *are* a nurse, and you said that this doctor is a specialist . . ."

"And you should wait to hear whatever he has to tell you." Jeanette found Libby's hand again and squeezed. "Best I can tell you right now is that your friend is in real good hands."

"Is this the family member for our Jane Doe?" A man's voice, confident and aware.

Libby pulled her hand from the nurse and turned sharply. "Who is he calling a *Jane Doe*? That means unknown, doesn't it? Is he talking about Marlea? Her name is Marlea."

"It's all right," the nurse soothed.

"No, it's not all right. She ain't got no family, and she ain't got nobody else to turn to. She ought to at least have the dignity of a name!"

"It's all—"

"No," the man interrupted. "She's right, and I apologize. I'm Dr. Reynolds. I came in with your friend."

"Libby. Belcher. And what do you mean, *came in with?*"

"Dr. Reynolds was on his way to the hospital. He found your friend. He was the one who called for the police and the ambulance. He's taken on her case . . ."

"Jeanette, I believe we can do without further broadcast."

"Fine, doctor." Chastened, Jeanette touched Libby's arm. "I'm glad you showed up for her, and if you need anything else . . ."

"Is Marlea going to be all right, for real?" Blue eyes wavered behind a screen of unshed tears. "There's only me to call. There's no other family."

"She's been stabilized, and now they're prepping her for surgery. I'll see her in about ten minutes." Reynolds kept his eyes on Libby, but nodded to Jeanette Washington as she slipped from the room.

"You'll be honest with me, right?" Looking up at Reynolds from her seat, Libby gnawed at her lower lip. "She trusts me, so I need to know, 'cause like I keep sayin', she ain't got nobody else."

———*∽∾∽*———

"How did it go?"

"How am I supposed to know, with you sneakin' up on me?" Jeanette hissed, slapping at Connie's arm. "I'm trying to hear."

Connie opened her mouth, but closed it again when Dr. Reynolds brushed past. Sneaking a look around the edge of the waiting room door, she watched the black-haired little white woman bury her face into her hands. Her shoulders shook and she hiccuped a time or two. Connie went back to her Baptist roots and hummed sympathy.

"Chile, this is so sad. Who is that?"

"That's her friend, her coach. She told me that the girl has no husband, no parents, no brothers or sisters."

"So sad." Looking over her shoulder, Jeanette caught a glimpse of the doctor as he entered the surgical suite.

"The poor girl has so many *ain't gots*, it's a shame," Reynolds overheard one of the nurses whisper. And before it's all over, Dr. Parker Reynolds knew she would have at least one more.

Striding long and pushing through the double doors of the surgical suite, he tried to ignore the nurse's words. "Let's get this show on the road," he announced to the assembled team as he headed for the sinks. "Let's get scrubbed and get in there and do what we do best." The show of bravado was just that—a show, and Parker hoped that he was the only one who knew it.

"Doctor, you keep scrubbing like that, and you're going to pull the skin right off your hands," one of the OR nurses teased. Reynolds managed to dredge up a smile and stepped away from the sink.

Now I know how Lady Macbeth felt, he thought. Shakespeare's murderous conspirator had scrubbed long and hard trying to get imaginary blood off her hands, too. *At least I didn't murder that young woman*, he told himself, but his heart wouldn't let him off that easily. *You don't know. What if she doesn't survive the surgery? What if she's maimed for life? How will you live with yourself then, Dr. Savior?*

Reynolds's eyes went back to the sink, but he refused to give in to the urge to scrub his already scourged skin one more time. *Washing your hands is not going to wake her or make her whole again. Washing your hands is not going to ever cleanse them of her blood. Ever.*

Why did the nagging voice in his head insist on sounding like Desireé Johnson? He could hear the lip-smacking tartness of her lazy drawl in every word. *Great. Now she's not only suing me, she's also going to be the voice of my conscience?*

Aw, hell, no!

I'm a doctor, a very good doctor, and I'm not going to second-guess myself on this. I'll do what I have to do to make up for what happened to this woman, but I can't . . . I won't let her or Desireé cost me the life I'm entitled to. It was an accident, damn it. I'm sorry it happened. I'm sorry if this Marlea Kellogg has to go through some pain, but at least she's alive. I'll help her if I can, but that's it. Determined, Parker stood straighter and accepted the surgical gloves he was offered.

I shouldn't have let my mind wander, and . . . My car! The Corniche was parked in his designated slot at the hospital, but how long would it take for someone to look at the car and ask the logical questions?

It didn't look bad when I checked it, just surface damage to the fender, but I was in a hurry. What if I missed something? What if it's worse than I thought? A hand-built custom Corniche is not the kind of car you allow to get scuffed, scraped, or dirty. What if one of these nosy people checks it? What if they find damage? And when they do and they ask questions, what will I say? Oh, that little ding? I hit, ran, nearly killed a woman, and scraped my car up in the process?

But to have the bodywork done . . . where can I take it? After all, you don't casually take a quarter-million-dollar custom auto to the local fix-it shop and say, "Can you hook a brother's ride up?" now do you?

There has to be a place. People are always getting things done, under-the-table. Surely, this is no exception. Thinking fast, Parker assessed his list of friends, his social and business acquaintances—nothing and nobody came to mind. His mother, the social butterfly of another generation, represented another group, but again, nothing.

That left Desireé and a host of men and women who could and would do a lot of things for money. And if you paid them enough most of them would forget that they had done those things for you. And Parker Reynolds had plenty of money.

I just need to call Desireé and make some kind of arrangement, he thought. *I'll have to be careful, though, because she's going to love having the chance to get her hooks into me again, but if I can lead her on just long enough to get what I need . . .*

"Doctor?" The young intern's curious green eyes peered over her surgical mask. "Is there a problem?"

"No problem at all," Reynolds snapped. "I have everything under control." Looking around for his waiting team, he felt control reassert itself over his domain. Buoyed by renewed confidence, he lifted his head and strode toward the surgical arena.

Passing two blue-gowned men assigned to his team, the surgeon heard their hushed comments. "I hear he's the best," said one. "In a case this severe, what do you think he's going to do?"

I'm going in there to do what only I can do for her. Parker smiled and kept walking.

CHAPTER 5

Lost in a thick black vortex edged with light, Marlea struggled to reach the edges, to touch the brightness, and was rewarded with the sound of voices. All around her in the shifting morass, echoing and resounding, Marlea couldn't quite make out what they were saying. Trying to sift something recognizable from the steady thrum, it comforted her to know that they were there . . . just out of reach, but there all the same. Not alone, she wanted to make them know that she heard, and tried to reach out to them.

So heavy . . . she mused, feeling herself nearer to the light. Willing herself forward, she was pulled hard, then stuck fast. Trying to see beyond the rising darkness, she wanted to push it aside to make her break. She wanted to run, and was terrified when her feet and legs refused to obey. Mouth stretched wide, she tried to scream. Fear claimed her completely when no sound left her body, and the voices swirled and rushed past her again. There was something wrong, and she knew it as she fell deeper, drowning in the darkness.

Marlea Kellogg tried to find her life for the second time that day. Again, the voices, and again, she saw the light, a bright, thin corona, arching like a cold, new moon, defined the darkness. Opening her mouth, trying to answer the voices around her, Marlea braced herself and scrambled for the light.

The light stretched and mounted in her vision, burning like white fire when she opened her eyes, blinding her, making her close them reflexively. Determined, knowing somehow that her real life lay on the other side of that light, Marlea fought to open her lids and then lay exhausted from the effort.

Something was wrong—*control,* she thought, *why can't I control this?* Her sore, scratchy eyes moved crazily about the room. White walls and curtains, mixed clumsily with stainless steel, people in white with blue plastic basins and trays, and the whole place smelled like antiseptic.

Where is this?

The room slipped sideways, and Marlea moaned softly.

A pretty brown-skinned woman turned swiftly. She said something. Marlea knew that the woman in the white dress said something. She saw the woman's lips move, but her voice was a part of the crowding rush. Marlea squeezed her eyes closed, then tried to open them. The effort nearly slid her back into the black tide.

"Lemme see her!"

Okay. Marlea stretched her eyes wide. *I heard that.*

A small woman with spiky black hair pushed past the first woman. Her face was panicked and her blue eyes were wreathed in dark circles. Marlea wondered if she had been in some kind of accident. Gently, the small woman's pale fingers found Marlea's. "How you doin', sweetie?"

Marlea opened her mouth to tell her—at least she thought she did. She tried to speak, and heard nothing. She tried again, and pain slapped hard, traveling from her head to her chest and extremities. *I'm not supposed to be feeling like this!* She wanted to say the words; instead a ragged moan escaped into the air around her. Panic threatened to strangle her, and Marlea sucked hard for breath, feeling the pressure. She wanted to scream, "Help me," but couldn't find the way.

"It's okay, Marlea. For real, it's okay."

"Ms. Belcher, if you please." It was a white-jacketed man this time. His hands went to the little woman's shoulders and moved her briskly to the side. The woman in the white dress offered a blue tray. Marlea's eyes opened wider as the man's hands moved to a tube at her side.

What are you doing? She hoped she had said the words aloud, but realized she hadn't when a salty tang invaded her mouth, making her swallow. Feeling the edges of darkness curl over her like a thick and unwanted blanket, Marlea fought to stay where she was. *Libby*, she suddenly remembered, her mind swirling, and her eyes finding the black-haired woman's. "Libby," she whispered, and fell into the darkness.

Libby reached for her hand again, and was rewarded with a light squeeze of her fingertips as Marlea succumbed to the drugs the doctor had administered. Releasing Marlea's fingers, she watched the nurse adjust the bedcovers.

"Ms. Belcher?" The doctor slipped an arm around Libby's narrow shoulders and ushered her from the room.

The door closed behind them. Pulling away from the doctor, Libby stopped walking and folded her arms around her body. She was suddenly very cold. "So she's out of the coma now, right?"

"Ms. Belcher," the doctor said slowly, "we've already reviewed the procedure of the medically induced coma with you, and—"

"And it's time you got off your medical high-horse and talked some common sense to me, Dr. Reynolds." Libby stretched herself to her full five feet and looked directly into the doctor's chin. "That's my friend you've got in there, and she doesn't have an idea in the world about what's going on. You're playing God with her life, puttin' her to sleep for days at a time, waking her up when you feel like it . . . You need to talk to me!"

"Right, then." Reynolds swept his teeth with his tongue, and then tucked it into his cheek. "Two days in the coma has pretty much done its job, and she's healing."

"Uh-uh. That's not what I'm talking about," Libby frowned. "What I want to know is, when are you gonna wake her up and tell her? She deserves to know."

"And so she will. At this point, that's the best answer I can give you." The doctor turned on his heel and walked away from her.

"You arrogant SOB," Libby muttered, going back into Marlea's room. "You know you owe her some kind of explanation, and you need to be here to give it to her."

The nurse murmured something as she quietly left the room. Libby heaved a sigh and went back to the blue, vinyl-covered chair where she had left her stash of magazines. Flopping low in the chair, she watched Marlea's sleeping form and was grateful for the gentle rise and fall of her chest.

"But one day soon, you're gonna wake up. Then what?" Libby promised herself that Hal would understand if she spent another night at the hospital. "I'm his wife," she said softly, hoping Marlea could hear her, "but I'm your friend. I'll be here when you wake up, Marlea. I'll be right here."

Libby had no idea when she had fallen asleep, but she knew it was her name that awakened her. Her eyes moved fast, taking in her surroundings. *Hospital. Oh, yeah. Marlea.* She carefully pushed herself erect in the hard blue wooden-armed vinyl chair and looked across the room.

"Libby?"

Libby held her breath. Marlea's head moved on the white pillow, then her hand against the stark white sheet, the fingers lifting slowly. "Hey, girl," Libby whispered, rising slowly. Easing through the shadows, she made her way to the bedside. Marlea's breathing was shallow and raspy. *She sounds tired,* Libby thought, looking into her friend's slack face. *It's like she's been drained of herself, and this shell is all that's left of her. I hope it's enough.* It was willpower alone that kept her from falling to her knees and weeping. "How you doin'?"

"I . . ." Marlea coughed and then cleared her throat. "Where . . . what . . ." She closed her eyes and coughed again. Her eyelids fluttered, settled almost long enough to cue sleep, then fluttered nearly open. "Where . . . what . . ."

"I know," Libby said softly. "You want to know where you are." Marlea nodded. "What happened." Marlea nodded again.

Debating whether or not to lie, Libby dropped her eyes and wished for the intervention of a night-stalking nurse. When none showed up, she took Marlea's fingers between her hands. She felt the cool fingers tense, anticipating. "You're in the hospital, Marlea. You're at Grady."

"Hospital?" Marlea's head moved against the pillow, her face a study in confusion, as she struggled to stay awake. "Why?"

Oh, Lord, don't make me have to answer this girl, Libby prayed, turning her eyes to the ceiling.

"Why?" Marlea whispered along the edge of a yawn.

Libby was still trying to find the right words when she felt Marlea's fingers slip free of her own. Marlea had succumbed to sleep.

Grateful for the reprieve, temporary as she knew it to be, Libby uttered another prayer on her way back to her vinyl chair.

—≈≈≈—

It was hard to break free of the seamless black sleep, but hearing the electronic drone around her, Marlea found a way to open her eyes. Without moving her head, she let her eyes travel from left to right. Picking out bright metal and gray-toned monitors stacked on a rack beside the white-sheeted bed where she lay made little sense. Ignoring the strain, her eyes tracked, and her brain struggled to register sterile white walls, a side-pulled curtain above the bed, closed doors, and a wall-mounted television.

This place looks like a hospital. Did Libby say I was in a hospital? Hospital. The word gave her a strange feeling. *Why would I be in anybody's hospital? Besides, if I am in a hospital, wouldn't I remember being brought here? Wouldn't I know the reason for being here?* Her eyes tracked the white-walled room again. *Wouldn't I?*

Marlea sighed hard and felt a dull, unspecific total-body ache. *Kind of like what you would feel if you were in a car wreck,* she joked to herself.

Car wreck. That's a good one, but if it's a joke, why am I in bed? A hospital bed? She dragged herself up on an elbow, surprised at how tired she was. The white room was draped in shadows and bluish electric light. *Damn, this sure does look like a hospital room.* She tried to remember. *What was it Libby said about a hospital?* Marlea's fingers probed a tender spot on her head. *When did I hit my head? I don't remember doing it, but I must have hit it, 'cause even thinking hurts.* She closed her eyes and took in a deep breath. *Damn, this place even smells like a hospital.*

Across the room, Libby slept in a blue vinyl-covered chair. She was twisted to one side, her head curled down toward her chest and her knees tucked high. She was snoring lightly, sleeping hard. *If this is a hospital, and Libby is all curled up in a chair, why am I in a hospital bed?*

The last thing I remember is driving away from Piedmont Park. She looked toward the windows. It was dark outside. How could that be? Her sigh was shaky against her dry throat. Something was very wrong; she felt it in the pit of her stomach. *It couldn't have been close to noon when I left the park, and now it's dark. How?*

This is way too close to The Twilight Zone *for me*, she finally decided, pushing the covers back. Moving too suddenly was a mistake, her swimming head told her. Fingers still caught in the edges of the crisp sheet, she gave in to a wave of nausea and lowered her head to the pillow behind her. Head on pillow seemed to trigger the lowering of her eyelids.

Two minutes, Marlea promised herself. *I'm going to keep my eyes closed for two minutes, just until I feel better, then I'll get to the bottom of this.*

And she saw her feet pacing the distance across the cinder track, could feel the cool breeze prickling the thin sheen of sweat along her neck and shoulders.

"Runners, take your mark . . ."

She approached the start, coiled low, and pressed her heel against the block. Breathing hope, she dropped her head and waited.

"Get set . . ."

The sound of the gunshot freed her. Long legs working with hydraulic precision, her feet ignored gravity. Marlea felt speed and adrenaline pump through her muscled thighs at 100 meters. At 200 meters, all she could hear was her own breathing. Chasing time, riding the wind, she barely saw the competition. Breath pulled tight through her nose and rushed out past her open lips. Her mouth felt dry, her lips were parched, but her legs felt as though she could run for an eternity.

". . . Marlea Kellogg . . ."

It seemed she heard her name in the distance. She couldn't remember the finish line, and her head ached with the effort of trying to hear. . .

"Ah, you're awake. I just wanted to check on you before I left for the night."

"Awake," she echoed dully. *But I was running. How?* Her weary thoughts tried to balance logic. *The race was a dream.* Her eyes were tired, felt as if they had been filled with sand, and Marlea struggled to open them wider. Focusing on the slender peanut-colored man at the foot of the bed, she swallowed a wave of nausea. Something was wrong. The fast, cold creep of gooseflesh along her arms was a bad sign, and she knew it. "I'm awake."

"That's a good sign." He snapped an expensive-looking pen from his pocket, made fast notes on a chart, then clicked both pen and chart back into place, and headed for the door.

"Hey," Marlea ignored the shiver that ran through her. "Good signs are fine, but why am I here? Have I been here all day? And who are you?"

An indelicate snort erupted from the chair in the corner, and Libby's head popped into view. Fully alert, she stared from Marlea to the doctor and back again.

Aware of Libby's silence, Marlea aimed her questions at the man in the white lab coat with the stethoscope tucked into the pocket. "Your nametag says doctor. Is that for real?"

"Yes."

Not trusting the indulgent smile and confident voice, Marlea lifted her right hand. "Somebody stuck an IV in me, and I'm lying in a hospital bed. You've got the degree, so I'm guessing you can tell me why."

"I can do that."

"What's your name, anyway?"

"Reynolds. Dr. Parker Reynolds. I'm a trauma surgeon, and I was your doctor. There was an accident. You were driving and you had an accident."

"Accident? No." Marlea's full lips thinned. "No, no accident. I would remember if something happened to me."

Moving closer to the bed, Reynolds reached for her wrist, then hesitated when she pulled free of his grasp. "I don't know you like that, and I don't know anything about an accident, either."

"Ms. Kellogg, I'm not entirely surprised that you have no memory of the accident, but I assure you, it did happen."

"What kind of accident?" Searching her memory, coming up with nothing, and waking up in a hospital bed with a doctor in front of her was bad enough, but seeing the anxious look on Libby's face was frightening. Marlea struggled to hold on.

Dr. Reynolds straightened his shoulders, and though he tried to arrange his features, Marlea saw something flit across his face. "It was a car accident," he said.

"Car accident, huh?" *Okay.* Marlea willed herself to relax and think. *That means I'm going to be sore for a while, and I guess I'll be in bed. It will throw my training off, and I'm going to have to scramble like a crazy thing . . .* A memory edged around the headache. *Because I missed*

. . . something . . . Why are they looking at me as if my puppy just died? It was just an accident. Is the doctor edging closer to that door? "I had an accident, and now I'm here for observation, right? How soon will I be able to leave? How is this going to affect my training schedule?"

"It's a bit more involved than that." Reynolds's voice went deadly calm and clinical. "You've had some surgery. We'll monitor your progress, and then I can give you a more definite release date." His hand was against the metal doorplate, and he was pushing. There was no sound from the chair in the corner. Libby had stopped breathing.

"Wait a minute." *He said I was in a car accident, just a car accident!* Marlea's eyes darted to her hands and her hands flew to her chest, moving on to check her face and her head. Finding them intact, she held her hands to her cheeks. *What's happened to me? What is he not telling me?* "What kind of surgery?"

The doctor shoved his hands into his pockets and allowed the door to shut softly at his back. "I am a trauma surgeon, Ms. Kellogg. I specialize in immediate treatment of life-threatening injury."

"Uh-huh." The shivers that began in her belly radiated, and the hands at her cheeks fisted. "You . . . treated . . . me?"

"Yes, I did. In your case, the treatment was radical."

"Radical." The bed began to rattle around Marlea's shaking body. "What does that mean?"

"You have to understand; you had to be cut from the wreckage of your car."

"And you cut me. Where?"

"The area of concern was your foot. Traumatic amputation was necessary to save your life."

The rush of darkness that claimed her kept Marlea ignorant of Dr. Reynolds's last words.

"She fainted," Libby whispered, rising from her chair. "She still doesn't know."

Nodding toward Marlea's unconscious form, Parker glanced at her chart, then turned to leave.

"Wait a minute," Libby laid a hand on his arm. "What kind of doctor are you? Where's your compassion? You're gonna leave her like this? She passed out before you told her everything."

"Not unusual," Parker muttered, shaking off the offending hand and crossing his fingers behind his back. "She's still under anesthesia. We'll have plenty of time for discussion when she awakens."

"And when she wakes up, what is she gonna do?" Libby wondered aloud. "Running is her life."

"Was," Reynolds said, escaping through the door.

CHAPTER 6

"Can you believe they even raised the price on the coffee? With what we make, you'd think they would give it to us for free."

Parker Reynolds cursed the sludge that passed for cafeteria coffee and kept his eyes on the floor, hoping that the square-nosed woman was talking to anybody but him. *If I have to listen to one more of these lazy creatures harping about how little they're paid* . . . He walked away from the counter in silent sanctimony.

But at least the nurse had stopped talking about Marlea Kellogg.

Lately, it seemed that Jeanette had developed a talent for showing up wherever Parker was, praising 'doctor' for his quick action in saving the patient's life. "If it hadn't been for doctor, this. And if it hadn't been for the doctor, that."

The woman is wearing my nerves to a point beyond thin. The doctor swore silently, trying to ignore the guilt he wore like a dirty robe. It was so palpable that he wondered if people could smell it. Waiting for the elevator, he tried to ignore the naked hero worship in Jeanette's eyes as she passed. *Some hero. I haven't slept since we brought that woman in here. My nerves are just about shot.* Stepping into the empty elevator, Parker ignored the dents, scrapes, and greasy fingerprints and slumped against the back wall, glad that he was alone.

The doors slid closed. *I hit that woman.* He couldn't help thinking what he would never willingly say aloud. *Damn it, it was my car that hit Marlea Kellogg.*

There. I said it. In his logical heart, Parker Reynolds knew it wasn't the fault of his car, but the car's driver—him. But he couldn't admit to more. That would be too much like a confession and he would never do that—he couldn't. Confessing always had consequences.

He tried taking a sip of the coffee. It was bitter and cold—just like an admission of guilt. The elevator stopped on the third floor. The doors opened, but nobody got on. Parker barely noticed.

Marlea Kellogg was on his mind. He couldn't help thinking about her again this morning, as if he had been able to restrict her nonstop presence in the days since the accident. It wasn't just Jeanette's doing. From the moment he had heard Marlea's moan, locked within the wreckage of her car, she had been in his head. Lodged deep in his thoughts, she had plagued his sleep and his waking hours as well. First, it was the need to do what it would take to save her life. Now it was the need to keep quiet about it.

I did what I had to do. I did the right thing. I went back, I got her help, and I did the surgery.

His hand never faltered during the surgery when he had cut away so much of what had been her life. *She's alive because of me.*

When she opened her eyes, even before she had started to ask questions, before she tried to make sense of life after her accident, there was something special about her. Now a week later, with time between them, there was still something special about her—shining nobility, tarnished by confusion and loss.

And Parker Reynolds refused to take the blame for it.

She's a smart woman, a survivor. She'll find a way to make a life for herself, Parker assured himself as the elevator doors opened on the fourth floor. A sweet-faced woman with silver hair shook her head at him and the doors closed. He tried the cold coffee again as the elevator rose.

By the time the elevator reached his floor, he had given up on the coffee and dumped the cup in the first trash can he saw. Still troubled by Marlea Kellogg, Parker squared his shoulders and headed for his office.

She is an interesting woman, the kind of woman I might have been able to take home to meet my mother—if my mother weren't such an old guard, born-and-bred snob.

But it wasn't all his mother's fault, even if she still demonstrated a preference for pale skin, "good hair," and thin noses. It was her background, the quality upbringing she had diligently shared with her son that had Sarah Hollis Reynolds dragging the practice of the paper-sack test into the twenty-first century.

Marlea could pass the test—just barely. With skin the color of perfectly creamed coffee, *café au lait* his mother would call it, she could pass. The thought slipped through before he could stop it. *I'm just as guilty as my mother is,* Parker knew. *Maybe even more so, because I know better.* Not that elegant, insulated Sarah Hollis Reynolds would have cared.

Tossing curt nods to a pair of his peers, Parker almost felt bad, but was shielded by inborn superiority. Neither of the men he had greeted were truly his peers, though Regan was a better-than-average neurosurgeon. Dark-skinned and kinky-haired, neither of the pair would pass the paper-sack test, and both had attended college and medical school on scholarships. *Not my equals. Low class, no class. That's what mother would think, though she had been too much of a lady to say it out loud.*

Parker was truly his mother's son. *Being born to a certain class did entitle one to certain . . . privileges.* That was the rule, wasn't it? Medical school at Harvard had been Parker Reynolds's birthright, a part of his family's legacy, much like the money and creature comforts he took for granted. His place at Grady Memorial Hospital had been assured the second they saw his name. *Being born to a certain class entitles one to be excused from certain . . . errors.*

Marlea Kellogg's accident had been an unfortunate error. *Pity that Ms. Kellogg comes from nothing.* Parker's feet slowed, nearly stopped, and then changed direction.

Her prospects would be so much brighter if she had a family of note, a name. But she didn't. From what he could remember of the family history her coach had recited, Marlea Kellogg's background wasn't all that different from Desireé Johnson's.

She's nothing like Desireé Johnson. Desireé is what my mother once called "as cheap as a copper penny." Marlea Kellogg was dainty and considerate—a lady in spite of her reduced circumstances. Her native "class" was evident, even when using the plastic dishes and cutlery favored by the hospital. Her manners were delicate and genteel, without exception.

Marlea was intelligent and inquisitive. Now that she was awake and recovering, she was reading information on her changed condition as fast as he could get it to her. But it was her courage that was most remarkable. Where most people, male or female, would have been locked in a stupor of regret, Marlea Kellogg was focused on understanding what had happened to her.

Commendable. And though she had been born an orphan and raised by an aunt, Marlea Kellogg found a way to be a societal contributor. A special education teacher, loved by her students, special in her own right. *A very special young woman*, Parker thought, moving to avoid the old man in the wrinkled blue-and-white cotton robe who was slowly maneuvering his wheelchair down the center of the hallway.

What did I do wrong? How did I manage to miss out on a woman like her? Then he thought of Desireé spreading her legs atop the green baize of his antique brass-cornered billiard table. *Yes, yes, I let myself get sidetracked*, he thought angrily. *I got sidetracked, all right. I got so involved with flea-market flirtation that I let her talk me into promising her things that she was just learning to dream about. Now she's slapped me with this palimony suit. If it hadn't been for that damned suit . . .*

Marlea Kellogg would still be running.

Culpability bent the doctor's shoulders and slowed his feet at Marlea's door. Hand on the brass doorplate, he carefully arranged his face. It wouldn't do for her to see regret. She deserves better.

Unexpectedly, the door hissed inward before he could push.

"Yeah, right. You let me know when you figure it out." Nurse Anne Keith's blue eyes and small mouth were both tight when she turned to face Parker. Jamming her well-padded hip against the door, she moved aside to let him enter.

"You're gonna want to be careful with that one today," she hissed, angling her head toward Marlea. "I don't know what crawled up her butt, but that heifer probably had to hobble through the gates of hell to get here . . ."

"I heard that," Marlea called from her bed.

"You're on your own," Anne warned, scurrying from the room.

"You certainly made an impression on her. So?" Letting the door close behind him, Parker came closer. "What's going on?"

Marlea sat wordless, ignoring him as she fingered a small silver box resting on the table beside her. Without much effort, Parker saw a tiny pair of silver running shoes and a crayon-endorsed homemade card. *Something from one of her children,* he guessed.

"I know that the accident affected your foot. I didn't think we had removed your tongue, as well." Parker pulled a chair to the foot of the bed and sat. "Hearing damaged, too? Perhaps I'm not as good a surgeon as I thought I was."

"I . . . don't have anything to say."

"Really? That's not what I just heard from Nurse Keith. She seemed to think you had quite a bit to say." Parker ignored both his patient's shrug and the cool breath of blame that brushed his skin when he leaned forward. "Ms. Kellogg . . . Marlea, she was here on my orders. She was here to help you get moving again."

"She needn't have bothered." Marlea whipped back the cotton blanket, revealing the cotton/spandex sock covering her foot and leg. "As you can see, I'm not going anywhere."

"Marlea, you lost two toes on one foot, not the right to live."

"Do you know what that means to a runner? Two toes . . . that's everything. How am I supposed to run with half a foot? I might as well have died." Her brown eyes glistened when she brought her thumb and forefinger together. "Do you know what this is?" She moved the pads of her fingers against each other as she held the doctor's gaze. When he said no, she smiled bitterly. "It's the world's smallest violin." A tear rolled down her cheek. "I feel like it's playing for me."

"You obviously don't know fine music." Ambushed by shame, Parker reached out and closed his hand over her fingers.

"You're holding up my pity party."

"Marlea, you have so much to offer. It would be a shame to lose you, so you may have to work on this, but you don't need a pity party. You have more than half a foot, and you will walk again, but we have to get you up and moving. A part of that is beginning therapy as soon as possible."

"Therapy," Marlea sniffled, but the tears fell in spite of the effort. "You don't want me to feel bad about what happened, but you want me to happily accept the results and just forge ahead. I don't get it."

"You don't want to, and as endearing as your stubbornness might be under other circumstances, now is not the time for it. We need to get you moving to keep you viable." Her frown told him that he had used the wrong word. "Circulation is critical in your recovery. Moving will help to get you back on your . . . uh, get you moving again."

"It hurts." Marlea pulled tissue from the box on the table at her side.

"But you're alive, and as long as you're alive, there's a chance to fix the problem." Parker squeezed her hand and felt rewarded when she squeezed back.

"Is that what they mean by 'bedside manner'? Giving me hope where there may not be any?"

"There's always hope." Straightening and willing himself not to say more, Parker held his breath. Guilty, but not guilty enough to admit his part in the runner's loss, he exhaled when Marlea nodded.

A light tap on the door made him release her hand and turn.

The door whispered open and a tall, round man, followed by a slender, doe-eyed woman, pushed his body into the room. "Ms. Kellogg?" Marlea nodded at the thin-haired man with the big belly. "I'm detective Gene

Brighton. This is my partner, Linda Palmer. We're here about your accident."

Police. Parker's pulse jumped. *Calm down, they're peons, mere redundancies—nothing like the characters on* CSI *or* Law and Order. *They're not worthy of my concern.* His heart fluttered a bit when the detective offered his hand and his card. *He looks like the old version of Al Roker. And the woman is a plain little duck.* That was something his mother would have said about another woman. *And I am her son.* He nearly giggled as the pair got down to business.

Detective Palmer, for all her plainness, seemed to be the sharper of the two. The doctor felt her eyes begin a sly assessment of the picture he presented. *You knew that as soon as Ms. Kellogg was conscious it was just a matter of time before the police would show up. They're not here to talk to you; you're the good guy in this. You saved her life; besides, you have a story. Keep it straight and stick to it. Stay calm, listen to what they have to say, and if they ask, just stick to the story.*

Linda Palmer murmured something in a softly musical voice. Marlea nodded again, and the odd couple crossed the room. Brown-skinned, brown-haired, brown-eyed Palmer pulled a pen and a small notebook from her pocket, and Brighton's gravelly voice took over.

Parker crossed his legs at the knee and leaned back in his chair.

"Okay, Ms. Kellogg," Brighton smoothed a thick, coffee-colored hand over the bulge of his belly. "Let's start with what you remember about July Fourth."

"Independence Day. Uh . . ." Straining to think, Marlea finally gave up. "Nothing."

Palmer scribbled something in her notebook. "You ran the Peachtree Road Race."

Interested, Marlea leaned forward. "Did I finish?"

"You sure did," Palmer smiled. *She's pretty when she smiles*, the doctor thought. *She should smile more often.*

Palmer glanced down and flipped a page in her notebook. "You had a pretty good time, too. Just over forty minutes."

"*Over* forty minutes?" Marlea made a face. "Does Libby know?"

"She knows," Brighton chuckled.

"She's mad, huh?"

"Nah." Brighton chuckled again. "She's glad you're okay."

"I guess she didn't tell you that losing my toes in an accident wasn't on my list of 'okay,' did she?"

"Actually, that was the first thing she told us." Turning slightly, Brighton faced Parker. "And doctor, you were the one who found her."

"Yes." *Breathe.* "I was on my way in for an ER shift, but I decided to stop for a bite to eat, and happened upon the accident site." *There. Short and to the point.*

"Didn't see any other cars?"

"No. None."

"All that highway, in the middle of the day, and you were the only one out there. Talk about a coincidence." The big man angled his gaze. "Funny how that could happen."

"Funny? Not at all. It was a holiday weekend, and the traffic is often irregular." *Careful, you're talking too much. This could be a trap.*

"Yeah, you're right. Holiday traffic can be unpredictable on the interstate. Good thing you came along when you did."

"Yes." Suddenly Reynolds didn't trust the big detective any farther than he could throw him. The doctor recrossed his legs and looked pointedly at his watch. The detectives didn't take the hint. Fifteen minutes later, they were still talking, still taking their infernal notes, but they were through with him.

Brighton seemed satisfied when he led Marlea through a final recitation. "If you'll go over it one more time," he said, "I think that'll do it."

"Okay," Marlea closed her eyes. "I was wearing a white Nike shirt, I remember that. The run wasn't hard, kind of long for me, though. I do the 400, so 6.2 miles was more than usual. It was crowded. A man tripped me; I remember that, too. Then I woke up here." She opened her eyes. "That's all."

Palmer finally closed her notebook, and Parker hoped that neither detective heard his sigh of relief when they each gave Marlea a card and urged her to call if she remembered anything else.

The door had barely closed behind the detectives when Marlea's frustration surfaced. "So strange," she whispered. "I can't remember anything between the park and here."

"It's not unusual," Parker said, relieved by Marlea's lack of recall. "Short-term memory loss is often a by-product of the kind of trauma you've experienced."

—⁂—

"You know she's going to remember more as time goes by."

"Yes, that's the way it usually happens."

"I'm guessing that her remembering will make someone very nervous."

"Yeah, but Gene, there's no way to know how long it will to take her, is there? Then too, there's no way to know how much she actually saw."

"If she saw anything." Brighton thumbed the elevator button. Pulling sunglasses from the breast pocket of his shirt, he delicately placed the glasses on the bridge of his nose. "Got me a feeling though, partner. Based on what we know, I'm getting a feeling."

"This is the slowest elevator I've ever seen." Palmer jabbed the elevator button. "Your 'feeling' means you've got a theory, and your theory is what?"

"Maybe the woman saw something—a make or model or a color while she was driving. According to the report, the other vehicle came from behind and swiped her right rear enough to make her veer into the wall."

"The crime of it isn't just in hitting her; the report implies the car that hit her was heavier than hers—it didn't just scrape and move on. She was pushed."

"After the accident, she was there 'til the doctor found her."

"How likely do you think it is that whoever hit her thought she was somebody else?" Linda Palmer looked at her partner, then changed her mind. "Okay, that was reaching."

The elevator doors slid open and the detectives boarded, riding in silence to the parking deck as a couple of women in flowered dresses chattered away.

Two steps off the elevator, and the silence was too much for Palmer. "Okay, Gene, look. The doctor was too cool, too calm, too determined to remain in the room when the woman was being questioned. He's hiding something."

"That's kinda like my feeling," Brighton agreed. "What does he drive?"

Waiting for Brighton to open the car door, Palmer pulled her notebook out and flipped pages. "It's an Acura, or at least that's what the garage attendant said he was driving today."

"Wonder if he owns any other cars?"

"I'm just guessing," Palmer traced a line in her little book. "Dr. Parker Reynolds strikes me as the kind of man who is easily tempted, and he probably enjoys the fact that he is one of *THE* Reynolds—the ones with all the money."

Brighton turned the wheel, steering the sedan out of the garage and into the sunlight. "Prob'ly got a whole stable full of cars."

"Stables are for horses," his partner noted, "but with his money, he's probably got a whole stable full of them, too."

CHAPTER 7

"Dude." AJ looked up from the sports medicine text he was reading. Dench stood in the middle of the spacious office holding a massive flowering plant that neither man could name. "These just came. For you." He held the flowers away from his body. "Who do you think sent them?"

"Looks like something Bianca would do. Where's the card?"

"No, dude. Not Bianca. Thought she was finished with you when she smelled the gravy runnin' on another train." AJ's eyes slashed him, and Dench wondered if he had said too much. "Sorry, dude, but she's not exactly 'happily ever after' material, now is she?"

"You've got a point." AJ found the small white envelope tucked among the blossoms and flicked it open.

"Who?" Dench tried to see over the broad clutch of flowers.

"Told you." AJ flipped the card onto the desk. "Bianca."

"Wonder what she wants?" Both men asked, studying the plant.

"You," Dench suddenly realized. Setting the heavy pot on the desk, he stepped back and eyed the thing as if it were poison ivy. "She wants you back 'cause she knows, man. It's the endorsement—been all over the news since before you got cut. It was played up because everybody was so surprised that Muscle Force kept you on, and with such a major contract. Dude, she's back 'cause she's smellin' money, and she smells it on you."

Damn it, Dench. Why you gotta go and be right? Looking past his friend, AJ gazed out the windows. It was a little too much to look Dench in the face and admit he was right. Looking out the windows didn't make it much easier. He had been right about Bianca every time he spoke her name. She was a gold digger, with a knack for ferreting out the man who could do the most for her, and she did have a way of turning up in AJ Yarborough's life when it was most convenient for her.

Like that first time, the game with the Browns . . . AJ still recalled wondering how a woman as exotic and enticing as Bianca had found her way into a locker room buried in the bowels of a stadium in Cleveland, Ohio. And yet there she was, sitting with her long legs crossed in the middle of the locker room.

Walking in, most of the team went nuts, good-looking woman like that, but she found me like I was on radar, AJ remembered. It took some fast talking to get her out of there, and once 'rescued,' she had lots of suggestions for showing her gratitude. *Hell, the stuff she had in mind— she turned my head like it could screw on and off . . . and she was nothin' like shy about it.*

A year of exotic and energetic sex, a near-engagement, and then she disappeared for eighteen months. *Took the Mercedes and all the jewelry I bought her, then turned up on*

Grainger's arm at that benefit, saying that he was the only man in the world to have ever shown her true love. And I had to be the one to take on the challenge. Me, trying to define love for a woman who would never understand it. Then she sold the co-op and left me lookin' like a fool five months later . . .

Rissa and Dench had both prophesied the doomed outcome. *Fact is, Rissa hated her instantly, and my sister's no fool. I shoulda listened.*

"Ain't nothing out there you haven't already seen," Dench said, moving between AJ and the window. "That terrace and the pool won't be movin' today, dude."

AJ shifted his gaze and Dench flinched at what he saw in his friend's eyes. "You, uh . . . wanna talk about her?"

AJ shrugged. "What's to say? She sent flowers. From any other woman, something like that would have been over the top. Coming from Bianca, they're simply par for the course."

"The ones she picked are kind of like her, aren't they? All fragrant and showy, just the thing to appeal to someone with a need for publicly displayed attention." Dench pressed a hand to AJ's shoulder and shook his head. "She don't know you very well."

That's an understatement.

Bianca Coltrane had never known AJ for the man he really was. She never much bothered after she checked the salary figures and collected a ton of credit cards. She simply seemed to see AJ, and every other man she encountered, as tactile proof of her superiority to every other woman in the world.

"She say where she is? Is she here? In Atlanta?"

"She didn't say."

"If she is, are you gonna see her? Would you want to?"

AJ looked at Dench's open face and knew he wouldn't tell him the truth, and he hoped his buddy wouldn't guess. *I'll take it to my grave.* What man wouldn't want to know if she could still push his buttons, a woman like that? Standing close to her was almost worth the risk of getting burned, even if almost wasn't good enough.

But hey, bad as it was, it wasn't all in vain, because what I shared with Bianca had nothing to do with love and everything to do with lust, and now I know the difference. At least I can honestly say I learned from her. She was an expensive lesson, but I learned. . .

The phone rang and AJ lunged for it—anything to keep from having to answer Dench's questions.

"Hello?" He could feel Dench's stare, and even before she spoke, AJ knew it was Bianca. *It's almost like she sends heat over the phone line*, he marveled, stumbling over further greeting.

Listening, trying not to enjoy her dulcet tones, he kept his answers as short as possible. No point in giving Dench any more ammunition.

"Thanks for the flowers. It was a nice gesture."

"Gesture, my foot! After what she put you through, she should have gestured with a hell of a lot more than a pot of posies!"

AJ half appreciated the support, but he shrugged Dench off and pointed to the door. Covering the mouthpiece with his hand, he whispered, "Close the door behind you."

"Uh-huh, I'm gon' close the door all right," Dench said, shambling toward the door. "Just you be sure not to open it for her."

Knowing he was stepping out on shaky ground, AJ turned back to the phone.

"I'm at the Ritz," Bianca sighed into his ear. "On Peachtree. You remember how much we used to like the Ritz, don't you?"

"It's a nice hotel, Bianca. I hope you'll enjoy your stay." *Now either get off my phone or enjoy listening to the dial tone.*

"AJ, honey, why are you so short with me? Honey, I know that we have a lot of history between us. I'm the first to admit that some of it wasn't so good, but you have to admit that when we were good, there was nothing better." She waited, letting him think.

AJ pulled the phone from his ear and glared at it. Not sure of what he would say, he pressed the phone against his ear and listened to her breathe—slow and steady, sure of herself. "What do you want, Bianca?"

"Dinner with an old friend, AJ, that's all I'm after. I'm in town for an Apparel Mart preview of my new clothing line, and I thought it was just polite to look you up. Since it's been so long, I thought we should talk."

"You could have called or e-mailed a long time ago, if that's really what you wanted."

Her laughter was bright, intriguing. "Would you have answered?" When he said nothing, she laughed again. "I thought not, so here I am."

"Here you are."

"I've missed you, AJ. I wanted to surprise you, work through what's come between us, and share some closure with you."

She's working on me, AJ warned himself. *She's working on me, and it's wearing me down.* He tried hardening his voice. "It's been three years, Bianca. I call that closure enough for both of us."

"Twenty-two months and four days, AJ. Even the days matter to me."

"They used to matter to me, too. I think it's better if we let sleeping dogs lie."

"AJ, I don't want you to hate me."

She sniffed, and he imagined a single tear shimmering against her blushing cheek. Bianca Coltrane was the only woman he had ever met who could even cry pretty. "I don't hate you, Bianca."

"Then why are you making this so hard?"

Because you picked my pocket, drop-kicked my heart, left me trying to pick my face up off the floor, and now you're back to shred what's left of my dignity. I can't let you do that.

"AJ?"

"I'm here."

"You didn't answer the question."

His deep breath caught in his throat, and AJ tried to talk around it. "Maybe because of the little indiscretions that drove us apart?"

"They were mine, AJ, and I admit it. I was wrong," she whispered. "I was scared."

"Scared. Huh." Facing the broad windows fronting his terrace, AJ closed his eyes. "I heard you weren't scared of any of my teammates." Bianca's gasp told him that he had struck a nerve.

"That was mean, AJ. You were never mean before."

"No one ever hurt me the way you did, Bianca."

"I . . . know. I'm ashamed of what I did, how I left things between us."

Silence hung in the air, and AJ unexpectedly felt something for Bianca that he had never felt before—pity.

"I'm sorry, AJ. Won't you let me try to make it up to you?" She waited. *Timing my mood.* AJ knew it instinctively.

"I can't give time back to you, AJ. As much as I want to, I can't make the past go away. But I can, I am, asking your forgiveness, and I can buy dinner. At a really good restaurant for a really good man." She was smiling. He could hear it.

"I don't know, Bianca."

"Think about it while you're getting dressed," she pressed. "It's four o'clock now. Meet me at six." She waited and, when AJ hesitated, her warmth surged over the line on a satisfied sigh. "Drinks at six, then dinner, AJ. I'm looking forward to it."

AJ heard the click when she disconnected the call. "What the hell am I thinkin'," he muttered, looking at the closed door across from him. "How am I gonna get dressed and out of here without running into Dench?"

An hour later, showered and shaved, dressed in neat dark linen shirt and slacks, AJ sorted through the keys on his bureau top. "The 300M," he decided. "It's the quietest. It'll keep Dench out of my business." *And it'll impress Bianca.*

Surprised at his luck, AJ made his way through the house to the garage without encountering his sister Rissa, or Dench. *That would be all I'd need, runnin' into my self-appointed consciences.*

There would be Rissa, with her finger up in my face, using all those grammatically and politically correct words I paid for her to learn, trying to tell me how to live my life. Actin' like somebody's mother, like she's not my baby sister. Trying to protect me. Then Dench—not much better. Both of 'em trying to watch my back, telling me which way to walk. But this time, my eyes are wide open. I know what I'm doing, and I don't need that pair in my way.

Pausing to listen, he could hear the sound of music drifting up from his home theater. "Good. They're watching a movie. *Ali*, from the sound of it."

Pleased with his good fortune, AJ hurried through the breezeway relaxing only after he had driven through the estate gates. *I've gotten this far without seeing either Rissa or Dench. That's gotta be some kind of a good sign. If fate is with me, then maybe seeing Bianca again is not as stupid as I thought.*

"I sound like I'm whistling in the dark, trying to keep bad things from touching me," AJ told himself as he guided the big car onto the highway. Fiddling with the car's stereo system, he settled for jazz. By the time AJ handed his car over to the Ritz valet, Dave Koz was calming his soul.

The young guy looked hard at AJ. "Sir? I hope you won't think I'm being, you know, pushy or anything. I'm a fan, though. Aren't you AJ Yarborough?"

"Yeah, man," another white-shirted valet added, pumping an arm in the air. "I saw you in that game with Philly. Man, you were one runnin' son of a bitch! Back in the day, you was the bomb!"

The first kid ran his hand over his shaved head. "I had you figured for the Hall of Fame. Still do; probably happen in a couple of years."

"Thanks." Feeling older than Namath, AJ signed a handful of autographs on his way to the lobby.

The concierge directed him to Bianca's sixteenth-floor suite. Standing outside her door, he wished he had stopped for flowers, then immediately dismissed the thought. "Flowers, no flowers, I'm here now." He knocked at the door.

The door swept inward and Bianca flowed from the room and into his arms. "AJ! Oh, honey!" Standing nearly six feet in high-heeled strappy sandals, she pressed the generously curved length of her body against him. Warm and tight in all the right places, she slipped her leg around and through his. "It's been too long."

Damn, she still looks good, and she feels as good as she looks. His arms rose as if of their own accord, accepting her. *This would be a whole lot easier if she was fat and tired.* AJ nodded against the luxuriant sweep of her soft honey-gold hair and held her tighter. *Always did like the way her hair felt, the way she smells.*

Tilting her head and arching her back, Bianca looked into AJ's face. She laced fingers tightly behind his neck, and he could feel her heartbeat beneath the thin silky knit of her short summer dress. Trying to force his thoughts from beneath the buttery gold of her little dress, AJ responded to the soft kiss she offered. Assuming his acceptance, she deepened the kiss.

Parting his lips, expecting more, AJ was surprised when she dropped her hands from his neck. Keeping her eyes on his, she took his hand, she led him into the suite.

Billie Holiday's voice, sultry and sensual, filled the rooms. *She always liked Billie. Still travels with her, I see.* He knew that if he found the hidden CD player, Sarah Vaughn would be the next choice. Proud, AJ grinned. *That's what I taught her, to love good music. Especially jazz. Before me, the deepest music she was into was a little R and B. Nothing wrong with it, but there's so much more . . .*

Bianca's fingers trailed along his shoulder and down his arm, gently steering him into the sitting room. Deep and long, the suite's sitting room was exactly as AJ remembered. Velvet sofas, highly polished wood and brass, with obviously expensive, tasteful artwork and deep custom carpeting—precisely Bianca's taste. Unable to stop himself, his eyes strayed toward what he knew would be her bedroom. Self-conscious, he pulled his attention away from the door and was embarrassed when he saw her noticing.

Dang! I was trying not to go there. To his great relief, she let it slide.

"How about a drink, AJ?" He watched her glide across the room to a brass-articulated highboy. She opened the brace of doors, revealing the bar. Assuming his preference, she clinked ice into a short thick glass and added a generous splash of brandy. Moving effortlessly, swirling the richly colored liquid, she returned to AJ's side and offered the drink.

"Still drink brandy, AJ? It's the good stuff."

"It is good," he said behind his first sip.

"Sit," she smiled, gracefully indicating the nearest sofa.

Sitting and tilting the glass to his lips, AJ nearly missed her glancing at her small gold wristwatch. As if on cue, there was a knock at the door. *What's up with that?* he wondered, his eyes going to Bianca.

Moving quickly to the door, she smiled and opened it. "Dinner. I thought we would eat here."

"I thought we were going out."

"Why?" AJ didn't answer. Ignoring his frown, Bianca directed the waiter. Supervising the setting of the small table, she took control of the evening.

AJ sat where she told him to and watched the obsequious waiter seat her. *I thought the plan was to meet her here at the Ritz and walk to the restaurant. Aw, man. . . hope Dench was wrong.* Across the table, Bianca smoothed the napkin across her lap. *Wonder what she's got up her sleeve?*

"Still a meat and potatoes man, AJ?" Teasing, Bianca touched her fork to the sirloin on AJ's plate. "I ordered it rare, just the way you used to like it."

"What is this about, Bianca?" AJ used two fingers to nudge the plate. "Really?"

"I don't know what you mean." She busied herself with her plate. "Two friends having dinner. That's what we are, aren't we?"

AJ turned his silverware. "I'm not so sure."

"How can you say that? I went out of my way to contact you—for old time's sake. I planned this dinner." Her hazel eyes widened and then she pouted prettily. "I thought it would give us more time together. I thought it would give us a chance to share what we've been doing. You haven't even asked me about my business."

"How's your business?" AJ asked dutifully.

"Well, you know that I've always loved clothes. I had a chance to do some modeling, found a few backers, and here I am." Pushing her plate aside, she leaned forward. "Now I'm ready to expand. How about you?"

"I got cut by my team." AJ toyed with his fork, stopping when she placed her hand atop his.

"Stop playing with the silver, AJ. I heard you've been very busy, that you put that little physical therapy degree or certification, or whatever it is, to work." When his face clouded, Bianca's fingers gently stroked the back of his hand. "Oh, don't get me wrong, AJ. I think it's wonderful that you worked with that kid and that he's all better now. Writing the book together was a wonderful idea, uh, cathartic even."

Okay, AJ thought, *now it's all starting to make sense. Dench was right. This is about money.*

"I saw on TV the other night that the book is not even out yet, and there's already a movie option. That must be exciting for you." AJ moved his hand, but Bianca captured it between her warm palms. "Then there's that wonderful contract with Muscle Force. It must be great to be you."

"Oh, yeah. Just great." *How big a damned fool do I have to be not to see through this?*

"And you look so fine to me. It's like no time has passed at all. I know we talked about friendship on the phone AJ, but now that I'm here with you, I'm wondering . . . do you think we could try it again?"

AJ's hand jerked, then pulled free. "Try what?"

"Silly." She reached for him again, and AJ recoiled. "Us. As a couple."

Standing so fast his chair toppled, AJ backed away from the beautifully set table. "A couple of what?" *Like I don't already know!*

"Maybe I should have waited until I had you in bed to broach the topic," Bianca simpered.

"Wouldn't have made any difference." AJ tossed his napkin to the table. "You know, when we were together, I used to look at people—young people, old people, married people, couples—and wonder how they did it. What did they know that I didn't know? Then we broke up and I've had . . ." he looked at the woman who stood across from him shaking back her hair, "almost three whole years to think of an answer."

"What's the answer, AJ?" Bianca's breasts heaved dramatically.

"It's not what they know, it's who they are. What they've learned they want and need from each other. Who they're matched with. For me, I want a woman who will have more feeling for the man in her life and the family that they build together than she has for a closet full of designer clothes."

"I am what I am, AJ." Bianca smoothed slow hands over her hips. "Would you have me lie to you? I would rather we start off honestly."

"Same old Bianca. You are what and whoever suits you at the moment."

"Baby, there is nothing old about me, and as long as I can find a good doctor and an on-call trainer, there never will be." Easing the soft golden knit of her dress high enough to display taut, satiny skin and tight, gym-bred curves, she smiled. She pulled the dress over her head, then watched his face when she held it at her side, displaying the sheer and scant icy-blue lace of her bra and panties against the tawny blush of her flawless skin. "Like it?"

What's not to like? AJ closed his eyes and prayed for strength. He opened them in time to see her make the toss. Reacting, his hands closed on the softness of her dress.

"Best hands in the NFL, and you can still put 'em on me," Bianca purred.

AJ cursed his reflexes. He desperately wanted to throw the dress back. *I do, and she'll think she punked me.* He dropped the dress across a nearby chair back.

"They say that nothing feels as good as silk. Except me." She preened easily.

"You know, Bianca, I believe that." *She thinks she punked me.* "I believe that 'they' really do say that about you."

Hips moving, she shifted her shoulders and let her hair fall forward in a lush and moving curtain.

Undulating to music only she could hear, Bianca danced in a small circle. "Trust me," she whispered over her shoulder, "they're right, but you already know that. Now the question is, how long are you going to stand over there?"

"Same old Bianca . . ."

Suddenly exasperated, she stopped dancing and propped a hand on her hip. "When are you going to grow up, AJ? Quit playing that game, you know, the one where we 'cat and mouse' around: me, playing the seductress, and you, playing the noble innocent? Believe me, nobody is that innocent—I know."

Standing hip-sprung in stiletto sandals, toying with the clasp of her lace bra, Bianca eyed him. "You wanted me once, AJ; you wanted all of this once. Well, now I'm telling you that you can have me. Free and clear. I'll even commit to being a one-man woman, if that'll make you happy, but you'll have to marry me to guarantee it."

"Marry you? I remember a time when you ran from the ring I wanted to give you. And now that I think of it, there was another time when I couldn't find a ring big enough to make you happy."

"That was then, this is now."

"I don't think I'm in the market for what you're selling, Bianca." AJ took a backward step, ready for the door. "When I wanted you, I wanted a wife, a friend, a companion, a woman to love for a lifetime."

"And I'm telling you that you can have that—now." She took a step toward him, the fine lace of her thong panties shimmering at the sweet juncture of her slender thighs. "I would make a good wife, AJ." Close enough to stare up into his eyes, Bianca caught his hand and slid it slowly over her tight, flat belly. Her grin was sly; she knew she had his attention. "I would even risk this body for a baby . . . with you, AJ."

"What the hell am I supposed to say to that?" AJ struggled to keep his eyes on her face as she pressed close, her palms planted against his chest.

"Make it easy on both of us; say yes."

"I don't think so, Bianca." Willpower gave him the strength to step out of her arms. "I think I'd better leave."

Crossing her arms tightly beneath her breasts, Bianca watched the door close behind him. "It's never that easy, AJ. I thought you knew that by now."

CHAPTER 8

"Eight-fifteen on a hot July night, and here I am. Alone in Atlanta."

Curiosity lit the blue eyes of the woman waiting next to him at the elevator. Her clear, oval face was framed by a careless mane of auburn hair and distinguished by a full and generous mouth. Her smile telegraphed want and need so intensely that AJ had to look away from her. Evidently, he didn't *have* to be alone.

But company like hers wasn't going to solve his problem. *This sure wasn't the ending I had scripted for tonight,* he thought. *But what else was I expectin'? It's like Dench said; I knew who she was when I walked through the door. And I did walk through it, all on my own.* AJ pushed his hands deep into the pockets of his linen trousers and tried to remember what made him think Bianca would ever change. *You knew who you were dealing with, and ain't no sense in trying to fool yourself by pretending that you thought she had changed just because she told you that she 'just wanted to talk'.* A fleeting image of Bianca shedding her dress and posing in her shimmering bra and panties crossed his mind. *Bianca has never wanted to 'just talk'.*

When the elevator reached the lobby, his blue-eyed companion cleared her throat and lifted a sculpted brow. Her eyes were smoky, her intention clear. "Have a good evening," AJ muttered. Her brow fell. *Pass incomplete.* Leaving his car and the beautiful woman behind, AJ crossed the Ritz lobby and emerged on Peachtree Street.

He scanned the street. *Now that you're out here, where are you trying to go?* People, looking sure of their destinations, rushed past. And AJ stood still. He didn't have a clue which way to go—it wasn't as if he had anyone waiting for him. *South*, he was tempted, *but for what?* So his feet turned north.

He had no idea how fast or how far he had walked. Though born and raised in Atlanta, it had been many years since he had last walked on Peachtree Street. Buses, horse-drawn carriages, pedestrians, and a couple of spandex-clad men on bikes passed before AJ realized where he was and how far he had come.

Standing at one corner, waiting for the light to change, he saw the Fox Theater across from him and the Georgian Terrace Hotel on the other corner. *Ponce de Leon Avenue*, he realized.

Okay, now that I know where I am, what am I going to do about it? Dinner was a bust. I could eat. Or I could drink. He crossed the street, passed The Fox and headed for the bar at Churchill Downs, the little bar on the corner, never realizing that he had finally settled on a destination.

The high-energy beat of soca and the heady aroma of Caribbean foods greeted him. *Not real hungry, but conch fritters might be good . . .*

━◦∞◦━

Peachtree Street was never meant to be seen like this. I've never liked taking the streets through this town in the summer. Parker Reynolds checked his door locks. He had the distinct feeling that the multi-layered guy leaning against the lamppost watching traffic knew the cost of his car and the amount of money in his pocket. *You have to be careful of people like that,* his mother always said. *They would just as soon pick your pocket as smile at you.*

Oh, Lord . . . is that vagrant stepping into the street? Panhandling? What next? If not for the accident on I-75 and the unholy mess the highway had become, I would be home by now, off these crowded, dirty streets. Parker thumped the leather seat of his Porsche and wished he had chosen a different car for the day. *Something with an automatic transmission—I hate having to shift in city traffic. That's not what this car is made for . . .*

Crawling past Crawford Long Hospital, he fumbled with the radio, listened to a traffic update. *An accident with injuries. At least it happened farther north of the city—it's a Kennestone Hospital problem, not Grady's, but this traffic is not going to break up for hours.* Sliding low in his seat, he shuddered deep inside, glad to be excused from possible trauma-surgery duty—something he felt more and more often since Marlea Kellogg had come into his life.

Suddenly, Reynolds had no energy for driving. *This rolling death march is going to be the death of me,* he sighed. *It's not nine o'clock yet; I could stop for a drink, maybe a bite to eat.* Crossing the traffic-choked intersection, searching for a landmark, his eyes found the

Georgian Terrace Hotel, and he knew where he was. *Where's that place? The one Desireé took me to? It wasn't half-bad . . .*

Peachtree Street didn't help his attitude as dinner and theater traffic seemed determined to bar his progress. Spying Churchill Downs, he jammed the Porsche into gear to make a quick, dirty, and totally illegal turn into the parking lot. Impatient, he parked quickly and walked from the lot.

They just go and give anybody a license these days, Parker fumed when a ragged Ford convertible narrowly missed him as he crossed the street. Holding a hand high for attention, Parker had to skip hurriedly between stop-start paced cars. Tempted to use his third finger, but afraid of the repercussions, his breathing eased when he made it to the other side of the street.

Casting a scornful glance over his shoulder, he headed for the restaurant doors and managed to jam a hand directly between the broad shoulders of the tall man in front of him. Startled and blinking rapidly, straight arm still extended, Parker fell back a step. Then another. "I . . . I beg your pardon. I wasn't looking . . ."

Looking down, the big man seemed to find Parker's stammer amusing.

What the hell is this big gorilla standing here smirking about? "I didn't see you . . ."

"Right."

All right, perhaps that was funny. This ape stands about seven feet tall, probably weighs in on the light side of three hundred-plus pounds, and he's wearing this ridiculous orange and yellow striped shirt, and I didn't see him. "I hope you'll excuse me."

"No prob, man."

A pretty woman in a matching shirt joined the ape, and watching them walk away, Parker's mind leapt to Desireé. There was something evocative and morbidly attractive about the rolling motion of the woman's wide hips in the white Capri pants. *Like Desireé. Maybe I should try calling her again.* Pulling on the heavy door, he patted his pocket, just to be sure he was carrying his cell-phone.

Maybe I shouldn't bother. It won't do to let her think I'm too eager. She'll think she has me over the proverbial barrel; me trying to reach her so urgently, and the calls coming so close to her serving me with those papers. Eventually, I am going to have to do something about her and those damned papers. His head began a dull throb as he crossed the restaurant.

From the corner of his eye, he noticed a curvy woman in a red cotton dress when she stood and raised her glass to her friends. The red dress was tight and cut low, clinging to her lush body like paint. *Like Desireé.* Her friends laughed at her words and she slipped back into her seat—and noticed him noticing her.

Parker looked away and aimed himself at the bar.

"Vodka gimlet," he ordered, climbing onto a tall stool. *It's bad enough to have to call Desireé, now her clones are following me.* He pulled out his cellphone and tapped in the number he knew by heart. He let it ring three times, then clapped the phone closed. Dropping it to the bar, he twirled it with his long fingers. *Where can she be? Every time I've called, I've gotten her answering machine.* The barman set the cold glass before him, and Parker nodded. *Sure, let him run a tab.*

Then his thoughts went back to Desireé. *She's been away from the phone all damned day long! I wonder how many of her galpals it took to record her "Hoochies Gone Wild" phone message?* He sucked at his drink, surprised by the short time it took to reach the bottom.

All I need to do is tap into her little circle. Surely there is someone in that group who knows a bit about car repair. Propping an elbow on the bar, he lifted his empty glass, signaling the barman. *Those people always seem to have an innate intelligence about this sort of thing, and Desireé is the kind of woman who knows people who know people.*

Waiting for his fresh drink, Parker folded his hands around his glass and looked idly into the smoky mirror he faced. *Anybody Desireé digs up is going to be some kind of con artist or thief. They'll take one look at the Rolls and try to charge me an arm and a leg, and I'll have to pay it.* He sighed. *I suppose you always have to pay for what you don't know. . .*

Watching people coming and going, enjoying the company of friends on a hot summer night, Parker felt like an outsider. He took an urgent sip and tried not to look like a solo drinker. *Everybody knows that drinking alone is one foot on the dark path to alcoholism.* Never mind that every evening he spent a couple of solitary hours in the company of a tall bottle of Grey Goose vodka.

Sipping in sanctimony, Parker watched the other three people sitting at the bar. Two were white-shirted waiters on a break. The third was a big man dressed in dark linen sitting a couple of stools over, and he didn't look much like an alcoholic. In fact, he looked quite sober. *And he looks familiar.* Reynolds watched him in the mirror. Shuffling faces from the hospital, his mother's social set, and Desiree's cadre of deadbeats through his mind, he came up blank. *But I know his face.*

"How 'bout I freshen that up for you, Mr. Yarborough?"

There was unction or possibly awe in the barman's voice, but it was the hint Parker needed; the face clicked into place. *AJ Yarborough, the football player. I should have known he was not someone Desireé would have known.*

Parker knocked back the rest of his drink, signaled the barman, and then did something that should have horrified him. Reaching over, he touched the football player's elbow, and then sat grinning when the other man's eyes found his. Embarrassed, he reeled his arm back across the seats. "I don't usually do things like this, but . . . you're AJ Yarborough, the football player, aren't you?"

"Yes."

The single word was cautious, and Parker didn't blame him. "I'm sure that every Tom, Dick, and Harry runs up to you looking for an autograph. Well, I'm not Tom, Dick, or Harry." AJ said nothing. "Parker Reynolds, I'm a fan." Parker used the arrival of his fresh drink to disguise his awkwardness. Raising his glass, he smiled. "Can I get you another?"

AJ tapped his Red Stripe bottle and shook his head. "I'm fine."

"Look, before you either write me off as crazy or decide that I'm trying to hit on you, which I'm not, I just want to say that I'm a doctor. I specialize in trauma surgery, and I've followed your career for quite a while. Lately, I've seen some items on your work with that high school kid, Bobby, uh . . ." Irritated that his memory failed, Parker snapped his fingers, trying to summon the name.

"His name was Robert."

"Right, right . . . Crown, I believe. Robert Crown." Sliding across to the next stool, Parker warmed to his topic. "What was he, about twenty? Felled by a stroke, and you stepped in to work with him. That was pretty impressive. Most people, even active ones, wouldn't have had a clue how to approach him, but you had football in common with him, and you just stepped right in and instinctively handled things. That's certainly not what I've come to expect from men who make their living on the gridiron." Parker held his breath and offered his hand. He started to breathe again when AJ accepted it.

"Thanks, but I want to clear some things up."

AJ's open smile was wide and clean. Parker began to trust the football player. "Sure. Like what?"

"As of June, I'm a *former* football player. My team cut me. "

"I know. Damned shame, too."

"You're *really* a fan?"

"Yes, though I never played." Parker didn't like the stress the football player placed on the word, 'really'. "I'm a surgeon. Have to watch my hands." The doctor held up his hands, stretched his fingers. "What else did you want to clear up?"

"Quiet as it's kept, everything I did with Robert wasn't based on instinct. I'm a degreed physical therapist."

"Really? Well, that certainly makes a difference."

AJ leaned back and eyed the doctor. "Why? You figure 'cause I've got a little brawn working for me, I can't have brains?"

"No." *Yes.* "It's just that it was never mentioned in any of the articles or programs I saw," Parker said, backpedaling.

"I see."

"Please, don't get me wrong. I didn't mean . . ." Parker was embarrassed by the look of understanding on AJ's face. "Will you continue your work? I mean, now that you've written this book and set out on the road of celebrity?"

"You're givin' me too much credit," AJ grinned. "I'm off the football field for good, but I've got the PT background and a small practice."

"You're a physical therapist with a practice? Really?"

"Yes. Why is that so hard for you to believe?"

The wisdom in the football player's face almost shamed Parker. Almost. "I, ah . . . just assumed . . . PT schools are pretty competitive."

"Almost as hard to get into one as it is to get into med school."

"Touché." Parker bobbed his head and tried to remember if he had given his full name. He didn't want the player supposing, even correctly, that it had been name alone that had gotten him through his prestigious medical education. "Where did you go to school?"

"Emory."

Damn. He's even smarter than he looks and sounds. "Emory is an outstanding school."

"And I was an outstanding student. I completed my work during the off-season."

Like a part-time job.

"And before you say it, I never treated school like a part-time job. My course and lab work was a priority, and I did have to hustle to get through. Just so you know, an NFL season is no walk in the park; adding school . . . well, I wanted it."

Parker emptied his glass and signaled for a refill. "You seem serious. This is more than just a hobby for you."

"I like workin' with people, seeing bodies find motion and wellness . . . Yeah, it's far more than a hobby, and I'm going to stick with it."

"Does your athletic past influence you? Did that last hit you took, the one that ended your career, have anything to do with your choice?"

"Maybe." AJ emptied his Red Stripe, remembered the bone-shattering crunch of his knees, and sat looking down at the bottle.

Thinking, Parker guessed, when he licked his lips and leaned forward on his stool. "Let me ask you a hypothetical question—as an athlete. When you took that last hit, what went through your mind? What did you think when you couldn't get up; when you had to be carried off the field on a stretcher?"

"Man, you don't mind gettin' personal, do you?" AJ shook his head heavily and drew a deep breath. "I thought my life was over, that nothing would ever be the same. I thought . . ." he looked at the doctor, and released the breath slowly. "This is going to sound silly to you. I thought I would never run again."

"And after the surgery?"

"That it hurt, but I was glad I could feel it." The corner of AJ's mouth lifted in a mirthless smile. "That I was the biggest fool in the world, and that if God would let me run again, I would never stop."

Pushing his lips together, Parker nodded. "Can you run now?"

"Yeah. Matter of fact, I ran the Peachtree Road Race a few weeks ago. Wasn't perfect, wasn't pretty, but it felt good to do it. Like at least part of me was back in my real life." AJ accepted another cold bottle from the barman and took a deep swallow.

"What if," Parker asked, "what if you could give that to someone else? Another runner?"

Suspicion crowded AJ's brow. "I don't know what you mean."

"I have a patient. A runner. She's refusing therapy now, but if I could convince her to try, would you consider taking her on as a new client? She just might consider it if she knew how hard another athlete had worked."

AJ laughed. "Where did that come from? You don't know anything about me. I could be fifty kinds of fraud for all you know."

"You were acting from concern for wholeness and health when you took on Robert Crown."

"Robert was different."

Parker tried to pin AJ with his eyes. "Different how?"

"He was a man, a football player." AJ saw the shift in the doctor's face. "Before you say it, no; it had nothing to do with gender. It's just that with football, well, you learn to work through the pain. It's a different mindset, and I wouldn't be right for her."

"Is that what they taught you at Emory? To walk away from a potential client because they didn't participate in your sport of choice?" Parker twirled the glass. "I thought they had a better curriculum than that."

AJ glared at him, and Parker had the pleasure of realizing that he had just hit a nerve. "You sound like a man seeking a challenge, and I can promise that this patient will be a real challenge for you."

"What's her condition?"

Got him! "Basically very good. She did lose two toes, though."

"Ouch." AJ flinched.

"From all that I understand, she was a highly competitive runner with Olympic aspirations. You ought to be able to identify with that."

"Yeah, going all out for a goal makes a lot of sense to me, but what's your stake in this woman's recovery?"

"Stake? Stake implies a gamble." Parker grinned too easily, then assumed a more sober visage. It wouldn't do to have the other man think he was being suckered. "This is no gamble. With proper therapy and support, her recovery is certain."

"Certainty is relative. You said she was an athlete, Olympic class. That takes a certain kind of pride and sacrifice," AJ said slowly. "What's your guess as to how she'll see this recovery that you've got planned for her?"

"About as you'd expect. I'm a healer." The doctor shrugged, knowing that AJ was probably thinking back to his own playing days. "My interest is in seeing my patient as whole as she can be . . . under the circumstances."

"Under the circumstances? What 'circumstances' would those be?"

"She's never going to have the body she had. She's never going to run the way she once did."

"That's pretty honest. You getting tired of baiting me?"

"She has an excellent, well-conditioned body. She's used to working hard. That's half the battle, isn't it? Come on," Parker lifted his glass in salute, then downed the end of his drink. "What have you got better to do?"

Good question. I sure won't be spending the time with Bianca. AJ raised his bottle and returned the salute. "Tell you what, I'll meet her, do an initial assessment, then we'll decide whether or not I'll take her on as a patient."

Parker signaled the barman and nodded as he watched the liquor cover the ice in his glass. "That's the best you can offer?"

AJ nodded. "For now."

"Then it will have to do," the doctor said, offering a handshake to seal the deal.

CHAPTER 9

"I really hate trashing through these reports." Palmer pushed the dog-eared stack across her desk. Leaning back, she stretched hugely and yawned. Recovering, she primly tugged her peach cotton top down over the exposed inch of her tight brown skin. When she was sure her partner had missed her display, she folded her hands on the worn blotter covering her city-issue desk. "Reading vehicular reports is definitely not the fun part of the job I signed up for. And the pictures—ugh!"

"Don't go actin' like a girl on me." Brighton licked his thumb, and turned the page. "We gotta read the reports, and the pictures are a part of that. Sometimes what's left of the car is the only witness we've got."

"No kidding." Palmer used her short-nailed fingertips to push the stack even further away. "On this Kellogg case, we've got pages and pictures of the wreck and the condition of the weather and the road at the time of the accident, and not a single living soul has come forth to say that he saw anything."

"That would just be too easy, now wouldn't it?" Brighton turned another page. A few unattached sheets slipped from Brighton's grasp and fluttered to the floor. Nudging one or two with his loafer, he ignored them and kept flipping.

"You gonna pick those up or not?"

"Not." He flipped another page, then watched it fall from the folder to join the others. "See? I'll just wait 'til I finish, then get all of them at once."

"Lazy."

"No, just conserving energy." He licked his thumb again. "You shouldn't be so critical."

Palmer ran a finger along the edges of the stack of reports. "Did you take a look at the reconstructionist's report?"

"For all the good it did. Deacon's pretty resourceful. He used a total-station system, and pulled in some crash-scene measurements." Brighton lifted a glossy sheet from the file and turned it so that his partner could see it. "Makes a nice kind of 3-D picture, don't'cha think? We can see what she must have seen during the accident."

"Sure we can. Looking at that thing we can see everything except the car that hit her." Standing stiffly, Palmer eyed her partner, then headed for the papers drifting toward his feet. "You knew it would get to me."

"What?" Brighton feigned innocence, but the flick of his eyes gave him away.

Palmer growled something about his being raised in a barn and collected the pages. Scanning as she slapped the pages together, she frowned. "From what I can see, they were able to collect evidence showing the principal direction of force, trace evidence, like gravel and road debris, and they found some paint scrapes on her car."

Brighton placed the folder on the desk in front of him. "They test the paint?"

On her knees, Palmer shuffled the pages. "Looks like they checked the speed from the skid marks, got the stopping time and distance, and after doin' the math, it adds up to a lot of nothing. And I don't see a single thing on the paint."

"Not even a hint of the color?"

Palmer sucked her teeth and frowned. "Did you just hear me say that I didn't see a single thing?"

Forgiving, Brighton grinned. "Then I say we go old school. Let's start with trace evidence, find out the color, and check out the one other person we know was there."

"The doctor."

"Exactly. Plug his name in and let's see what kind of cars come up under his ownership. Then we'll just . . ."

"I've already got it." Palmer pointed to her desk.

"Oh, you're a sly one. Open it up and let's see what we've got."

Reaching across the space between their desks, Palmer snagged the report, while Brighton flapped a questing hand across his desk.

"Looking for these?" Palmer offered his reading glasses.

"Yeah, thanks." He jammed them on his nose and peered over them. "That's better." Noticing her smirk, he rolled his eyes. "Don't ever get old, partner. Life is hard when your arms are too short to read."

Palmer tried not to laugh. "I'm seeing four . . . five . . . no, six different cars listed here for Dr. Parker Reynolds, including a Corvette, a vintage Porsche Targa, a Rolls Corniche . . ."

"Rolls Corniche. Nothing quite like hand-built luxury, is there?"

"When you can afford the very best . . ." Palmer left the thought hanging.

"Not on what I make." Brighton looked at her over the top of his glasses. "Wasn't he driving a Lexus when we were there?"

"Yeah, a really nice new one."

"Is it on the list?"

"Uh-huh." She drew a finger across the list. "Got it right here."

"Did you see the tag hangin' on that baby? 'C Y I WRK'."

"He's a regular one-man fan club."

Brighton's chair moaned when he rocked back and closed his eyes. "True dat."

※

"Who was the bright person who decided that this was flesh-colored?" Marlea pulled the thick beige surgical stocking over her foot. "It doesn't look a thing like my flesh."

"Is that humor?" Reynolds glanced up from his Palm Pilot, smiling. "Coming from you, I suppose it is, isn't it?" She pulled the leg of her sweatpants down over the sock. Ignoring the surgical shoe, she tucked one leg protectively behind the other.

"You're coming along quite well. We'll need to arrange for your continuing therapy."

"You've got jokes, right?" Marlea's crooked smile was hopeful. "I already told you, I don't want therapy."

She looks about twelve years old, sitting there on the bed in that sweat suit with her hair pulled up like that, pouting. Parker tried to distance himself from her vulnerability, from the way she looked.

"Marlea, I understand that you're reluctant to talk about it." *I would be, too.* "You'll be leaving the hospital shortly, and we need to come up with a plan that will get you back on your feet."

"You know what? I'm not reluctant, I'm pissed way the hell off!" She slammed her hand against her thigh and her eyes burned into the doctor's. "What good will therapy do, 'cause even if *I'm* on *my* feet, *we* won't be running, will *we*?"

"Life is not just about running; you should know that by now."

"Easy for you to say." Narrowing her eyes defiantly, she dropped her chin to her chest. "You've never been committed to anything, have you?"

"I'm a doctor. I'm committed to life." Parker tried to smile.

"Running is, was, my life."

Her head stayed low, and Parker's usually agile mind flailed about, seeking the right words. "Running has absolutely nothing to do with the kind of teacher you are, or the quality of woman you are."

"That sounds good, but . . ." When she lifted her head, her brown eyes held more pain than Parker would have ever imagined. "Next thing I know, you'll be standing there trying to tell me that not only am I lucky to have survived, which I agree with, but that no one worthy of me will mind the changes in me."

"Your friend Libby doesn't seem to have a problem."

"Libby loves me. She would be my friend if I grew two more heads and a hump on my back. It's not the same thing." Marlea's shoulders rose and fell. She untucked her stockinged foot and held it in front of her. "My foot will never work the way it used to. It'll never look normal again, not even to me. You've already told me that you can't attach any more toes to it. You can't fix me."

"Marlea . . ."

"Uh-uh." She cut him off with a decisive shake of her head. "It's not like I have a man who will mind, but I might want one some day. If I was your woman, would you want me cuddlin' up to you with my stumpy ol' foot? Think about it. How many men do you know who are out there looking for a woman like me? I'm not talking about some freak collector. I'm talking about an honest, decent, intelligent, loving man—somebody to plan a life with? And what about children? How would I explain it to them?"

Father, can I get a break? Parker prayed, feeling undeserving. *Looking into her pain is too hard.* "I think you're getting ahead of yourself. You're a beautiful woman, with a talent for teaching children; there's no way around that. You would make a wonderful wife and mother. Your life path is up to you. But I think that if we, if you, are going to make positive steps, you have to commit to therapy."

"You really believe that?"

"Yes, I do." Parker saw himself through her eyes for the first time, and guilt poured over his head and shoulders, sticking like tar. Remorse edged into the tiny bends and crevices of his heart, but it wasn't enough to stop his heart from breaking for her. *She trusts me*, he knew. *I want to give her a promise I can keep.*

"I'm not going to lie to you. I can promise that your recovery will be faster and far more complete with therapy than without it." Surprising himself, he reached for her hand, and was pleased when she didn't pull away. "Try the therapy, Marlea. I promise you won't regret it."

"Promises, promises . . ." Pressing her lips thin, she looked at their joined hands.

"How about this one. I promise that you will walk again. Maybe," he smiled, "you'll even dance again."

"But will I run? Will I ever run again? And if I could ever have that dream come true, what about my balance? My speed?"

"We're getting ahead of ourselves. Haven't you ever heard that you have to walk before you can run?"

"Jokes," Marlea muttered.

But at least she smiled! "There are no promises here, but there is an excellent physical therapist in town, and he's available. His time is at a premium these days because, in addition to his practice, he's working with the Federal Awareness Coalition on a diversity amendment, and he has some other ongoing business ventures. Very bright man, though. Did I tell you that this guy is a former NFL player with a very big heart?"

"You didn't tell me anything about him. Big heart, huh? Is that why he's a 'former' NFL player?"

"Enough of that, you little smartass. You know what I mean. He's one of the best and most motivated therapists I've ever met."

"Yeah?" Marlea teased, "but is he cute?"

"That would require a highly subjective judgment, and as of this moment, I am not prepared to offer an opinion as to his degree of cuteness—unless that would get you to commit to working with him. In that case, he could certainly be called cute."

"You've already talked to him about me?" Marlea probed, pushing her tongue into her cheek.

"Please don't look like that." *Please!* "This man is a professional. I couldn't very well ask him to take on a case without telling him something about you, now could I?"

"Did you call me a victim when you talked to him?"

Parker made a face. "Now would I do a thing like that?"

"I'm not sure. You might."

"Is this that 'pity party' thing again? Because if it is, I'm not buying into it." Parker took an exaggerated look at his watch. "And if you are, then you've got about five minutes to get over it. You have a two o'clock appointment with Mr. Yarborough."

"Two o'clock? You're kidding!"

"No, I'm very serious. Two o'clock."

"Men! You've been here examining me for almost twenty minutes, and this is the first you've said about this person coming to see me. What the heck were you thinking?" Marlea gripped the walker at her bedside and slid one foot to the floor. A sloppy hop-shuffle brought her to the tiny hospital bathroom. "You made an appointment for me, and I look like this?" She pushed her face close to the narrow mirror above the sink and groaned. Raking numb fingers through her ponytail, she glared past herself to Parker's reflection. "The first time I meet this amazing therapist, and I look like the loser in an ax fight. I can't believe you did this!"

Amused, Parker crossed his arms and watched. "Why are you worried? This is a hospital, not a tearoom. He's here to assess your condition, not take you to the prom."

"More jokes." Marlea rubbed at her eyes. "Last thing I need."

"Can we get you back over here?" Parker swept an arm toward the bed.

"Why not? There's not a whole lot more I can do in here." She wiped her hands on a small towel and tossed it aside. "So what other surprises do I have to look forward to this afternoon?"

"If you're going to be surly about it . . ." And she was, he could already see it. "I don't think I'll tell you, though I believe knowing might help you to better appreciate this particular therapist."

"Why? What makes this one so special? Has he got a magic wand or something?" Marlea managed her hop-shuffle back to her bed and sat. She folded her hands in her lap and made her face attentive. "I'm all ears. You can tell me now."

"I don't know," Parker began. "Perhaps it would be better if . . ." A light tap on the door interrupted him.

The door moved slowly inward. "Oh," he began, realizing that he was about to introduce his perfect solution. "Come in! We've been waiting for you."

AJ pushed the door wider and stepped into the room.

"Marlea Kellogg, I would like to introduce you to . . ." Marlea's mouth dropped open.

"You!" she finally managed, gaping at AJ Yarborough.

CHAPTER 10

"You two already know each other?" Parker Reynolds reached for the foot of Marlea's bed when he felt the earth move under his feet. His whole world shifted, and he didn't feel very well.

"Oh, yeah." Marlea elbowed herself higher in her bed. "Yeah, I know him. He's the man who tripped me, the SOB who cost me everything!"

"Whoa! Lady, I just walked into the room." AJ raised a hand and looked closely at the woman in the bed. "You don't know anything about my parentage, and frankly, my mother would take extreme exception to your characterization of her as a . . ."

"You know him?" *From where?* Parker wondered, premonition giving him an instant headache. *How could she have pulled his face out of her Swiss-cheesed memory?*

"I don't know him, but I remember him."

"You remember him?" Parker forced himself to release his grip on the bed's footboard.

"You remember me?" Hand still on the door, AJ was too curious to leave but unsure whether he should stay. "Where do you think you remember me from?"

"From before." Marlea's chest heaved with effort.

"From before what?" The doctor's head jerked toward Marlea. "You remember him from before what?"

"Remember what?" AJ released the door.

"The park and the race! You, I'm going to remember for the rest of my natural life!"

"What race?"

"You remember being in the park, and you remember the race?" The doctor's face froze. "And after the race?"

"Some of it, just the parts I told you about. Nothing else, until I woke up in this bed missing half my foot. But I remember him." Marlea glared at the therapist.

"Nothing?"

"I keep telling you . . ." She slapped at the bed. "No, I don't remember anything I haven't already told you about, nothing at all."

"Hey!" AJ's shout got Marlea's attention and her eyes raked his strong form. Her expression left AJ with no doubt that, given half the chance, she would gladly use her good foot on him. "What race are you two so worked up about?"

Marlea's lips curled. "Like you don't know!"

"I don't know." AJ felt compelled to defend himself, since nobody else in the room was bothering to do so.

"The Peachtree."

"Road race?"

"Yes, you tripped me!"

"That was you?" And suddenly, the world—and her fury—made sense. AJ remembered the pretty woman with the ponytail and the endless legs. Getting tangled up with her hadn't exactly been the high point of his day, but when he looked closely at the angry woman glaring across the room . . . yep, that was her. "Small world. So how are you?"

"Aside from sitting up in this hospital, I'm just fine. Thanks for asking." Marlea couldn't believe the question. "Seriously, how do you think I'm doing?"

AJ came closer and grinned. "You sound a little angry, to tell the truth. But since we didn't get to exchange names earlier, I'm AJ Yarborough." He stuck out his hand; she ignored it.

"So you're gonna leave a brother hangin', huh?" He dropped his hand but held his knowing grin.

"A brother ought to go someplace he's wanted." Marlea's eyes hurled daggers at him.

"As you can see, our Ms. Kellogg is in rare form today," Parker offered from the sideline. "Since you already know each other, I'm going to leave you to work out the therapy details." He gave Marlea's knee a pat and quickly left the room.

AJ took the doctor's place at the foot of the bed. "I still don't know why you're so mad at me. You got your shirt, right?"

For only the second time since he had entered the room, she looked at him, really looked at him. "Shirt? You think that's what this is about? A shirt?" Eyes blazing, Marlea looked ready to fly from the bed on willpower alone. "No, brother, this is about far more than a shirt. I've dreamed of the Olympics all my life. I can't even tell you how much I wanted it, how hard I worked, and I was two points away from a dream, then along you came. You big-eared, big-headed, big-footed . . . big . . . big . . . lummox!"

"Lummox, huh? Never been called that before."

"Whatever." Her ponytail bobbing, she reached for a narrow book, pulled it into her lap, and studied its creamy pages. AJ cleared his throat, and she turned another page. Determined, she kept her head low, but her eyes followed him when he pulled a chair close to the bedside and sat.

Tipping his head, he managed to catch her eyes; for a long moment, they sat in uneasy silence.

"I'm not going to do this," Marlea finally said.

"Your choice. But it would be your loss."

Marlea closed the book. "No great loss. I'll just do the practical thing; get myself an electric wheelchair and roll around for the rest of my life."

AJ pulled one leg across the other and waited. She seemed determined to wait him out. "Heard you once had goals, Olympic aspirations."

"I reevaluated."

"Did you reevaluate your thoughts about the children who depend on you, too? I hear you're a teacher—and damned good at it."

"You listen to everything you hear? What's it to you?"

"The real question is, what's it worth to *you?* Even if you're prepared to give up running, are you willing to give up on the good you can do, have already done, for kids who love you?"

She hesitated. "And you think you can do something about that?"

"Yeah, I do." Her face dared him, and AJ refused to back down. "You and I have more in common than you think we do. We'll need to talk about it one day."

His confidence was well-chosen armor, and Marlea was tempted to take a run at it. He saw it in her face, but she didn't do it. This time she just looked at him.

"Tell you what." AJ fixed her with an unwavering stare. "I've agreed to take your case on. That means that we're going to be together for a while, and that you and I are going to have to find a way to get you rehabilitated, so I'm going to make you a promise."

"Oh, goody. More promises."

AJ shook his head. "I promise that you will work with me and learn to like it. You've talked about a dream, a dream I cost you? Well, now you're going to help me give that dream back to you. Before I'm through with you, Miss Lady, you will not only walk for me, but you are going to dance with me."

"In your dreams."

―∿∿∿―

This can't be happening.

Slipping from Marlea's room, Parker fled, rushing down the hall as though he was being chased. Gnawing at his thumbnail, he pushed through a chattering cluster of interns. He ignored their curious glances and hurried on to his office.

Once inside, he pressed his back to the door and his teeth worked around to the cuticle of his thumb. *She's starting to remember. How long will it take before she remembers the accident?* Parker passed a hand over his head and tried to calm himself. *I wonder if she got a good look when . . .* He thought about the odd little scratch Steven found when he took the car in for detailing. *As a houseman, he's always been discreet. He'll never say anything about the damage. I pay him too well.* And to keep the secret, Parker was willing to keep doing it.

But if the police ever get around to suspecting me, there can be no damage. It has to disappear . . . His stomach rolled and he nearly gagged. *I was safe enough when Marlea awakened and remembered nothing about the accident, but then the police came along with their infernal prying and prodding. They will be back, and like water against stone, they will chip away at her mental block. They're going to quiz and question her until they break through or crawl over the mountain that obscures her memory. That would take time, or at least I thought it would.* Then AJ Yarborough walked in and jogged her memory.

Me and my bright ideas! I should have just left well enough alone. Stinging pain made Parker pull his thumb from his mouth, jarring him away from the door. Pacing, trying to breathe normally, he squeezed his thumb and watched the welling blood.

Damn! Desireé. How did I forget? She'll know what to do, who to contact. She always knows the slick way around things. Pulling his cellphone from his pocket, he punched in her number as he walked.

She answered on the third ring, and Parker wondered if she had checked her caller ID before picking up the phone. *Trying to pay me back for all the times I did it to her,* he thought. *It would be just like her.*

Might as well get this over with. "Hello, Desireé," he said before she could get a word out. "I wanted to talk to you about something."

"I thought you might once I got your attention. Don't think that just 'cause I wasn't born in Buckhead and educated in private schools that you can talk your way around me."

"That was never my intention." *What the hell was I thinking when I got involved with her?* Feeling his stomach curdle, Parker made the obligatory apologies and tried not to say anything she could hold against him later. He managed, just barely, to talk his way around her palimony demands by offering a preemptive settlement. "A few thousand dollars to tide you over—just until we can sit down like civil people and come to a resolution."

He listened to her puff and breathe while he summoned nerve. It was more than a little disconcerting to hear nothing but irate breathing over the phone. "Desireé, I called because I wanted to ask you about something else."

"Really? Well, Parker Aaron Reynolds the Third, let me give you an answer," she snapped. "I am not about to do no booty call with a man who thinks he can throw money at me to tide me over. You want something from me, then you can start by apologizing for tryin' to treat me like your whore. I don't do on-call ass for nobody!"

"Oh, Desireé, I . . . that was never my intention, and again, I apologize if I gave you that impression."

"Smug as always, but I accept your apology."

Feeling like two cents waiting for change, Parker swallowed his pride. It was a cold, hard lump. "Desireé, I have a problem that only you can help me with."

"How can I help you, Parker?"

"Could you . . . would you meet me to discuss it?"

"I'm getting my nails done, but I can meet you if you want me to. Where?"

Okay, the hard part is done. Relief flushed tension from his body, and Parker realized he had been holding the phone in a vise-like grip. He loosened his fingers and smiled. "I'll be happy to pick you up."

Twenty minutes later, Desireé skipped down the sidewalk toward Parker's Corniche. Without waiting for an invitation or his assistance, she flashed her crimson nails, grabbed the door, and dropped into the leather passenger's seat.

If chivalry is dead, then Desireé killed it, Parker thought. On another day, under other circumstances, Desireé's short, white strapless dress and red ankle-wrapped sandals might have been quite fetching. But today, she looked like one of those girls Rick James used to sing about . . . *the kind you don't take home to mother.*

"Okay, tell me now." She tugged at the seatbelt, made herself comfortable, then turned heavily made-up eyes on Parker. "What happened?"

Pulling into traffic, eyes straight ahead, Parker experienced a moment of something he didn't want to call fear. *If I just say it the way I rehearsed it, I'll get through this,* he promised himself. "I had a little fender-bender, and I don't want to report it to my insurance company."

Her eyes leaked avarice, and Parker could feel her measuring him for a payoff. "Oh, now you need me?" she grinned knowingly. "What's in it for me?"

"Desireé, I just know that you know people, talented people. I just thought that you might know a mechanic who would like to pick up a few dollars. That's all."

"Don't go getting all huffy with me," she warned, pushing her tongue into her cheek. "Which car?"

"The Rolls."

She hissed laughter between her teeth and scooted around in her seat until she could look into Parker's face. "You talk like you think I'm a fool, Parker. It's bad enough that you think I'm a whore, but I ain't stupid. You want work done on your Rolls, you take it to a specialist. It's more to it than you're telling."

"Desireé . . ."

"That's okay, I don't have to know everything." Pushing her lips together, appraising him, she came to a decision. She pulled a small phone from her bright purse. Opening it, she kept her eyes on Parker. "I'm going to make this call for you, but just know that I will never do any jail time for you, so whatever this is, don't ask me for anything more."

Parker's eyes went from traffic to Desireé and back. "I would never . . ."

"No, baby, and you never will."

"Desireé, I wouldn't have come to you if I hadn't known that you were a woman I could trust. I came to you because . . ."

Holding the phone to her ear, listening, she straightened in her seat. "You came to me because you didn't have anywhere else to go."

He would have answered, but she raised a hand and held a low-voiced conversation he couldn't hear. Off the phone, she grinned like the Cheshire cat and began a stream of directions. As he followed her directions through southwest Atlanta, Parker hoped he hadn't made promises that he might have to keep. They stopped behind a pink Victorian-era house on a tree-lined street near the Atlanta University campus. The wizened old man who approached the Corniche looked homeless enough to make Parker cringe.

"What's his name?"

"You don't need to worry about that, you won't be around long enough to be friends with him. All you've got to know about him is that the man is a car genius," Desireé promised. "And you ain't got to worry about thanking me, baby. This is just one of those little things a woman like me does for her man."

I've just sold my soul to the Devil! The look in her eyes made him itch.

Standing beneath a massive oak tree, Parker watched uneasily as the 'car genius' bent low and walked around the car twice, finally pronouncing the custom frame dented and the paint damaged. *Well, hell*, Parker thought, *I know that*. It must have shown on his face, because the 'car genius' strolled over and squinted up at him.

"Rolls Royce builds a nice piece of machinery, and good thing for you, I can help you out," the old man said, pulling at his chin. His long brown fingers were deeply embedded with grease and grime. Parker was glad he didn't offer to shake hands.

The mechanic walked back to the Corniche and squatted next to the fender. Running an experienced hand over the damage, he paused. "Hand built, custom car like this takes a lot of special work, and that makes things tricky. You've got this special paint job, looks like Rolls Royce Tan—got to order that special." Turning back to Parker, he took a moment to spit on the ground in front of him. "Give me a couple of days; I can make it look good enough to report the car stolen."

"Stolen? Why?"

"You want it in your possession when they match it up to that girl's car? It ain't no great trick these days, you know."

Parker's pulse jigged. "What girl?"

The 'car genius' sucked his teeth and shook his head. "Mister, might as well tell you now, my momma ain't raised no fool. Oh, and I got cable. I saw it on the 24-hour local news where that girl got hit back on the Fourth of July. It was a hit and run up on I-75. They say she's gonna be all right, but the police sure would like to git hold of the one that hit her."

"What makes you think it was me, that it was my car?"

"Saw some pictures in the paper. She had a silver Accord. Vehicle height 'bout matches your damage. Then, too, I found this." The man held up his hand, displaying the silvery patina adhering to his fingertips.

Parker blanched. He looked at Desireé, and her greedy eyes glittered as she slipped her arm through his, pulling him close. "He can fix anything, baby. He'll make that car better than new. You just pay him, and life will be good—just pay him whatever he asks."

"How much?" The number given was staggering, and Parker felt his life spinning further out of control. "That's far more than the dealer would charge."

"Yeah, but I won't call the cops on you." The shade-tree mechanic sucked at the inside of his cheek and looked amused when Parker stumbled back a few steps.

When the 'car genius' kept his saliva to himself, Parker looked relieved. Then he looked at Desireé on his arm.

"S'up to you," the 'car genius' said.

Parker was aware of the cloud that slipped between him and the sun, and he prayed that it was not an omen.

CHAPTER 11

How many nurses does it take to draw blood? Doesn't much matter, because it always hurts when they do it for the fiftieth time. Marlea poked at the cotton ball taped over the sore spot on her arm. *At least I'll be out of here soon, and I won't have to go through this much longer.*

Out of here and back to my own life. She turned to face the window; the morning sun was still high in the sky. *". . . blue skies, sunshine, please go away . . ."* The start of an old song by the Temptations . . . but the words felt right. No day should be this bright and sunny when your life held so little hope.

A small bird landed on the windowsill. Though it sat outside, she could hear its quick chirp. *Looking for its mate, or just glad to be alive,* she thought. *Me, I've got nothing to sing about.*

I always knew that I wouldn't be fast forever. I just thought that it would be long enough to . . . I know that nobody stays competitive forever, but I came so close this time. I had this one last chance. I know that I should be grateful to have survived, and I am, but I thought that if I wanted something so badly and worked so hard to get it . . .

I get out of here; I go back to my life. At least I can still teach. Nobody can take that away from me. I get to work with the children I love . . . and then what? She closed her eyes and tried not to dwell on the depression she felt shrouding the beginning of her day. Marlea Kellogg wrapped her arms around herself and wondered what else she would do for the rest of her life.

Before this accident, everything was always so clear. I had a path and an identity. I never worried about sports or classes at the gym. I knew that I was a runner and a teacher—now I'm only half of what I once was. I'm a teacher who loves what she does and that's going to have to be enough.

She opened her eyes. A small package rested beside her on the bed. *What the heck is this?* She picked it up and read the return label. It was from Katie Charles. *Katie. She must be . . . maybe twelve years old now? She was a brave kid.* Marlea smiled, remembering the little girl powering her way through the halls of the Runyon School in her specially built wheelchair.

She opened the package and found a videocassette—and a note.

Hi, Ms. Kellogg,

I know it's been a long time, but I heard about what happened to you. I am sorry to hear about it, but I know that if anybody can hold her head up and make the best of a bad situation, it has to be you. You have a way of making good things better and finding your way around bad things. I know that you will find your way around this, too.

Your friend,

Katie

P.S. Do you remember that time our class sang for assembly? We sang 'Tomorrow' and my mother taped it. This copy is for you. Don't forget, the sun will come up tomorrow.

Marlea folded the note, and let the cassette slide from her lap. Katie was just a kid, maybe two years away from believing in Santa Claus.

It was sweet of her to think of me. Marlea's palms pressed the note flat and tucked it back into the package. She leaned over to slip the package into the drawer of her bedside table and caught motion from the corner of her eye.

"Is it okay for me to come in?" A white cloth fastened to a stick crept through the slight opening of her door. Moved from side to side, it looked like some kind of flag.

Cocking her head, half-waiting for the rest of the show, Marlea hesitated.

"You decent?" The flag waved again.

"Uh, yes?"

With a final wave, the flag disappeared, only to be replaced by the strong figure of AJ Yarborough. "How are you today?"

"Not that it matters, but I'm doing as well as might be expected under the circumstances. What's with the flag?"

"Just a symbol, a declaration of faith." AJ looked at his makeshift flag. "It's a white flag to let you know that I come in peace."

"Are you spelling that with an *i* or an *e*?" If pressed, Marlea might have admitted that his white smile and the clean lines of his sun-burnished skin were appealing, but nobody was pressing, and she wasn't about to give him the break. "Why are you here?"

"We have a date. Remember?" Stepping into the room, AJ dropped his flag on the brown vinyl chair in the corner. Still smiling, he reached for the wheelchair parked in the corner and pushed it close to Marlea's bed. "I thought I would pick you up in style."

"No way." *No matter how graceful he looks, I'm not falling for it.* "I'm not getting in that thing, and I'm not going anywhere with you, not today, tomorrow, or any other day."

"Why not?"

"'Cause you're no Richard Williams is 'why not.' "

"Who is Richard Williams?" Briefly stumped, AJ grinned when the answer dawned on him. "What has Venus and Serena Williams's father got to do with anything?"

"He got them to do what he wanted them to do, when he wanted them to do it, and you are not my daddy."

"No, ma'am. Think of me as a trainer."

Marlea fanned a hand. "I already have a trainer, thank you very much."

"Yes, ma'am. I've met her, and Ms. Libby Belcher is about as good as they come—for what you used to do. We talked it over and agreed that for what you are going to need in the future, I'm the one to get you ready."

"You talked to Libby about me? You had no right!"

"No, ma'am. I disagree with you; I had every right."

"Quit calling me ma'am! You had absolutely no right to . . ."

"Marlea, then. Look, when I signed on to your case, I took on responsibilities. I owe it to you to do the very best for you that I am able to, and a part of that was talking to your coach. My job, as your physical therapist, is to pinpoint your weaknesses and to build your strengths."

Marlea's lips tightened into a straight line across her face. "You always showing up in my life. Is that a weakness or a curse?"

"Marlea, I'm sorry I tripped you; I was clumsy. I'm sorry for the loss of time, but I can't give it back to you. I am very sorry that you were in the accident; you don't deserve this kind of pain." AJ stepped around the wheelchair and reached forward, capturing her hands between his. Tender steel beneath his warm and certain flesh kept her from pulling her hand away. "I'm not going to apologize again for tripping you. It was an accident. Get over it."

Blinking, Marlea's lips parted, and she ran her tongue over them before taking her hands back.

"I'm not going to argue therapy or treatment with you. I'm not going to argue where you've been versus where you thought you were going. At this point, I am not going to ask your preferences or solicit your choices, but I am putting you on notice: You are going to work with me. You are going to walk."

"Oh, now you're a miracle worker, too?"

"No, but I am going to take a hands-on approach to my part in your recovery. You know I've been called in to work with you on exercises—how to use your body to regain strength and mobility, and to prevent reinjury."

Eyes low, Marlea's mouth opened and closed. No words escaped her.

"Nothing to say?"

"Not to you." The corner of her mouth hitched. "Would you listen if I did?"

"If I thought it would do you any good." Parking a hip on her bed, AJ looked at her and waited. Marlea shrugged. "You might be able to convince me. Care to give it a try?" She shrugged again. "That's not an answer." His voice went low and respectful. "I saw some film on you yesterday. You were good."

"Yeah. I was."

"The way you were running, it was like you were cutting the air, girl. And the look on your face . . . you were a fierce competitor. I never would have figured you for a quitter."

Her head snapped up and AJ watched her shove pain from her face. She really was tough.

"I'm not a quitter. I simply hate you, that's all."

"You don't even know me."

"I know enough."

Her body tense, she folded her arms across her chest and crossed her legs. *Dang,* he thought, *Psych 101 says she's through with me.* "What do you think you know?"

"I know that you and Dr. Reynolds think you're going to save me from myself. You coming in here like some fifty-cent savior. I know that's not going to work for me."

Wonder if she talks to her kids like this? AJ smiled. "You know that things have changed for you. You know that you could have died in that accident."

"A part of me did."

AJ brushed the words aside. "You're still here. When you get tired of feeling sorry for yourself, there's some stuff you'll need to know—for self-preservation."

Sullen, Marlea tried not to look directly into AJ's face. "Like what?"

She acts tough, but she sounds scared. "Like what will happen to your body and your quality of life if we don't get you up and moving."

"I think you're just trying to scare me into doing what you want."

"No, I just want you to understand the limits you're placing on your recovery. Without therapy, you can look forward to poor circulation, infection . . . little things that could make your situation a lot worse."

"Little things." *What is he talking about? Is he trying to say that if I don't work with him, I'll lose the rest of my foot? Is he trying to say that I'll be a freak?* Marlea recoiled, imagining what lay beneath her bandages. *That's what he wants me to think, that I'll be a freak.*

"It's not like you're going to be a freak," AJ said, reading her mind. "I understand that you've worked with children who have had to learn to deal with physical and mental challenges."

"I have, and not one of them was a freak."

"Exactly. You've lost digits Marlea, not a limb. You're going to do more than just survive this; you're going to triumph over it. That's what I'm here for—to help you over those hurdles." He winked when she grimaced at the word *hurdle.* "Why not give it a try?"

"I already told you that I'm not going to give anything a try. I don't want to. There's nothing you or anybody else can do to give me back my toes or my life, and I don't plan to fake it." Drawing back her good foot,

Marlea shoved hard against AJ's hip, bouncing him off the bed. "And don't sit on my bed; it's not sanitary."

"Inhospitable, that's what that was," he said, looking at the bandaged foot she tucked defensively beneath the covers. "You know, in all fairness, in any game, you get three strikes. Today's visit? We're just going to call it strike one. You might want to keep track of that, 'cause there will be no 'do-overs,' and you have two more times to tell me 'no.' Meantime, have a good day, and I'll see you tomorrow."

"That's up to you," she muttered, watching him return the wheelchair to the corner. She said nothing as he left the room.

After the door closed behind him, Marlea flipped back the light blanket and drew her other leg up on the bed. Careful with her bandaged foot, she pulled both knees high and looped her arms around them. *Mr. AJ Yarborough has a lot of nerve.*

"Who does he think he is? Telling me I have three chances. To do what? Get it right? Or maybe he thinks that he's going to come in here and somehow save me from myself? Next thing I know, he'll be hovering over me, saying something like, 'resistance is futile.' " *And with that voice, he'll make me believe it.* Chin resting on her knees, Marlea bit her lips and huffed. "That's just ridiculous, and if he thinks that he's going to win me over by being condescending, well, he's just got another think coming.

"The last time I detested any one human being this much was . . ." She couldn't think of a single time, not even when Libby forced stair drills into a successful training routine. *And then he had the nerve to try to recruit Libby as an ally.* "Wait 'til I tell Libby that he had the nerve to tell me that I have three strikes . . ." *Two*, she remembered.

"Threatening me, that's what he did." *With what?* A common sense question: hard to dismiss. Unwilling to be deterred by logic, Marlea shifted her focus to her doctor. "It's really his fault. He hooked me up with this domineering, egocentric megalomaniacal . . ." She had to stop when she ran out of adjectives.

Her eyes went to the clock on her bedside table, and she recalled what AJ said about little things. *Am I running out of time? He said that I had to work with him. Why him?* Her mind sketched AJ Yarborough, then inspected him inch by inch. He was perfect. *Just because he's good looking is no reason to hold on to him,* and her mind went immediately to Piedmont Park. For some reason, her memory chose his muscles to remember, his body to claim.

The crush of her nipples, then her breasts, against the hard wall of his chest, his breath hot against her skin couldn't be ignored. Hands on sweaty skin, pulses shared, locked in motion and in time, made her heart beat faster. The rush of their sudden impact, his arms closing around her as they folded against each other, was undeniable. His leg climbing hers, his dense and commanding weight moved her as no man ever had. Marlea closed her eyes and swallowed hard, feeling him again, hating that he stirred her. *It was damned near orgasmic.*

Why him? Why did Dr. Reynolds pick AJ Yarborough? And why did Libby go along with him? What makes AJ Yarborough the 'one' for me? "Has fate just got it in for me?"

"I'm sorry, what did you say?" The gentle voice snagged Marlea's attention and made her jump. It was Jeanette, the nurse who had called Libby. Entering the room, she used her hip to open the door wider.

"Just talking to myself," Marlea improvised.

"A little prayer goes a long way." The nurse dimpled when she smiled. "I came by to change the dressing on your foot."

Knowing that it was a job that had to be done, Marlea slid her legs free of the covers. Jeanette pulled a short stool forward and sat. She deftly snapped open the cover of the plastic tray she had brought with her and went to work. "This doesn't look too bad," she said pleasantly.

Marlea turned her eyes away from her foot. "I met the PT that Dr. Reynolds wants me to work with."

"Mr. Yarborough? Yes, this is the first time he's worked with us. I hear he's very good, though." Jeanette winked up at Marlea. "You're a lucky woman, getting all that attention from a fine specimen like him."

"Lucky? You think so?"

"Humph! It could be a lot worse. I broke my ankle last year, and you should have seen the frog I got stuck with. All chunky and bent over, shriveled up like a raisin, whistled through his false teeth when he talked, and he had the nerve to try to feel me up, too. Kept saying he was trying to maintain the circulation around my damaged joint, walkin' his fingers up my leg, like I wouldn't notice." She gave a final turn to the bandage and smiled. "Honey, I'm a nurse and I know where my ankle is. Don't you think that old fart could have come up with something better to tell me—anything but that?"

"Like what?" Marlea giggled.

"Oh, I don't know." Jeanette began to tidy her supplies. "At least he didn't have to treat me like a blonde nurse."

"A what?"

"Okay, here's what I mean." Jeanette crossed her legs, obviously ready for a visit. "Why did the blonde nurse take a red magic marker to work?"

Marlea shrugged. "I don't know."

"In case she had to draw some blood . . . get it?"

"Uh, yeah . . ."

"I actually tell better jokes than that." Jeanette leaned forward and whispered, "How 'bout this one? These two women, Maisey and Daisy, were having a glass or two of wine and talking about their boyfriends one night. Maisey wasn't the sharpest knife in the drawer, but she mentioned that her boyfriend had dandruff. Daisy didn't see where this was such a big deal, so she said, 'When my boyfriend had dandruff, I gave him Head & Shoulders.' Maisey thought about it and thought about it. She didn't want to sound too stupid, but she finally had to ask, 'How do you give shoulders?'" Jeanette slapped her thigh and whooped, tickled by her own joke.

"Anyway," she wheezed through her laughter, "any man who wants to feel me up should buy me jewelry, or be able to tell a good joke, or . . . at least be as good-looking as AJ Yarborough."

Sharing the laugh, Marlea tried not to wonder if AJ Yarborough would ever have the nerve to feel her up.

CHAPTER 12

Why him? The question still nagged at Marlea as she rode along in the sticky vinyl-seated wheelchair. *AJ Yarborough is not the only PT in Atlanta, and he surely is not the only man left in the city, yet here we are together again.* The irony was not lost on her as AJ moved her smoothly across the threshold into Grady's green-walled physical therapy area. She tried ignoring him and the therapy tables and machines.

Cutting her eyes toward a mirrored wall, she watched him. Muscles bunched in his arms, and his white shirt was molded nicely across his chest as he pushed her chair. Judging from the pleasant expression on his face, AJ either didn't notice her ignoring him or was ignoring her back—she couldn't tell which. Parking her next to a leather exam table, he didn't seem to mind her silence. With his back to her, he pulled a white sheet from the basket next to the table and snapped it efficiently into place.

"I'm not altogether sure why we're doing this." Marlea drummed her fingers against the chair's armrest and watched the way his butt curved into his thighs. *Some men really know how to wear khaki shorts.* The thought caught her off-guard. *Enough of that nonsense! I can tell Dr. Reynolds that I'm not satisfied. Or that I'm self-*

conscious. I can tell him that I'll do the therapy, but I prefer working with a woman. That'll get this man out of my life.

AJ opened a small black case and removed a black box. He pulled two long wires from the box and affixed flat plastic pads to the ends. "We're doing this because physical therapy treatment should begin as early as possible. Early treatment can help prevent chronic problems and decrease the length of recovery time."

He didn't even look at me. "I'm all for that."

"I'm sure you are," AJ grinned, setting the black contraption aside. Offering a sculpted bicep, he beckoned. "Grab hold and let's get started."

Marlea gripped AJ's arm and looked up at him. She waited for him to nod before giving him her full weight. *Ooh! He's strong,* she marveled silently, hoping her admiration didn't show on her face.

"You're welcome," he said, his eyes on her feet.

Oh, Lord! Marlea checked herself. *I didn't say that out loud, did I?* She stole a glance at his face—all business. Her weight shifted against his arm, and she looked down at her feet: one perfectly good Nike and a big, blue, thick-soled surgical shoe. *At least I'm dressed for the occasion.* Dressed in blue shorts and a white Runyon School shirt, Marlea discovered that neither of her well-shod feet would support her weight. Clinging to AJ's arm, she let him swing her onto the white-sheeted exam table.

"What's that evil-looking thing?" She eyed the wired black box.

"Part of your therapy." AJ lifted his eyebrows in imaginary menace. "It's an electronic muscle stimulator. We're also going to be using some stretching, cold packs, and moist heat to get you through this. Don't worry, you'll like it."

"I thought this was going to be like a trip to the chiropractor."

"Chiropractors rely on joint manipulation to decrease pain. My job is to get you moving again." He paused to take a stack of towels and a frosty-looking blue bag from a petite, short-haired woman with obvious hero worship in her eyes. "Thanks, Anita."

Anita seemed to see Marlea for the first time. She made specific eye contact, her heavily made-up hazel eyes seeming to check for imperfections as they moved over Marlea. When they found the surgical shoe, a look of superiority glazed her features and creased her plump lips. She didn't say anything. She didn't have to. She simply made sure that her hip-slinging walk made the statement for her.

And why do I care? Marlea wondered, glad when the doll-like woman with the stripper's strut drifted away. She felt a small triumph when AJ didn't seem to notice.

"I'm going to start with an exam, take you through some stretching, and finish off with something to soothe you," he said. Patiently, he guided Marlea on the table. Leaning forward, the heat from his body engulfed her, and Marlea held her breath. Seeming oblivious to her reaction to his closeness, his hands were firm and sure. "Just breathe through it and relax."

But she couldn't relax. *How am I supposed to relax with him all up on top of me, telling me to relax? That's like going to the dentist and being told, 'This won't hurt—much.'* She flinched when he removed her shoes and began to stroke the bottom of her feet.

"What are you doing?"

"Testing your reflexes." He moved a finger along the base of her toes on her right foot. "How does that feel?"

"Okay." It sent tremors straight to her core and brought water to her mouth. She forced herself to remain still and closed her eyes.

"And that?"

"Fine." The word shimmered across her lips, long and lingering. *Oh, Lord. Did I stutter?* She cracked one eyelid. *Did he hear me?*

His questing hands and ministering fingers moved past her toes and over her foot.

Oh, Lord! I've heard . . . I thought it was just a rumor . . . that some women are sensitive . . . sometimes orgasms from kissing, receiving a back rub . . . triggered by certain smells, and even breast-feeding babies . . . but my foot . . .

Rivers of sensation climbed her legs and teased beneath her shorts. Mortified, determined not to be broken by his possession of her body, Marlea endured the testing, trying to do little more than grunt when he spoke to her.

Her thoughts were more free than her body, and all she could think of was Jeanette talking about the doctor she had when she broke her ankle. *". . . any man who wants to feel me up should buy me jewelry, or be able to tell a good joke, or . . . at least be as good-looking as AJ Yarborough."*

It took the better part of twenty minutes for him to reach a decision, and his hands never stopped moving. Nearly panting, Marlea stole a look at him as he bent close. He looked like the type who might buy jewelry, or at least the way she imagined such a man might look.

AJ pressed his warm palm flat against her cool sole and Marlea gasped. He nodded and whispered encouragement. *Wonder if he knows any good jokes?* She sighed.

Trying to read his face, she saw more than she had ever intended. Catching him unawares, the way she had, the well-honed lines of his manly face nearly overshadowed the hint of tenderness in his eyes. Calculating measurements, his mouth moved, and Marlea nearly gave in to the hypnotic stroke of his long finger against the arch of her foot. *This man is as pretty as a jungle cat,* she marveled. *No wonder that woman was in here flirting so hard. Strong enough to lift me and put me anywhere he wants, moving like a dancer, and he's certainly not stupid.* Marlea heard Jeanette's words again.

"That about does it," AJ smiled casually. He made marks on a chart, then hooked it to the end of the exam table. "Let's get you stretched out." His hand slipped beneath her leg, touching her bare skin, and Marlea gasped in spite of herself.

"I didn't expect you to touch me like that."

"Not a problem."

Maybe not for you, but I . . . did he think that was an apology? He said the words too easily. *He did!*

"Well, it ought to be a problem." Marlea pushed at the long-fingered hand he had placed on her bare knee, then at the one braced against her hip. "You didn't ask me, but I don't like this stretch. It's too . . . invasive."

"What do you mean, 'invasive?' " Moving his hands away from her, AJ looked confused. "Marlea, this is a standard stretch, using an outside applied force."

"Next thing I know, you're going to tell me that it has a name, too, aren't you?" Struggling up on her elbow, Marlea labored for dignity—and came up short. "Because I don't have toes, I don't have any right to my own feelings?" Finally upright, her legs stretched in front of her, Marlea tried to make sense of her thoughts. "I don't like this. I don't like being 'handled.' "

"We don't have to go through that particular stretch today . . ."

Her leg and good foot jerked irritably. "I don't want to do it at all—ever!"

A shadow crossed AJ's face, gone almost before she saw it. "Marlea, I thought I made it clear. I am the therapist here."

"Is that why you and everybody else seems to think you've got exactly what I need?"

"Nobody is trying to take control of your life away from you. It's just that, as a therapist, I have to know more than your name, and we're not putting this to a vote. I've examined you, and . . ."

"*. . . any man who wants to feel me up should . . . be as good-looking as AJ Yarborough.*" Marlea could have sworn aloud when the corners of AJ's lips curved upward. *He's smiling.* "You're smiling. Are you enjoying this?"

"Sure." He reached for the small black box and straightened the wires with his fingertips. "I always enjoy my work."

"Well, you can just put that thing away, because your work with me is over for the day." Without his help, Marlea edged her body to the side of the exam table. Reaching hard, she was able to grab the wheelchair and tug it close enough to roll into it. The effort left her breathless and exhausted, but she would rather have died than admitted it to AJ Yarborough.

Gripping the chair's big rubber tires, she tried to turn them, but the damned wheelchair refused to move. She adjusted her grip and tried again. Nothing.

"I can help you with that," AJ offered.

"No, I'll manage." Marlea tried rocking in the chair, then twisted in the seat, looking for the magic lever or switch that would free her. The tip of AJ's shoe moved, flicking a metal lever, and the chair rolled forward. Embarrassed, Marlea refused to look back, even when she heard his parting words.

"Strike two."

━━━♦♦♦━━━

'Strike two.' Yeah, right. Putting his hands on me, touching me, making me feel like that. Marlea narrowly missed the wall as she steered her chair toward the elevator. *He knew what he was doing. I'll bet he took some kind of special course on how to touch women in just exactly the right way to . . . 'Strike two.' He's just talking, trying to*

build his confidence and wear me down at the same time. I don't know who he thinks he's playing with . . . .

Whatever he was doing wasn't helping her with her reluctant transportation. The wheelchair took more maneuvering than she had anticipated. Focused on her predicament, she failed to notice the slender uniformed woman watching her.

"Let me help you with that, Ms. Kellogg." The woman reached past Marlea's shoulder to press the call button.

"Thanks, 'cause I was . . ." Marlea looked up into Anita's hazel eyes. "I . . . I'm finished with my therapy."

"Great. I was just on my way up to see you."

Marlea looked at the small paper-covered tray the other woman held. *She's got awfully long nails for a nurse.* Opening elevator doors sucked at the air. Before Marlea could move, diminutive Anita gripped the chair one-handed and pushed. Neon blue-tinged panic ambushed Marlea for a second and she imagined some horrible slasher flick. *I saw the way she looked at AJ, the way she acted around him. What if this woman is some kind of unhinged stalker?* Marlea gripped the chair's arms and stared straight ahead as the doors closed. *I'm bigger than she is . . . I might be able to knock her down if I have to . . .*

The elevator rose, and she wondered, *What if . . .*

"You didn't ask why."

Marlea held her breath, glad when the doors slid open. *She just wants to talk?*

"I'll tell you anyway." Anita regained control of the chair and powered it down the hall. Marlea wondered if she could stop the chair by dragging her feet. "I saw you working with AJ today." Marlea could hear the smile warm her voice.

"Yeah," Marlea shrugged, looking for an ally in the empty corridor. "I was promised I could get out of here sooner if I tried the therapy." *She can't blame me for that, can she?*

"Good for you," Anita gushed, no blame in her tone. Reaching Marlea's room, she guided the wheelchair forward. "Do you want the chair or the bed?"

The telephone was near the bed. "I think I would prefer the bed. Please." *If she's crazy, there's no need to make her angry, too.*

Anita helped make the transfer to the bed and Marlea sat there, waiting.

"Oh," Anita said brightly, "I have something for you." She reached for the small tray she had brought with her. "Your meds. AJ asked if I would get them for you after you left him. A lot of patients are sore after a strenuous therapy session, and he had Dr. Reynolds prescribe these for you." She sighed. "He's so thoughtful."

Taking the tiny cup from the proffered tray, Marlea had no doubt which 'he' the nurse referred to. She tossed the pills to the back of her throat and chased them with water from the carafe on her bedside table. Swallowing again, she looked at Anita. *Well, if she planned to poison me, I've already swallowed it.* "Were those pills for sleep or for pain?"

The nurse's hazel eyes brightened with concern. "Are you in pain?"

"It's just," Marlea hesitated, not sure how to phrase it. "My foot, the one that's . . . you know . . . it's burning."

The nurse nodded. "Phantom limb."

"You say that like it's supposed to mean something, but . . ." Marlea wiggled her foot. "It really hurts, but I can't exactly rub it, or do anything for something that's not there."

"Hmm, that's true." Watching Marlea slide out of her shorts and shirt, Anita lowered her thick fringe of lashes. "Scientists are still studying amputees, trying to determine the cause of this pain. One of the studies I've read concludes that the pain occurs because the body doesn't understand what's missing, so the sensations go to other body parts."

She's trying to tell me that my toes are missing, so I get hot for the therapist? Lord, help me . . . "Way to make me feel better," Marlea muttered, ignoring the gown Anita passed to her. Reaching, she tried to massage her leg.

Anita made a show of turning and settling the wheelchair. "There's a lot of thought that says stress is also a large factor in phantom limb pain. "

"Stress?" AJ Yarborough's face crossed her mind, and Marlea stopped rubbing.

Anita noticed and smiled. "First time you've felt it?"

Marlea nodded and unfolded the gown. "But I'm not under stress." *Unless you count having that man touching me.*

"No, of course you're not." The nurse helped Marlea adjust the gown. "Don't fret over it now. It's not unusual, but we need to get you in bed so that you can get some rest after your therapy session."

Yawning, Marlea realized that the medication was a sleeping pill. "First it's surgery, then it's therapy, now it's 'phantom pain.' Can't wait to get out of here," she murmured, closing her eyes. *Every time I look around, someone else is stepping in and taking control of my life . . .* "You said you had something to tell me?"

"Yes, about AJ Yarborough."

Here it comes . . . Marlea tensed.

"I wanted to say that you are a lucky woman. He's good at what he does, and he works from the heart."

"Are you speaking from experience?" Marlea yawned.

"You could say that." Anita clasped her hands in front of her body and smiled demurely. "He worked with my brother after his stroke." She licked her lips and chuckled. "I hear you're reluctant to work with AJ, that you've been pretty stubborn about it, too. Well, you've got nothing on that hard-headed brother of mine. Shoot, that boy could give lessons to mules, but AJ got through to him."

Smothering another yawn, Marlea shrugged. "What's your point?"

"I've got two. The first is that you're too young to give up on yourself. The second is that you shouldn't waste a gift. AJ Yarborough is a gifted therapist, and he can help you get to where you can help yourself."

"You wouldn't be saying all of this because you . . . oh, I don't know . . . want to get close to him, would you?"

"Honey, please!" Anita laughed. "I might be if I wasn't married to a man I've loved since the first time I saw him." She took her small tray and flipped a hand toward Marlea. "That pill ought to be kicking in any time now, so I'm going. Whew!" She was still laughing as the door closed behind her.

Okay, that was embarrassing. Marlea rolled onto her side and plucked at the sheet pulled over her body. *Now he's siccing the nurses on me, too. What kind of spell has that man cast over everyone in this hospital? Everybody has something good to say about him, everybody has another reason why I need him in my life.*

The light in the room seemed to shift . . .

When did that happen? What time is it? Looking toward where the window should have been, there was nothing, not even a wall. Lost in space, she put out a hand and touched nothing. *Where am I? Am I dreaming?* Reality and cause had nothing to do with the sudden freedom of standing on her own two feet again. Turning in a slow circle, enjoying the luxury of dancing on her toes and the tease of warm, scented air on her bare skin, Marlea loved her wholeness and dismissed her location.

Twirling slowly, she discovered that she was not alone. In a soft corner, wrapped in velvet shadow, AJ Yarborough waited. Walking close, circling him, inspecting him, she walked right up to him, wrapped her arms around him, and delivered a kiss that could only leave him hungry for more. Not letting him move, taking all the advantage, she bound him with silk scarves, the kind a big man like him could shred in a heartbeat—if he wanted to. The thing was, he didn't want to. He didn't want anything other than what she willingly gave him. His satisfied, hungry moans seem to enfold her, and she began to wonder what it was that he wanted her to know; what it was that she couldn't seem to understand. His moans grew deeper and she tried harder to hear him. Suddenly, the moans stopped, and Marlea opened her eyes to find herself still in the hospital bed.

Realizing that she was not alone, she rolled over. *Where did he go?* She moved her hand over a sensitive nipple, peaked beneath her cotton gown, and then brought her fingertips to her lips.

"Dreaming?" the aide asked, rolling his protesting bedside table closer.

"I guess so." Eyes wide, Marlea looked at the young man, tried to place him in time and space. He was tall enough, but round and fleshy, nothing like AJ. With heavily freckled skin a shade past peanut butter and silvery gray eyes, he was different enough to convince her that he was right. *I was dreaming.*

He moved to help her sit higher in the bed. "Brought you some lunch."

"Thanks." Shaken by her dream, it took all Marlea's strength not to crawl free of the sheets and search beneath her bed. *A dream? Couldn't have been; it was too real.* Trying to hold on to what she had come so close to, she clutched the bed sheet. It was too real.

What in the world is he doing to me?

CHAPTER 13

"You know, this might go faster if you helped." Linda Palmer rubbed her dusty palms against her denim skirt.

"Aww, come on partner, you look like you're doin' fine. Besides, you know my forté is supervision." Gene Brighton stuffed the last lemony bite of his Krispy Kreme doughnut into his mouth and chewed happily. When Palmer closed her eyes, he grinned and selected another doughnut from the green and white box.

"If I had a nickel for every page I've turned . . ." Palmer flipped through a sheaf of computerized pages. "Damn, I would be a real rich woman . . ." Her fingers slowed, then stopped. "Oops, now what do we have here?"

"I dunno," Brighton said slugging down coffee. "What *do* we have here?"

"We have an official registration on a vehicle from Dr. Parker Aaron Reynolds the Third."

"Aaron?" Brighton turned up his nose and snorted.

"What?"

"Aaron." Brighton snorted again, "the Third. There were three of 'em with that name?"

"Technically." Palmer dropped into her desk chair and rubbed at the back of her neck. "See, the grandfather would have been first, so he would have been called

Senior. His son would have been Junior and the grandson would have been the Third."

"No number two?"

"No, number two is always called Junior."

"Assuming they know or care how all that formal crap works." Brighton used a paper napkin to dab at the sugar frosting clinging to his lips. "Who came up with that sissy rule, anyway?"

"Do I look like Emily Post to you?"

"Anyway . . ."

"Anyway, I was just thinking . . ." Palmer moved her hand over several stacks of paper before she uncovered a blue APD folder. "Here it is. This is the final accident report." She flipped the folder open, found what she wanted, then traced a line of print. Stopping abruptly, eyes shining in triumph, she jabbed at the page. "There it is, the paint they found on her car, just like I remembered."

"You got something?" Brighton levered his bulk from behind his desk and moved behind his partner. Reading over her shoulder, his eyes followed her fingertip, and his lips moved slowly. "You found it and it looks like a match. I always knew you were a smart girl."

"Woman."

"Whatever." He gave her shoulder a squeeze. "You're smart, puttin' two and two together like that; just take the compliment for what it's worth."

"Isn't it funny how easy it is to backtrack once you realize that the good doctor comes from money?"

"When your family has as much money as his does, you have to keep good records, and good records include

keeping track of vehicle purchases and registrations."
Brighton tapped the page.

"Wait a minute . . ." Inspired, Palmer used her elbow
to hold the page while she looked for a second report.
Flipping pages, she quickly found what she was looking
for and laid the two reports side by side. "Look at that."

"Only two cars in the city with that paint job."
Squinting, Brighton brought his face closer to the page.
"One of them is sitting on a lot up in Buckhead."

"And the other one belongs to Dr. Parker Aaron
Reynolds the Third."

"And son of a gun, there he is, owner of record."

"That's got to be him," Palmer agreed. "The DMV
report shows him owning a Rolls Corniche, and the color
is Rolls Royce Tan."

"Yep." Brighton pushed his hands into the curve of
his back and stood straighter. "That's exactly the color of
the chips of paint crushed into her factory-issue silver
paint job—custom-mixed, specially baked Rolls Royce
Tan; probably scraped from the inside of his fender when
he hit her. Bet he never even noticed the scratch."

"Maybe he didn't, but I'll bet he notices us when we
call him on it," Linda Palmer grinned, patting the stack
of photos and printouts.

———⁓⁓⁓———

"Somebody has got to get through to her, AJ. I really
think you're the man to do it. She needs to work with

someone who shares her passion, someone who has at least been close to the place where she is now. "

"You've got a lot of faith in me, Parker. I just hope I don't let you down."

"If you can get her up and moving, you will have more than justified my faith." The doctor's gaze dropped and then returned to AJ's. "Marlea's more afraid than anything else."

"Wouldn't you be? I know I would." AJ stood and offered his hand across Parker's massive desk. "Anyway, I just wanted to bring you up to speed on how things are going with her."

"Thanks." Parker stood and grabbed the other man's hand. "You're the right man, AJ. I know you'll get her through this."

"If she doesn't get me first," AJ laughed.

His stride was purposeful, but he was no longer laughing as he walked away from the doctor's office. Marlea Kellogg was on his mind, and he couldn't get her out of his head. *She's not trying to hear anything from me. She's fighting me every step of the way. Even went to Reynolds and asked for a female therapist. Thank God, he saw through it—knew that it was her fear talking.*

And why shouldn't she be afraid? The woman used to outrun almost everybody in sight. That listing of her races and times I found on the Internet showed that she had more than just potential—she was the real deal. Every article said she had the speed and technique; just never made it to the finish line she set for herself.

She knows what she was, and has no clue as to what her future includes. Only knows that she won't ever run the way she used to. Probably feeling like the Lone Ranger, too—like she's lost her identity and that this has never happened to anyone else in the world. Running his tongue over his teeth, AJ pressed the elevator's call button and tried not to look impatient.

"You think better when you're calm." Every coach he had ever played under had told him that, and now, thinking about Marlea Kellogg, he needed to be calm. *But she's not alone, and truth is, I want her to walk as much as she does. She just doesn't know how much she wants it—yet.*

He was still studying the tips of his shoes when the elevator doors opened. Stepping aside quickly, he managed to avoid running into the small black-haired woman who jumped out of the elevator.

"Hey! I know you," she blurted. "You're that therapist, right? AJ something?"

AJ paused midstep and looked down at her. Though she stood perfectly still, everything about her, head to toe, was frenetic—almost as if she was vibrating. She looked as though she would burst with energy. *And I should remember someone like this.*

"We've never formally met, just spoken on the phone. It's good to finally put a face with the name." Now moving from foot to foot, the woman grabbed AJ's hand and pumped it vigorously. "I'm Libby Belcher. Marlea Kellogg's friend. And I'm her coach, or at least I was." Dropping AJ's hand, Libby's teeth tugged at her lower lip, but her eyes remained fastened on his face.

Tenacious as a pit-bull, AJ decided when she blocked him, as the elevator doors closed. *What is she waiting for me to say?*

"I want to know about Marlea's progress. She's been in this hospital for a long time. You've had a chance to evaluate her condition, and I need to know what's going on with her." When he was slow to answer, Libby reached out and tugged at his sleeve, holding on tightly. "There is no way in this world I'm gonna let you walk around all closed-mouthed while you're working with my friend. She's had enough trouble to last her for a while, so you need to start talking to me right now!"

She cares. AJ looked down at the small hand on his sleeve and hesitated. *She truly cares.*

"Don't make me follow you," Libby threatened. "'Cause I will if I have to."

My client has the right to keep her business to herself. Still hanging onto his sleeve, Libby bristled, anticipating resistance. *But I need every ally I can get if I'm ever going to get her to work with me.* AJ thought of Marlea's determination to hold onto what she seemed to see as the last vestiges of her dignity and self-reliance. *And it's not getting her anywhere. Client confidentiality be damned. I can't get her attention any other way, and this little dynamo might be able to get her to move where I can't . . .*

"Let's move over here." He led Libby a few steps away from the bank of elevators. "I'm only talking to you because, while I have nothing to lose in her participating in therapy, she has everything to lose. And damn it, as hard as she is to get along with, I don't want her to be the loser in this."

Libby released his sleeve and focused on the wrinkles her death-grip had created. Smoothing her hand over the creases, she nodded. "You like her, don't you?"

"That's a hell of a question. I barely know the woman."

"Uh-huh," Libby grinned, patting her palms together. "Barely knowing her ain't got much of nothin' to do with how you feel about her. You like her."

AJ shrugged. *If it will make this go any easier . . .* "Yes. I like her."

Libby snapped her fingers and forgot his shirt. "I knew it!"

"But what good is my liking her going to do if I can't get her walking? She seems to think that the role of therapy in her recovery is optional."

"She ought to know better than that, and she can't stay here forever." Libby gnawed at her lip, thinking. "Well, things are gonna have to change. Soon."

"What do you mean?"

"I've had some family stuff come up, and it looks like I'm going to have to leave Atlanta, at least for a little while."

"Damn." AJ ran a finger along his jawline. A couple of the nurses had whispered about the relationship between the coach and the runner. Like sisters, they said. One or two of them even doubted that their patient would have come this far without her friend's support. "How long is a little while?"

Libby's hands wiggled and she grimaced. "Plus or minus . . . I don't know . . . six months or so."

"Six months can be an eternity when you're hanging on by your fingernails." AJ remembered his own recovery. *I had family in my corner, and it still felt like a lifetime. What would it be like to have to take every step alone?* According to everything in the record, Marlea Kellogg had no family—no one on her side other than this tough little lady. "You've been her rock."

"Maybe I was, once. But now, I think it's your turn."

"What?"

"You're big enough to be her rock." Libby gave him an appraising once-over. She ran a hand over his arm, squeezing the muscle as she went, smoothing the remaining crinkles on his sleeve. "Yes, sir, you're big enough for a lot of things. I'm going to talk to her." She checked her watch. "I've got to get going." She backed a step away, then waved as she turned. "Don't give it another thought. She's going to work with you—you have my word on it."

Determined little woman. Wonder if she's determined enough to wear that other one down? I hope so.

She's going to work with you—you have my word on it.

Libby said the words out loud, then repeated them in her heart—a mantra matched to her footsteps as she came to Marlea's door.

Funny how I've come to think of this as her door, like it's the door to her home or something. She pushed the door wide and stepped through. "Hey, girl!"

Marlea's head barely moved. Sitting on her bed watching a video, she seemed riveted by the children speaking into the camera. Her face mirrored their earnest openness.

"Marlea?"

Marlea's attention snapped into focus at the sound of her name, and she swiped at her tear-filled eyes before looking at her visitor. Using the remote, she darkened the television screen, then pushed the remote beneath her leg. "Libby."

"The Runyon kids getting to you? They wondering if you're coming back in the fall?" Libby let the door fall shut behind her and came closer. "You are planning on being there for them, aren't you?"

"You can't even come in and give me a hug without a million questions first?" Marlea opened her arms, and seemed relieved when Libby walked into them and squeezed her tightly.

"Okay, there's your hug," Libby drew back to look into Marlea's face. "What's this I hear about you not cooperating with AJ? Seen him a grand total of what, like two times? And I hear that all you're doing when you see him is lying there like a bump on a log."

"I did tell you who he is, didn't I? That he's the one who tripped me at the Peachtree and . . ."

"Quit trying to blow smoke up my ass. What's your point?" Libby's sandal slapped at the tile floor.

"Libby, you don't understand."

"Damned straight I don't." The sandal slapped again.

"Libby, it . . ." How to explain that the man's every touch felt sexual, that he stimulated her in ways only a lover should? "What I'm trying to tell you is that . . . maybe therapy isn't for me because . . ."

"Because, why?" Libby cocked her head impatiently.

"Because every time he puts his hands on me, it feels like sex," Marlea blurted.

"Is that a bad thing?"

"I'm not crying rape or anything, but . . . I don't have any control over it and I . . . I don't like it. The nurse said I would probably get over it in time, but until then . . . I don't think he can do anything for me." *Libby doesn't look pleased, but what do I care? She's gonna be able to walk out of here and get on with her life.* Marlea looked away.

"So you're not willing to try?"

"It's not that. It's the way it makes me feel when he touches my foot and I go spinning off into orgasmic rapture. I don't know him like that, and even if I did . . . I . . ."

"So you're going to ignore your doctor's orders? You're not even going to make the effort and give him a chance, 'cause your nookie is tickled? Marlea, I can't have you acting like this."

"You don't understand," Marlea frowned. "This is about more than a little 'tickle.' And *you* can't have me acting like this? What are you going to do, Libby? Make me run laps, do a few jacks to get over it, what?"

"I gotta tell you, even the doctor said you'd get over it in time. Did you tell him how you feel, and why?" Marlea's eyes widened. "I should have known you wouldn't." Libby did a little side-to-side dance, demanding attention. "Marlea . . . this is not easy, but . . . I'm afraid I'm not going to be here to make you do much of anything. Hal's parents are going to be moving. To Florida." Her blue eyes clouded. "It's his father's health, and of course, you know his mother's never been all that strong. Hal and I, well, they need us . . ."

"You're moving, Libby?" Marlea's lip quivered. "When I need you," she whispered.

"It won't be for long. Six months at the most." Libby reached for the hand that Marlea pulled back against her chest. "If you can hang on for a few months, I'll be back. You'll be healed up enough to go back to your own place, and then you can get on with your life and all."

"Sure." Marlea nodded. "Sure, I can hang on." *I mean, what in the world else am I going to do?*

"But in the meantime," Libby said, pointing a stern finger and shaking it for emphasis, "you've got to work with Mr. Yarborough."

Marlea sighed and generally made it plain that she was trying not to feel sorry for herself.

"You're such a brat, and you know it, don't you?"

"She's right, you know." Parker Reynolds pushed through the door and came over to the bed. "From what I hear, you've got decent insurance and a real chance of a solid recovery, but that will do you no good if you ignore the therapy. Oh, and you will have to move out of this room eventually."

"You're not funny," Marlea mumbled.

"I'm not intending to be." Reynolds stuffed his hands into the pockets of his white coat. "The usual stay for a procedure like yours is seven days or less. You've been here for, what? Fourteen?"

"Not 'cause I wanted to be. My plans had me up and running . . . somewhere."

"Well, if you got on with your therapy, you could at least be walking somewhere."

"Thank you for your wisdom." Marlea directed her scowl to Libby, who simply smiled.

"I'm going to get on with my rounds," Reynolds said softly. "You give some thought as to what your next step is going to be."

"Yeah, I'll do that," Marlea said to his back.

Resisting the urge to say more, Parker let the door close behind him.

"Dr. Reynolds?" The woman's soft voice made his name more of a statement than a question.

"Yes?"

"I don't know if you remember us," the big man stepped forward, offering his hand.

"Ah. . ." Parker accepted the meaty palm. For some reason, he knew both the man and the slender, bookish woman at his side. Parents or children of a patient? *No, I would have remembered. But they're so familiar . . .* And then the faces clicked into context.

"I'm Detective Brighton, and this is my partner, Detective Palmer."

"Yes." Parker nodded numbly.

The plain little woman came a step closer. She fished a small notebook from her purse. Then she looked directly into Parker's face, and her brown eyes were anything but timid. Her gaze was frank and carnivorous—and it gave Parker a deadly cold chill.

"Do you drive a Rolls Corniche? Rolls Royce Tan? Tag number BEST 1?" she asked, her tones clipped and acidic.

Parker Reynolds hesitated, blinking to buy time. "Yes, why?"

"We would like to talk to you about an accident involving your vehicle."

They know! Suddenly airless, the hospital corridor seemed to swim around him, and Dr. Parker Reynolds struggled to stay on his feet. "Ah, an accident?"

"Your insurance company was presented with a claim. State law requires that they follow up on the report with a computer listing, and as luck would have it, your paint job matches a sample taken from a hit and run on I-75/85 running through Atlanta."

"This is about the Corniche? It was stolen—I reported it . . ." *Right after I left it on the corner of Metropolitan and University, by the takeout chicken restaurant, with the lights on, the engine running, and the doors hanging open.* "I don't suppose you've found it?"

"We've found enough of it to draw some conclusions." The big cop stood back, letting the woman run the show, and Parker almost gagged, remembering the abandonment of his beloved Corniche and Desireé waiting at the wheel of his Lexus.

That had been a mistake, taking her with him. He had known it from the beginning. Yet, there she sat, ready for the caper, dressed in a skin-tight black catsuit and flowing blonde wig. She had insisted on accompanying him, and her logic almost made sense. "Who else you gonna get to drive the getaway car? Your high-society mama ain't the type, and you don't know a woman more faithful than me."

Afraid, knowing she was right, he gave in. Miserable because she was right, he slumped in the passenger seat and waited in the dark.

"Why have you got to go looking like a whipped pup?" Desireé frowned.

"What if . . ." Parker eyed the wire-thin dark man slinking around the corner of the greasy-windowed restaurant. Two others joined him, and the Corniche quickly became the obvious focus of their attention. Parker slid lower in his seat. "What if nobody takes it?"

"Like that could happen. They're already skulking around like hungry cats." Desireé sucked her teeth. "How in the hell does a Nervous Nelly like you go all up inside people and do surgery?"

"That's different."

Or at least he had tried to convince himself that it was different. At this moment, looking into the suspicious faces of the two detectives, he wasn't so sure. The doctor swallowed hard and consciously tried to slow his breathing and his pounding heart. Afraid and waiting, he damned Desireé and hoped that his imaginings would not become reality. "My insurance company should have followed up on my report . . ."

"Yeah, we saw that report, but our computer scored another hit . . ."

CHAPTER 14

He touched her again, and she had to bite her lips to hold back a scream. What she felt would be called ecstasy by most women, especially at the hands of a man like AJ Yarborough. She could see the strong muscles shift in his chest when his hands moved higher and an electric thrill climbed her legs, sending spiced sweetness to a place he had never seen.

Oh, this can't be right, she almost moaned aloud. Silently cursing the aphrodisiacal stimulation of the therapy, she looked up into his face. *He hasn't got a clue*, she realized, holding her breath. When he touched her sole, Marlea nearly wept. *And they wondered why I wanted a female therapist. Maybe that would make this easier . . .* His fingers moved and, knowing where her body was headed, Marlea's eyes closed, not wanting to see his face when she reached her undeniable destination.

AJ squeezed and she hoped he wouldn't see. Marlea hit her zenith like a NASCAR favorite at top speed. Her eyes crossed and her breath was a gasp of impossibility. Sweat leapt from her pores, leaving salty trace rivulets in its wake, and for long seconds, logical thought was a mortal impossibility. Willing her body still, Marlea fought for control. Determined thought saved her from total embarrassment, and she was able to breathe again. She swallowed hard. *Maybe I am better off with him. I don't know if I could stand a woman generating this kind of* . . .

"You're looking a little flushed," AJ said. Stepping back from the massage table, he reached for a white towel and looked at her closely as he wiped his hands. "Feelin' all right?"

Oh, yeah. Just fine. "A little tired," Marlea lied, grateful that the two of them were alone in the therapy room. Pushing up on her elbow, she tried changing the topic. "I'm a trained athlete. Why am I feeling like this? I've only been in this place for . . . how long?"

"It's not so much the time as it is the lack of activity and the resultant atrophy. You've been in bed, not using muscles that you've trained to use for most of your life, and coming back after surgery and a significant layoff has a cost," AJ said.

Marlea's head drooped. "It's kind of funny, you know. The same muscles I used to run the 400 are the same ones I need to walk."

"Pretty much," AJ agreed, working his strong hands against Marlea's calf. "Why did you choose the 400?"

"I . . . my speed didn't really kick in until after the first 200 meters." Marlea sucked air, her flesh yielding to his ministrations.

AJ's thumb found a tender ridge of flesh and followed it. "Ever try any other sports?"

"Other sports?" Marlea's teeth were on edge. "Look at me. I'm a tall woman, I was a tall girl. Of course they made me play basketball—at least they did until I got old enough to say no."

"Then you ran?"

"Then I ran." Marlea held her breath and blinked rapidly.

"They ever try to switch you to hurdles?"

"I ran around them." Her voice trembled.

"Got to give it to you." His thumbs tucked into her shin, and he watched her face. "You must have really wanted it, to work so diligently." The thumbs pressed hard.

Marlea's breath escaped on a quiver. "You sound like you respect female athletes. Is that like a bedside manner thing?"

"Nope. I played some ball, learned what it takes. I respect passion and hard work in anybody. My sister was heavy into basketball. Nearly made it into the WNBA."

"Really? Women's National Basketball Association, huh?"

"Yeah. She had game, but still got cut in the final round. And yeah, she's good. Earns respect on the court and in the court." The muscle wasn't cooperating, and AJ manipulated it to force her calf.

"In the court?" Marlea's voice rose, then fell an octave when a raw and twisted sensation crawled through her essence.

"She's a lawyer, and my agent."

"She sounds like quite a lady." Marlea grabbed his wrist and squeezed. The moan that escaped her throat was too close to guttural satisfaction, and Marlea bit at her lips to stop the rush of sound. At the back of her thigh, AJ's hand pressed.

"No!" *Not again! Please don't do that to me again!* Clutching at him, she snatched her leg away.

"Marlea, come on . . ."

"I said no!"

Her short nails raked hard against the back of his hand, drawing blood, and AJ jerked against the sudden sting. "That's three," he glowered, bringing his face close to hers. "Look, lady . . ."

"What, man?" Breathing hard, Marlea matched him, pushing her face a breath closer, daring him. "I told you no, and I meant it. What are you going to do about it?"

"I . . ." To be perfectly honest, if anyone else had asked him, AJ would have been forced to admit that he didn't know. *Hell, when I came up with that three strikes thing, it was more of a psychological tool than anything else. Now here she is, calling my bluff.*

"I . . ." He looked at her and wanted to strangle her. *Stubborn as she is, nobody would ever blame me. Just look at her!* All that thick, black hair pulled back, revealing the comely oval of her sculpted face and the fiery eyes of a hellion. His eyes checked hers, moved away, and caught on the lush bow of her full lips, the bottom one pooched so provocatively that it forced him to try to read her eyes again. *She's not giving an inch.*

And neither am I.

Alone in the therapy room, a glaring intimate party of two, laced and bound by frustration, neither of them could look away. The shared moment felt as if it was happening in slow motion, and neither of them could have cared less about the outcome.

Knowing and giving less than half a damn that it wasn't a generally approved therapeutic practice, AJ reached to cradle her in his arms and was surprised when she didn't resist. In fact, she seemed curious, if not downright willing, when he pulled her close. Slowly, his lips brushed her cheek, then the corner of her mouth. His lips touched hers, awakening something too long dormant.

His embrace answered the erotic fires licking at her body and soothed the anger they had so recently shared. Head tilted, she let her lips find his. Her eyes were wide, watching, but not the least bit timid, and AJ wondered what she was thinking as her eyes closed.

The sudden crush of his lips eased, becoming sweet, tentative, questioning. Quick breath, snatched and only when necessary, passed between them.

Wrong, wrong, wrong, but I've come this far . . . His eyes closed, blocking everything but the distraction of her lips on his. Her lips parted, leading and encouraging, and AJ fell deeper into the kiss, forgetting why he had begun this.

Unthinking in his arms, Marlea felt more than welcome relief in the surrender of a kiss. Touching him, being held by him, with the clean masculine scent of his bronze skin layered against her own, eased her body. His embrace was a safe haven, a respite from the nerve-driven frenzy that had tormented her. What had gone before was only natural in a man's arms, and no man had ever held her with more tenderness or compassion.

Acute awareness asserted itself, and Marlea's eyes opened. *Oh, Lord, what am I doing? I'm sitting up here in this empty room, kissing this man, and . . .* She pulled away. "You kissed me."

"I had to get your attention. You used up your three strikes."

"If that was three, what do I get when I reach four?"

"There is no four," AJ answered, his lips dangerously close. "There's just you and me, and your success." He pulled back enough to look into her eyes. "I promised you three strikes—and now, you know that I keep my promises."

"You promised me something else."

"That you'll dance with me." His face tightened. "I didn't forget."

"You and me, huh?" Dropping her eyes, Marlea brushed at an imaginary strand of hair. "Maybe you should keep those promises with someone who can meet you halfway."

She flinched when the pad of his thumb touched her cheek. "That would be you."

"Not hardly." Her eyes met his again, and she tried a small, uneasy smile when his arms fell away.

"We should talk about what just happened."

"No, Mr. Yarborough, we shouldn't. We should just treat it like it never happened." He took a breath, started to speak, and she shook her head. "It's okay, just a part of the therapy. No harm, no foul, but if it's all the same to you, I'm ready to go now." His lips parted again, and she raised her hand to stop him. "Don't say it. I'll work with you, but I have to go now. I've had all the therapy I can take for one day."

AJ's mouth thinned and his eyes stayed on her face. He pulled the wheelchair close and Marlea bit her lips. "I can do it," she said, watching him. "I don't need your help; I can do it myself."

"Are you sure?"

"Yes, I'm sure." She slipped from the table to the chair and looked up at him. "I've got it under control."

"I hope so, Marlea." He left her sitting.

Marlea watched the door long after AJ left, her mind wandering past that kiss.

I wonder how many other women he's kissed like that? As well as he did it, he's certainly done it before. Wonder how those women responded? Did their legs fall open? Did they say something memorable before they surrendered? Or did they sit in bed when he was finished, because their legs were too weak to support them?

Marlea propped her elbow on the chair's armrest and dropped her chin into her hand, trapped by question. *He kissed me. Was that kiss supposed to seduce me into working with him, or was it a prelude to something else? Was it pity for a poor cripple? Or was it supposed to make me just another notch on his belt?* she wondered bitterly.

Better his belt than his bedpost, I guess. All he has to do is touch my foot, and my panties get wet. The ache between her legs reminded her of what it felt like to have him touch her. She sat taller in the chair and instantly regretted the change in pressure. It felt like an echo of coition. *And he wasn't even trying to turn me on. What would it be like if we were together—really together?* She licked her lips, thinking of the way God designed man and woman and their interlocking body parts. *What if it was real? If he wanted me enough to* . . . Her body lurched, making her inhaled breath sizzle across her lips and teeth.

Working with AJ Yarborough was going to be a lot harder than expected.

———⟨∾⟩———

On the other side of the door, AJ clenched his hands. "Damned unprofessional. How did I let her provoke me?" He paced a few steps, crossed his arms, and paced some more. "Humph, the same way she's managed to goad me every time we've met.

"I guess I just lose my damned mind when it comes to women." Passing his hand over his closely barbered hair, he changed direction and headed for the employees' lounge. "Bad enough it took me all that time to get over Bianca, and she's still trying to push my buttons. Now I get this one. She's determined to do everything wrong, and I wind up kissing her. What kind of ethics violation is that? Man, I've got all the sense God gave a goose."

"Excuse me."

AJ almost ran over the corpulent man in the pink Izod shirt. Flanked by a slender woman in a sleeveless yellow cotton dress and two square-built uniformed Atlanta police officers, it was clear the man was in the area for something other than exercise.

"I'm looking for one of the doctors. Parker Reynolds. They said I could find him down here."

He let his voice rise on the last word so that it sounded like a question, but AJ sensed no question about the group. Something was up. "I saw him about an hour ago. Did you try his office?"

"Told you," the woman said softly.

"Thanks," the big man nodded. Motioning to the officers and the woman, he led the group back in the direction they had come from.

Watching them leave, AJ wondered what was going on. And why were they looking for the doctor? But he didn't wonder long. When his tongue crossed his lips, he tasted Marlea Kellogg and a kiss he couldn't forget.

A study in good taste, Parker Reynolds's spacious office contained everything a successful surgeon's should. Shelved walls of leather-bound medical texts and state-of-the-art computer equipment were designer-mixed with costly glass-encased antique medical memorabilia. Trendy ergonomic furniture was color-blended to complement framed Henry Ossawa Tanner and Romare Bearden originals. On the floor, costly hand-loomed Persian carpets topped dreary hospital-issued broadloom.

"The good doctor sure knows how to live and work," Linda Palmer said, as she pushed past the hospital security guard. Her fingertips pressed the door open wider. Gene Brighton peeked over her shoulder.

"You got that right. This place is almost as fly as his crib."

Palmer put on a sour face as she looked up at her partner. "I wish you wouldn't talk like that in public."

"Just 'cause I don't hang out at the clubs doesn't mean that I ain't hip. I know cool when I see it, and I can still get my groove on with the best of 'em."

"Now why did you have to go and put that image into my head?" Palmer shuddered.

"Whatever." Brighton stepped around his partner. "He's not here."

One of the uniformed officers stepped forward. "His secretary just called for him. He should be here directly." Almost on cue, Parker walked up. The second officer followed.

"Detectives Brighton and Palmer, right?" The doctor looked between the detectives and the blue-uniformed officers. When he looked directly at Brighton, his gaze clouded. Noting the watchful officer behind him, he didn't offer his hand, but he didn't try to run, either. "Has anything changed?"

Brighton and Palmer's eyes met, and Parker almost lost his lunch. *They know!* His eyes went back to the uniformed officers. *Is he pulling out . . . Oh, God, no . . .*

Brighton curved his thumb over the handcuffs hooked onto his belt and looked almost bored as he pulled them free. "A lot of things have changed, Dr. Reynolds."

Palmer gave her hair a pat and looked perky, for a change. *He's got the cuffs, but she'll be the one*, Parker knew with certainty.

"Parker Aaron Reynolds, you have the right to remain silent . . ."

The walls seemed to tilt as the doctor's knees gave out and he hit the floor hard. "What, what are you charging me with?" he stammered, realizing that the woman was still reciting his rights. "The charges, what are they?"

Glad to oblige, Brighton grinned. "They're real interesting, doctor. Started out as a simple hit and run, but you came up with some interesting modifications on the theme. Now we're looking at failure to yield, leaving the scene of an accident, and failure to stop and render aid. That one is arguable, since you did come back to the scene of the accident, but . . . oh, and then there's battery."

"Battery?" The room swam and Parker fought for consciousness. "But I'm a doctor."

"Yeah, we know." Palmer said, leaning close and tucking her bird-like features into a semblance of sympathy. "See, the thing is you were the one who caused the injury, and then when your victim was unable to give consent, you knowingly operated on her . . ."

Dr. Parker Aaron Reynolds never heard the rest of the detective's words. He never felt the snap and bite of the stainless-steel cuffs when they were clapped on his wrists. Dr. Reynolds simply keeled over and soiled himself.

CHAPTER 15

"I don't know, honey. I expect we'll hear something from him soon." Backing out of Marlea Kellogg's room, Jeanette smiled and tried to sound cheerful. The nurse may have sounded cheerful, but she didn't breathe again until the door closed behind her.

"She's asking for him again?" Connie Charles whispered, rushing to her coworker's side.

"Yeah. They told me not to tell her yet. Got me in there lyin' my tail off." Jeanette's breath was a whistled sigh and she shook her head. "She doesn't know, girl. She still trusts him. Trusts him with her life."

"Ain't that the truth," the second nurse muttered, shaking her head. "Lord, talk about misplaced trust. Still, it's too bad about the doctor."

"Connie, girl, yes! Were you up there by his office when they came to collect him? I heard it was an ugly scene. The police didn't give him any slack, not that he deserved it." Jeanette knotted her hands and pushed them deep into the pockets of her blue smock. "Who knew the man was guilty? And worse, who would have thought he would have gone so far out of his way to hide it?"

"Humph! Have mercy." Connie ruefully remembered Marlea's anonymous arrival. "Remember when they first brought her in? Nobody knew who she was or anything.

Then for him to come in here playing savior and operate on her the way he did . . . Jeanette, you know, it's a wonder the poor girl didn't lose more than a couple of toes. Lord, truth is sure stranger than fiction." Connie's eyes suddenly widened and she thoughtfully closed her hand over the pin clipped to the breast of her uniform. "Girl, what if her survival was, you know, an accident?"

"But he took such good care of her, Connie. Doesn't that prove that his heart was in the right place, that he's not entirely evil?"

"Humph," sniffed Phyllis Bridgewater, cruising by, close enough to hear and drop off an opinion. "You've got toes. You can still wear all of your cute shoes." She lifted her nose a bit higher and sailed on.

"Busybody," Jeanette huffed under her breath.

"Always trying to stir up something in somebody else's business, but this time, she's got a point." Connie waited for the head nurse to round the corner, then turned to her friend. "So who's going to tell her? About Doctor, I mean? They can keep putting it off if they want to, but sooner or later, that woman is going to notice when he doesn't show up."

"She's not crazy about television, thank goodness. At least she won't have the news dropped on her that way."

"So sad." Connie hummed sympathy and patted her flattened hand against her breast. "And she has no family, from what I understand. She's going to need a shoulder to lean on, for sure."

It took a moment to register, and then Jeanette drew back, shocked. "Why are you looking at me like that?

You think I should tell her? Uh-uh, not me. You have lost your damned mind if you think I . . . Why do I have to be the one to tell her?"

"Well, because. You know how friendly you are. Besides, she likes you." Pulling Jeanette with her, Connie stepped back against the wall to avoid a passing gurney. Back against the wall, she eyed the other nurse. "Look, girl, that woman has no family, and she's scared enough as it is. She's got the therapist for now, but with the doctor out of the picture, what will happen when she's discharged?"

"Assisted living, probably. At least for a little while." Jeanette pushed away from the wall, managing to dislodge Connie's grip.

"But Jeanette, think about it: The doctor injured her, lied to her, did surgery on her, and now she has no one else. You and I both know that she's too young to be just, just set adrift among a lot of senior citizens. She needs to be with people who will challenge her and help her to see how much life she has left, even without her foot."

"It's her toes, not her whole foot, and I don't see where it's my job to tell her, or to go stepping in and trying to manage her life." Jeanette moved her shoulder to avoid Connie, and set off down the hall with the other woman racing behind her. "None of this is really my business, or yours for that matter. Besides, the coach will probably take her in—you know that's her real friend."

"No," Connie puffed. "That's not gonna happen. Didn't I hear you say that the coach and her husband were moving to Florida? Family problems you said, if I remember correctly."

"I heard she's already gone, but it's not my business."

"Damn, you move fast for a full-figured girl." Connie picked up her pace. "Think about it, Jeanette. Somebody's got to do it."

"Connie, get off my back," Jeanette fumed, stopping short and frowning when Connie rammed her back. "I don't see you rushing off to the rescue. That girl's health-care is going to be a lot of responsibility, and down the road she'll have all the legal dealings with the doctor, and I'm not her mother. I'm not her family. I do like the girl, and I feel bad for her, but that's where it ends. My job is to take the best possible care of her that I can while she's here, not deliver bad news. I don't work for Western Union, and she's a patient, not a puppy. I'm not taking that girl home with me!"

"Sounds serious. Who are you talking about?"

Caught arguing, the women froze and looked guilty at the sound of the man's voice. They simultaneously clamped their full lips together and looked back at the man. AJ Yarborough stood tall and imposing, waiting for an answer.

"It's nothing," Jeanette mumbled, hoping he would ignore whatever he had overheard.

"Nothing, my foot; it's a patient," Connie volunteered.

Jeanette's eyes widened and her nose flared, sending a warning. Connie widened her own eyes. Adding a hard-angled elbow to her argument, Jeanette flared again. Not to be outdone, Connie dug into Jeanette's ribs with her elbow. Nudging each other, waggling their eyebrows and wanting the information out but not willing to be the one to tell it, neither of the women would meet AJ's gaze.

"Oh, come on." He watched them send signals back and forth again. "Somebody say something; both of you know what's happening."

"Well . . ." Jeanette bit her lips.

"You can't tell anybody we told," Connie blurted. "You've got to swear you won't tell."

"You're acting like I'm forcing you to tell," AJ said. "Look, ladies, I don't know what this is about, but you looked and sounded pretty serious." The nurses looked at him hard, and AJ jokingly crossed his heart. "You can count on my discretion. Can I help?"

Connie and Jeanette stood still, hands clasped over their hearts and stared.

"What do you think?"

"Quit whispering, Connie. He's standing right there. He can hear you."

Jeanette sighed. "Well, if you can't help, at least your knowing what's going on can't possibly make things worse—now can it?"

"You want to tell me?"

Jeanette looked at him and sighed again.

Waiting, AJ stood tall and gorgeous, one large hand splayed across his chest and the other in his pocket. Looking at him, both women were willing to talk, but Connie found the words first. "You know, this is a violation of her confidentiality, and I don't want to be the one telling her business, but . . ."

"It's not exactly only her business," Jeanette butted in. "It's really the doctor's business. We all saw how they grabbed him up out of here."

"I didn't see, and now you've got me completely confused." AJ looked blank. "Tell me what happened."

"Not here," Connie whispered. The nurses looked over their shoulders, then back at AJ.

"Come on." Jeanette's fingers touched his bare arm, then she crooked a finger at him. "Let's not put it out here in the open. Come on." She led the way into the nearest patient's lounge and closed the door behind them.

"This is going to shock you," Jeanette announced, pushing her back against the door.

AJ didn't look convinced.

"Let me start. Okay, the police came in today and took . . ."

"Connie, if you're going to tell it, tell it right. Start at the beginning." Jeanette's face betrayed her concern. "You know that our patient Ms. Kellogg was injured on the Fourth of July . . ."

"And nobody knew anything, until we went through her clothes. Ooh, honey, it was a holy mess . . ." Connie's hands flew through the air, pantomiming her side of the story.

Jeanette sniffed. "We were helping out in the ER that day because of the holiday. We were the ones who found her name and her contact. I was the one who talked to the trainer . . ."

"And it was the doctor who hit her!" Connie blabbed, ignoring Jeanette's disapproving frown. "That's right, he hit her. Then he brought her in here and did surgery on her. Dr. Do Good did bad, and today the cops came in here and snatched him up for it." Folding her arms, she nodded sagely. "Dr. Parker Reynolds was the one who hit that girl and damn near killed her. He's the one who did it, all right—I heard they got proof and everything."

AJ looked from one woman to the other. They both nodded.

AJ remembered the first time he had seen the doctor with his patient. Compassion, dignity, and resolve were all very much in evidence. *And he was the one who found me. He was so dedicated to her recovery that he wanted to be sure that she had a therapist who was empathetic as well as skilled.* AJ remembered sitting on a barstool next to the doctor.

"When did you hear about it?"

"This afternoon, about two hours ago. Chile, they handcuffed him and took him right on out of here. I still can't believe it."

AJ tried to remember life two hours earlier. *Two hours ago I was with Nat Jenkins, a sixty-year-old golfer who was trying to get right after a broken ankle. It was simple, and I didn't have a clue about any of this . . .* He looked at the anxious nurses and shook his head. *This can't be right, they've got this all confused.*

"Can't believe it, right? Well, neither can anybody else," Connie announced.

"It's, uh, hard to believe." Dropping into the nearest chair, he had to remind himself to close his mouth. *It was bad enough when she trusted him, and now this betrayal. She only trusted me because of him. How is she ever going to move past this?*

"Somebody has to tell her," Connie prompted, sliding into the chair across from AJ.

"We were trying to prepare her to leave," Jeanette said softly. "She's not quite ready to be on her own, and she told me she lives in a townhouse. That means stairs, and she's not ready for stairs yet, is she?"

Thoughtful, Connie couldn't help asking, "Why can't she use the first floor only?"

"Because she outfitted it as a gym right after her last training partner left the city," AJ said. "She knocked out the walls and had it rebuilt so that she never had to have a break in her training—she's got a treadmill in there instead of a sofa. She told me."

Jeanette pressed her palms together, held them at her heart, and moved a step closer. "I don't think anybody has told her coach yet, either."

"You're waiting for me to fix this, aren't you?" AJ's shoulders rose and fell with his breath. Neither of the nurses said anything. "Somebody from the nursing staff will call her coach, and Ms. Belcher will tell her. It'll help to have a friend tell her."

"Ms. Belcher left town with her husband a couple of days ago," Jeanette volunteered.

"Won't be back any time soon, from what we hear," Connie added.

"And you're telling me that she has *no* friends, no relatives?"

"Her mother and brother are deceased, so that's it for family." Jeanette shrugged. "Apparently, no friends she trusts enough to share her situation with. She's gotten a few cards and notes since she's been here, but no visits from coworkers or anybody, any none of us have heard her call a friend. You have to be able to trust the people you call friends. With the doctor gone, that leaves you and the coach."

"I guess its time she made some friends," AJ said. *She barely trusts me.* Then he remembered kissing Marlea. *She let me kiss her . . . we both seem to have survived that, but would she trust me enough to let me help her through this?* "I don't know how to tell her without making things worse."

"But . . ." both women began.

AJ raised his hand, silencing them. "I don't know how to tell her about the doctor—yet. But I think I can help out with her other problem. My grandma used to say that God never closes a door, unless he opens a window. I might know how to pry open a window or two."

"What does that mean?"

"It means I'm going to have a talk, a serious talk, with my client." AJ stood and Connie hopped up from her seat. Jeanette managed to keep pace with him as he headed for the door. "Alone," he said. His raised finger and stern face stopped the women in their tracks. "I'll let you know how it turns out."

Watching him leave, the two women looked at each other.

"Well, I'm glad that's handled," Connie said.

"It's not handled yet," Jeanette answered.

"Uh-uh. That's just ridiculous. I can't just go moving into your house all willy-nilly."

"Sure, you can. Why can't you?"

"Because . . . well, I can't. I mean, I have my own place. I'm not some kind of pet, and I'm not a cripple. Isn't that what you've been telling me? I have responsibilities, and bills, and . . . and a life. Then, too, I won't be working for a while, you know."

"But in the meantime . . ." AJ wished he had more convincing words, but none came to mind.

"I'll be fine in my own place," Marlea repeated. "I won't be underfoot. Besides, my townhouse has always suited me, and I'll be glad to get back to it."

"Two stories?"

"Three," she said, suspicious. "Why?"

"What about the first floor gym? You can't sleep on a stair master or a treadmill. You would have to get up the stairs, and you'll need some help adjusting."

Marlea's face tightened. "There you go again, trying to make me need something."

AJ threw both hands up in the air. "Probably for the same reasons you're so determined not to need anyone or anything. Marlea, you're a whole and independent woman. I get it. Hell, everybody in the Western world gets it. You can stop hitting us over the head with it now."

Stubborn as ever, Marlea stiffened on the bed. She stared into space for a long moment. "You know, it's really strange, Dr. Reynolds just up and leaving the way he did." Looking thoughtful, her tone changed. "Why didn't he tell me he was leaving? And he simply left my case in your hands? Without asking me or telling me anything, and now you want me to move to your house? I'm not so sure about this—it sounds kind of fishy to me."

I don't even know why I expected this to be easy. Defensive, AJ raised his hands. "You're making way too much of this. You knew that you would have to leave the hospital sooner or later—or did you plan to make this hospital room your permanent residence? Your time is up here, Marlea. Bottom line: your post-surgical follow-up will be done by another doctor, and your therapy stays with me. Meanwhile, they need the bed and you're well enough to move on."

Marlea toyed with a cup from her bedside table. "It would be nice to be out of here, but with you?"

"What's wrong with me?" AJ looked down at himself then back at her.

"A lot of things." Marlea tried hard but couldn't quite bite back her smile.

"Like what?"

"You don't take direction very well, for one thing." Marlea tried not to think of what she had felt the last time he touched her. A rivulet of memory teased her core, and she pressed her thumbs hard against the cup.

"I'll try to do better, and your stay with me won't be for long, just until we get your therapy back on track."

"And what about when Dr. Reynolds returns?"

Not gonna happen! AJ swallowed audibly. "I'm still only handling the therapy end of your case, and I think you're making way more of this than you need to." *Lord, please let her buy this before my thin lie falls apart.* Leaning against the wall, AJ tried to look cool, but it was a struggle.

"What about your wife, or your woman, or your . . . whoever? What will she think if you drag me home and move me in?" AJ threw his head back and laughed. Marlea pressed on. "I'm telling you right now, I'm not about to be a charity case, and I'm not trying to pay room and board by being your 'something on the side.'" He was still laughing. "Don't laugh. Whoever she is, she deserves better than that."

"The only women at my house are my sister and the housekeeper. Other than that, there's nobody." He grinned.

"Why?"

"What do you mean?" AJ crossed his arms and stared. When she said nothing, he shook his head, amazed. "Nosy, aren't you?"

"You just invited me to move into your home—right after my doctor ducked out without so much as a fare thee well, and you're claiming that there are no strings attached. I have a right to know what I'm getting into, don't I?"

"So you're at least considering it?"

"I still don't know why I can't go back to my own place."

AJ thanked a generous God for the topic change and felt his chest loosen. "Because you would be alone, and your home is not set up for your needs. How will you get up and down the stairs, or what if you fell, Marlea?"

"I guess I didn't think of that." Her eyes shifted, and she gave him a look that made him think of his mother.

"You never answered my question," she insisted, setting the cup aside. "Why is a man like you out here in the world all alone?"

"I could ask you the same thing."

"But you won't, 'cause I asked you first." Sliding her hands over her legs, Marlea leaned forward as though trying to x-ray him to get to the truth.

What kind of man does she think I am? Thinking of the little she knew of him, a couple of sadistic images ran through his head. *She probably thinks I'm some kind of . . . what the hell am I about to get myself into?*

"I guess you could say I never met the right woman." *That's an understatement.* "But that has nothing to do with your making this temporary move. My house is large enough, plenty of room to safely accommodate you." *It's not like I can tell her about the women who used to follow the teams, or the ones that send the drawers in the mail.* "My office and a small clinic are right there, so you can't beat it for convenience."

"You're dodging the question, aren't you?"

Is it that obvious? "I don't know what you're talking about."

"Yeah, right." Marlea's hands smoothed along the satiny track of her thighs again. "C'mon, you can tell me. Why aren't you in a relationship? Why are you still available?"

She said the last word slowly, her teeth and tongue massaging every letter. *I SURE can't try to explain Bianca—I don't understand her myself.* "I'm kind of selective. Got no babies, no baby's mamas, and therefore no baby/mama drama. How about you?"

"I could say the same thing—pretty much." Her eyes dropped, hiding something that they denied when they rose again. "So if I move in—just 'til I can take care of myself again—I won't have to deal with any drama?"

"Not unless you bring it." He offered his hand. "Want to shake on it?" She dropped her eyes and blushed. *Now what's up with that?* he wondered.

Her firm grip met his before he could ask.

CHAPTER 16

Man, look at me. I'm actin' worse than some old lady, AJ grinned. Strangely elated, not sure why, he headed for his jeep, feeling as if he had won something good—something real good.

I can't believe it. She agreed to leave the hospital—with me! He felt like an old lady again. *What the hell do I know about preparing for a lady houseguest? Whew! This is nothing like getting things together when Bianca was around. Then all I had to do was make sure that the sheets were clean, the bath salts were expensive, and that there was plenty of that champagne she likes.*

He left out the part about making sure that there was money in her accounts and that her bills were paid. *And damned if I didn't do it.* He shook his head as he walked, careful not to speak out loud. It wouldn't do to have people thinking he had completely lost his mind.

But his thoughts still were still haunted by the bruised memory of Bianca. *Guess I was still young enough to believe in love at first sight, and falling in love with the perfect woman. Bianca looked perfect, and I fell for it.* Dench had a word for that—punked. He had a saying, too. He always said, *"Just 'cause you fall in love, you ain't got to fall into stupid"*.

"And the boy ain't never lied," AJ had to admit. He had no plans for getting punked like that ever again.

But this time is different. Marlea Kellogg is nothing like Bianca Coltrane, and our situation is entirely different. She's not my lover, though she could become a friend. In the meantime, this is about her health and business, and if I don't make a list, I'm sure to leave something out, and I don't want her to be without anything.

Sitting in his jeep, he reached for his Palm Pilot and started making notes. First on the list: where to put her. Dench was in the guesthouse, but the small suite at the end of the main floor would be perfect for Marlea. She would have privacy—a bedroom, a sitting room, a bath, and she would be close to the elevator.

He scribbled the note and searched his memory for other things he knew about Marlea. Television—she didn't like network television, but she did like videos. The kids from her school kept sending her stuff. She would need a VCR and maybe a DVD player, too. He scrawled another note. By the time he reached item eleven, he remembered where he was: the parking deck at Grady Memorial Hospital.

"Got too much to do to spend my time here, and I've got to get this list home." He tossed the Palm Pilot onto the passenger seat and jammed the key into the ignition. "Mrs. Baldwin's gonna love her," he figured, thinking of his housekeeper. "One more body in that big house, another mouth to feed, and a mind of her own. Yep, Marlea's her kind of girl."

Wheeling the jeep away from the hospital and onto the highway, AJ thought of Marlea's impact on the rest of his small household. Dench would fall in love with her because she was an athlete, a pretty athlete, even if she wasn't on the track these days. She might not be Rissa, but she would catch and hold his buddy's attention, for sure. And Rissa? Marlea Kellogg would be another human target for her insatiable curiosity.

Reaching to tune the CD player, AJ had to laugh. *My little sister is nosy like nobody else I've ever known. And to top it off, the girl's mouth won't hold water. She digs up the information, and then tells it as fast as she can.*

She had been that way for as long as anybody could remember.

"Like when she was four and found our Christmas stuff. Couldn't even read. She took one look at the pictures on the boxes and came running to me as fast as her little legs could carry her, told me Daddy lied to Mom. Bad enough she snooped and found the stuff Santa Claus was supposedly bringing, but then she had to put two and two together and come up with six. Since Dad told her about Santa, she figured he told Mom, too. 'Cause the toys were in the house, Daddy had to have brought them in, then lied and said Santa did it, and Rissa couldn't wait to tell it. Lord, that child couldn't wait to carry that tale from me to grandma and Aunt Kate, Cousin Art, and a bunch of the neighborhood kids."

The memory was funny and good, and AJ hooted as he turned up the CD volume. Randy Crawford filled the jeep, and he pulled onto I-20 still thinking about his sister. "Man, I still remember the time she . . ." His ringing cellphone stopped him. Thumbing the call button, he opened his mouth to speak, but Rissa Yarborough beat him to it.

"Hey, AJ, how you doin'?" she drawled into the phone.

"I'm good. You were just on my mind," he said, nodding to the pair of flirting redheads in the Mustang on his right.

"That's what I like about you, brother dear. You always have a good thought."

"I do what I can." AJ wondered which of the red-haired women was steering the car when the driver lifted her shirt and extended a bare-breasted invitation. Declining, he raised a hand and sped up. The Mustang changed lanes behind him.

"I tried you at home, and Mrs. Baldwin said you were out. Where are you?"

Eyes on the rearview mirror, AJ caught sight of the Mustang. "I'm headed home now. You?"

"At the office. I just left the courthouse and I'm about ready to go home. That all-day mediation was rough, but we finally came to an agreement, and I filed the papers. You were just on my mind."

AJ almost wondered what he would do if the Mustang caught up with him, but the women found a more likely target for their charms. A man's arm emerged from the driver's side window of a big black Expedition and waved. It looked like a done deal—so much for that.

"AJ?" Rissa's voice was sharp, bringing her brother's attention back to her.

"Yeah, yeah, I'm here. Listen, I was gonna call you. I just wanted to give you a heads-up on something. I'm going to be bringing a patient home to stay for a while."

"Today?"

"Tomorrow, more than likely. She hasn't been released yet."

Rissa hummed into the phone. "Why are you bringing her to the house, AJ?"

"She's an amputee, and we'll be working on balance and functional training."

"Why, brother dear, did I hear you say 'she'?" AJ could almost hear his sister's pique. Her sharp mind was racing, looking for signals, testing for possibilities. "You're being very . . . shall we say, clinical? And I really don't want to use the word 'circumspect,' but it almost sounds . . . interesting. What's her name?"

"Marlea. Marlea Kellogg."

"Marlea," Rissa repeated, trying it out. "Marlea Kellogg. Pretty name. How do you spell it?" Reaching for a pad and pen, she doodled the name as AJ spelled it, then waited a beat. "Is she going to be . . . interesting?"

"Rissa," AJ laughed. "She's an athlete, if that's what you mean."

"Okay, if that's how you want to put it." Rissa underlined the name with broad strokes. "She must be something special if you want to bring her home. How long have you known her?"

"Rissa, I barely know this woman. She's been a patient at Grady since her accident. All I want you to do is help me make a comfortable place for her for as long as she needs it."

"She's been at Grady? What kind of accident?"

"Car accident. She lost a couple of toes when they had to cut her out of the car." AJ gripped the steering wheel. No conversation was ever easy with Rissa.

"Toes?" Rissa circled the underlined name. "Are you kidding? Which toes? Is that bad?"

"It is for a runner. Messes up their balance, gait, speed, all that."

"That's sad, but you barely know this runner and you want to bring her to the house? Where's her doctor?" AJ could hear her thinking and wished she would stop.

"That's part of the problem. He's been arrested."

"Arrested?" Rissa's pen slashed diagonally across the page. "What kind of mess is that? Why was he arrested, AJ? What were the charges—do you know? What's his name? Would I know him? When was he arrested?" Rissa's mind ticked over what she had seen and heard at work.

"You know I can't tell you any of that."

"No fair," she pouted. "You can't just tease me like that, AJ. Who's the doctor?"

"Rissa," he warned.

She wrote 'doctor' on her pad, followed by a string of question marks. "Okay. It is your house. So you've got it, big brother. How old is she? Does she, did she, run for a living? Where is she from? Where's her family? How does it happen that you're stepping in to . . ."

She caught herself and AJ could almost hear her asserting self-control. The questions stopped. If the woman was coming out to the house to stay, there would be plenty of time to get all the answers. She put her pen down. "It might be fun to have another woman around the house."

"Thanks, Rissa. I knew I could count on you." AJ aimed the jeep for the Cascade Road exit.

"Of course you can, AJ." Rissa waited for her brother to disconnect before she hung up the phone and smiled. Leaning across her desk, she touched the intercom button. "Helen, I'm going to be leaving for the rest of the day. Please hold my calls." Then she had another thought. Reaching for the button again, she almost changed her mind—but curiosity got the better of her. "Helen, can you get that folder together for Grady? No need for a messenger; I'll run it over. It's on my way."

Glancing at her watch, she wondered about traffic. "I should be able to get there in about ten minutes. That'll give us a couple of hours for a visit." Collecting her Prada bag, Rissa Yarborough hit the wall switch on her way out. Grady Hospital wasn't that far away.

She couldn't imagine why she hadn't sat here before. There were enough chairs in the room; she just had never thought to use one before. Yet today, this afternoon, sitting by the window and looking out at the people coming and going seemed the most natural thing in the world. The setting sun splashed light along the marble windowsill, reminding her of the passing time. *It's nearly five o'clock and still light,* Marlea noted. *It's still summer.* So much had happened in the last few weeks. *How can it still be summer?*

A quick knock and the creaking door broke the silence in the room. Startled, Marlea turned in time to see the tall woman's fingertips come around the edge of her door.

Stylish to a fault, the woman's lightweight suit draped her figure to graceful perfection. Belted at her narrow waist, the jacket stopped above her hipline, and the narrow skirt stopped at her knee, revealing a pair of the best legs Marlea had ever seen on another woman.

Marlea brought her hand to the throat of her white tee shirt. Just looking at this woman made her feel totally dowdy, and she didn't have a clue as to who she was.

"Hi, I'm Marissa Yarborough, AJ's sister."

"Oh," Marlea managed. *Well, I knew she wasn't a nurse. She kind of looks like him, though. Same eyes and mouth, but softer. But what is she doing here?* Disconcerted by Rissa's designer suit, flawless makeup, and her short and sleek razor-cut hair, Marlea self-consciously smoothed her own hair, making a vain effort to catch the strays that had escaped her ponytail. She touched her chapped lips, wondering how she had managed to forget makeup.

Checking her appearance. She hasn't had many visitors; doesn't look too bad, though. Making no effort to hide her appraisal, Rissa moved into the room, took Marlea's hand, and forged ahead. "I hope you don't mind my dropping in, but I thought we should meet. I talked to AJ and he told me that you would be with us for a while."

"Only until I can get back to my own place."

"Of course." *Defensive,* Rissa noted, releasing Marlea's hand. *That's not a bad thing.* "But if we're going to live together, we might as well get to know each other, and frankly, I'm content to wait for AJ. So here I am." She smiled, then looked for a chair. "You mind? I've been in court-ordered mediation all day, and I could use the seat."

Politely waiting for Marlea's nod, she turned the chair toward the window. "This is nice, kind of peaceful, you know?" Leaning back in the chair, she kicked off her shoes and grinned. "Hope you don't mind, but since we're going to share a house, you might as well know that when nobody's looking, I break down, girl. I get real comfortable, real quick."

She used the toes of one foot to massage the other, then closed her eyes and moaned with relief. When she opened her eyes, Marlea was staring.

"Oh, my goodness! Was that rude? Am I being insensitive?" Rissa's mouth fell open and her eyes shot to Marlea's feet. "Oh, I am so sorry. I . . . I don't know what to say . . ."

"You pretty much just said it all." Marlea pressed her lips together, but the smile crept around the edges. "If we're going to live in the same house, you can't go around apologizing every time someone says something about a shoe, or a sock, or a foot. What happened happened, and there's nothing either of us can do about it. But I would feel a whole lot better if we didn't have to make an issue out of it. Is that okay?"

"Fine by me." Rissa pulled a leg beneath her in the chair. "How did it happen?"

"I honestly don't know. Mostly all I remember is the Peachtree Road Race and being in Piedmont Park. I really don't even remember most of that." Marlea took a deep breath and looked out the window. "I was just sitting here marveling at the fact that it's still summer—out there."

"You haven't been outside since you got here, have you?" Rissa guessed. "You are so going to love it at the house. We call it 'the house,' but it's really a small estate. It sits on four acres on the southwest side of the city. There's a pool and some other stuff, but I think you'll like the windows and the terraces best. Lots of privacy and lots of space. Lots of places for you to get back in touch with nature and with yourself, you know? Places to catch up on some of the time you lost being here."

"I look like I need that?"

"Yeah, you do. You look like you need a little sun, some good food, some good gossip, and a little girl time." Rissa reached across to tuck a few more hairs behind Marlea's ear. "Sister, I'm gonna hook you up!"

"Thanks, I think." Marlea plucked at her hair again. "I am getting a little tired of always getting what's supposed to be good for me in here."

"Please." Rissa blew air between her teeth. "Nothing a hospital issues is good for you. I'm a lawyer, I know."

"You're funny. What kind of law do you practice?"

"Sports and entertainment, thanks to my brother. He was my first, and my star, client. He's got some interesting contracts that I'm handling for him right now." Rissa did a little dance in her seat and rocked a fist in the air. "In case you didn't know, my brother is the bomb!"

"He's worked hard with me."

Why is she looking so uncomfortable? It's not like I caught her doing the nasty with AJ. Rissa's brows lifted. *Or is it?* When Marlea didn't continue, Rissa used her toes to pull her shoes closer to her chair and decided that it was still her turn to talk. "So what do you do in the real world? AJ said you were a runner."

"I used to be a runner. I wanted to run in the Olympics." Marlea licked her lips and shrugged. "I'm a special ed teacher."

"Really? Where?"

"The Runyon School. It's small and private, up in Marietta."

"I guess rich kids need love, too."

"Okay," Marlea jabbed a finger in the air between them. "Now that's insensitive. I'm not at Runyon because of the money, I'm there because in a multicultural environment, there's a need for role models and strong educators—that applies regardless of whether the kids and their parents are rich or poor. I'm the first, but I hope not the last, African-American special ed teacher they've ever had at Runyon. I'm also a damned good teacher, I love what I do, and it's a great school. But you have to remember, I would be a great teacher in any school."

"Excuse me. *Mea culpa*." Rissa brought her palms together and bowed her head. "No shame in your game, girl."

"None at all."

"So you dating anybody?"

"Say *what*?" Marlea's face showed her amazement. "Talk about no shame!"

Rissa shrugged. "My brother's a single man, and he's bringing a woman home." She cleared her throat pointedly. "You do the math."

"It's not like that."

"Uh-huh, I believe you. Is that a no?"

"That's a definite no." Marlea blushed.

Now there's something you don't see every day—a grown woman who blushes, and she does it when I mention my brother. Hmm . . . Stretching lazily, Rissa kept her eyes on Marlea . "I have another question."

"What else is new?"

"I'm gonna ignore that." Rissa stretched her legs out in front of her. "What was your doctor's name?"

"Reynolds. Parker Reynolds. Why?"

The name clicked immediately. *That can't be right!* Rissa leaned forward in her chair. *AJ said the doctor had been arrested, but he didn't tell me the doctor's name.* "What did you say his name was?"

"Parker Reynolds," Marlea repeated.

"He's in the news today." Rissa remembered catching the scene on the tiny TV her secretary kept on her desk. Helen had been thoroughly irritated when the breaking news story interrupted *The Young and The Restless.* "Was he with you when he was arrested?"

"Arrested? That's ridiculous. I don't know what you're talking about. My doctor wasn't arrested. He's consulting on another case—somewhere."

Rissa pressed a hand to her lips and wished she had never said anything.

Denial weighted Marlea's voice. "Where did you hear such a preposterous thing?"

"I spoke out of turn . . ." *If Helen wasn't addicted to those damned soaps, I never would have seen anything, then I never would have had anything to tell, and . . . and*

Daddy always did say, 'if IF was a fifth, we would all be drunk.'

"You're a lawyer. You would know, wouldn't you?"

Rissa's clear eyes and intelligent face said what her lips could not.

"Why?"

"I spoke out of turn."

Marlea reached across the space between them and gripped Rissa's wrist. "You can't stop now. Why? You have to tell me; why was he arrested?"

"Damn, girl. You've got a mean grip on you." Rissa pulled her wrist free and took a deep breath.

Marlea grabbed again. "Oh, no. There's no way you're going to have a crisis of conscience now. You've told me he was arrested, now you need to finish. Why was he arrested?"

How much to tell? Rissa's eyes darted to the window, then back to Marlea. "He was arrested for a hit-and-run accident. Yours."

"Mine?" Marlea's golden skin faded, leaving her face an ashen gray. "His was the car that hit me? Then he brought me here?" Fast tears filled her eyes. "He lied to me? The doctor who took off two of my toes and ended my running career lied to me?"

"I don't think he saw it that way."

"That's mighty damned big of you." Marlea's eyes went back to the window. Two fat tears fell, staining her white shirt. Outside, the sun was lower in the sky, still shining, but it meant nothing to her. "How do you think he saw it? Make this good, 'cause it's going to have to last me a lifetime!"

Nobody's ever rendered me speechless before, Rissa marveled, wishing she could say something to erase the horror on Marlea's face. She didn't have the words, and settled for stammering, "I don't know what to say."

"At least you're honest." Marlea's head drooped. Rissa pushed her feet back into her shoes and used the silence to escape.

Fleeing, Rissa rushed past a pair of nurses in matching blue and lavender paisley print uniforms. One of them said something, but Rissa was too busy digging through her Prada bag. Coming to an emergency exit, she plunged through the door and darted down the stairs.

Practically running, she ignored the metal handrails when she found her phone. Dreading the call but knowing she had to make it, she hit the speed dial. She was rewarded with the slim phone's burring ring. "AJ," she whispered furtively when he answered her urgent call. "Where are you?"

"Grocery store," he said, hefting the last of the bags into the jeep. "Why? What's going on? And why are you whispering?"

Rissa's heels clattered on the metal stairs, as she passed the second floor. "Don't fuss, but I'm at Grady. You'd better get down here quick, big brother, 'cause I've thrown both our asses into the fire! I didn't know that she didn't know. You didn't tell me."

"Okay, this doesn't sound good." AJ climbed into the driver's seat and pressed his hand over one ear, trying to hear better. "What didn't I tell you? And what did you do?"

Rissa swallowed hard. "I told Marlea about the doctor getting arrested."

"You told her what? You don't even know her! You had no right . . . you . . . you . . ."

Pushing through the door on the first floor, Rissa stopped in the middle of the marble-tiled lobby. She pulled the phone from her ear, glared at it, then slammed it back to her ear. "Don't you holler at me, AJ. What do you mean, I shouldn't have told her? You shouldn't have told me. You know I can't keep a secret."

On his end, AJ shook his head. It was true. Rissa's mouth couldn't hold water.

So how do I fix this? he wondered, making the wide U-turn out of the parking lot and onto Cascade. Thinking hard, he tried several ways of turning the subject to his advantage and came up with nothing by the time he piloted his car down Butler Street and made the turn into Grady's parking deck.

CHAPTER 17

Belted into the jeep's passenger seat, Marlea sat stock-still and tried to think grateful thoughts. As Libby said last night; Yes, *the doctor lied. And yes, a lie by omission is still a lie, but you're going to have good care and good company—even if his sister IS the nosiest creature on two legs. He promised to take care of you, and he will do right by you.* For some strange reason, Libby had faith in AJ. *You said yourself, AJ and his sister are not to blame for anything, didn't you?* Yes, she had. *So be thankful and get well.*

Solid long-distance counsel.

They drove past a McDonald's, a Wendy's, a couple of banks, and a few other stores, and Marlea's misgivings lingered. AJ crossed an unfamiliar intersection, and the street narrowed, becoming two lanes, and she felt no better. Five minutes later, AJ made one turn, then another, finally pulling to a stop in front of a massive wrought-iron gate.

"Where are we?" Marlea asked, half afraid of the answer.

"Home," AJ told her.

He lives behind these big gates? She lifted her sunglasses to see better, and it didn't help. She folded the shades and dropped them into her pocket. *Are these gates here to keep something in or something out? Like maybe, the police?* She watched him punch numbers into an electronic keypad and waited as the gates swung wide. *Oh, Lord, don't tell me, this man is a drug dealer! A drug dealer who practices physical therapy on the side?* She cut her eyes to the side. AJ drove through the gate, oblivious to her inspection. *He looks harmless enough. Just wait and see,* she cautioned herself.

AJ steered the jeep along a twisting, tree-lined cobblestone path. Marlea leaned forward a little, trying to see better. She was able to pick out several houses sitting back from the road and ringing the stone drive. She squinted, picking out little details. One of the houses was high-walled and turreted like a castle, or at least that was what it looked like from where she was sitting. Another sprawled along a high ridge marked by a natural break of pine and spruce.

This is a compound, Marlea noted, awed and wondering what just one of these places might go for. *That's at least five million dollars worth of house,* she guessed, as AJ steered the jeep along the curving drive toward what looked like a mansion anchoring the circle of houses. Touching a remote in the center of the jeep's sun visor, he cued a second gate that opened as he followed the rising driveway onto his property.

Did I say five million? Marlea tried not to gape. *That was before I saw the rest of it! If this brother is dealing drugs, this is a hell of an investment!*

"Well, this is it." AJ looked at her, slapped his thighs, and climbed out of the jeep.

From the front seat of the jeep, Marlea looked out at what she imagined must be a garage. *A garage with eight doors? Even with his sister and the housekeeper in residence, who needs eight cars?* A basketball court and a swimming pool were visible in the distance.

Marlea bit the inside of her lip and waited. Give him a chance, that was what Libby said. *Now that I'm here, what else can I do?* From the rearview mirror, she could see him pulling her bags from the back of the jeep. AJ had already told her that Rissa and the housekeeper, Mrs. Baldwin, had gone to Marietta and brought down the rest of the things she would need for her stay. *So here I am.*

Leaning hard, she shoved open the door of the jeep and managed to climb down. Not fully sure of what the front of the house looked like, she took a good look at the side. Brick and tuck-pointed mortar had never been done so perfectly. Cozy ivy climbed the narrow white banister bordering a small stone porch. Neatly flanked by mani-cured shrubbery, the side entrance to his house looked harmless enough.

The door to the house had lead-paned windows that offered a view into what looked like the kitchen, but it was the breezeway that connected the house to a smaller building that intrigued her. The small building was con-structed mostly of glass. High doors, glass ceiling, and walls. She tipped her head and squinted. Plants inside, some tools, long tables, and stacks of assorted red clay pots answered her question. It was a greenhouse. *Oh, Lord, he grows the stuff here!*

"My grandmother stayed here a while. She loved gar-dening. Rissa uses it now. She says it's her therapy."

"Oh," Marlea breathed, her pulse slowing.

"Here, you might need this. For a little while, anyway." Holding one bag under his arm and another in his hand, AJ offered the cane she had deliberately left in a corner of her hospital room.

"I don't . . . why would I need that?"

"The house is new to you, new surfaces underfoot." He shrugged. "Just until you get used to it."

She took the cane, then looked down at the arm he offered.

"Allow me to escort you into my home?" She took his arm and walked with him up the curved ramp and through the side door.

"You made it!" Rissa bounced down the stairs and planted herself solidly in front of Marlea and AJ.

"Yeah," a man's voice said from behind the door.

"Come out from back there, Dench. You're scaring her."

"Me?" The tall, barrel-chested man stepped out, frowning. "I'm not the one zooming down the stairs like . . ."

"Never mind all that. Meet Marlea." Her tone was almost as suggestive as her expression when Rissa reached for Marlea's free hand. "Marlea Kellogg, meet Dennis Charles Traylor. Dench, to his friends. Now that you're here, you can call him Dench, too."

Marlea opened her mouth to respond, but Rissa had taken charge and was moving her away from the men and down the main corridor of the house. "AJ and Dench will bring the rest of your stuff later. Dench went up to

Marietta with me to collect your stuff. How did you ever find that cute little townhouse? I can see why you miss it, but you're going to like it here. Smell that? Mrs. Baldwin made a special lunch for you. Girl, wait 'til you taste her cooking. Fabulous, that's all I can say."

How does she manage to talk so much? When does she breathe? Oh, I forgot, she's a lawyer. It must be a job-related skill. Marlea listened and kept walking.

Rissa stopped outside a set of double-hung mahogany doors and grinned. "This is the library, and I love showing this off." Flinging the doors open, she stepped into the room and turned in a small circle. "Don't you love it? Floor to ceiling books, and AJ everywhere you look."

The library was a small gem of a room. Set in a corner of the house, high-polished green marble sparkled underfoot, and recessed lighting blended softly with the light from wide windows cornering the room. Dark mahogany shelves housed leather-bound books. Marlea couldn't help herself. She leaned on the cane and reached out to touch the handsome volumes. Books by Chaucer, Charles Dickens, William Faulkner, Langston Hughes, Zora Neale Hurston, Richard Wright, and a host of other authors were discreetly lined up like literary soldiers. Two rows down, she found a mix of paper and hardback romance novels. "Eclectic taste. Does he actually read these?"

Rissa flipped her hand. "He reads the literary stuff; I read the romance. It gets me away from the day to day. You ever read any?" Marlea shook her head and giggled. "You don't seem the type, but if the notion ever strikes you, they're here."

"Maybe . . ." Marlea hoped she sounded polite.

Rissa kept moving. "There's a couple of things I love about this room. The furniture is great." She brushed a languid hand across the backs of a pair of sand-colored leather chairs. "You can have music if you like." Rissa touched a panel in the wall and soft music filled the room. "The mate to this room is at the other end of the house. AJ uses it as an office, but if you need to handle business in here, you can always use one of these desks." She went to the wall, between the windows and pressed a decorative latch. The desk folded out from the wall complete with a computer docking station. Marlea squeaked in surprise.

"But," Rissa pressed her hands together, obviously pleased, "my most favorite part of this room has got to be this wall." She walked toward the doors they had come through, and Marlea saw the photos—hundreds of them.

So the doctor didn't lie about everything. And here was the proof, a wall of AJ in his uniforms from peewee leagues to pros. "He really is a football player." Then it dawned on her. "Oh, is he *that* AJ Yarborough? The one they call 'the nicest man in football?'" *And not a drug dealer.* "Well, there are certainly enough pictures of him."

"Don't take it so hard. They weren't AJ's idea, but Mom and I think they're sweet," Rissa volunteered.

"I told you this is where she would bring her," AJ muttered.

"Yeah, that's what you said, man. But I thought for sure she would take her to the kitchen." Dench said.

"And pass up the opportunity to embarrass me? Don't be silly."

"Well, I just thought," Dench passed a big hand over his belly. "Lunch is ready and all."

"I hope you're not too bored," AJ said, turning to Marlea. "Our mother has been taking these shots for a long time. She kept them, no matter what anybody else said. Then when I built this place, she insisted I put them up, and she wanted them all together, so they're in here. When I retired, she added more."

Leaning on her cane, Marlea took a closer look and smiled. "You're cute . . . I mean, as a kid . . . you were cute."

"How about now?" Rissa's smile was knowing.

AJ ignored his sister. "She took a lot of them with her very own little Brownie Starfire. It's a box camera that Kodak used to make. It uses flashbulbs, can you believe it? And she loves it. It's something she had as a child."

"And it still works," Rissa added. "Mom has promised that she's gonna use that camera to take pictures of her grandkids." She nudged AJ. "One of us better hurry up. You know that camera is real old."

Embarrassed, AJ took Marlea's elbow and steered her toward the door. "Please ignore my sister. She was dropped on her head as an infant."

"But he loves me, 'cause I'm special." Rissa blew her brother a kiss. "Come on, Marlea, I'll help you get settled in."

"Then lunch," Dench said, making it plain what was on *his* mind.

"Ten minutes, sweetie."

"That means at least an hour," Dench mumbled, following AJ. "Think Mrs. Baldwin will let us start without them?"

"You know, I can wait to do this," Marlea offered.

"Honey, please." Rissa fanned a hand at the departing men. "Does Dench look like he's missed any meals lately? They'll be fine, I promise. Let's get you settled."

Leading the way along the broad parquet-floored corridor and talking nonstop, Rissa finally pushed open a second set of mahogany doors. "What do you think?"

"I think this is bigger than my first apartment." Marlea stood in the doorway, leaning on her cane. She looked at Rissa and wondered, half hoped, that this was the person with the fine eye for decoration. *No way a man did this; it's just too pretty.* The shining textures of taffeta and silk caught her eye and her imagination. Done in cool shades of blue and green with flashes of yellow and mauve, the small sitting room had a welcoming aura. "This is lovely."

Crossing the hardwood floor, Marlea admired the oriental rugs. To her mostly uneducated eyes, they looked like antiques, their colors warmed and muted by time. Walking further into the room and pausing at the first doorway she came to, she discovered a bedroom and looked back at her hostess with wonder etched on her face. "I'm going to feel like a princess in here."

"A four-poster bed with a canopy will do that to a girl, won't it?" Rissa preened, glad she had chosen it. "The bathroom is over here."

Marlea followed her pointing finger. Stark-white porcelain and swan-shaped brass fixtures were complimented by towels and curtains done in blues, greens, and teals reminiscent of the sitting room. "This is gorgeous. I can't tell you how much I appreciate . . ."

"No, girl. I appreciate the smile you put on my brother's face. AJ only smiles like this when he's excited about a project or . . . Oh! Not that he thinks you're a project or anything. It's just . . ." Rissa stopped and twisted her lips. "Something about you always has me putting my foot in my mouth. What is it?"

"Rissa, I have the feeling that that is a trick you manage all by yourself."

"Anyway, let me show you where we started putting your things."

Moving to one of the walls, Rissa laid her palm against an almost invisible panel. Marlea gasped as the wall rolled back to reveal a dressing room. Touching another hidden switch, Rissa bathed the room in light. Marlea hoped that she didn't seem like too much of a bumpkin amid the obvious luxury.

"I didn't know if you'd want dresses or skirts, so I only brought a few of each."

Marlea smiled, not wanting to say that she only owned a few. "I mostly wear the running stuff, anyway." Open drawers in the chest that stood in the middle of the room revealed stacks of tee shirts and running shorts. Aware of Rissa's eyes on her, Marlea moved to close the drawers.

"Your shoes are over there." Rissa pointed out a wall of shoe racks. Six pairs of Nike, New Balance and Reebok shoes waited. "I'm not sure how they'll fit, but AJ said you had an appointment with a ped . . ." she moved her hands and shrugged. "He said you had an appointment with a man to make some shoes, so I just thought that in the meantime . . ."

She didn't bring any pumps, Marlea thought miserably. "Thanks, but . . . Thank you for doing this for me." She closed another drawer.

"Well, that's all there is to see in here." Rissa stepped back into the bedroom. "Oh, hey, are you tired?" She grabbed Marlea's arm and steered her toward the bed. "Sit."

"Dang, Rissa, I'm not a puppy."

"Right. Let me try that again."

"No need," Marlea's raised hand backed the other woman off.

"It's easy to see why you and AJ get along."

"I don't know if that's a fair statement."

"Well, I do, and I know why, too." Rissa dropped heavily onto the bed and wrinkled her nose. She patted the comforter, inviting company. "You're both control freaks, can't let anybody else help you out. He's always been like that, even when we were kids."

Crossing her legs, she looked at Marlea. "Big kid picked on me, said he was gonna beat me up because I couldn't keep a secret, and AJ made him eat dirt. I told him not to, but he said he had to because I was his little sister. Kid was bigger than him, too, but he never hesitated. Said it was 'cause he loved me."

"And that's a bad thing?" Marlea eased herself to sit.

"Never said it was bad." Rissa looped her folded hands over her knees. "AJ is just one of those people who have to know how things are going to turn out—have to find a way to control the outcome. Like with you. Okay, I'm talking too much again, but it's true." She lifted her chin and studied Marlea's face. "He coulda let you go on your way, but that would have meant that your full recovery was out of his hands, and there's no way my brother would ever let that happen."

"It's easy to see that you adore your brother, and that's sweet." Marlea sounded sad and a tiny bit jealous.

"I could give you a lot of other examples," Rissa grinned.

"I'll bet you could."

"Oh, child. Could I ever." *I could start by telling you about my brother and the women in and out of his life,* Rissa thought. *But I wonder how you'll fit?*

Marlea took a deep breath and looked away. Rissa rocked, fingers still locked around her knees.

Bianca Coltrane, bless her pointy little head, had never fit. The girl was so into material things that she made Madonna look like a nun. Glad she's out of the picture. Rissa rocked and sighed, and hoped it was true. *Bianca is like a poster girl for Murphy's Law—if it could go wrong, she probably caused it.*

And poor AJ. When that witch sank her claws into him, it had taken every ounce of her brother's formidable integrity to walk away from her. That had to be hard. If there was any truth to the rumors, Bianca was a fierce competitor when it came to men, and it was said that her sexual arsenal was downright awesome.

And I think he really loved her . . . he wouldn't listen to me. Rissa glanced at the woman sitting beside her. She was still staring intently at the print on the walls.

Maybe this is the right one, Rissa sighed, *and maybe I'm going to have to help him figure it out.* Not that love was foreign to AJ; he just didn't fall easily. He hadn't brought home a lot of women, didn't even do a lot of dating—especially not since he got the news about his contract.

"AJ hasn't brought home a patient since Robert Crown," Rissa murmured.

"Who's Robert Crown?"

"Oh, did I say that out loud?" Rissa's eyes slid low and she stood slowly. Crown was unexpected, too. A twenty-year-old UGA running back, he needed help recovering from a stroke. AJ did it *gratis*, said that working with the young man was an investment." Moving across the room, Rissa picked up a pair of sweatpants and folded them over a hangar. Sneaking a glance at Marlea, she slipped the matching jacket onto the hanger. "Crown was an investment, but you're different."

"How?"

"I'm not sure yet. For now let's go get some lunch. Maybe I'll fill you in when I know." Rissa closed the closet door and stuffed her hands into the pockets of her jeans.

"Thanks, I think."

"Don't thank me yet," Rissa smiled. "I only said *maybe*."

"You know you can't take me, Dench."

Pointing a thick finger across the table, he shook his head. "You're going to get enough of teasing me, Rissa."

"Oh, yeah. Like you gon' school me." She threw back her shoulders, managing to look runway ready in spite of her jeans, tee shirt, and lack of makeup. She dug into the pocket of her jeans and came up with a bill. She placed it flat on the table, her hand beside it, and let her eyes drill Dench. "I've got a twenty here, and Ben Franklin says you can't take me in eight ball."

Dench checked his pockets and pulled out his own twenty. Eyes on Rissa, he held the bill to his ear, then pressed it to the tabletop. "Ben says he's lonely and he always wanted a twin." He stood. "Let's do this."

"Oh, we gon' do it, all right." Rissa stood and led the way from the room.

"This won't take long," Dench muttered, behind her back.

"I heard that," Rissa shouted, heading down the stairs.

"Are they always like that?" Marlea asked when it was finally quiet again.

"Always. They're in love and don't even know it." AJ leaned his elbows on the table and pushed his unused knife closer to his empty plate. "They think they're friends, though I think Dench is starting to figure it out."

"In love and not know it? That's a funny notion. Where did you get an idea like that?"

"It happens, I'm told."

"Hmm, I don't see it. You're either in love or you're not."

"Ever been in love?"

"No time for it. How about you?"

"Once. It didn't work out, so I settled for being in love with football."

Marlea's eyes fell, and she seemed to reach a decision. "Dr. Reynolds said you were a football player, and I saw the pictures. Sorry to say, I didn't remember your name before."

"That's okay . . ."

"*Nicest man in the NFL . . .*" she grinned.

"Yeah, I really was an NFL player. Running back," AJ told her. "That's the big man who's expected to get down the field and get the job done fast."

"I thought that was the quarterback."

"Glory boys," AJ chuckled, liking the bright flash of her teeth when she smiled with him. "That's what they would like for you to believe, but I've outrun many of 'em in my day."

"So how did you come to football, if you were so fast?"

"How did you come to running?"

Her lower lip jutted out. "No fair; you can't answer a question with a question."

"Sure I can, if it's the best possible answer."

"Okay. Well, it was just the best thing for me. It was the thing I did to feel alive and like . . . it was like a blessing." She shrugged when no more words came.

"I feel you. It was the same for me. Catching the ball, flying across the field, even running down someone on the other team . . . it was what I was born to do. The field was where I was most alive. The rest of it—school, hobbies, other kids, eating, sleeping—that was just stuff to do until it was time for the next game."

"I feel you, too." Marlea smiled wistfully. She reached for her cloth napkin and began twisting the ends.

Suddenly aware of the nervous gesture, she let the napkin fall to the tabletop. "Josh, my brother, actually he was my cousin, but I didn't find out about that until some wretched neighbor kids blabbed . . . but he used to run with me."

"Family's good that way," AJ agreed, leaning toward her. "You said, 'was' . . ."

"Long story."

"I can wait." He leaned back in his chair, prepared to do exactly that.

Marlea dropped her eyes to the dining table between them. "Well," she sighed, "since you seem so determined to get into my business, and I am living in your home . . . Josh was . . . he was really my cousin, but I mostly grew up thinking he was my brother. His mom was really my aunt, but I thought she was my mother." She pushed a hand through her hair. "Is this making any sense?"

She waited for his nod before continuing. "It's not a long story, or a pretty one. My father was a musician, and he was a gambler. My mother was a beautician. They fell in love and made me, end of story. What about your family?"

"Come on, Marlea. How many times do I have to tell you to play fair? Finish the story."

"My daddy was probably a better musician than he was a gambler, 'cause he was caught cheating. Cheating got his throat cut and sent my pregnant mom out looking for revenge. My mother was no Foxy Brown, and she was brutally beaten for her trouble. She died of her injuries ten days after I was born. That left me with her sister, my aunt Cyndra, who became the only mother I have ever known. She's the only woman I've ever called *Mom*."

"A little family, with a whole lot of love."

"Yeah, until I lost them. Josh was killed in Iraq, a peacekeeping mission they called it. Mom died last year, I think of a broken heart. So . . ." she blinked back a tear, "I run . . . ran." The tear rolled free and Marlea brushed at it with a slash of her hand." What about your family?"

"Not much to speak of," AJ said slowly.

"Oh, come on. I told you about Josh and my mother."

"I love my mother, I'm crazy about my weird sister, and I wish I had found a way to love my father better." He threw an arm over the back of his chair and drummed his fingers. "That's the biggest regret of my life, that I didn't get along better with my father when I had a chance to."

"I suppose we all have something in our life that we regret."

"Mine starts out kind of stupid. My name." Her face hinted at the question she didn't ask. He drummed his fingers harder. "My father was like most men—first born kid, a big, healthy son. It was his chance to 'man-up,' his chance for immortality. He insisted on naming me after himself. Tagged me a 'junior.' Antoine Jacob Yarborough Jr. It's funny now, but as a kid, I felt robbed of an identity. I spent most of my life feeling like my father treated me and my name like leftovers."

"All kids have identity crises," Marlea offered.

AJ sucked hard air through his nose. "Maybe, but my dad made it clear that he wasn't trying to entertain my psychological trauma. My old man worked construction. It was hard, honest work, and he figured that if it was good enough for him, then it was good enough for me. He wanted me to follow him. He was good at what he did and made good money. He figured that it was as good as it would get for a black man workin' in the South.

"Don't know if Rissa told you or not, but all those pictures in the library were taken by my mother. My pops thought that my running and football were just games. 'What good does all that playing do a black man?' he used to say. Even when I got the football scholarship, he thought it was useless. He said, 'Break your back, break your legs, then what'll you have? Nothin', that's what!' "

Marlea looked around, taking in the expansive kitchen and the view beyond the terrace and pool. "You could have done worse."

"Yeah, I could have, but my dad wasn't trying to hear it. He never supported my ballplaying, not even when I got drafted. That's when I changed my name: twenty-one, with a pro contract, I changed my name legally and learned to keep some distance between my father and myself. I can still hear him sometimes: 'You shamed a' me, boy? Gave away my name like it was nothin'.' "

AJ shook his head and sniffed. Marlea watched his eyes for tears and saw none. "Guess you could say I gave away his name so I could be something, so I could be my own man. It had nothing to do with hurting him.

"My dad's gone now, five years, and I still regret not having found a way to make some kind of peace with him. Still, I learned a lot from him: that a man needs work he can be proud of, to respect and take care of your family." AJ pulled his arm from the back of the chair and straightened in his seat. "I learned something else, too. I'm resolved to be a better father, when the time comes. In the meantime, Rissa works with me, and I get to concentrate on her and our mother."

"Will I get a chance to meet your mother?"

"Sooner or later. Mostly Moms is off being the merry widow, and she deserves the privilege. Not to play my dad cheap, but she was the one who bulldozed me through school, made me promise to get the degree even after I went pro, and stayed on me to be sure I kept the promise. She's enjoying travel and freedom after a thirty-year marriage. This month, she's in Puerto Rico."

"She sounds like the reason for your drive and one of your reasons for pushing me."

"Could be." Relaxing again, AJ propped his elbows on the table and leaned close. "What is the one thing you wanted most in the world?"

Marlea lifted her glass and took a sip, her gaze steady over the rim. "That's easy. A gold medal in the 400. How about you?" She set the glass down. "If I remember correctly, you earned a Heisman, then you played with the big boys, so . . . what? What else is there for you? Something like . . . a Super Bowl ring?"

"Well, yeah, but more than that," he explained, his face taking on a boyish cast. "So far, fewer than ten men have rushed for more than 2,000 yards in a season—O.J. Simpson, Eric Dickerson, Barry Saunders, and Terrell Davis—I wanted to be one of them, but I guess I ran out of time. Knees couldn't take it."

"Hall of Fame," she whispered reverently. "So what did you put in place of the game?

AJ thought about Bianca, and wished he could say that he had put his family, his wife and children in place of, and in fact ahead of, the game. *But hey, that wasn't meant to be.* "I put my physical therapy practice in that place."

"And right now, in your house, that means me?"

"Yeah," he said, thinking about it for the first time. "I guess it does."

Marlea carefully placed her hand flat on the tabletop. "Then that gives me some responsibility for how things turn out, right?"

"Huh?"

"If your practice, what you do with me, has to replace the most important thing in your life, then I guess we had better get it right."

His voice softened when he looked at her, and he tried not to think of ripe and lurking possibilities. "Yeah, Marlea," he agreed, his hand closing over hers. "We'd better get it right."

CHAPTER 18

Rissa musta heard wrong. No way a woman who looks like this doesn't date often. AJ kept his eyes on his plate. *My sister can't keep a secret, and she does have a tendency to talk too much sometimes, but she's usually right in what she reports.* He looked at Marlea. *Wonder why?*

Sitting across from AJ, Marlea tried to look comfortable. Kind of an effort, considering where they were going after lunch, but it was nice of him to offer to spend the time with her. Ray's on the River was scenic and kind of romantic—lots of crisp white napery and a full view of the Chattahoochee River. The food was wonderful and the company was good, but she was a little nervous about the suit Rissa had talked her into. *Is this really an appropriate outfit for a visit to a podiatrist?*

A podiatrist, no, that was wrong. AJ said that this guy was more than just a foot doctor. The thought of a doctor made her skin crawl. *I don't think I could take another doctor right now.* An icy sliver of betrayal stabbed her, and she reached for her wineglass. The quick swallow of Chablis didn't do much for her, so she tried another.

He didn't exactly spring the trip on me, but . . . she caught her breath and let it out slowly across her wineglass. *This man is a pedorthist, not a podiatrist—and this is certainly not a trip I was looking forward to.* She sipped again, then set the glass aside, glancing at AJ. *I don't want him thinking I'm a drunk on top of everything else.*

Everything else. I don't suppose I would ever really be ready, and now Rissa has me all dressed up . . . She crossed and uncrossed her legs under the table, knowing that she would have been just as willing to have worn one of her Nike wind suits. A passing waiter filled her glass, and Marlea tried to keep her hands still. She didn't know what to do with them; slipping them over her lap again would only betray her nervousness.

Like he doesn't know already. Rissa probably told him that I don't get out much, and he's a nice enough man to spring for this mercy date. Marlea cringed inwardly. *Humph! This is not a date, and I don't need to forget that. This is just a good-looking man trying to be nice.* She forgot her resolve and fingered the lapel of her borrowed suit. Slate blue and faced with matching silk, the Dreen original hugged her curves and rested suggestively against her breasts and hips. Rissa said that the color brought out the red in her skin and made her eyes more exciting.

Like I need exciting eyes! Stealing a glance at AJ, she was pleased to find his eyes on her. *At least, I look good— sitting.* Marlea pushed her feet further under the table and wished for something other than the clunky surgical shoe that encased her damaged foot.

Pushing her fork into the tender stuffed tilapia, she looked up, catching AJ's eyes on her again. "Something?"

"No." He pretended interest in his scalloped potatoes, then gave up and put his fork aside. "Yes."

Steeling herself, Marlea forgot the fish. "What?"

"You've got something on your mind. No, don't deny it. I figured it out after I spent five minutes talking to you, and you just sat there looking out the window."

"Did I . . . AJ, I . . ."

Leaning close her, AJ planted his arms on the table. "I know that with everything that's happened to you, time has to be skewed and your life has to feel crazy, but what we're doing today, this is a good step. Have you given any thought to how this is going to affect your teaching?"

Trying not to look at the cane resting on the chair next to her, Marlea shook her head.

"What about your children?"

He's seen the cards and letters from the Runyon School. She remembered his walking in on her. *I don't know what made me think that I wanted to watch that damned video in his theater. I could have just as easily watched it in my sitting room.* But the idea of seeing the faces she knew and loved so well on the big screen had been irresistible. *And he walked in on me.* One of the parents had helped the children to produce the video and he had caught her watching it. *They've sent me cards and letters, and I haven't answered a single one.*

"At the rate I'm going, I don't know when I'll get back to teaching." Her lids fluttering, she swallowed hard. She tried to lighten her tone. "AJ, whether I walk or not has nothing to do with the children."

"You're lying to yourself, Marlea, and you don't have to."

The corners of her mouth quivered and she toyed with her fork. The fish was cold now. "So I don't get a break, huh? You're just going to sit there and judge me?"

Now she's trying to pick a fight? AJ shook his head. *I'm not going to let her take me there.* "Marlea, it's not about judgment. You've come a long way, but you're not alone. I'm here. I believe in you and your recovery, and I'll be here for you."

"And that's supposed to get me back into the classroom?" She looked dubious. "I'm not afraid of the kids. I was born to teach, and I'll always be good at it. Rissa said that you do a lot of work with special groups, so I know you understand how it feels to follow your heart for others. I'm a teacher. I'm going to teach again."

"Glad to hear that. Now when do you plan to get back to the rest of your life?"

For a second, Marlea wanted to curse Rissa for the skillfully applied eye makeup. If she hadn't been afraid it would run and leave her looking like a raccoon, she probably would have cried.

"It's waiting for you, you know," AJ continued. "Marlea, I promise that the only thing that has changed in your life is the way you choose to live it."

"That's an easy promise for you to make, AJ, but think about it. I can teach because a teacher is what I am. But on the other hand, you know what my foot looks like, and you've seen me try to get around on it—not exactly the picture of grace and elegance, am I? What man is going to want a woman like that? I'm not willing to plan a family without a husband, and I would need to be whole for that, and well, I'm not exactly that. Not any more."

Reaching across the table, AJ took her hand and stared hard into her eyes. "And here I was thinking what a smart woman you are. Marlea, don't you realize that if a man truly loves you, if you truly love him, it doesn't matter how many toes you have or what kind of shoes you can or can't wear? And last I heard, toes and the way you walk ain't had nothin' to do with makin' babies—if that's what you want."

Leaning away from him, she took a moment to regain her composure. "Now you're trying to embarrass me."

"No way, just callin' it like I see it." His grin moved to laughter, and Marlea couldn't resist laughing with him.

"Okay, you've made me laugh, got me feeling like a fool for short-changing myself. Tell me about this place we're going to."

"Jim Crocker is a pedorthist. When it comes to shoes, prescription footwear, rocker soles, orthotic inserts, you name it, he's the man. There's not a foot on this planet that I wouldn't trust to Jim. I've known him to customize or fabricate shoes for everyone from diabetics to athletes."

"You're sure I can't just wear some of the shoes I already have?" Marlea's teeth clamped down on her knuckles.

"You've already tried, haven't you?"

Damn that big-mouthed Rissa! "So I'll have better balance in a custom-made shoe?"

She was still asking questions when AJ's Rover crossed Cobb Parkway into the landscaped office park that housed Marietta BioPed. AJ moved to leave the vehicle, but Marlea sat looking at the sign.

"It's just a step, Marlea."

Her eyes were huge and haunted, glistening with unshed tears. "It's just a step I never thought I would have to take, AJ."

Reaching across the seat, he gripped the hands that lay so limp and cold in her lap. "It's a step you don't have to take alone."

"Promise?"

"Cross my heart." And he did.

Marlea followed AJ into Marietta BioPed. Jim Crocker was waiting for them.

He stood at the rear of the neatly appointed reception area talking with two young men. The taller and blonder of the two noticed them first and pointed them out. Moving with sprightly ease, Crocker handed over the folders he had been sharing with the two men and crossed the room.

"AJ, good to see you. It's been too long, my friend." Warm and welcoming, he could model for Santa Claus figurines, Marlea marveled. From the snowy white hair and neatly trimmed beard right down to the rosy cheeks and round little belly, the man was a dead ringer for every red-suited Santa she had ever seen.

"You didn't tell me," she whispered with a smile.

"Thought you'd like the surprise."

Crocker shook Marlea's hand, then tucked his thumbs into the narrow pockets of his open vest and rocked on his toes. "I often cultivate my resemblance to the red-suited one; it builds confidence."

Okay, I can see the confidence thing working here.

"Knowing AJ, I'm sure he's explained what I do here," Crocker chuckled. "Do you have any questions before we get started?"

"I . . . I do have some questions." Marlea looked at AJ, then made up her mind. "I would like to speak with you alone, though, for just a few minutes."

"But . . ." AJ frowned. *What was it she was always saying about me trying to make her need me? Damn it,* his heart surged, *she does need me, even if she does look as if she thinks she doesn't.* He gave it one more try. "Are you sure?"

"Yes."

"Right this way, then." Crocker wasted no time in mediation. Instead, he ushered Marlea into a green-walled consultation room. She settled into an upholstered tweed armchair and faced the pedorthist. Crocker dropped into the chair facing her and looked concerned. "What shall we talk about?"

How to begin? Alone with Jim Crocker, she fought embarrassment. *I can't believe I'm sitting here with Santa Claus, trying to figure out how to ask his advice about how to stop my world from rocking every time that, that . . . therapist touches me!*

"A little shy, are we?" He rocked back in his chair. "Is this a delicate matter?"

Intently examining her fingertips, Marlea nodded. "See . . . every time he puts his hands on me, it feels like . . . sex," she finally blurted. "I'm not crying rape or anything, but . . . I don't have any control over it and I . . . I don't like it. The nurse said I would probably get over it in time, but until then . . ."

"How long has this been going on?

"Almost from day one."

"Are you in pain?"

"No," she said, shaking her head and dropping her eyes. "I almost wish I were; maybe that way I wouldn't feel so guilty about it."

"And you don't get the same, ah, sensations when you duplicate the exercises on your own?"

"Never. Not even when one of the female nurses tried to help me at Grady. It only happens with him."

"You could change therapists."

"Don't you think I tried? Every time I tried, something came up. First, I couldn't seem to get rid of him. Then all of the recommended therapists had full caseloads. After that, my insurance began to limit who I could see and for what. Then I sort of had to . . . move in with him. So now I have a therapist who turns me on every time he lays a hand on me. Every time."

"Ahh," the old man sighed, lifting his thick white brows. "That has got to be a young man's fantasy, to be able to trigger ascendancy in a beautiful woman with the briefest of touches." His eyes sharpened behind his thick-lensed glasses. "But you don't have that kind of relationship, do you? At least, not yet?"

Okay, maybe I should have kept this to myself. "No, we don't have that kind of relationship, and if I had known that you were going to make fun of me, I would have kept this to myself."

"Forgive an old man's prying." The specialist smiled softly, his round cheeks dimpling. "To answer your question, though, in time you can expect the sensations to diminish."

"But what do I do for now? This is so humiliating. There's nothing I can take for it, and cold showers aren't helping. I understand that I need the therapy, but he's driving me nuts!"

"You trust him?" She nodded, and he spread his hands apart as though that explained everything. "Then stop thinking of your body as betraying you and let him help you."

"That's it? I should just lie back and enjoy it?"

"That's it. Think about it, Miss Kellogg. What you're feeling is real, there's documented evidence of it. I've talked to AJ and there is no salacious attachment, only the concern of a dedicated therapist. Your therapy is not going to last forever. My advice to you is to get back on your feet and back to your life as soon as possible."

Chastened, unable to look at the old man, Marlea nodded. "You won't tell him what I told you, will you?"

"Never." Eyes twinkling, Crocker mimed zipped lips. "Shall we rejoin him?"

"Okay." Marlea followed him from the room. "Wait." At the door, she laid a hand on his arm. "You really won't tell?"

The elderly man put his palm over his heart. "Never." When Marlea hesitated, his silvery brows rose above his bright blue eyes. "Is there something else?"

Marlea looked at him shyly. She tapped the cane lightly against the floor. "After you do the fitting and make the changes, will I need this?"

Crocker's smile made her heart lift. "Only as a souvenir."

"I can think of better souvenirs than this."

"How about a good sturdy shoe that will take you wherever you need to go?"

"That will do me fine," Marlea smiled, following him across the hall to his studio.

"I was beginning to think you two had forgotten me," AJ said, rising from his seat.

"Never fear, my friend. We've got business to do in here today. This lady tells me that she's ready for a pair of shoes."

"Then let's get down to business." AJ pulled a chair forward for Marlea.

Sitting carefully, she glanced around, relieved when AJ sat beside her. Not altogether different from other shoe stores, the main area of Marietta BioPed was fitted as both an examination room and shoe salesroom. Crocker brought a selection of boxes and tools with him when he pulled a stool close enough for analysis. Behind him, more scales and forms were assembled in Plexiglas cubbyholes behind a desk. *For measuring foot lengths and widths,* Marlea guessed. Shoes ranging from the practical to the pretty were displayed on small wall-mounted platforms, and she found herself hoping that she could have something stylish.

"Let's try this." Crocker bent to slip the surgical shoe from her foot, and Marlea held her breath. Tensing, she stretched her fingers, then closed them tight.

"It's going to be all right," AJ whispered, squeezing the fingers she had thrust into his grasp.

Aware but discreet, Crocker opened one of the boxes stacked at the foot of his stool. He pulled out something that looked a lot like a cross between a baked potato and a house slipper.

Marlea's face crumpled. "That goes on my foot? That's the shoe you want me to wear?"

"You wound me, my dear." Crocker let the corners of his mouth droop slightly, then smiled. "I would never have a pretty lady wear such a thing; this is just for sizing. We're going to do a mold first. Your part of this is easy. Just relax." Guiding her foot lightly, Crocker slipped the form over her toes, then lifted it into place over her arch and heel. Filled with a cool and soft material, the mold felt fine; comfortable, in fact.

"I don't know if this is really my style, AJ. Does it come in a pump?"

"This one, no," Crocker chuckled. "Eventually, we'll get you into that pump. Meanwhile," he gave her foot a pat, "we'll let that set."

When the pedorthist bent to shuffle the boxes at his feet, Marlea leaned close, her cheek brushing AJ's. "Do you really think I'll ever get to wear a real shoe again?"

"Marlea, you can get almost any style of shoe you want; you'll just have to learn to walk in them."

Her fingers tightened around his, and she reached for the courage she saw swirling in the coffee-toned depths of his gaze. "Then what I really want is a running shoe, because I plan to do more than walk. You promised."

"That's a promise I'm going to keep, Marlea. You can bank on it." *Lord,* he thought, *if you made anything better than this woman, you kept her for yourself.* "Did you hear that, Jim? Running shoes. Two pairs. She's going to need them."

CHAPTER 19

. . . This season, the team counted on much more than big plays from the 27-year-old Yarborough. Built to get the job done at six-foot-two and 210 pounds, Yarborough is a starter and primary tailback—a role distinguished in the league by freakishly talented runners like Barry Sanders . . .

Yarborough has gained attention as one of the NFL's best all-around backs. This season, he has led his team with 875 rushing yards and 93 receptions, so far. He has also scored an even dozen touchdowns . . .

With his NFL-caliber body and extraordinary talent, Yarborough was destined for the game, says Coach Newell. "Intangibles have set Yarborough apart. If I ask him to work hard, he works harder. He's focused and coachable . . ."

Marlea turned the page for the rest of the article.

"She been sitting there long?"

"About two hours," Martha Baldwin whispered back, selecting an apron from the pantry drawer.

"What is she reading?" Rissa asked, craning her neck. "Looks like one of the scrapbooks Mama made for AJ."

"It is. She's been going through them all week. All by herself, here in the kitchen, going through them page by page. She ought to know all about him by now," the housekeeper said.

"And you in here keeping her secret?"

"Somebody has to." Mrs. Baldwin dodged the nudge Rissa aimed at her. She shook the folds out of her apron and slipped it around her waist. "And we both know that you can't."

"You know you've only got two things going for you, don't you?" Rissa made a face, propped a hand on her hip, and pointed her finger. "AJ can't get enough of your cooking, and I love you."

"Saves me every time," the older woman smiled, eyeing Rissa. Taking in the tailored flat-front pants and the matching jacket folded over her arm, she guessed her favorite pain-in-the-neck was headed for work. "Want your usual, or do you have time for a real breakfast this morning?"

Rissa craned her neck again. Marlea still sat in the same place at the table, turning pages and learning about AJ Yarborough. "I'm going to make time for a real breakfast this morning," she decided.

"I thought you might."

Bills star AJ Yarborough engaged . . . For no reason she could imagine, Marlea couldn't seem to get past that headline. But like an onlooker at a train wreck, she couldn't look away, either. Planting her index finger on the page, she traced the lines of print and began to read.

Heisman Trophy winner and first-round draft pick AJ Yarborough, dubbed 'the Supersonic Man', has become engaged to his girlfriend of one year, designer Bianca Coltrane, his publicist Greg Harper announced Wednesday . . .

. . . It will be a first marriage for both 30-year old Yarborough and 24-year old Coltrane.

A wedding date has not been announced . . .

And it never happened. The thought was so sharp that it blurred her vision. *Why the hell does it matter to me?* Marlea wondered, looking up from the page.

"Whatcha readin'?" Rissa drawled, sliding into the chair across from Marlea.

She knows damned well what I'm reading. Marlea closed the book on her hand. "Nothing."

"Oh, we're gonna play games, now? Looks like one of AJ's albums," Rissa said, reaching across the table to touch the cover. "Did you find that one in the library?"

She knows exactly where I 'found' this . . .

Mrs. Baldwin moved to the table and pushed her food-laden tray between the women. "I've got your coffee here." She moved the sterling-silver pot over both their cups and shot a cautionary look at Rissa. "I b'lieve you both take cream and sugar." Her eyes made Rissa close her mouth.

"I've got toast and, well, I believe I have everything you need." Pointedly turning her face to Rissa, Martha Baldwin smiled sweetly. "If you need anything, and I mean anything at all, you ask me. You hear?"

"Yes, ma'am." Rissa pressed her lips together and decided not to press her luck, even when Marlea opened the album again. Busying herself with scrambled eggs and toast, she managed to stay quiet as Marlea turned two pages. She couldn't stand it any more when Marlea turned a third page.

"AJ's done a lot of stuff," she blurted, then could have slapped herself when Marlea grinned.

"I knew you couldn't do it."

"Do what?"

"Keep your mouth shut, not even after the look Mrs. Baldwin gave you."

"You saw that?" Rissa slid a little lower in her chair.

"It almost sizzled, girl."

"Yeah, she's got that 'mother' thing workin' for her. I never want to disappoint her."

"Then you need to learn to mind your own business!" Martha called from the sink.

"I guess she told you," Marlea whooped.

"She's always telling me," Rissa laughed. "Seriously, though, if you want to know more about AJ, you ought to ask him."

Marlea pushed the album to the side. "Why don't you just come on out and say that you want me to ask him? And why is it such a big deal to you?"

"I think I told you once my brother is the bomb. Besides, there are not a lot of guys like him around. I mean, there's Warrick Dunne with the Falcons and the work he does with single mothers, and others who do stuff, but I know AJ. I grew up with him—he's my brother and I love him."

"And he's special?" Marlea's fingers traced the leather edges of the book beside her plate, but her eye stayed on Rissa.

"Yeah, he is." Rissa sat up straighter and began to recite a list of AJ's favorite charities and events. "On top of that," she finished, "he also sponsors several annual sports camps and clinics for Special Olympics."

"Wow." *Way to make me feel selfish.* Marlea thought of the cards and letters she had gotten from the children at the Runyon School—the ones she had yet to answer. *I guess I know what I'll be doing this afternoon.*

Licking apple butter from her fingers, Rissa couldn't help herself. "AJ is really good at what he does. So do you like him?"

"I like him fine, I guess."

"Don't play coy with me; you know what I mean."

Marlea's whole body went cold. "No, I'm pretty sure I don't."

"I mean, like, forever. Like marriage. You want that?"

"AJ said you were nosy."

"And he ain't never lied, but ain't no shame in my game, girl. So are you looking for a little nookie for now, or now and forever?

Scooting her chair back from the table, Marlea lifted her foot from the floor. "Look who you're asking. It's not like I could run a man down, now is it?"

"Something tells me that running a man down might not be the best way to get the one you want to keep." Rissa looked down at the front of her neatly wrapped white shirt and brushed off a few toast crumbs. "You might just have to stay still to get him."

"Is that . . . some kind of . . . hint?"

"Do you need a hint?"

⌘

"Dude, what's up?"

"Not much. Stretching, trying to get a workout in. Want to join me?"

"You're kiddin', right?" When AJ shook his head, Dench spread his hands and backed toward a black vinyl-covered bench. Sitting, he tried to explain. "Man, it's off-season. I get to take a break from running behind a bunch of knuckleheads, and I appreciate it. I ain't tryin' to do anything I don't have to."

"It's on you, then." Hands knotted behind his head, AJ bent left and right.

"Rissa said you got Marlea fitted for shoes. So what's next for your pretty houseguest?"

"Hand me my gloves, will you?" AJ took the finger-less black leather gloves from his friend. Pulling them on, he debated what to say. There was a pretty good chance that Dench would repeat everything to the Mouth of the South, and Rissa would tell Marlea. *Better to only tell what we all already know*, he decided.

"I guess you know that the doctor who handled her case was the person who hit her. I can't imagine Rissa didn't tell you. Anyway, he's been arraigned and his trial date set. Rissa talked to Marlea, and though she's refusing to show up in court, she's willing to settle on damages."

Dench ran a wide hand across the top of his head. "That's gonna leave her pretty well set for money. She can afford to recuperate just about anywhere she wants to, right? You think she'll stay here with you?"

"She will because she needs me. I'm what's best for her." AJ knew he was hoping out loud.

"Sounds to me like you at least need to ask the woman out, get to know her as more than a patient, before you decide that you're what's best for her."

"Trouble with you, Dench, is that I didn't ask you for your opinion."

"Uh-huh." Dench plucked a towel from the floor, balled it up and tossed it toward AJ. "You might not have asked, but if you want her to stay with you, you'd better think about it."

AJ snatched the towel from the air and sailed it back. "Say you're right. Say I date her, then what?"

"Ain't nobody in here said nothin' about dating," Dench chuckled.

"But you're thinking it."

"What I'm thinkin' is not the question. The real question is, what are you thinking? And on that note, I'm leaving. You want the door open or closed?"

"Leave it open." AJ watched him leave, then returned to his workout.

Stepping from the elevator, Marlea was careful. Even though she had used them for a few secret treadmill workouts, the bottoms of her new shoes were still more slippery than any running shoe she had ever worn. Not trusting them, she trailed her fingers along the wall as she made her way down the hall.

AJ's scrapbook was still on her mind. She found a collection of fan letters at the back of the last one she had looked at this morning. Pages and pages of fan letters from people who seemed to think that he really was the nicest man in the NFL. *Well, those and the ones from the women who thought he was a walking work of art.* Marlea had to suppress a giggle. *Yeah, his fans were something else—especially that sister who promised to be the most flexible woman he had ever met! And he doesn't seem stuck up about it,* she marveled.

The rhythmic clang of working iron guided her to his workout room, where they were to meet. *I'm early, but I don't suppose he'll mind.* From the doorway, Marlea held her breath, silently appreciating his working body.

He wore black nylon shorts that accentuated the length and breadth of his long, muscled thighs. His ripped torso was bare and bathed in light and shadow from the broad bay of windows separating the gym from the indoor pool.

Ripped was the term body builders applied to finely built and carefully defined musculature, but AJ Yarborough had more. What he had could only be referred to as chiseled. *If I turned my hand just right . . . I'll bet if I tried, my fingers could fit . . .* She had to look away to stop the thought.

Keeping her eyes on the floor came nowhere near helping Marlea to ignore him. After all, there he was, everywhere she looked. Reflected in mirrors surrounding the gym floor, the precision and symmetry of AJ's rippling muscles and perfectly taut molten chocolate skin was in evidence.

Eye candy.

I have no business thinking of him like this. Marlea pondered the mystery of AJ Yarborough. *All that running and working out with weights, what kind of energy is he trying to channel? Maybe it has something to do with that woman he almost married* . . . There was no photo with the article, and that struck her as odd. *Maybe his mama didn't like what's-her-name* . . . *Bianca. Bianca Coltrane. The article said she was a designer, but it didn't say what she designed, and I've never heard of her. I wonder what she was like?*

Tall, probably. AJ doesn't seem like the type of man who would be threatened by any woman, but she was probably pretty. No, I'll bet she was beautiful . . . *like beauty-queen beautiful. He was playing in the pros then; she would have had to been a match for the lifestyle.* Feeling ungenerous, Marlea tried to fix the thought. *Maybe she was smart and had a good heart.*

There had to be something special about her, something that drew him to her. But they never married. Wonder why? Maybe she broke his heart. That was . . . Marlea tallied the years in her head . . . *almost seven years ago. And they never reconciled? They never found a way around whatever it was that came between them?*

Maybe they're still friends, at least. But I'm pretty sure that Rissa would have said something by now. What would it take to drive a man like him away, for good?

There's nothing bitter about him, though. He seems to have gotten over her, but who or what has he put in her place? Changing the load on his bar, AJ made a change in his routine.

Leaning against the doorframe, she watched him. Well worth watching, AJ's body tensed as he balanced his weight. Reaching to grasp the overhead steel bar, AJ used the strength of his arms to hoist his body, gracefully curving his hips to coil his legs up, over, and around the suspended bar.

I'm about as bad as Rissa, digging into the man's past. It's not as though we have a future and I have a right to know anything more than what he's willing to tell me. He's going to get me walking again, and I'm going to walk right out of his life. She looked down at her new running shoes. *No, I'm going to run—right out of his life. He promised.*

Hanging from his knees, arms crossed at his chest, AJ began the punishing repetitions that were his habit. Tightening the muscles defining the length of his torso, the blocks of his stomach in matched pairs, he tucked his chin against his chest. Curling his body, releasing his breath in slow, controlled exhalations, his movements slow and deliberate, AJ worked through a range of motion designed to define and separate. A thin line of sweat crept along the tight dark skin of his bare chest, drawing deep-walled lines of fiber and flesh.

"How many more of those are you going to do?" Marlea whispered, wishing he would never stop.

Her low voice barely disturbed the air between them, and he heard her voice but not her words. "Marlea?"

"Yes." She took a step closer, hoping he wouldn't accuse her of voyeurism. "We were supposed to meet this morning."

"Right. You mind if I finish?" He curled his torso, bringing his head and shoulders higher. His back curved and his behind tightened in the black shorts, promising much.

You mind if I watch? Marlea kept the words to herself, but shook her head at the regal sight.

Continuing the series of crunches, AJ pointed to the rack of individual weights. "Hand me those, will you?"

"How heavy?"

"Can you lift the twenties?" he grunted.

Hesitating, Marlea looked over her shoulder. "If I do them one at a time."

"I can wait."

Breathing hard, Marlea frowned and took her time delivering the weights, proud that she was still able to lift the poundage. He took them from her hands and mumbled his thanks.

Breathing harder with the added poundage, his skin shining, slick from the sweat of exertion, AJ finished his work. Dropping the weights to the rubber mat beneath him, he reversed his grip and managed to chin himself neatly before dropping easily to the floor. *Damn, he looks good doing that.* His forearm swiped his chin, catching salty drops of water, and Marlea's knees softened.

Rissa was right; he does work hard. "That was quite a workout. How often do you do it?"

"Got to do something every day. I feel kinda lazy if I don't. Hold on, I've got one more set." Dusting his hands with chalk, AJ reached high and began a series of pull-ups that strained the cords in his arms.

Silently, Marlea counted the reps. "Must be the result of all those years of football and training." *He did forty without stopping . . .*

"You know about that?" Completing the set, AJ dropped to his feet, resting his hands on his knees while he gathered breath. "How?"

"I . . . uh . . . I went through some of the scrapbooks in your library." She handed him the towel on the bench beside her. "I hope you don't mind."

"No, I don't mind at all." Recovering, he accepted the towel Marlea offered and worked it vigorously over his shoulders and torso before tossing it into the corner hamper. "I see you've got your shoes on. Does that mean you're ready to get to work?"

Marlea's stomach flipped when AJ pulled a white cotton tee shirt over his head and chest. "Yeah . . . uh . . . yeah. I'm ready." A small part of her mind was grateful for the humble shirt—he was too disturbing without it. "Where do you want me?"

"Over here," he said, indicating a series of mats. "We're going to start with some stretches, then build into some flexibility."

Oh, no. Not again! The flexibility training meant her lying down and him leaning close, bad enough, but he would have to touch her. Looking down at her shorts and tee shirt, she came close to swearing. *At least he wouldn't be able to touch my skin if I had worn long pants—not that it would help.* Her lip quivered. *I know this man is honorable. He's only trying to help me . . .* She had been repeating the words to herself regularly since her talk with Jim Crocker. She had even shared them with Libby over the phone, hoping that confession would help her.

I know this man is honorable. He's only trying to help me . . . Steeling herself, knowing what his touch would trigger, Marlea let him lower her to the mat.

"This is getting easier," AJ said, helping her to roll onto her side.

Not for me. She swallowed the unspoken words. *I know this man is honorable. He's only trying to help me. . .*

The mantra should have helped, should have marshaled her thoughts and cued her body for work and rehabilitation. Instead, her pulse raced and her nipples tightened in anticipation. *I know this man is honorable. He's only trying to help me* . . . AJ's hands began to move, first against her hip, then a warm palm pressed to the inside of her thigh, and Marlea tried to hold onto herself. *I know this man is honorable. He's only trying to help me* . . .

She thought of the open and intelligent face that looked up at her from his scrapbooks. *His mother took those pictures.* She thought of those fan letters tucked in the back of that last scrapbook, all of them from women who would pay money to feel what she was feeling right now. *But this is medical-related,* she thought weakly.

Electricity lapped at her leg, following the path of his hands. *I know this man is honorable. He's only trying to help me* . . .

His hand moved again, and her breath quickened. *I know this man is honorable. He's only trying to help me* . . .

"I want to try something new, Marlea." AJ's fingers pressed. "Here we go."

I know this man is . . . Closing her eyes, biting her lips against the roaring tear of ecstasy, Marlea knew that only God could help her now.

CHAPTER 20

Marlea took a deep breath. "School has already begun. If I'm ever going to get back, I have to do this." Slowly, delicately, she shifted her weight onto her right foot. "I can do this. I did it yesterday and the day before." Slowly, delicately, she shifted her right foot into place. "I walked all over this house last week without that danged cane, and I know I can do it again."

Knowing that Martha Baldwin was the only person in the house who knew what she was doing, and she would never tell, Marlea took another step on the marble tiled floor.

Reaching the Precor treadmill had been her first goal. Then she had managed to step aboard and get it started. It was amazing how scared she had been, using a machine that she had trained on for almost half her life, walking that first half-mile. "Took me almost fifteen minutes."

But she had worked at it, and her confidence and strength grew. Earlier this week, she had managed almost two miles in less than thirty minutes. "Now, it's a matter of picking up my time and gaining distance. And even if AJ does know what he's doing, there's no way I'm going to tell him about this—not him or Libby, either. They can just be surprised with the rest of the world."

Glancing at her watch, she figured she had a couple of hours to sneak in her walk. "AJ and Dench went to a publicity photo shoot with Robert Crown, Rissa should be in her office until around seven, and Mrs. Baldwin is on her way to church—plenty of time. What could be better?"

Programming music for her workout, she had a fleeting image of herself running and pushed it away. "Yeah, that would be better, but I can't live on what was. The best thing for me now is getting back to school." A tremor of delight quickened her step. She could see herself, almost hear the children around her. "I can't wait to walk through the doors at Runyon. I wonder if the kids have given up on me?" They were still sending cards and letters. "Nah, no way."

Realizing that she had begun to pick up AJ's habit of self-conversation, Marlea looked around, glad to see that she was still alone. "Good thing nobody's around to hear me talking to myself."

Stepping onto the treadmill, she stood wide, her feet riding the rails as she programmed the machine. It hummed response, then the tread began to roll slow and smooth between her legs. Maneuvering carefully, she set her feet on the belt and began a slow, trudging warm-up. Eight minutes later, thinking of AJ's promise, she increased the speed. "I can do this. If he can promise that I'll run, I can do this." She kept walking.

"But he made another promise, too. He said I would dance—with him." And even beyond thanking him, Marlea couldn't think of anything she would rather do.

Two miles later, soft and solitary applause startled her and made her reach for the treadmill's rails.

"I knew you could do it." AJ's voice was soft, a shade past a whisper. Walking closer, he peered at the treadmill's display panel. "Damn, when you push, you don't play around, do you?"

Slowing the speed, liking the admiration in his face and voice, Marlea swiped at the salty water nearing her eyes. "I had to try, and I did it. I got through three miles today with no cane, no holding onto the rails, just walking all by myself."

"You did it, baby." He brought two fingers to his forehead in salute. "Running is just around the corner. Now we have to work on balance so that you can go farther, faster, and over different surfaces. Balance," AJ said. "Everything we do from now on is about balance."

"Right." She stopped the treadmill, and when he offered his arm, she took it gratefully.

Accepting his help felt better than she had anticipated. Marlea finally found her breath and a chair. Dabbing at her face with the towel he offered, she blew hard. He squatted low before her chair, hips dropping and tightening the cotton fabric of his drawstring pants. *Don't look.* "Did you finish your photo session?" *Ask a stupid question . . .* She tried to concentrate on his face.

"Yeah, but what you did was amazing. All on your own."

Marlea deliberately moved her measuring eyes from the juncture that hailed so naturally from between his thighs. *Don't look.* And his thighs—long and strong, thick and muscled—didn't they look . . .

Aw, damn, she fussed silently, *I looked.* She moved her eyes again and settled on his left shoulder. *Uh-huh, that ought to be safe enough.*

"Marlea? Did you hear what I said?"

"Yeah, balance. You said balance."

"Good. Now we're going to work on balance." He stood easily. "Slow and easy, something like core training. You'll hold me here." He slipped his bare forearms beneath her palms. It took her a while to remember to breathe. "I'll hold you here. Just lean on me."

I can do that. She placed her hand in his. Bringing Marlea to her feet, AJ partnered her, melding their strength, mating his body to hers.

Beginning with a glance and a nod of assent, Marlea let her arms snake around AJ's shoulders, feeling his right hand warm her back. Taking a moment to feel each other's balance, the slight dip of his body led her smoothly into one backward step and then another.

Holding her breath, praying not to stumble, she followed his lead into a figure eight, a turn, a pause. Her left foot was weightless, touching his right, and when his foot slid out, hers went along willingly. His knees bent and his hips led. She tried not to limp as he accepted her weight and carried her into deeper undulation. They stepped forward and shifted back, their legs twining and feet lifting before gliding on to another move, pulled along by the music's melodic search and soar.

There was a moment when Marlea's leg trembled and took on a defiant sweep. Fearing failure, she gave in to it. She leaned forward against him, her cheek brushing his, in complete trust. They both listened and succumbed to a rush of stringed instruments, crooning vocals, and the wail of what seemed like a clarinet under exquisite torture. She felt his breath in sync with hers as he moved with and between her steps, anticipating ending perfectly together on the last note of the song.

Now how am I supposed to balance this? "What are we doing?"

"We're dancing," AJ whispered, guiding her gently.

Dance is a vertical expression of a horizontal desire; George Bernard Shaw said that, Marlea recalled. *Wonder if AJ knows that.*

Still holding her, AJ stopped moving. "Maybe we should start this from the beginning."

"I'm confused," Marlea admitted, trying not to grip his hard body.

"You know that walking, dancing, finding the natural grace you were born with, it's all a part of who you are. Whatever we do has to be functional."

"Dancing has a function?" The Shaw quote came to her mind again, and she hoped he didn't feel the shimmer of her nerves, but she had no intention of moving from where she stood.

"Socially," AJ paused. "What if you were on a date?"

Okay, enough of this. Marlea took a step back from him and reluctantly dropped her arms. "I don't date much, and I don't think anyone is going to ask me to dance. It's kind of hard to get your boogie on with a cane."

"You did pretty well on that treadmill without a cane."

"That was different." Turning slowly, she made her way to the chair she had started from.

"But what if, Marlea? What if this were a date? What would you expect from me?"

Hardly daring to look over her shoulder, Marlea kept moving. "This is silly." Sitting hard, she wrapped her arms around her body and looked away from him. *I don't know, AJ. What would a woman expect from a man like you? What did Bianca Coltrane expect from you?*

"We could start with this."

Looking up, Marlea saw AJ's extended hand holding a little blue wildflower. *Where did he get . . .* She remembered the ceramic vase by the door, the one he had stood next to watching her walking on the treadmill.

"You gonna leave a brother hangin'?" He held the flower closer.

Remembering the first time she had heard him say those words, Marlea pressed her lips together, keeping the smile to herself, she was determined to keep that hospital room and her stay at Grady a distant memory. "What's this for?"

"If this were a date, I would bring you flowers." They both looked at the single blossom. "Okay, spur of the moment. I brought you flower, a flower."

"Thank you." The silly smile broke free and Marlea accepted the flower. "What next?"

"I might . . ." AJ looked around the room. "I might bring you a gift, too . . . something I know you like."

"The flower wasn't a gift?"

"Not exactly. Pretty women deserve flowers."

She passed a hand over her ponytail, tucking in stray hairs as if it wasn't too late for him to notice. "Just for being pretty?" *Wonder if he bought truckloads of flowers for Bianca Coltrane?*

"Something like that." Smiling, he held up a finger and backed away from her. Reaching the side table, he picked up something and held it behind his back as he walked toward Marlea.

"What is it?" She tried to read his face, gave up, and bent to try to see what he hid.

"M&Ms!" she squealed when he held his hand out. Grabbing the bag, she ripped it open, tossed a few into her mouth, then thought better of it and offered the bag. "I guess I could share."

AJ refused. "Would you like a drink?"

"No, thank you." Marlea bit down on more candy, studying AJ as she chewed. "Why?"

"Because if this were a date, we would share something, and I can't think of a lot of things more intimate between two people. When a man is with a woman, she has to know that he thinks of her, has to think of her. He has to be as willing to know what she wants and needs as he is willing to have her anticipate and meet his needs."

"I don't want anything." Marlea dropped her eyes and shifted in her chair. "The question is, what do you want? What is this leading up to?"

"We were going to dance, remember?" AJ moved to the small gray wall panel. Touching buttons, he waited for the softly changed music to fill the air around them. "I want my dance."

Marlea folded the tip down on her bag of M&Ms. She tucked the bag between her leg and the chair and waited. The music was soft and soothing, almost too intimate, and it made her want to move with it. "I know this song." She tried to remember the artist and the words.

Turn out the lights, and light a candle . . . Teddy Pendergrass.

"Is make-out music a part of my therapy?"

"No way," AJ grinned, opening his arms to her. "Remember what I told you about core training. The slow transfer of weight will aid in the balance you're eventually going to use for running."

"Dancing as functional training. What happened to, 'if this was a date'?"

"First things first."

"Why not?" Placing her hand in his, Marlea stepped into his arms. The familiar sense of urgency began where her hand met his and grew, spreading warm, then hot and sacred as it headed to her core. Eyes closed, her breath fast, Marlea gave in to the music and the man who held her. Her body softened against his and suddenly, she knew. "It was honesty, wasn't it?"

His cheek moved against her hair. A single broad palm braced her back as he held her close, and she knew without question that she was right. She saw the whip of pain in his eyes. It only lasted for a second, telling what words could not. Marlea's feet stopped and she stood, breast to chest, with AJ. "It was honesty that broke you apart, wasn't it?"

AJ looked away first. Dropping his eyes, still holding Marlea close, he shook his head. "I should have known that Rissa couldn't keep her mouth shut."

"It wasn't Rissa. I saw the engagement announcement in the scrapbook." Marlea dropped her head to his shoulder and looked up at him. "I saw it and I did the math. Do you still see her?"

His feet began to move again, slower this time, searching for the music. "Yeah, occasionally," he finally said. His voice was husky and filled with unspoken words. "It's not the same, though. It'll never be the same."

"You value honesty that much, that you would give up everything for it?"

He sighed. "Without honesty, what would we have? I was ready to hand my life over to that woman, Marlea. She would have been my wife, the one I was meant to turn to in the best and the worst of times. She would have been the mother of our children . . ."

I like how he said 'our' children.

"Bianca's loyalties never lay with me; they were always with my bankbook—or the one that was bigger." He pulled Marlea closer. "You know how it is when people say and do whatever they think will get them what they want from you." He moved with Marlea in his arms, his breath soft against her sleek hair and she wondered if he felt the shivers rippling beneath her skin. "Yeah, it was honesty that broke us apart."

"You really value honesty that much?" *Maybe I should tell him . . .*

"Yeah, I do. Don't you?"

267

AJ's eyes changed again as he found Marlea's, and she wondered what that woman had done to hurt him. Warm and trusting, there was an unplanned innocence that she found hard to deny. Her fingers tightened in his grasp and she nodded.

"You know, uh . . ." Part of her mind was screaming loud and reverberating denials, but her heart urged her forward. Marlea went with her heart. "Since we're talking about honesty, I need to tell you something."

He looked at her, and her once brave heart began to beat like a hummingbird's wings.

"Do you remember when I . . . gave you such a hard time about the therapy, especially in the beginning?"

"Do I ever."

AJ turned them in a small circle, making her a little dizzy. *Okay, I guess I could blame this on being dizzy . . .* "There was a reason." She waited. He waited. She took it as a signal to continue. "AJ, I know you know what phantom limb pain is, but did you know that sometimes people get phantom limb orgasms?" She held her breath.

"Oh." AJ kept dancing. "How long?"

He's taking that better than I thought he would. "Since the very first time."

"Oh." The music changed, and still holding her in his arms, AJ kept dancing. "Still?"

Marlea nodded. "Still."

His feet stopped, but he didn't release her and she had no urge to go. "You could have told me, Marlea. You should have told me. It all makes sense now, but I thought you hated me."

"I don't hate you," she said sheepishly, resting in his arms.

"Why didn't you tell me?"

"Now you're just talking crazy." Marlea sucked her teeth. "How was I supposed to say that to you?"

"You could have trusted me to understand."

"You were a stranger, and I was dealing with something way out of my usual experience," she said. "You're a nice man, AJ, and a really good dancer, but can I tell you something else now?" He nodded. "I'm getting pretty tired."

"Sorry. We dance so well together, that I forgot how tired you must be," AJ grinned.

"Yes, I'm really beat, but . . . dancing with you was nice."

His lips never moved, but his eyes said something Marlea couldn't translate. Wishing him closer and afraid to hold on, she felt like a fool. *He's like no other man I've ever known.*

With most of the men she had known, she had always felt obliged to be less in the effort to make them feel like more. But with AJ there was an undeniable willingness of spirit, wholeness, and the interest it takes to be a part of someone else's life. *When someone gives you something as special as this man is giving me, makes you feel as special as he is making me feel, what do you do? I could say . . .* "Thank you for the date, AJ. This is the best date I've had since . . . forever. I want to give you something."

Reaching behind her head, she pulled the band from her hair. Long and thick, her hair fell to her shoulders. A perfect frame for the coppery oval of her face, it shielded her from him. Taking his hand between hers, she slipped it over his hand to his wrist. "My kids made this for me. I wore it when I ran my best 400, and I want you to have it."

"I don't know what to say, Marlea." He turned his wrist beneath her hand. "This has to be precious to you."

"You gave me a flower and M&Ms, and a chance to dance. That's precious to me. The band is from my running, my past. Up until tonight, it was one of the most precious things I owned. Tonight, you gave me this date and a little taste of my future. That's precious to me, too."

"Does that mean our date is over? It's still early. Are you saying goodnight to me?"

"For now."

She saw him, knew that his face was coming closer, and she made no effort to get out of the way. Her arms rose of their own accord, her fingers locking behind his head, then pulling herself closer, Marlea met him more than halfway. Slowly, her lips brushed the corner of his mouth. Letting her lips find his, the sudden sweet crush of his lips challenged her, distancing control and reason. Questing tongues steered them toward an unspoken destination, and they both went willingly. Surrender should have sought a different name. In his arms, Marlea claimed as much as she gave. Holding her, AJ could not have asked for more.

It took energy, time, and the need to breathe to separate them.

"You're a really good kisser," Marlea admired.

"This surprises you?" AJ teased.

"No, what surprised me is that you're really a good dancer. It makes me wonder what else you're good at."

He kissed her again, slower this time. "You let me know when you're ready to find out."

———※———

She was gone, but he could still feel her. The little band from her hair seemed to carry an intimate hint of who she really was. It surprised AJ how much he wanted to feel deserving of her trust. He remembered the last time he cared so much about what a woman thought of him.

Bianca.

I got down on my knees and asked for her hand in marriage, like some sucker in a fairy tale, and look where that got me.

Kicked in the teeth—and more than once.

He wrapped the band around his fingers and almost thought he could feel Marlea's ebbing warmth. Dancing with her had been therapy—for both of them. Holding her in his arms felt like the most natural thing on earth. Letting her go had been harder than he would have ever imagined.

Out of thin air, he remembered sitting at the table with her on her first afternoon at the house. They had watched Rissa and Dench make their silly bet, and he had told Marlea that they were in love and didn't have the sense to know it.

She laughed and said that she couldn't imagine being in love and not knowing it.

AJ's fingers caressed the hair band and he sighed. *Maybe Rissa and Dench aren't the only ones.*

CHAPTER 21

"Man, this is almost like planning a war." AJ pushed his chair back from the table and stretched. "To tell the truth, when I volunteered for this, I figured all I would have to do was pose for some pictures and write a check."

"In your dreams," Harriet Blake laughed, tugging her green printed blouse down over her hips. The sound of her laughter was a lot like Harriet—big, round, solid. Brown-skinned and full-breasted, hers wasn't exactly the body type most people would picture in a road race, but everybody in AJ's library that morning knew that Harriet Blake didn't hesitate to put her foot where her true heart was. The woman would run for anything that would benefit man or womankind.

"I told you up front that this was going to take a lot of work, and what did you say to me? You said," Harriet deepened her voice, "you said, 'I'm up to it. I'm fully committed.' Those were your exact words, if I remember correctly—and I'm sure that I do." She plopped an elbow on the desktop and laughed again. "But at least we're getting the Hammond House for this."

The historic Victorian house in Atlanta's West End would be perfect for the reception. Dedicated as a museum, the beautiful old building housed an exceptional African-American art collection. The carefully landscaped backyard was large enough to hold a tent for the anticipated overflow crowd.

Sitting back in his chair and holding a gold-rimmed china saucer daintily beneath his coffee cup, Charles Wade said, "She still hasn't told us why it has to be held in a tent."

"It's September in Atlanta," Harriet said, as though that explained everything.

Charles frowned, prissy to a fault. Unconvinced, he added, "She hasn't told us how they're going to hang chandeliers in the tent and keep it cool enough for a thousand people to mill around in there, or why we need to decorate the rooms with topiary, either."

"It's decoration to set the mood, hon. That's what party planners are for," Sophia Edwards soothed, motioning Harriet to be quiet. "I've gotten volunteer commitments on everything, including manpower. We will be serving a full buffet supper, and we are going to have china dishes and real silverware and crystal glasses for the drinks. I've buttonholed every business and service provider I can think of to make sure of it. We're going to set an appropriate tone for this event, and it will be reflected in the bottom line." She gave Wade's almond-skinned arm a solicitous pat. "It's all going to be just fine, Charles. I have everything well in hand. You'll see."

He grumbled something unintelligible, clearly not pacified.

Mitch Foster strolled back to the table from his place by the windows. A small man, quiet and compact, he seemed to take comfort from viewing the gardens whenever he attended one of these meetings at AJ's home. "It seems that we're finished with detailing race logistics, staff, and sponsors. Am I right?"

"Unless you know of someone who wants to lace up his shoes and run this thing for me," Harriet snickered. Charles Wade groaned. "Or if they don't want to run, they could pick me up in a limo, or maybe a stretch Hummer," Harriet said.

"We don't have those kinds of sponsors, babe." Sophia's long nails flashed dismissal.

AJ dropped his chin into his hand and waited. "Ladies?" Sophia and Harriet turned to flutter their lashes in his direction.

"This is why this thing takes a year to plan," Charles reminded everyone.

"Before we break up, I just want to do a final review of our donors." Mitch opened a bright yellow folder. He passed a clutch of stapled sheets to everyone around the table. "This is my final list. I just want to make sure that none of you can think of a name to add."

Even Charles Wade admitted that the list looked complete, and Harriet and Sophia were impressed by some of the names from the entertainment world.

"Omigod, looka here!" Sophia screeched, honing in on a name among the Ws. "I know he's got a daughter at Spelman, but do you really think he'll show up to run in our little race?" She sighed like a schoolgirl. "I've loved him since he was on television."

"Ooh, girl, yeah. I remember when he was on *ER*. He was so young and so fine."

"Now he's got an Oscar, and he's just grown finer with time." Sophia bit her clenched fist.

"Could you two come back to the here and now?" Charles Wade snapped his fingers under the women's noses. Trying not to laugh, AJ looked down at his own list.

"We're up by a couple of thousand early entries," Mitch explained. "I expect there will be about 1,500 more at the race site that day."

AJ turned pages. "Man, I remember back when I was still in school and this race was only an 8K, drawing a couple of hundred die-hard runners, total."

"It's you, man—your stepping up and calling attention to the cause. I still can't believe you're willing to write a fat check, help us out with the media stuff, and put your foot on the road, too." Mitch grinned proudly. "I can think of a whole bunch of brothers—some sisters, too—who would pay a bunch of money to run with you."

"Some of 'em are already paying a bunch, thank goodness," Harriet laughed.

"It's for a good cause. I'm glad to do it. But let's get back to this list. I want to see if there are any donors that I can talk into upping their donations."

"Good idea; research can always use more money." Looking over AJ's shoulder, Mitch pointed to a name. "There's a buddy of yours."

Dench Traylor's name was in the middle of the page. AJ smiled. "If you can get that old boy to run, then I already know that my sister's name must be on this list somewhere."

"Yeah, she's on there, a few pages back. Flip back a few pages to the beginning, and I think you'll see some others you know."

AJ flipped to the first page, and came across the names of a few old friends. Turning the page, he placed his finger at the top of the column and Bianca Coltrane's name leapt out at him.

"Take this one off," AJ said brusquely, causing the volunteers to look at him curiously.

Straining to see, Mitch strained to read the name over AJ's thick shoulder. "Bianca Coltrane? But she's already accounted for. Her check cleared, and she'll be at the reception and everything," he protested.

AJ was adamant. "No, she can't bring anything but trouble. Tell you what, I'll write the check. Cash it and get the money back to her."

"AJ, that's just silly. Money is money, and she gave us hers. She wanted to make the donation from the goodness of her heart."

"Not this one." AJ's finger tapped the sheet. "She never does anything from the goodness of her heart."

"You sound like you know something," Harriet said, looking at him closely. Then it obviously dawned on her. "Oh, was that this Bianca Coltrane?"

"Coltrane?" Charles Ward repeated. "Was she the one you almost . . ."

AJ was saved from answering when Marlea and Rissa slammed through the kitchen and rushed down the long hall arguing.

Moving backward, Marlea rushed through the open door first. "I beat you!"

"Did not!" Hot on her heels, Rissa wasn't giving an inch. "Dench, you saw. We ran the length of the driveway, but I got here first, didn't I?"

"You did not, I left your slow butt in the dust. That back you were following? It was mine!" Finally noticing the startled group gathered around the table, Marlea stopped moving and lowered her voice. "Uh . . . excuse me . . ."

"Uh-uh." Desperate, Rissa swiped her forehead with the back of her wrist and appealed to Dench again. "Who won?"

No fool, Dench Traylor raised his hands. "Far as I could see, it was a dead heat, and you've got company here, in case you didn't notice." Loping across the marble floor, he snagged a muffin from a silver tray and glanced around. "Morning, all. Sorry for the intrusion—what did we interrupt?"

"Putting finishing touches on the plans for the reception tonight." AJ turned to the committee members. "This is my sister, Rissa." She raised a sweaty hand in greeting. "And these two are our house guests, Marlea Kellogg and Dench Traylor."

Sophia tapped her cheek. "You comin' tonight?"

"Long as I don't have to run, I wouldn't miss it," Dench promised, jamming a chunk of his muffin into his mouth.

"Will there be dancing?" Marlea's voice held enough longing to prompt everyone in the room to look at her.

"No," AJ said slowly, "it's not that kind of party." Lowering his eyes, he shuffled papers. "This is more of a meet and greet kind of thing—something to get the donors and sponsors and the media excited about our cause."

"What is your cause?"

"Special Olympics," Rissa answered. "I told you about the fundraising support AJ gives them."

"Are you going to come?" Harriet looked to Marlea and Rissa.

"No," Marlea said, "I'm gonna pass."

"The heck you are!" Rissa jammed her hands against her hips. "No way are you playing Cinderella up in this camp."

"I wasn't planning on anything like that. I don't have anything to wear."

"Like I can't find something in my closet to fit you. Oh, I know the perfect thing. Dreen did this original wrap dress for me, and it is so your style."

Marlea took a step backward. "No, I wouldn't dream of wearing something that was designed and made especially for you. Besides, I don't have any shoes besides these—and what do you mean, my *style?*"

"Shoes are not a problem. I know exactly what to do about that. We'll use that foam stuff that makes your running shoes fit." Rissa looped her arm through Marlea's, ignoring the pert style question. "We'll do your hair up, and I'll loan you my emerald necklace and earrings."

"But . . ."

Dench shook his head. "Might as well give it up, girl. In case you don't know, that's Rissa-speak for 'you're going'."

Rissa was already tugging her from the room. "And you're going to look good when you get there, too."

—❧—

Dench Traylor looked good in the midnight-blue summer-weight wool shirt and slacks. He wore the tailored clothes well, but his best accessory was the smile on his lips. He looked like the big winner in the Lady Lottery, a beautiful woman on each arm. Tall and statuesque, Rissa Yarborough closed a possessive hand around his upper arm and smiled at him. Utterly charmed by the molten gold of her perfumed skin against the smoky gold-threaded cloth of her ankle-length dress, Dench flexed muscle he had almost forgotten he owned.

Seeing his sloppy grin, Marlea's fingers became light on his other arm. Feeling like a third wheel, she let her hand drift to her side, setting the tall man and the object of his affection free to mix, mingle, and admire each other.

AJ saw them enter and smiled from the other side of the tent, immediately forgetting anything the man in front of him had to say. *Rissa was right.* Looking past Dench and barely seeing his sister, his eyes locked on Marlea. She was elegant in a way he had never seen before. Turquoise silk flowed in a sleek river of tiny pleats, from the halter at her throat to the wide-legged pants brushing the tops of the flat golden shoes she wore.

For a moment, AJ shifted into professional mode. He watched her walk, her gait smooth and even, her strength and balance apparent. Then the man took over and he lost himself in the curves of her body and the shift of her hips.

Her runner's body, solid and gravity-defiant, teased and invited beneath the flowing silk. True to her word, Rissa had done something enchanting with Marlea's hair, taking her workaday ponytail high and entwining it with gold. *She looks like a goddess.* AJ tried to come up with the name of some African equivalent to Aphrodite or Diana, the huntress. *I got nothin',* he finally admitted, *but damn, she looks good.*

Totally unaware of her beauty or her presence, Marlea looked around the tent in awe. Her eyes rose to the crystal chandeliers adorning the tent's roof and she smiled, fascinated. A pair of athletic-looking men stopped talking and headed in her direction, more than willing to explain the suspension of the lighting fixtures.

I don't blame them; she's stunning. Just gorgeous.

"You know her?"

The words snapped AJ back from the sight he had been enjoying. "She's a house guest," he said, eyes still trailing Marlea.

"Think I could meet her?" Kennedy Wharton, owner of Atlanta's Best Bread asked, nudging AJ with an insistent finger.

"Maybe later." The look on AJ's face made the other man back off.

"And maybe not," Wharton muttered, watching AJ head for the captivating figure in turquoise. Fortunately, he decided, spotting a pretty newspaper writer in a red minidress, the tent had an abundance of lovely women. He followed the mini-dress.

"Having a good time?" The familiar voice at her ear brightened Marlea's smile and marked AJ's territory as she turned to accept the slender flute filled with something golden and fizzy. "Ginger ale," AJ smiled back.

Recognizing the arrival of the alpha male, Marlea's two companions mumbled gentle excuses and left with regretful glances and private promises to return as soon as the former-pro interloper turned his back.

Marlea never noticed. "I am so glad I let Rissa talk me into coming tonight."

"I'm glad you did, too." AJ offered his arm and felt like a king when she took it. Walking through the tent, stopping to introduce her to several sponsors and loyal long-time runners, he admired her social grace, especially when confronted with recognition.

"Kellogg," a dark panther-like man in khaki looked at her closely. He repeated her name another time or two. "This isn't your usual kind of race, is it?"

"Marlea won't be running this one, Kessler." AJ felt Marlea stiffen at his side. *Maybe I should have let her handle that one on her own*, he thought belatedly.

Cranking his jaw to one side, Adrian Kessler studied Marlea. "I'm a writer for *Sports Today*, and I do some things for *Atlanta Sports and Fitness*, and I know you . . . Didn't you run the 400?" He fingered his ear, then stroked his chin. "Yeah, you did—you're the 'glamazon'. Tall for the race, but fast as lightening. I saw you take first in St. Louis a few months ago, then you dropped out of sight. Everybody thought you were a cinch for the Olympic team, but you haven't applied. What happened?"

"I, uh . . ." Marlea's eyes fell and then rose. Her hand tightened on AJ's arm. His hand covered hers and squeezed. "I had an accident, and it kind of changed my plans."

"Accident." Kessler looked thoughtful. "Sorry to hear it, but you're looking well—exquisite, in fact. Will you be competing again soon?"

Marlea's dimpled smile was confident. "Who knows what the future will bring?"

"You're right, but in the meantime . . ." The writer looked thoughtful and was silent until both Marlea and AJ directed questioning looks at him. "Would you consider being a part of a series I'm researching? Competitive female athletes living in Atlanta would be my focus, and your recovery and future would be a perfect centerpiece." He glanced at AJ, seemingly asking permission. "I'd like to call and set up a time, if you don't mind."

Putting a finger to the writer's chin, Marlea redirected his gaze. "I'm sure he's flattered, but I make my own decisions, and I'll consider it." Marlea turned and gave her glass to AJ. "Will you gentlemen excuse me?" She left the men with the soft whisper of silk.

"Magnificent woman, beautiful and with a mind of her own," Kessler murmured, raising his glass as he moved off into the crowd.

"Yes, she is," AJ agreed, watching her cut a path through the growing crowd.

"Still talking to yourself, AJ?" Cool fingers trailed his collar as the woman stepped around to face him. "Charming habit."

"Bianca."

"In the flesh." Her back and midriff bare, Bianca's wrapped knit dress clung to her like a second skin. She moved closer to AJ. Her fingers lingered, tracing the open neckline of his jacket. "You know I've never been one to let our little disagreements turn into grudges." Her alluring smile framed perfect white teeth and her sweet breath warmed his skin.

"This is not the time or the place." Gripping her wrist, he removed her hand and turned away.

"But a time will come, AJ, and you can name the place. You just need to resign yourself."

"I'm not interested."

"Don't be silly; of course you are." Bianca's eyes narrowed and followed AJ's to find Marlea's back. "Oh, that's your new playmate?" Her eyes, feral and determined, returned to his. "She looks harmless, AJ. Just remember, I'm not, and I saw you first."

"You're being ridiculous, and it doesn't become you." AJ brushed her fingers aside. "I'm here on business, and you came to play. Why don't you run along and do that?" Almost on cue, Harriet Blake rushed to his side, stood on tiptoe, and whispered in his ear. He nodded and followed her without another word.

Bianca's eyes flashed icy anger, and she nearly swung on the man who strolled close enough to offer her a glass of champagne. "No, thank you," she said through gritted teeth. Brushing past him, she followed the path she had seen Marlea take.

Entering the small bathroom, Bianca found her quarry at the vanity mirror, applying lipstick. "Nice shade," she said, managing a smile behind the benign words.

"Thank you. It's borrowed, but I like it, too." Marlea blotted her lips delicately.

"This is a lovely party, don't you think? But then, AJ always has nice affairs."

AJ? The name caught her attention and Marlea turned from the mirror. "You know him?"

"I've known him for years and years," Bianca snapped open her purse and studied the contents. "I almost married him. How do you know him?"

Almost married . . . Unless he's almost married more than one woman, this is Bianca Coltrane. Surprised, Marlea fought to keep her face from telling on her. "I'm a patient . . . a client of his."

"How interesting." Bianca's eyes traveled over Marlea, examining her from head to toe, trying to find the flaws. What she found was good skin, the color of caramel. The golden whisky-toned eyes were intelligent and the lushly bow-shaped lips seductive. She tilted her head, looking down at Marlea's feet. "Pretty shoes, but I think I would have opted for a higher heel."

"After my surgery, high heels weren't advisable." Marlea looked at her feet and tried not to feel ugly.

"Surgical patient. Did you break something?" She looked Marlea up and down again, applying the new information. Noting the swell of her breast and the fine bend of her waistline as it flared into her hips, Bianca gave her points. "You certainly look athletic. Will you be running this race?"

"I'm afraid not. AJ doesn't think I'm ready yet."

"And of course, what AJ thinks is important to you." Bianca's hand-trimmed fake lashes brushed her cheek and she wrinkled her nose. "Running is such sweaty work."

"I was a competitive runner."

"Was." Bianca hummed sympathetically. "No wonder he took you on. AJ has always had a soft spot for the underdog. That's one of the things I'll always love about him, even when we're old and gray." She wound a lock of hair around her finger, then leaned close to the mirror to inspect the resulting ringlet. She needn't have bothered; her hair and make-up were flawless, but she already knew that. She wanted the chance to watch Marlea's reflection.

"It must be hard to be treated like a pet by a man you can never have. He's mine, you know. But it's nice for AJ to have a pet, even if it can't perform."

"It must be even harder to know that whatever you did turned his heart from you, and you can't find a way to turn it back."

Bianca's eyes went flat and reptilian. "You don't know me like that, little girl. You don't want to start a fight with me; you don't have the ammunition." Bianca's tone was deadly, her meaning clear. "I always get what I want, and I want AJ Yarborough."

"People in hell want ice water." Marlea said the words, then had to force herself not to try to feed the borrowed tube of lipstick to the evil woman walking past her and out of the powder room. "And you can't have AJ. I won't let you."

"As if you have a choice."

Marlea had a clear vision of herself shoving Bianca's head through the mirror, and she was still holding onto it when Rissa pushed through the door to find a hard-breathing Marlea standing in the midst of Victorian porcelain and gilt splendor. "I just saw Bianca slink out of here. What's wrong?" she asked cautiously.

"I just met Bianca Coltrane."

Oh, hell. No wonder she looks like she's ready to breathe fire. Wonder what that witch had to say? Not sure what to say, Rissa took the lipstick from Marlea's hand and dropped it into her small evening bag.

"I'm ready to go home."

Okay, so whatever she said, it was about AJ—like I didn't already know that would be the case. She handed the bag to Marlea and felt insane relief when she took it.

"Marlea." Rissa's hand was cool and firm when she touched Marlea's arm, betraying none of what was in her heart. "If you leave now, she wins. You give her all she wants. You become the weak little nobody that she can push around anytime she wants to—and I know that's not who you are. You have to stay. Suck it up, work that winning smile of yours, get drunk if you have to, but don't leave, and don't let that gold-digging heifer win."

"I'm staying—until she leaves. Then I'll be ready to go." Straightening her shoulders, Marlea lifted her head and deliberately arranged her face. She could still see the mean veneer of smarmy self-congratulation cross Bianca's perfect face before she swept from the powder room. When she looked harder, she could see the fine cracks in Bianca's façade. On closer inspection, Marlea could name what she saw leaking through.

Fear.

It must be hard to be treated like a pet by a man you can never have. He's mine, you know. But it's nice for AJ to have a pet, even if it can't perform.

The words were harsh, but Marlea knew the lie when it shattered against a wall of her determination. Marlea headed for the door with Rissa hard on her heels. "That woman is only afraid of what she can't be sure of, and she knows that I touch a part of AJ she can never reach." Hand on the door, Marlea put on brakes and faced Rissa.

"What?"

"You know her." Marlea's voice was low. "Is she a runner?"

"Does a chicken have lips?" Rissa blew amused air. "No!"

"Then that's what she's afraid of. " Marlea pulled the door open and stepped into the reception's bright din. "It's what she thinks he loves about me. It's what she can never give him. She only wins if I don't run—and I'm running."

"Running?" Rissa smiled apologies at the people she brushed against in her rush to follow Marlea. "After AJ?"

"This damned race." Marlea said, and renewed fire swirled deep in the whisky gold of her eyes. "I'm running."

CHAPTER 22

"AJ, I want to do the race, too." Sitting on the stone wall surrounding the terrace, Marlea laced her shoes and looked ready for the challenge. "I won't try to run much, no more than I can do comfortably. I'll walk if I have to."

"Yeah, I can just see that, you walking anywhere you can run." AJ pulled the laces tight on his shoes. He took longer than necessary tying them and refused to face her. "The race is tomorrow. You've been here for six weeks, and you just started running distance again. Do you really think we've trained well enough?"

"Man, AJ," Marlea countered, her eyes sweeping the blue sky, "you really want to try to hard sell me on that? Two to four hours a day in the gym? Every day? Five miles, three times a week? All the walk-running I've done? Running with Rissa?" She smiled slyly. "All the walking we've done—together?"

Marlea thought about putting on her specially padded running shoes and climbing the wooded acreage surrounding the house. She thought back to how secure she felt when AJ took her hand to help her over some obstacle, back to what they had shared on those walks. *We've talked about everything on those walks, including Bianca Coltrane.* According to AJ, she was beautiful and smart.

I would sure like to give him an earful, tell him what I think of her. But deep in her heart, Marlea knew she would never tell him about her encounter with Bianca. *I wonder if Rissa said anything?* Looking at AJ under a cloudless blue sky, with a soft breeze touching them, she guessed that AJ's sister had somehow found the strength of will and character to keep her mouth shut—for a change.

But AJ is a smart man. It was hard to understand how Bianca's real personality got by him. Driven and goal-oriented, he called her. *More like cold and calculating when Rissa told it, though.* Even Mrs. Baldwin in a weak moment said that the woman had a cash register for a heart and an ATM for a soul.

Frowning, AJ was still lecturing. "Walking is not running, especially not under the Georgia sun. This is still September, and the day is subject to break hot."

"Come on, AJ, I've been outside before."

AJ looked dubious.

"Before you say no," Marlea rushed on, "I talked to Libby and told her about the reception last night. She said she was sorry she missed it. I also told her that I wanted to run this race, and she agreed. She said I was probably ready to tackle something harder."

"She probably did, but she doesn't work with you every day like I do." AJ stood and pulled the Nike sweatshirt over his head. Balling it up, he dropped it at his feet and began to stretch. "Libby is guessing long-distance."

"But she's right," Marlea insisted. "I've done three-and five-mile runs with Rissa and Dench and did just fine. And I've walked the malls and a couple of tracks with Jeanette and Connie. They're nurses. They would have said something if I had shown any sign of trouble."

"They're not runners." He was adamant.

"I can do better than six miles on the treadmill, and I can do it at better than five miles per hour. AJ, you know that even with programming, the treadmill is a sanitized course, nothing like a real outdoor course, and you wanted me to gain confidence." She took a deep breath. "I can do this, AJ. I know I can." She blew out hard and waited.

"Let me think about it," he said, jogging off the terrace.

"Don't think too long! The race is tomorrow," Marlea yelled at his back.

"He's gonna say no, you know."

"What makes you so sure, Rissa?"

"You." She stretched her long legs and nodded in the direction AJ had gone. "That man? My brother? Honey, he's falling . . . No, I take that back. He has already fallen so hard for you that he's afraid."

"Afraid?" Marlea looked hard at the woman in the three-striped sweatpants and matching shirt. "Not AJ. He's one of the bravest souls I've ever met. He's not afraid of anything—least of all me."

"Believe that if you want to. He's afraid of losing you."

Marlea swung her legs to the terrace floor and stood shifting from foot to foot, testing her shoes. "You're kidding, right?"

"Nope," Dench said from his place by the terrace door. "She couldn't be more right if she had to be."

Rissa brought her palms together in soft applause. "Well said by the brother in the corner. I'm a lawyer, girl. You know I do my research."

"Then what are we going to do about it, because I'm going to run that race, start to finish." Marlea couldn't help it; challenge cut her heart when she heard Bianca's words infiltrating her mind again. *It must be hard to be treated like a pet by a man you can never have, but it's nice for AJ to have a pet, even if it can't perform.* Intentionally cruel, the hateful words bore a threat she couldn't ignore.

But I'm going to have the last laugh. I'm going to run the hell out of this race. "How are you going to help me?" Marlea demanded, approaching Rissa.

"Slow your roll there, sister." Dench came close and rested a protective hand on Rissa's shoulder. "If you register, even late, I'll bet he'll know about it. You have to have a number to run and if you try to get one, he'll know about it. I can't think of anybody you can ask, at this late date, either."

"There's you." Light suddenly shone in Marlea's eyes. "You have a number, and you don't really want to run, do you?"

"AJ wouldn't like that," Dench drawled.

"But who's going to tell him?" Rissa grinned, pulling her feet into the chair and hugging her knees. "I know what you're thinking, and I can so keep this to myself."

Thinking fast, Marlea dropped into the chair beside Rissa's. Looking up at Dench, she hummed. "You two don't run together, do you?"

"No way. He's seeded and usually way up in the crowd. I'm back with the sluggers and plodders."

"Sluggers and plodders?" Rissa made a face. "Nice to know you think so highly of me, sweetie."

He gave Rissa's shoulder a squeeze. "Present company excluded."

"I'll settle for plodding. Can I have the number?"

Unconvinced, Dench shook his head. "I don't know, Marlea. What if AJ is right and you haven't trained enough. What if you can't make it?"

"Come on, Dench. I can make it; I know I can."

"I don't know . . ."

"I'll run with her," Rissa volunteered. "I'll stay with her every step of the way."

"Like you can keep up with me," Marlea sneered.

"Go ahead, bite the hand that feeds you. I'm just trying to help you out, but if you think I run too slow, and you don't think my help is . . ."

"No, Rissa, no! I never meant anything bad. Run with me, please run with me."

Her pride salved, Rissa relented. "Since you're begging . . ."

"What's in it for me?" Dench was in a bargaining mood, and Rissa's grin was sly when she placed her hand over his on her shoulder. "Oh, well, you want the number, Marlea, you got it. How we gonna make the switch?"

"Easy." Rissa obviously enjoyed plotting. "We'll all dress and head for the race, just as we planned, but we're going to run late. I'll figure out something to stall us. We don't need a lot of time, about ten minutes ought to do it. Once we're there, Marlea and I will hang back at the car, doing girl stuff. AJ will become impatient and run off to handle whatever it is he's supposed to do. Plus, as you said, he's seeded. He'll never see you hand over the number, and by the time he finds us at the finish line, she will have run and what can he say then?"

"Cool. Sounds like it'll work." Dench looked at Marlea. "But why are you willing to go to such lengths to run a race?"

Because I am not a pet. Marlea shrugged. "Part of me wants to do the run as a personal challenge, but another part of me would be lying if I didn't admit that I want to do it as a surprise for AJ."

"And she met Bianca at the reception," Rissa blabbed.

"Mouth like a sieve," Marlea sighed. "Yeah, I met her and she made it sound as though my not being able to run made me less of a person." Biting the inside of her lip, Marlea kept the rest of Bianca's words to herself.

"Don't let her push your buttons like that," Dench counseled.

"No, it's not about her. This run is for me."

"He looked at you funny, but AJ never said a word about you being dressed out. My brother can be so oblivious sometimes."

Trying to stifle the tremor of excitement that threatened to make her scream, Marlea pulled at the snaps on her windpants, then stepped free of them. She made a stab at folding them before tossing them on the jeep's back seat. "I can't believe your plan actually worked."

"The beauty of simplicity," Rissa smiled, reaching for the safety pins she had gone back to the house to collect, thus causing the ten-minute delay in AJ's schedule. "Can you believe he was so ticked off with me that he just ran off without a backward glance?"

"Leaving this for you," Dench grinned, handing over his race number.

Marlea's fingers trembled when she took it from him. Reverently pressing the sheet against her shirt, she accepted pins from Rissa. Once her number was secure, she looked up at both of them, tears in her eyes. "Thank you. Both of you."

"Girl, you're going to make me cry." Rissa folded her into a hug.

Dench couldn't help joining in. "You'd better hurry and find your time group if you don't want to miss your race." He sniffed and stepped back. Planting his hands in the small of his back, he looked skyward. "Good luck."

"He's a big ol' softy," Rissa whispered, keeping an eye out for AJ.

Finding their place behind the starting banner, Marlea had only a second or two to cherish the excitement of the race. Granted this was slower and longer than her beloved 400, but it was a race, and adrenaline shot through her veins in a hot rush.

"Runners, take your mark . . ."

Shaking off anything that had nothing to do with the run, she planted her right foot and prayed for the all-important balance that would carry her over the distance. Coiling her body, she gave her foot a twist, digging the toe of her shoe into position.

"Get set . . ."

Breathe . . . find the rhythm, hold the balance.

". . . go!"

The banner fell, trampled instantly by eager feet, but Marlea was more than ready, as her body broke free. Long legs working with hydraulic precision, Rissa at her side, her feet found their path. Marlea could hear her own breathing and feel the gravel crunching beneath her feet.

A mile into the run, Rissa looked across at Marlea. If there was a problem, she couldn't tell. "How're you doing?"

"Fine."

Three miles later, the answer was the same, and Rissa wondered if she was the only woman running through Welcome All park wishing that the race was over.

Marlea's answers were automatic because Rissa's questions barely registered. Her feet, trained for more years than she could count, ran where she directed them. Her thoughts ignored her control and ran straight to AJ.

Great day for a run, clear skies, not too hot. Wonder what his time will be? I know he's slowed down, and runs about an eight-minute mile. She checked the steel-banded chronometer on her wrist. *We're an hour into this race, which means he should be finished.* Curving along the asphalt turn of the street encircling the park, a bit of memory brought a flash of AJ and the first time she had seen him.

Funny, that day was a 10K, too. I never saw him until he fell out of nowhere and into my life. She smiled and remembered caramel skin, closely barbered dark hair, and a neat mustache over a nice . . . no, that day, nothing about him was nice—the big sweaty oaf!

Even features and broad shoulders and feet the size of Texas. Towering over her five feet, eight inches, he had barreled into her, knocking her flat. When her body was tangled with his, he seemed all broad shoulders and long, strong-muscled legs. *And as bad as it seemed then, things have changed . . . fate sure does have a sense of humor.*

Her breath pulled tight through her nose and rushed out past her open lips. Her mouth felt dry and her lips were parched. Her feet burned and she was pretty sure they would be blistered, but her legs felt as though she could run for an eternity.

Abuse, complaint, and agony, Rissa thought, hating Marlea just a little when she sprinted up the hill ahead of her. *Ninety minutes of my life that I will never see again, and I'm running behind a woman! But I guess it was worth it.* All she could see of Marlea was her back as she took the turn toward the finish line.

Her feet slapped the ground, but her pulse was still racing as she crossed the finish line, and Marlea wondered if AJ was right about the training. *Man, I'm sucking wind like a . . .*

"We did it," Rissa exalted, slapping an arm around Marlea's sweaty shoulders. "Ooh, girl, we did it." Grinning and laughing, she hugged Marlea. "I must really like you to do something like this. I don't work this hard at my real job."

Marlea hugged back and checked her chronometer over Rissa's shoulder. "And we did it in less than ninety minutes, that's . . . uh-oh . . ." Her arms fell and her face grew wary.

"What?" Rissa turned to find the imposing shadow of her big brother's presence darkening her optimism. "Uh-oh."

"What the hell were you thinking, running 6.2 miles on a new shoe?"

Though their mouths opened, neither of the women could find words in the face of AJ's anger.

"And you let them, helped them to do this?" he said, turning to Dench. "You know better!"

"They're grown." Dench shrugged and yawned, making it abundantly clear that he couldn't have cared less.

"Let me speak for both of us." Walking backward, facing her brother, Rissa threw both hands into the air. "As far as Dench and I are concerned, we did you both a big favor. You wanted to be sure that Marlea could go back to her life, now you know she can. She wanted to run again, and now she knows she can. What's the problem?"

His sister's words hit home. AJ stopped walking and shook his head. He checked the runners still crossing the finish line and then looked at Marlea. His gaze and voice softened. "You ran the whole race?" She nodded, and he did the time and distance math. "Pretty good time. How do you feel?"

"My feet hurt."

His face clouded. "Serves you right, Marlea. I told you . . ."

"But I finished, and you owed me a tee shirt anyway."

"I'm getting nowhere with you, am I?" AJ finally laughed.

"The tee shirt line is over there," Marlea pointed and headed for the line with AJ following.

"Looks like she handled that," Rissa giggled.

"Like he was going to refuse her anything." Dench used his thumb to catch a stray drop threatening Rissa's vision. She stood patiently, letting him mop her sweaty brow, figuring that she deserved the small pampering. "Old boy was pretty mad there, at first."

"Meant nothing," Rissa said with finality. "Those two couldn't be separated if their lives depended on it."

"Suppose we find ourselves another ride back to the house." He kissed the top of her head. "Let them have some time to figure that out for themselves."

"I think we can do that." Rissa tipped her head to offer her lips—it felt like the natural thing to do. Well, that and the fact that she liked the way he kissed, and he didn't seem to mind doing it at all. She was beginning to figure out some things for herself.

CHAPTER 23

"Are you sure you didn't want to go with Rissa and Dench and the rest of the committee to eat?" AJ swung the door of the jeep wide and offered his hand.

"No, I'm glad you were willing to pass." Slipping her hand into his, Marlea eased from her seat and winced in pain when her foot touched the ground.

"What's wrong?" AJ looked down and saw the crimson flush climbing her damp sock. "Marlea, your foot is bleeding."

"Oh, God." She reached for the door and leaned heavily.

Grim-faced and wordless, AJ surrounded her with his arms and scooped her close to his body. Holding her close enough to share heartbeats, he carried her past the cozy, ivy-covered, narrow white banister and across the small, stone porch.

A wave of vertigo threatened, and she raised her arms, linking her fingers behind his strong neck. Closing her eyes, trusting his strength, Marlea let herself be carried through the lead-paned door and into the kitchen.

"Oh, Lord! What happened to this girl?"

Marlea opened her eyes to find Martha Baldwin's worried face and fluttering apron heading her way. "I'm okay, Mrs. Baldwin."

"You don't look okay. You look bad, is how you look." Martha's eyes accused AJ, and she flapped the apron again. "What did you do to her?"

"I told her not to do what she did," AJ said, proclaiming his innocence. "I'll tell you about it later."

"You'd better," Martha fussed as AJ passed her.

"She's going to get you, you know." Marlea dropped her head back to AJ's shoulder and moaned softly when he lowered her to the chintz-printed chair in her bedroom.

Kneeling in front of her, he loosened her shoe, then gingerly removed it. He watched her bite her lip, fighting not to cry out. "Hurt?"

"A little," she lied. Her foot hurt like hell.

"Let's see what I can do about that." Rising, AJ went into the small bathroom. Marlea heard him run water, but was still surprised when he emerged with towels and a basin. Kneeling, he pulled rolls of gauze from the stack of towels and set them to the side. Pulling over a small tapestry-covered stool, he sat and tenderly brought her foot to the towel draped across his lap. Rolling her blood-tinged sock away, he exposed her foot.

Wanting to protest, but craving the comfort, Marlea submitted to his ministrations. It was nice to have him take charge, and she was glad that he was there to do it. Warm salted water covered her foot and the pain began to ebb. Beneath the water, his hands were sure and soothing, and Marlea was able to forget about the touch of his palm against her skin.

The towel he used to dry her foot felt so good that it made her sigh. Completing his task, AJ used the gauze to deftly wrap her injured foot, then held it in his lap. Marlea sighed again. It wasn't loud, but it was enough to make him smile as he looked up at her. "Better?"

"Much better, and for a change, it didn't make me . . . you know."

"Are you blushing?" He leaned forward and looked up into her face. "You are." When she started to move her foot, he lay a still hand across her ankle. "Thought we had gotten over that, that we could talk about whatever came up between the two of us."

Her breast rose and fell before she could voice the words. "You're right."

"Then what was the real reason for running today?"

Hesitating, Marlea measured her words. She debated a lie, but said, "I met Bianca Coltrane at the reception." When AJ waited, Marlea knew she would have to say more. "She said that . . . she kind of . . . dared me to run."

AJ's face shadowed. "And you couldn't take a dare?"

"No, AJ, I couldn't let that dare pass unaccepted." *You didn't hear what she said to me, and you don't know how much she meant it!*

"Well, I know how Bianca can push buttons, especially when she puts her mind to it."

"AJ, do we have to talk about her? I ran a race today, a 10K, and I owe it to you." Leaning forward, Marlea held AJ's face between her warm palms and dropped a light kiss on his forehead. "Thank you, AJ."

"Since you were the one who did the running, maybe I owe you a little credit, too." AJ lifted his face enough to brush Marlea's lips with his own. "Are you up to taking any other dares?"

"I think so." Smiling against his lips, Marlea prayed that she was on the right track. "AJ, you told me to let you know when I wanted to know what else you do well. Think you could show me now?"

"I'm good at a lot of things," he drawled, looking deep into the intoxicating whisky and gold of her eyes. He traced a finger along the sweet curve of her cheek. "You want to be a little more specific?"

"How about something we could do in this room? Together?" She moved her gold-flecked eyes pointedly toward the four-poster bed, then back to the man.

"Marlea, is this gratitude talking? 'Cause I'm not into thank-you sex."

Kissing him, isolated by the enticement of her lips on his and the entreaty of his tongue, she knew that she was right. What she felt had nothing to do with gratitude. "You know what?" Marlea released his face and pushed herself up from the chintz chair. "You wouldn't even get this invitation if I didn't mean it. I'm only going to ask you one more time; after that, I'm going to hop over there and show you what you almost missed. So do you want to make love or not?"

"Since you put it so romantically, yeah," AJ said, standing to sweep her sweaty body into his arms. "But I think a shower is in order first."

Marlea buried her face against the strong column of his throat and whispered into his skin, "I like the way you think, but what about my foot?"

"I think we can manage. I'll rewrap it later."

Taking AJ's hand, trusting, Marlea followed him to the bathroom. Grasping the chrome handle of the shower door, AJ pulled. Opened, the shower displayed shelves holding an assortment of soaps and shower gels and a chrome basket of assorted brushes, but neither Marlea nor AJ saw them. Reaching in and adjusting the water temperature seemed an empty gesture, a play for time. They were together, and nothing else mattered.

Standing close, AJ's thumbs claimed the bands of her panties and shorts, sliding them down her legs and off her feet. Letting him lead her, Marlea surrendered to AJ's familiar hands as they moved along the length of her legs. His touch had always called to her, and surrendering, she welcomed it now.

He gave her a quick kiss before gently sliding her shirt over her head. An intimate glow of pleasure warmed her, sending a flush that began between her breasts and rose high along the dusky column of her throat. AJ's fingers on her cheek, she closed her eyes, savoring his touch.

He kissed her once more, teasing her, pulling away before she wanted him to, and the spiked flush of cinnamon surged through her veins again. Marlea pulled back the shower curtain and stepped inside. "Are you coming with me, or do I have to do this alone?"

AJ's eyes lingered longingly on the lushness of her naked flesh beneath the silvery fall of water. "No sooner said than done." His voice was husky, but his movements were sure as he swiftly stripped away his shirt and shorts to join her.

Bracing his hands on the shower wall above her, he shared the fall of water. Turning slowly, Marlea let warmly persistent water drum along the curve of her spine. When his hands moved over her naked back, the shiver of unrelieved anticipation left her blinking.

Behind the embroidered curtain of the shower enclosure, warm water and scented soap stroked the smooth silk of Marlea's skin, bringing her against the rougher maleness of AJ's skin. His gasp at the exquisitely tender sense of her hand against the tight flatness of his male nipples touched her with more than anticipation. Marlea knew she would never regret what she was committed to giving.

"Marlea." His voice made her name into music and Marlea felt blessed and christened by the water passing over them. Golden late-afternoon sunlight poured generously from the skylight, gilding their bodies as warm water liquefied their joined passion. She moved beneath the vibrating flow of water, almost gasping when it touched her.

Her hands moving over his broad shoulders brought his chest to meet the tilting slope and weight of her rounded breasts. Dark coffee-colored nipples, lifted by the cut and tease of her thoughts, stood out and reached for him. Drifting lower, his hands found the sweet curve of her waist as it bent into the lush swell of her hips and he pulled her tight against all that was most male.

But the shower alone was not what they would come craving. Opening the shower door a crack, not wanting to be chilled by cool air outside the stall, Marlea grabbed for the thick sea green Turkish bath towels hanging from a brass rack. She offered one to AJ, wrapped herself in the other, and stepped out.

At the bedside thick towels slid to the floor, landing in a heap at their feet. AJ knelt in front of her, like a servant bowing before his queen, his hands moving along the length of her long legs. When his large hands framed her hips, he softly kissed her stomach and slowly worked his way down to the groove between her thighs.

Feeling his touch, the sweet stir tempting her wetness, Marlea gripped his shoulders, and released a deeply hungry breath. AJ took his time, exploring and savoring her luscious femininity. He moved a hand inward, delicately spreading her to reveal more. She welcomed him— no part of her would escape him.

Not believing how sweet she tasted, AJ found Marlea's gaze locked on him and smiled when her fingers tenderly touched the side of his face. His probe deepened, and she crumpled to let her breath fall hot on his shoulders, her fingers tightening there. "Oh, Lord, AJ. Quick, before it's too late, top drawer, nightstand."

It took a second for him to understand, but when he did, he reached for the golden coin he found in the nightstand. "Wait." Marlea shifted to meet his gaze, and her hand covered his. "Let me do it," she said. "Please, I want to."

The coin glinted with stolen light as she forced his hand open. Releasing the condom into her smaller hand was more difficult than he had imagined. Relinquishing control did not offend his manhood. It was that no woman, not even Bianca, had ever been so bold, or so seductively giving as to share in this intimate ritual—and certainly, he had never asked.

"I want to," Marlea said again, as she folded back the gold foil. "Doing this for you, for us, gives me pleasure. It lets me share more of who you are and what you have for me—what we have for each other." Her voice was almost as soft as the lips that brushed his chest as she bent to her task.

Her tender fingers were maddeningly slow, moving with responsive deliberation that made him want her all the more. The magic of her moving fingers unrolling the thin latex shield amazed him as she shaped and molded the only barrier that either of them could allow.

When she finished, his long arms wrapped her with a protective grip that threatened to press the very air from her lungs. "This is right," Marlea whispered, banishing the threat of Bianca Coltrane.

Falling into bed with AJ, Marlea quivered, rocked by the oceans he stirred within her, and he held her, working his way along the seamless band of her silken flesh. Tracing her navel, he slowly, steadily, loved everything in his path. Pulling him closer, her eyes still on him, Marlea's legs seemed capable only of holding AJ.

His entrance stunned them both. Infinite, warm, and perfect, their joining felt as though their bodies had been created only for the mating of one to the other. Delicious and complete harmony, what they shared was both essential and as necessary as air. Bound to him by silken bands of muscle, Marlea lost track of herself. Clutching him, sobbing and weeping as he strained against her, her entire body felt overcome by his possession—a possession she never wanted to end.

Holding him tightly, Marlea wanted to absorb him into her very skin. She could feel the shivering edge his body skated, and she met him with all her strength. Without warning, her body convulsed around him. She could feel him grow rigid, hear him calling her name as he joined her in a seemingly endless dance of heat, desire, and satisfaction.

Threading her arms around him, she clung tightly, unaware of the desperation of her embrace. Losing track of time, minutes, hours later, bodies entwined, they lay together. AJ relaxed against her and Marlea tried not to think of his ever moving any farther away from her than he was at that instant.

He gently traced the lines of her face and whispered her name over and over again, a song in the growing darkness. Not long after, he was asleep, pinning her beneath him. In AJ's arms, pressed by the weight of his body, Marlea had space for only one thought.

Never the same again. I'll never be the same again.

CHAPTER 24

Lying there with his arm draped across her, Marlea opened her eyes—barely. Seeing him through the screen of her lashes, she tried to isolate the moment it happened. Her thoughts roamed, sifting through their time together, and tried to pick out the exact moment she had fallen in love. *And fallen is the right word.* Life changed irrevocably, from the very second she had fallen into AJ Yarborough.

Her lashes fluttered when she realized the weight of her thoughts. *I used the 'L' word.* Eyes wide, she moved them to AJ's face. Strong and clean, even in his sleep, his wide brow, high sketched cheekbones, and the lips that stole a bit of her heart each time they touched hers, were impressive. *Yes, he's handsome, but it takes more than good looks to make a woman fall in love with a man . . .*

She thought of the brutally erotic agony of his touch in her therapy. *It didn't hurt, it never hurt. I was just embarrassed,* she recalled, glad that she had finally told him about it. *One thing's for sure,* she wiggled her toes beneath the covers, *I'm feeling it in all the right places these days.* The nurses were right, the frenzy his touch ignited in her confused body after the loss of her toes had shifted, finding a time, place, and rhythm. Clinging to him in the clean-sheeted nest they created with their joined bodies, Marlea couldn't have felt more right.

This is right, being here with a man who completes me. He makes me laugh, he hears what I say, and he speaks a language I understand, right down to my bones. With him, I always know what comes next. With AJ, I feel included, I feel . . . Her gaze caressed his face. *I feel loved.* His snoring was light, his breath touching her shoulder, and Marlea tried to take comfort in the sound. *But he's leaving,* she thought, and the loneliness had already begun.

Without really trying, she could see the numbers click into place on the digital clock standing sentry on the nightstand. 7:00 A.M. and she already felt cheated. *He's supposed to leave for the airport at eight. I ought to wake him, maybe slip in some last minute loving.* But laying beside him, his touch felt so good, so intimate, that she was loathe to lose what she had right then.

Her bed-warmed fingers stroked the arm he had enclosed her with, and her secret smile promised that she had memorized every hair and every pore in his skin. Inhaling deeply, she closed her eyes and knew that she would know him anywhere and anytime. *I would know his scent, his touch . . .* She stroked his arm again. *Shoot, I would know this man in braille.*

Libby used to have a saying for it, for how she felt about her husband, Hal. Marlea's eyes went to the window. It was going to be one of those pretty bright-sun, blue-sky days that Georgia was known for. *But how did Libby put it?*

Oh, yeah, she used to say, 'This man is my all-day study and my midnight dream.'

Closing her hand and arm over his, Marlea rolled to her hip and pressed her body closer to his. *'My all-day study and my midnight dream.' The girl ain't never lied.*

At her back, AJ's breathing lightened, and Marlea's eyes went back to the clock—7:10am. *Fifty minutes left, then I'll have to say goodbye.*

He would only be gone a few days—back on Friday. She moved carefully, matching her curves to his planes and lengths. *He's going to New York on business. He's going to sign a few contracts, shake a few hands, maybe do some publicity shots, and then he'll come back home—to me.*

Come back to me? Now when did I get so possessive? The hand of his encircling arm closed on her shoulder, and she reached to guide it lower. His hand followed her lead, teasing as it went.

He's awake, and he's mine: at least, if sleeping with a man for seven nights in a row gives me any kind of right . . . Time has nothing to do with what I have with AJ.

"Morning."

Soft and throaty, his early-morning voice was all the invitation Marlea needed. Her eyes told him what she wanted. Barely breathing, never fearing rejection, Marlea moved closer, letting him travel her skin; all that lay between her soul and the world. Accepting her touch in return, they teased, and almost as if by unspoken agreement, avoided the places God made to create sexual energy.

His fingers touched her face, bringing a hint of his familiar manly scent. It was a smell so deeply ingrained that it must have been there when he was born, and when

311

he folded back her palm, Marlea wondered what he smelled on the skin of her hand, but wouldn't ask.

Caressing and being caressed, she could have stayed there for more time than a clock could tell. Stroking him incited familiar heat between her legs, and she knew what he would find if he touched her there. *When*, she sighed.

His fingers traced circles, intricate and arcane patterns on her breasts. Questing, his fingertips seemed to taste her, like a gourmet delicacy. Provoking, lingering, he took his time sampling her skin. Her nipples hardened and he played with them, sometimes aggressive like turning the buttons of an old radio, other times delicate like a shimmering brush of feathers.

Simmering, ready, and knowing that it was no secret, Marlea tried to keep pace with him. Moving across her belly, down her legs, stroking at her thigh, a single finger tracing where he would not yet go, she knew he felt her heat. His touch was soft and intoxicating, bearing promise and threatening fulfillment.

Almost floating over his skin, Marlea's hands followed their own quest. Finding swollen expectancy, she was almost afraid to touch what she had awakened craving. When he rolled, taking her with him, she gasped, feeling him thicken, readying for her. Her fingers claimed him, stroking. Touch changed him, more at the bottom than the top, as her fingers wrapped around, exciting him to grow in her hand.

His breathing changed, but his touch was unrelenting. His search brought him low to find her true center exposed and welcoming, and he touched her as she might have touched herself. Finding what he sought, with fingers dipped in the dew of her passion, he touched the bud within and it rose to greet him. Marking the same pattern at her core that he had imprinted on her swollen breasts, AJ drew her closer beneath the comforting blanket of his long-muscled body.

Trembling along the thin lip of orgasm, she heard him moan and understood. Her fingers twined through his and she wanted to echo his cry as thought blasted her away to a place where clocks held no sway. AJ's bare leg swept hers and he took full possession of her, laying claim to all that she so willingly offered.

But the clock was still there when her heavy-lidded eyes focused. 7:55 A.M. She felt him move. "AJ?"

"Shh," he whispered. "Don't get up."

She heard his bare feet whisper over the oriental carpet beside the bed. She heard his steps move farther away. She heard the shower come on in the bathroom. "AJ?"

Then he was beside her again, his kiss a lick of fire at the nape of her neck. "Shh, I'm fine. You should go back to sleep."

She felt him move across the room again, knew when he was in the shower. She heard him moving beneath the fall of water and thought of his words: *'You should go back to sleep.'*

She threw back the covers and made her way across the floor. *'You should go back to sleep,'* he said.

Like that was gonna happen.

~~~

"Seems like I'm going to be taking a later flight," AJ said into the phone. "Yeah, dude, I know it's not like me to miss a flight, but I had a good reason this time." Oblivious to the stares his sister and housekeeper directed toward him, he bent to kiss the ear of a blushing and obviously happy Marlea. "I'll be at Kennedy by two, and your office no later than four." He listened, then raised a thick eyebrow in Marlea's direction. She shook her head. "No, man. I'll be alone, this trip."

Sharp-eyed, neither Rissa nor Mrs. Baldwin missed the interplay.

Finishing his call, AJ dropped the phone on the counter and walked over to the table. "You're sure?"

Marlea looked up at him, the soft glow of her skin striking in the light. "I'm sure, and I'll still be here when you get back." She raised her hand, offered her little finger, and never took her eyes from his.

AJ linked his finger to hers and brought it to his lips. "You'd better be, 'cause I promise I'll always be there for you."

Marlea pulled the joined fingers to her lips and smiled. "Now where else would I go?"

When she released his finger, AJ was slow to move away from her. "I'm just sayin', is all."

"Could you two just say goodbye so we can get to the airport?" Dench leaned against the doorframe, his words breaking the spell Marlea and AJ shared.

The phone rang as Marlea opened her mouth. "For you," Martha Baldwin said, offering the phone to Marlea.

Surprised, Marlea took the phone from the older woman's hand. "Hello?" She frowned, then brightened.

"Of course, I remember you, and today is fine." She listened, looked at AJ, then nodded. "Well, I'm not sure what I have to offer . . . but, yes . . . I can do it. Two o'clock, and here is fine."

Hovering and curious, Martha Baldwin took the phone from Marlea's hand, making sure to stay close enough to hear.

"So who was it?" Rissa slid across a chair to get closer.

"Adrian Kessler, from *Atlanta Sports and Fitness* magazine. He wanted to follow up on his suggestion from the reception."

"What was his suggestion?" Dench came close enough to grab AJ's raincoat and laptop.

"You're gonna do it, right?" AJ urged.

"All these questions; just a moment, please." Her brows rose, but her grin matched AJ's when she directed her attention to him. "Aren't you the man who just promised that you would always be with me? I do this interview, and where will you be?"

"With you in spirit, but I still have to get to New York." He bent to kiss Marlea's cheek, managing to catch her mouth in the process.

Dench shifted the laptop to his other hand. "You gotta get to the airport first, dude."

<hr />

Sliding into the small booth at DayBreak's, Bianca Coltrane tried to hold onto what had begun as a good day. "I had the appointment, all I had to do was get there." She looked down at her hand. She was still clutching the broken heel of her Via Spiga pump. "Useless thing," she muttered, tossing it onto the tabletop. Pulling her cellphone from her sidewalk-sale Prada handbag, she scrolled through the phone numbers until she found the right one.

A server materialized and raised an eyebrow.

"Coffee. Whatever you have in a French roast, and a paper, *The Times*," Bianca snapped, turning her back on the white-shirted woman. Staring through the broad plate glass, she cursed the passing taxicabs. *Where the hell were they when I needed one?*

She pressed the numbers on her phone and waited. Finally connected, Bianca tried to control her frustration, but she wasn't used to trying and not very good at it.

"Look," she huffed into the ear of Guilliame du Verriers, scion of The House of du Verriers, when she ultimately got through to him, "I've broken the heel of my shoe, can't find a cab, and can't possibly get to your office in less than an hour. We'll have to change my appointment."

Guilliame's very Gaelic hum came clearly over the line, and Bianca didn't like the sound of it. When she pressed, he hummed again. "Look, Guilliame, we had a deal and you're going to stick to it. You're just going to have to change my appointment; pull out your date book and pencil me in!"

"Perhaps this is not possible—not today. Perhaps next month . . ."

Bianca's choking cough clogged the phone for a second. "No, that's not acceptable, Guilliame. We both know how much I have invested in this line, and I'm not going to let you back me down. You're going to do business with me, and you're going to see me."

Monsieur du Verriers did not take well to pressure, especially when it came from an overdone, simplistic American bent on using her good looks and fabulous figure to compensate for a lack of talent. He drew a sonorously deep breath through his long and aristocratic nose and then passed it through his thin-lipped mouth, phrasing his answer. When he finally spoke, his accent thickened, but he enunciated clearly. He didn't want her to miss his meaning. "We can certainly do that for you, Mademoiselle Coltrane. We will change your appointment—to next spring. You will contact me then. *Au voir.*"

"Hello?" She took the phone from her ear and stared at it. *Oh, no, he did not hang up on me!* She clamped the phone to her ear—nothing. *And told me to call back next year?*

Stunned, Bianca flapped a hand at the server. She barely saw the olive-skinned, sloe-eyed, sometime actress, sometime model as the young woman set coffee, cream, and the day's *New York Times* in front of her.

Folding her phone, her mind raced. *I should have listened to Roy. He warned me about mortgaging the condo. But I had so much faith in my line and du Verriers's promise.* So why hadn't she had more companies interested in it? *People loved it in Atlanta.* But none of them called her office in New York. She pushed a hand through the thickness of her hair. The House of du Verriers had been the only one she had to pin her hope on—now a broken heel had toppled that hope. Well, a broken heel and a funky French attitude. *Guilliame probably found somebody else's chest to drool down.*

Thinking of the first time that the vainglorious, smarmy, over-perfumed man kissed her didn't help. *Wrapped his arms around me, pressed his lips to mine, and came all over himself. Yeah, that was funny and I didn't even laugh out loud. And to think of how many dinners I let him buy, just so he could hope that I would crawl up in a bed with him and let him press his fat hairy belly on me— ugh!*

But this is not over—I won't let it be. She thought hard. *I know powerful men, men with money, and they are only men. One of them will come through for me.* She opened the paper, habit taking her to the sports pages. *Someone I know must be flush enough to bail me out.*

Seeking a familiar face, Bianca looked down and there he was, like the answer to a prayer. The *Times* photo was in color, and it was a good one. Tight, toned, brown eyes gleaming with intelligence and health, he looked perfect, and it was almost more than she could take. Eyes flying over the story, her keen toed heel-less pump spanked the tile at her feet. Giving the paper a snap to straighten it, she reread the article.

"Unbelievable. All this money for a man who is out of the game." Bianca folded the paper so that her finger could trace the line of zeros following the one-two-five. "Retired, with all this money, and they still call him 'the nicest man in football'."

She read further, finding the other line she wanted. "He's in New York to finalize contracts on his book and an upcoming movie. Impressive. All that money is just the down payment." She reread the paragraph and thought of those dollars again. One hundred twenty-five thousand dollars would pay for a lot of shoes.

"No mention of an accompanying woman," she smiled. "AJ Yarborough is all alone in the big city."

Closing the paper, Bianca tucked it away for future reference. She lifted her cup and sipped. "All alone—but not for long."

———

"So how did it go?"

"It was amazing, AJ. I never knew I had so much to say, and it felt good to say it. Man, I had a chance to clear the air on some highly misunderstood conceptions of female athletes. Oh, AJ, not only that, but I talked about my accident. I had a chance to talk about what it's like to be an amputee."

"Marlea . . ."

"Wait, AJ, let me tell you. I know that it could have been worse, that I could have lost my whole foot or a leg, but I talked about everything."

"Everything?"

"AJ . . . okay, I didn't talk about that, but I talked about everything else. Oh, and I didn't talk about how much I care for you. I'm saving that for when you get back to Atlanta. We can have a private conversation, just the two of us."

He heard a smile in her voice and felt his chest tighten. "That's great, Marlea. How are you going to celebrate?"

"I hadn't thought about that," she said slowly. "He's going to fax an advanced copy of the story, and I could share it here at the house with Rissa and Mrs. Baldwin."

"No, baby. You need to really celebrate."

"I could wait for you," Marlea offered.

"That's generous, but until I get back, you should be with friends."

"Not a bad idea." Marlea gave his suggestion a little thought. She had never really had girlfriends the way other women did. So who did that leave? She let her mind ramble. "Libby's back in town for a few days, and I can get Rissa and Jeanette and Connie—we could do something fun. Maybe go out for dinner and drinks . . . And then I'll see you on Friday."

"Yes, ma'am. Friday it is; oh, and I'm going to bring you something special."

"Oh, a gift. I like that, but I love you, AJ." Her gasp was swift over the phone line as she realized what she had said. "I didn't mean to tell you like that, but I do, AJ—love you."

He cupped the phone in both hands. "Me, you, too."

"I'm glad," she whispered. "Bye." The single word was soft but final, almost as though she had run out of things to say. AJ set the phone aside reluctantly.

Sitting on the sofa and watching AJ as he talked to Marlea, Bianca plucked at the pearl buttons on her shirt.

Wondering if it would have made a difference if she had entered the room naked, she waited for AJ to end his call.

"You didn't tell her about me. Should I guess why?"

His back stiffened. "No need to guess. There's nothing to tell."

"Really. I guess I'll have to see what I can do to change that." The pearl buttons moved easily as the blouse fell away. She let her skirt slide over sleek skin and smiled. She had always liked the look of a man perched on the edge of Purgatory.

CHAPTER 25

Sounds of the televised game bounced off the walls, and the rocking music floating on the air was almost as loud as the conversation from the next booth. The waitress in the green Jocks 'N Jill's tee shirt leaned close, swiping at the table with a cloth before setting the tray of drinks down.

"So what are you ladies celebrating?" she asked, rubbing hard at a slick-looking spot.

Jeanette and Libby licked sauce from their fingers, trying to speak. Connie forked cole slaw into her mouth, content to let them try.

"Her," Rissa volunteered, pointing at Marlea and pulling copied sheets from under Connie's elbow. "She was just interviewed for this marvelous article. Take a look." Then she went back to her fries.

"Cool. What did she do?"

"I ran a race," Marlea used her fork to push food around on her plate, "and that's only a draft of the article."

Rissa put the tender rib aside and came up for air. "But read the article—the draft of the article."

"Sure." The waitress, whose nametag read 'Cassie', set the tray down and wiped her damp hands against her short apron. Taking the stapled sheets from Rissa's hand, she ignored Connie who passed out the drinks from her tray. "Aw, man," Cassie breathed, surveying the pages. "They had to cut off your toes? Damn!" She drew the final word out in amazement when Marlea nodded.

Cassie's smoky gray eyes met Marlea's and fell back to the pages. "Dang, you almost made it to the Olympics. And now?" She turned the page, read the last few words, and looked up with a smile. "He says you're still running? That you did a race a week ago?"

"Something like that," Marlea nodded.

"The article says you use a special shoe. Are you going to keep running?"

"Yes, but I don't know if I'll ever do the 400 again. Besides, I'm over thirty, that's kind of long in the tooth for a runner."

"Will you listen to grandma, over there?" Libby plucked a lime wedge from the white china saucer in the center of the table and pinched it into the mouth of her Corona, watching the pale juice run into the golden beer before taking a long drink from the long-necked bottle.

Cassie shyly turned the pages back to the beginning. "It says you're a teacher, too. Bet your kids are proud of you."

"Are they ever. You should have seen the cards and letters, the videos and stuff that she received in the hospital. Those kids love her." Jeanette reached for a handful of napkins and shared them with Rissa and Connie. "Now ask her when she's going back."

Marlea wished she had the nerve to stuff Jeanette's mouth with the damned napkins, but with her luck, the woman would eat them. "I'll be back in the classroom at the beginning of the year. I've already talked to the administrators at Runyon."

"I didn't know, you didn't tell us." Jeanette plucked paper tissue from her sticky fingers, frowning at a particularly stubborn clump when it fell into the lap of her denim skirt. When Cassie handed her a premoistened towelette, she smiled her thanks.

"I'll bet AJ knows," Connie mumbled.

"AJ is your man, huh?" Cassie read the look on Marlea's face and knew that she was right. "Ohh, that's so sweet, so noble. He stood by you through all of this. You mind if I take this with me? I want to share it with some friends."

"No, feel free. That's a draft," Marlea said. "We have other copies, take it if you want it."

"Thanks." Cassie hurried away with her tray and her copies. Ten minutes later, she was back with a tray of fresh drinks. "Hope y'all are thirsty. You have an admirer over there and he sent these over to you."

"Who?"

Unloading the drinks, Cassie tossed her head toward the bar. "Him. Over there."

"Jeanette, please," Rissa's lips rippled with suppressed laughter. "Sitting over here trying to act like you don't take drinks from strange men. However, as cute as I am," she straightened her cotton sweater, " I'm not surprised."

"Not you, hon." Cassie tapped Marlea's denim jacket. "Her."

"Me?" Marlea almost slid out of her seat when Jeanette snickered. "You have got to be mistaken." She chanced a glance around Cassie, catching the eye of a long-legged, chocolate-skinned man. "Oh, no. He did not wink at me."

"He probably did," Cassie grinned, taking her tray. "I left your article on the counter while I was filling orders and he read it, then he told me to bring you whatever you all were drinking and to pick up your dinner tab, too."

"I like him already," Libby offered brightly, waggling the Corona.

"You're married, remember? You can't go around liking strange men just because they buy you drinks."

"I can if I want to; you're not the boss of me." Pretending to sulk, Libby sucked at her beer.

"Then you can talk to him when he gets here," Marlea whispered, sprouting a sudden and passionate interest in her quesadilla. "He's on his way over here now." Using her fork and her fingers, Marlea took a bite. She was still chewing when the man reached the table.

"Ladies." He planted a hand on his chest and parted his lips in a full smile—as if he had practiced. "I'm Vincent Welles, and I would truly enjoy the chance to sit and get to know you all better." He said *all*, but his eyes locked on Marlea.

Vincent Welles stood there looking as though he was used to women drooling over him—and in spite of herself, Marlea—and every other woman in the restaurant—could see why. He was tall and solid, packed with muscle, and had a butt you could bounce quarters off, if you had a mind to. Broad-shouldered, with a narrow waist, he flexed and stood poised for the inevitable invitation—it came from Connie.

Accepting, he slid into the booth, seating himself next to Marlea. Looking down at her as if she had just stepped off the menu, he leaned his elbows on the table and folded his hands.

He nodded toward the bar. "I was sitting over there, all by my lonesome, and I couldn't help noticing this table full of good-looking women. Then I saw the article Cassie left laying on the bar." He smiled and Marlea knew what Little Red Riding Hood must have felt like when she met the Big Bad Wolf. "So you're the one who had the surgery."

"Yes, that was me." Suddenly cold and greasy, the quesadilla didn't taste quite so good anymore. Marlea set her fork aside and tossed her napkin onto the tabletop.

"So what was it like? They took about half your foot, right?" Eyes eager, he leaned forward.

Rissa, Libby, and Connie were teasing Jeanette about whatever old song was playing over the stereo system. None of them heard Vincent Welles when he said, "Wonder what that's like? To feel that nub? Rubbin' up on it an' stuff." He licked his lips. "I heard where sometimes, after you lose a body part, the nerves get confused and all it takes is just a little touch . . ."

This can't be happening. Marlea's breath came in short little gasps and she couldn't stop it. *If I let this vulgar clown go on bullying and trying to intimidate me, how do I get through the rest of my life?*

"Look, Mr. Welles, you're out of order. I'm out tonight with friends and I . . ."

"I heard you could get your freak on like that," he continued. "Ever happen to you? Touch your foot and turn you on?"

How do I tell my children that they have to accept boundaries, but not limits, when I can't make this man understand that he's abusing mine? Refusing to look at him, Marlea couldn't find the difference between anger and embarrassment—and she didn't care. Drawing her own line, she realized the truth: *I do it by admitting that I'm mad as hell at Dr. Reynolds, and then I make a lie out of disability. I take myself back. Nobody can make a fool out of you if you don't let him.* She looked at Vincent Welles and reached another decision. "Mr. Welles, you need to leave. Now."

"Why?" He licked his lips and leaned far enough back in the booth to bring his mouth close enough to whisper, "You let me, and I'll suck that nub and make you scream my name like I was the second comin'."

"If you don't get the hell away from me, and I mean right now, I'm gonna make you scream *MY* name," Marlea promised, reaching for her fork.

"All I want to do is make you feel good," he whispered.

"Then you won't mind this."

"Damn, bitch," Welles yelped, simultaneously leaping from the booth and trying to pull the fork from his leg, a slow and obviously painful process. Wincing, he worked at his wound. "You trying to give me tetanus or somethin'? All I was trying to do was . . ."

"Crawl up on me, you nasty . . ."

"Watch who you're callin' a bitch!" Jeanette hissed.

"Oh, hell, no!" Rissa pushed to her feet behind the table. She pointed a finger at Welles and shook it like a weapon. "You know, there's a name for people like you, and I happen to know what it is—got a 1600 on the SAT back in the day, and sat at the head of my class at Emory Law, yes I did. You're an acrotomophile, mister. That means you've got an amputee fetish."

"And I would see a doctor for it, if I were you, 'cause man, you are one sick puppy," Connie added, getting loud.

Jeanette was on her knees in the booth and pointing. "She already told you, you need to leave. She's got a man."

"And a lawyer. Frankly, I think my brother would be real happy to kick your sorry butt, but I think the cops could get you out of here a bit faster." Rissa pulled out her cellphone and started pressing buttons.

"You ain't got to call the cops," Welles frowned, tossing the fork back to the table. "No need to go making threats or anything." He turned wounded eyes on Marlea. "I just thought you might be looking for someone to make you feel whole."

Reaching for the fork, Marlea held his eyes. "I'm not prey or in need of pity, and I certainly don't need that kind of 'help' from you."

Libby's bright eyes flashed fury. "She's about as whole as one person can get, and if you don't go far away from her, I might have to show you how whole I am."

Phone to her ear, Rissa's eyes slid sideways, taking in Libby's ire. "Humph." Her voice went low. "Must be the Black Irish in her."

"I heard that," Libby sniped.

"I'm just sayin'."

Vincent Welles moved his head from side to side, his neck creaking in the process, then eased away from the table, limping and muttering something about "crazy women" under his breath.

Watching him stop at the bar to pay his tab, Rissa closed her phone and laid it on the table. "Men like that make you glad that there are decent men in the world like AJ."

"Tell the truth and shame the devil, chile." Jeanette's shoulders rocked as she sipped her drink. Then she got seriously tickled and laughed until she was gasping for air. She had to slap her breast to clear her throat. "Remember when you first met AJ?"

"How could I ever forget?" Marlea dropped her head and laughed. "No one will ever say I went looking for love. He just earned it."

Marlea's obvious comfort in being so close to the man was not lost on the trainer. *Aw, shucks now! No wonder she's still living at his house and wants him in on her training. She figures he knows her body—even better than me, and under the circumstances, I guess he does. Wonder how long they've been sleeping together? And why didn't she tell me?*

Probing a tooth with her tongue and watching the woman across from her, Libby recalled how very fine AJ Yarborough was the last time she had seen him, and had to raise her beer. "Well, I ain't mad at you."

"That makes two of us," Connie giggled, clinking her glass against Libby's bottle.

"Oh, my goodness." Jeanette worked a hand over her mouth, trying not to laugh. "And how about how he got you up and walking?"

Marlea's mouth dropped open. "You know about that?"

"Honey, Grady's a big hospital, but we were all talking about you and AJ."

"And how he got you to walk," Connie chimed in, dodging Jeanette's elbow. "Of course I can only repeat what I've heard, but I heard he was a pretty good kisser."

"Now where did you hear that?"

"Hospital." Connie giggled again. "He looks like a good kisser, and you've got to respect that in a man. I know I do."

"Okay." Marlea raised her hands in defense. "I respect him. He earned that, too."

"Ooh, you're blushing," Rissa happily pointed out.

"Y'all are embarrassing me." Burying her face in her hands, Marlea shook her head. "Just stop it." Raising her head, tucking her hair behind her ears, she took a deep breath and tried to keep a straight face. "Can we talk about something else?"

"Okay, okay." Libby signaled for another round of drinks. "But back to you, girl. Congratulations on completing your first race since the surgery."

"Hear, hear!" Rissa drummed her palms against the tabletop. "She ran a great race, and I ought to know. I was behind her every step of the way."

Cassie materialized at the table, sweeping empty glasses and bottles onto her tray and setting down fresh drinks. "On the house," she said. "I just want you to know that I didn't send him over here, and I had no idea he was gonna act that way. I hope you'll accept my apology."

"For what?" Marlea fanned her hand. "You didn't raise him, and I'm not about to let his issues mess up my night out."

"I'm glad." Cassie squeezed her arm and smiled. "Y'all let me know if I can do anything else for you."

"That girl's gonna get a real nice tip from me." Libby grabbed the fresh Corona and squeezed the lime wedge into the beer. Tipping the bottle to her lips, she sighed and swallowed. "You took that real well."

"I did, didn't I?" Marlea swirled a straw through her drink and sipped.

"AJ would have been proud of you," Rissa said.

"I'm proud of myself. First, I run a race and now I move on past a dog—and I didn't even limp in the process." Marlea high-fived Connie and Jeanette.

"Anyway," Libby said, resting the bottle on the cocktail napkin in front of her. "I was just gonna say that I knew I could count on you to run again, and it sounds like you went and found a man in the process."

"You're real funny, Libby, and I can see that you think it's a joke, but you know how they say that the only things you can count on in life are death and taxes? Well, I can add two more things that I can count on." Marlea raised her glass for a toast and urged the others to do the same. "For better or for worse, I'll never run the 400 again, but I'll never have to doubt AJ Yarborough. Never."

Rissa quickly touched her glass to Marlea's, and the other women joined them in turn. Only Jeanette heard Libby murmur, "Never say never," as she brought her drink to her lips.

CHAPTER 26

. . . I've got him back in my arms again, so satisfied . . .
The old song played through Marlea's thoughts for the
thousandth time since she had awakened in AJ's arms.
*He's back from New York; he's back in my bed. Does it get
any better than this?* Turning from the broad library windows, Marlea pulled her thoughts back into the house
and cradled her mug of herbal tea. Looking over Rissa's
shoulder, her mind caressed thoughts too precious to
share, and her skin shivered beneath her cotton shirt,
remembering his touch.

*AJ's back and things are better than I could have ever
dreamed.* It seemed that he held her closer since his
return, treasuring her as never before. *I've never felt like
this about a man, and I swear that if anyone had ever told
me I could feel this good about another human, I would
have called him or her a fool.* Her skin remembered what
it was like to feel his warm length, and tingled.

Marlea lowered her face to the cup and sipped lightly.
It wouldn't do for Rissa to catch her looking so happy.
*She would only run off and tell her brother what he already
knew.*

"Darn, I thought I'd bookmarked it. I thought it was
DreenScapes.com. Am I right? Read the Website off to
me again. It's www . . . what's the rest of it?" Rissa looked

up from the computer's flat screen and waved her hand in front of Marlea's face. "Hello? Are you in there?"

"Yeah, of course. What did you ask me?" Marlea sipped more tea.

"That must be some awfully good tea," Rissa observed. "I asked if you remembered the DreenScape Website. I wanted to show you her new designs. She's got some things that would be perfect . . . Marlea! Are you listening to me?"

"Um," Marlea was saved by the telephone. She pointed to the one on the desk at Rissa elbow. "Telephone," she announced brightly.

"You're nuts." Rissa's eyes were on Marlea as she answered the telephone, and they changed to marked curiosity as she greeted the caller. "How can I help you, Mr. Charles?" She listened and nodded. "Could you hold for just a moment?"

Pressing the mute button, Rissa turned to Marlea. She held the phone out in front of her, but gripped it tightly. "This is Dexter Charles. He's Parker Reynolds's attorney, and he wants to speak to you."

"To me?" Marlea's fingers lost their strength and the thick mug fell to the floor, sloshing warm tea over her bare feet. "Why? What does he want with me?"

A dozen explanations rushed across Rissa's pretty face. "You'll have to ask him yourself."

"You never kept a secret in your life, Rissa. What does he want with me?"

Gesturing with the phone, she shook her head. "You'll have to ask him yourself."

Taking the phone, Marlea pressed the mute button. She could hear rustling in the background, but no voices. "Hello?"

"Good morning, Ms. Kellogg." Dexter Charles had a surprisingly pleasant voice, but it did little to calm the oily wave of anger-tinged fear that ambushed Marlea. "I'm calling at the request of my client, Dr. Parker Reynolds."

"Why?" Fumbling backward, the back of Marlea's leg found the edge of the deep leather sofa fronting the mahogany shelves. She fell to the cushions.

"I'm sure that you're aware that after his arrest, Dr. Reynolds admitted his part in your accident. His guilty plea was entered and accepted, subsequently the criminal portion of your case has been completed. Dr. Reynolds is currently serving his sentence in the Fulton County jail."

"That doesn't explain your calling me." Marlea held the phone in both hands and tried to keep it still against her ear. "How did you know I was here, and why are you calling me?"

"I admit that it took some doing to locate you, but Grady Hospital was helpful. The reason for my call is that my client has asked to see you."

"I can't imagine why. It's not like we have anything in common except, oh yeah, he's the man who nearly killed me in an accident, then cut off my toes and ended any chance I had at completing a goal I worked toward my entire life, and then lied about it. Gee, I'm not feeling very chatty, and especially not with him. Does this surprise you?"

"Certainly. Your feelings are highly understandable, so I'm not going to hold you," Dexter soothed. "But I would like to leave you with a thought."

"What is it?"

"You will have to face this if you intend to get on with your life. And you're a young woman, Ms. Kellogg. You'll be on this planet for, oh, another fifty or sixty years. That's a long time to leave hate and anger unresolved."

Drawing a long breath, Marlea tried to frame an appropriate response. She settled for, "Thank you. I'll think about it."

"He wants to see you, right? To make amends?" From her place at the desk, Rissa watched Marlea's face. The softly satisfied feminine glow she'd worn since AJ's return was gone. "You gonna do it?"

"Hell, no." Marlea dropped the phone to her side on the sofa. Wrapping her arms around herself, she slid lower into the cushions and shook her head. "It's enough that he's serving his misdemeanor charges consecutively. What possible good could it do for me to see him? So I could stand in front of him and call him a sorry son of a bitch?" She sucked her teeth and shook her head. "No, I can't see it."

"Are you really willing to let him off that easily?"

"What?" Marlea's eyes searched the other woman's face. "You want me to pursue a civil case? Cut him off at the fiscal knees for what he's done?" She made a face. "The settlement we've already come to is fine, and he won't be able to practice for a while. All he can do is offer more money, so what is there to talk about?"

"How about closure, Marlea?" On the desk, the computer screen snapped into darkness for a long moment before the screen saver activated, bringing bright tropical fish to roam the screen. Rissa's fingers drummed the desk and her lips twitched. "Part of your healing lies in forgiveness, in letting go of the pain and getting on with your life, doesn't it? How much more of your life are you going to let him take away from you—even by accident?"

"Is that part of the 'Lawyer's Creed', or something? That's basically what Charles Dexter said."

"Don't get crabby with me, girl. Even though I practice a whole different kind of law, Marlea, I don't want to see you cut off your nose to spite your face."

"And it's such a pretty nose." AJ stepped into the library and headed straight for Marlea. Dropping heavily to her side on the sofa, he stretched a long arm behind her, and seemed satisfied when she pulled her knees close to her body and leaned against him. "What's going on? Why do you two look so tense?"

Marlea closed her eyes, anticipating the inevitable, and Rissa did not disappoint.

Standing, backing toward the door, Rissa tuned up. "Marlea just got a phone call." Pausing in the doorway, she delivered the pitch. "Charles Dexter is Parker Reynolds's attorney. He called because Reynolds wants to talk to Marlea, but she doesn't want to talk to him. I think she should, for closure, but she definitely should and as soon as possible. It might be easier if you went with her, AJ, but she should definitely go." And Rissa disappeared around the edge of the door.

"Big mouth," Marlea sulked.

AJ's brow rose. "You know, she's done that ever since we were kids, and I'm still surprised every time it happens." He sighed and looked down at the woman curled into his side. "So what do you want to do, Silk?"

Silk. The nickname made her smile and Marlea moved her hand across his chest, comforted by his solidity. *I never had a real nickname before.* Oh, sure, kids had called her 'Speedy' and 'Hotfoot' and such, but she had never enjoyed the intimacy of a name so private and connecting until AJ.

Returning from New York, embracing her in the night, holding her against his skin, he had told her that he had missed her, that he had never felt more whole. He had told her that she felt like silk, and held her closer than shadow. In silvery early morning light, he had called her Silk again, and she cherished the single word every time it crossed his lips.

"Silk?"

"I want to leave well enough alone, AJ. I want to run like I used to, but if I can't have that, I have you and I have teaching. I want to leave well enough alone."

"Can you do that?" Looking down, lifting her chin, he looked into the amber-flecked depths of her eyes. "Look, Silk, I've learned a few things about you. One, you're stubborn as a mule. Two, you don't give up easily. Three, things go real deep with you. So the way I figure it, if you don't face this, it's going to haunt you down the road, and sweet as you are, I don't ever want anything bitter or hurtful in your life. But it's on you."

Pressing her lips together, Marlea looked at AJ and frowned. *How do I plan a life with this man if I leave this big stone unturned? Sure, he'll tell me he understands, but every time I look at him, I'll know that he knows that I ran away from the tail end of a fight.*

AJ took the phone from the sofa and set it on a side table. "You need some time alone, Silk?"

So why see him? I didn't go to court, because I had nothing to say to or about him. I didn't go to his sentencing for the same reason, and now that he's behind bars he's asking to see me. Why?

AJ's fingers curled at her cheek, stroking gently, and she took comfort from the gesture. *He was so good at lying to me, though. He was so good at making me think that he was my friend, that he had my best interests at heart. What kind of sociopath is he? Still . . .* AJ's strong heartbeat sounded in her ear when she moved her face against his chest. *I would never have met AJ if not for Reynolds. And fate.*

Maybe it was fate that sent both our cars down I-75 on Independence Day. Maybe it was a stroke of independence for both of us—breaking both of us away from the lives we thought we were destined for. Me, Olympic gold; him, a life of privilege and pleasure. Humph. Wonder what his money is buying him in jail.

Okay, there's that bitterness AJ spoke of . . . maybe he's right. I deserve the chance to face him and say, "I'm mad as hell at you". I deserve to tell him that I'm glad he's paying for what he did to me. I deserve the chance to tell him that I hope he has to think about what he did for the rest of his life. I deserve . . .

"Silk? Come on, baby, it's all right." AJ rocked her slowly to and fro, and Marlea realized she was crying.

She swiped a balled fist across her cheek and looked at it. "That son of a bitch made me cry. Nobody makes me cry."

"'. . . and nobody puts Baby in a corner . . .'," AJ grinned, quoting the line from *Dirty Dancing*.

"That's your sister's favorite movie, not mine."

"I know, Silk. Yours is *Independence Day*. I'm still a little jealous of Will Smith."

"No need. I much prefer sexy good-looking football heroes," Marlea smiled against his lips. "But you can pass me that phone."

He did. "Want me to stay?"

"Nope. I can do this on my own."

"What's that line from the movie, the one you like so much?" he asked as he stood.

Marlea pressed the recall button and listened as the phone began to ring. *Welcome to earth.*

———❦———

"Marlea, you look wonderful."

How does he do it? Marlea wondered. Dressed in a bright jailhouse orange jumpsuit and obviously worn tennis shoes, Parker Reynolds entered the sterile visitor's area with all the grace and aplomb of a gentleman in his drawing room.

Wary, she watched him take a seat in the ugly green vinyl chair across the steel table from her. Her eyes went from his neatly shaved, much leaner face to the round, brown face of his portly police escort. The officer tried to look bored, as if he had done this hundreds of times, but this visit promised to be interesting and he didn't quite succeed.

This particular prisoner had only been here for a few weeks, and he hadn't had a lot of visitors. His attorney of record, Charles Dexter, came regularly, but the officer guessed that the big-bucks lawyer wasn't paying social calls. He was earning his fat fees. But the buxom sister who flirted her way past the guards was kind of a surprise. She didn't look like this prisoner's type at all, even though she claimed she was the doctor's fiancée, or *feeansay*, as she called it. Whatever she was to the man, all anybody could think was *pump the booty* as she swung by. Well, that and knowing that the doctor must have been praying for conjugal visits from his Desireé.

The only other visitor Parker Reynolds had was an elegant, silver-haired, butter-colored woman, with a full entourage and the kind of demeanor and voice that meant she never had to use the words, 'I'm better than you.' She just took it for granted that she was, and people let her.

It was rumored that the refined and genteel woman was his mother. She only came once, she and her retinue, but word at the desk was that she had reduced the prisoner to a quivering mass. *Probably was his mother*, the thick officer decided.

"I'm sure you're wondering why I requested this meeting," Parker began, his doctor's persona exerting itself. "You see before you a much-humbled man, and I beg your forgiveness."

"Oh, sure. You got any spare toes in your pocket?"

Parker dropped his eyes and a small muscle ticked in his cheek. "I suppose I deserve that."

"You do? When did you grow a conscience? You certainly didn't have one before you got caught."

The officer shuffled his feet in the corner, angling to see better. This slender, good-looking woman had some fire in her, and he didn't plan to miss a single word she said.

"Marlea," Parker passed a suddenly shaky hand over his badly shaven face. "I did feel bad, especially when I got to know you. It's just that this thing, this accident—and it was an accident—it took on a life of its own." Entreating, he held out his hand, but lowered his eyes when she recoiled. "I know you don't believe me, but I never knew how to tell you."

"Dr. Reynolds. Parker. Why did you do surgery on me? You knew what you had done, and still, you used a knife on me. What if I had died?"

Weak -eyed, Parker shook his head. "But you didn't die. I was on duty that day, and I may not be good at a lot of things, but I am a competent surgeon. I was in rotation, and it was my job to give you the best possible care I could, anyway. You weren't meant to die, Marlea— not that day, and not by my hand."

"So now you're God's agent? Why did you do it?"

"I was . . . weak . . . afraid. I didn't know what else to do."

Marlea looked at the officer who moved closer, standing directly behind Parker's chair. "You know, I'm not even sure why I agreed to come here today. I've had to learn a lot and make a lot of adjustments in my life— and not by choice. So the only question I have left for you is, what did you get out of all this?"

"I suppose you could say that I've had to learn to stand up and be a man." Parker's left shoulder rose and fell in a halting shrug. "My mother talked to the judge, you know, but it didn't do a lot of good. It was Judge Barrett. He lost his wife and daughter in a hit-and-run accident last year, so he didn't look kindly on me—even with my family name and my mother's intervention." Parker trailed a finger along the edge of the table. "Maybe it was because of my family. Anyway, he denied Dexter's motion to have me serve all of my misdemeanor sentences concurrently. I'll be here for eighteen months, then I'll do house arrest for a full thirty-six more months. Four and a half years to serve, and I won't be able to practice medicine for a total of five years."

"It took you less than a minute to run me into a wall," Marlea said softly.

"And now I'm paying for it. Marlea, I'm sorry." He dropped his head heavily to his chest. "What will you do next?"

"Go back to teaching. What else can I do?"

"You can run. It's a part of your gift, Marlea."

"I ran a 10K a little while ago, but it wasn't the same as the 400." She noticed the high-barred window in the room for the first time, and wondered why the building's designer had even bothered. Nearly six feet off the floor, what could anyone see out of it?

Parker's brow furrowed and his lips turned down. "Marlea, does this mean you haven't tried to run the 400 since the surgery? Why hasn't Yarborough tried it with you?"

"Maybe because the 400 requires toes. The need for weight balance is huge, not to mention the overall demand on the forefoot . . . but, you already know that, don't you?"

Parker pushed his chair back from the metal table between them and peered under it. The watching officer looked, too. Straightening, Parker looked at Marlea. "You've seen a pedorthist, and you've been fitted for shoes." He pointed beneath the table. "Those work for you?" Barely waiting for her nod, he demanded, "You have running shoes, too?" She nodded again, and Parker threw up both hands. "Then why in the world isn't he training you?"

"You've got a lot of nerve quizzing me. What are you talking about—AJ training me? For what?"

"For the 400, Marlea. You can still run it. You can still compete."

"You don't know what you're talking about." Marlea's whisky-toned eyes went back to the high little window and she understood why it was there: to prevent hopelessness. At least thought could hope for the promise of freedom that the body couldn't yet achieve.

"Marlea, I do know what I'm talking about, though I don't know all the particulars. You might not qualify for Olympic gold, but what about the Paralympics? Have you thought of that?"

"No, I never really thought about the Paralympics. I mean, I know that they run every four years and that disabled athletes compete, but I never thought . . ."

"You should." Eager, Parker leaned forward. "I'll bet they run the 400 and that you could qualify. It would be a chance for you to run competitively again."

Qualify? Run competitively again? Something in her heart stirred, and logic tried to beat it into submission. *I don't want any special treatment. All I ever wanted was to be the best, but this . . .* The dream reared its head and she almost felt the rush of the wind against her heated skin. "How do you qualify?"

"I'm not sure, but there most certainly has to be a Website."

~~~

She hit 'search' again and stared in fascination as the site swirled into brilliance on the flat monitor. "Are you sure of the spelling, Libby? It's *para*, not *paro*?"

"I'm positive." Libby's confident voice rang out from the speaker. "Tell you the truth, the only thing I'm not positive about is what brought about this interest in the Paralympics."

"I had a chance to talk to someone who brought up the topic. AJ and I discussed it, and decided that we needed to know more."

"I see," Libby hummed. "Did 'we' decide what event you would search?"

Marlea turned to AJ. He grinned and leaned back into the depths of his chair, checking the pages Marlea had already printed from sites she had found.

"We're looking at the 400, of course. I talked to Adrian Kessler this morning, and he wants to know if I would consider a series of articles based on my training and centered on female athletes and sports rehab issues. I told him I would, and I figure that if the Paralympics has an event and I can qualify, I think it would be . . . a good thing."

"It sounds like you've already made up your mind about this 'good thing'."

Marlea tried not to hear the implications lurking behind Libby's words. The computer search list jumped to life on the screen. Marlea checked the bottom of the page—more than thirty pages of results. "You were right."

"Have you decided on a coach yet? You know, I'm still mostly in Florida these days." She sounded as if she already knew the answer.

"I actually do have a candidate in mind, someone that I have the utmost confidence in." Pulling another copy from the printer, Marlea stood and flipped through the sheets. Satisfied that she had them all, she turned to drop into the chair facing AJ.

"That would be AJ, right?"

"Who else?"

Libby hummed. "Just don't get hurt, Marlea."

"Jealous, Libby?" AJ smiled and pulled Marlea's bare feet into his lap.

Libby cleared her throat loudly over the line. "Not me, because y'all are both grown, but I swear if you weren't at home, I would have to tell you to get a room."

"I don't know what you're talking about." Marlea sank low in her chair, almost ready to purr when AJ stroked her sole.

"Yeah, you do. I can hear it in your voice, and I don't have to be subject to your lust. I'm hanging up now."

"Now, look what you did," Marlea teased, moving her foot in AJ's lap.

"Me?" He looked down at his lap and her probing toes, then up at her with barely disguised glee on his face. "Hard to believe that just a few months ago, you were barely able to let yourself dream of walking again, Silk, and now here we are planning a competitive run."

"I can't think of anyone I would rather do it with."

"You talking about running?"

Her sensitive foot moved again, making him gasp. "That, too," she said.

CHAPTER 27

Cascade Center, NY

AJ, I don't know about this. Even with all they had done—finding the application, getting medical documentation, submitting verification on the shoes she wore to run, and the endless training—it was scary. *What if I can't make a legal start? What if I fall again? I haven't fallen in more than six weeks, but as nervous as I am, it could happen again.*

Think positive, she admonished herself, but it was hard.

It's been a long time. I said that, and AJ said I was scared. I'm not scared. I just don't want to fail—him or me. Marlea jigged from foot to foot, tried to shake the tension out of her shoulders and legs, and hoped none of the other women in the locker room would notice her jitters. Around her, women in various stages of undress paid her little or no attention.

Bending over her gym bag, Marlea pulled out her shoes and socks, looking at them as though they had appeared out of thin air. *These are the same kind of socks and shoes I've trained in. They're not magic. The magic is going to have to come from my heart and my feet. That's what AJ said.*

I hope to God he's right.

Her stomach cramped abruptly and she dropped a shoe—*not a good sign.*

A slender hand, skin bright as polished brass, caught the shoe before it hit the floor. "I can only stay a minute, but AJ thought it might help to see a familiar face before you ran, and they wouldn't let him in here," Rissa grinned, dropping to the bench beside Marlea.

"How am I gonna run if you hang onto my shoe?"

Rissa pulled at the shoestring then handed the shoe back. "The way you always do, girl." She slipped an arm around Marlea's shoulders and squeezed. "You're gonna run like it's the only thing in the world. I've watched you, and I know you can do it. AJ made me hold the stopwatch when he ran with you, remember? I know you're fast—even if you don't." She squeezed her shoulder again. "Oh, and I have something for you. It was delivered right after you left the house, and I know you're going to want it."

Curious, Marlea accepted the small white envelope and slit the flap cautiously. She took her time shaking the single page free. Opening it, she found a narrow bracelet, red, yellow, and orange yarn braided into a diamond pattern. "This has to be from one of my kids."

"You would know for sure if you read the note."

"Thanks, Rissa. I can always count on you to point out the obvious." She ignored Rissa's wrinkled face and began reading:

Hi Miss Kellogg,

My mom showed me your picture in the paper. It made me very proud, especially when they said that you were not a quitter and that you were going to run again. Looks like the sun really has come up for you. I made this bracelet so you would remember how much I love you. When you run, I think it will help you win.

> *Your friend,*
> *Katie Charles*
> *PS: Don't forget to smile when you cross the finish line!*

"Hey, that's one of your kids, right? You gonna wear the bracelet?" Without waiting for an answer, Rissa seized the bracelet. "Hold out your arm."

"Like I have a choice." Marlea extended her arm obediently and Rissa twisted the yarn into place.

The small talisman seemed to work instantly. Marlea's stomach stopped grinding and her heart lifted. "I can do this." She pulled her shorts and shirt from the bag, then plunged her hand into the depths again and found her bra. "You need to go find your seat and deliver a message for me. You tell AJ for me that I'm about to blow the dust off this old field."

"Wow." Relieved to see the change of attitude, a newly relaxed Rissa asked, "Anybody ever tell you that you're sexy when you're psyched?"

"Yeah." Marlea stood and unzipped her sweat jacket. "Your brother."

"And you believed him?" Rissa ducked when Marlea draped her jacket over her head.

"Every time."

—∞—

Exhaling slowly, Marlea counted eight beats and then sucked in another big breath and let it course through her long, lean frame. Exhaling again, she pushed through the heavy metal door and stood outside. Cool, early-fall morning air pricked at her skin, raising goose bumps and her spirits. She fingered the yarn bracelet and squared her shoulders.

Ahead of her, on a slight rise, she could see the track and the field. "Dang, I'm thirty-four and ready to giggle like an eight-year-old just because I get a chance to run."

"Me, too." Tall as Marlea and thin as a racehorse, the other woman smiled. "Kendra Asaou," she said, offering her hand. "This is your first race? I have not seen you before."

Marlea smiled. "Not my first race, but my first race since my . . . accident."

"The first one coming back is always a little hard." Stepping back, setting her hands against her lean hips, Kendra's black eyes roamed over Marlea. "What has changed? You look perfect—and fast."

"I'm an amputee," Marlea said, surprised that she didn't stutter. "I lost two toes in my accident."

Kendra's eyed Marlea's feet, inspecting her shoes. "Ah. What do you run?"

"The 400. What's your event?"

"Hundred meters and relay. The 400 is too much for me." Kendra ran a hand over her short, tight afro. "You said you had an accident?"

"Yes, it was a hit-and-run car accident. My car was struck, hit the wall, and I wound up in surgery. "

"The loss of the toes must wreak havoc on your balance and speed. You must be very strong, and one hell of a runner." Kendra realized that Marlea's eyes looked expectant. "Oh, me? I was raised in Canada, had an accident on my family's farm when I was sixteen. It's my leg, and believe me, I missed out on a lot of dances and races." She patted her thigh, the sound muffled by her long sweat pants. She smiled brightly when she saw the look on Marlea's face.

"I make my home in Florida now, though. The last name is my husband's."

"You're married? What about . . ."

"The prosthesis?" Kendra laughed. "My Paul couldn't care less about what I don't have. He loves everything about me that he does have. I love him, too. Mostly because he taught me to celebrate the blessings." She put a hand on Marlea's arm. "I kind of think that that's the reason we get challenges like this, so that we know what to appreciate in this life." She leaned close and whispered. "I know what you're thinking. And no, sex has never been a problem. Know what I mean?"

Marlea grinned and looked at her feet. She thought of AJ and blushed. "Uh, yeah, I think I do know what you mean."

"Oh, you're that lucky, are you?" Laughing, Kendra squeezed Marlea's arm.

A loudspeaker blared from the field. "Oh, my. Just when the conversation was getting interesting." Kendra looked annoyed. "They're calling the warm-up for my race." She gripped Marlea's hand and shook hard. "Best of luck on your race. Hope we'll meet again."

"Me, too. Best of luck, Kendra, and let's both qualify for the U.S. team." Marlea had just enough time to wave as the other woman trotted to the field. "Qualify for the U.S. team. Least I'm not dreaming small."

Visualizing herself heading for a lane and bending to the blocks, Marlea's fingers twisted the yarn bracelet as she concentrated on what it would feel like to release the power and run. *I can do this.* Sliding her hands over her sleek head, she walked to her assigned area. Ponytail intact, she tried to focus, to recall Libby's mind/body routine.

"Marlea!" For a moment, it seemed she had heard her name, but it was so far away, too far away to distinguish as she bent to stretch. "Marlea!" She looked up into the mass of faces above her and was struck by the abundance of movement and color.

"Silk?"

In her ears, the nickname made a sound like no other and claimed her immediate attention. Her head jerked high, and she saw him.

"You know I had to bribe two security guards to get this close?"

"But am I worth it?" Marlea straightened and jammed her fists against her hips.

"What kind of question is that? You know you are." AJ reached down from the stands, his fingers just close enough to brush the tips of hers. Truth was, he had handed over a couple of hundred in cash and signed a dozen autographs. But he would never complain, not when it earned him the look that danced in the liquid depths of her eyes and the smile that dawned on her face when she saw him.

Marlea's fingertips touched her lips before she reached to touch his fingers. "I'll see you at the finish line."

"It's a date," he promised.

In the distance, Marlea heard the call for the 400. Touching AJ's fingers again, she smiled. "I gotta go, but you'd better not stand me up."

"Ain't no way." He watched her face as she backed away from the stands. "I'll be right there to meet you, Silk," he whispered as she turned and ran toward her place on the track.

Pulling her thoughts away from AJ and focusing on the race took some effort, but she managed to find the number four slot without incident. "Number four," she whispered to herself. "That's got to be my lucky number. It was my number in St. Louis, and I ran the race of a lifetime there. It's going to be good for me here, too."

Hands on her hips, she walked to the start and took a deep breath. Looking at the three women on her left and the two on her right, she realized that she was running in a field of six. *I guess that either makes us six of the fastest women in the country without full use of one foot, or we're the six who never realized what we couldn't do.*

Kicking her toes along the dirt track, Marlea wiped her hands against her shorts, then pressed her hands against her thighs. Flushed with a sudden sense of kinship, she smiled at the women lined up next to her. It felt good when they smiled back, offering competition and fellowship. *Good luck to all of you,* Marlea thought, *but I'm taking this one. This is my race.*

"*Runners, take your marks . . .*" Four little words that anchored so much of her life sent shivers racing up her legs. But it was the tingling in her foot that made her think of the first time AJ touched her.

"*Get set . . .*"

The stance was slightly modified from the one that Marlea had used for most of her running life, but it kept her head up high enough to sight the finish line, and to see AJ's gold and white jacket move through the crowd.

"*Go!*"

Her face tightened and her arms pumped when she heard the crack of the starter's pistol. The first strike of Marlea's foot against the cinder track ignited the speed in her soul. With no thought for anything but the run, she picked up her pace and grinned at the struggling woman next to her, fighting to stay even and praying to pass.

Seeing challenge in the woman's eye, Marlea dug deeper and pulled on her resolve. *It's only 400 meters.* Driving hard, her chest burned and threatened to burst at 200 meters, but she could see the goal. *Breathe!* When the woman fell steps behind, Marlea could almost feel the push of time against her hot skin.

In the stands, binoculars found the number four runner and held. Her head was high, shoulders level, and her hips tight. Marlea had a nice long stride, the rhythm setting her ponytail swinging, and she seemed determined to finish fast. Her kick was high, and her speed unbound as she crossed the finish line well ahead of the other runners.

Marlea's arms came high and her head fell back as she ran, her throat was arched and tight with triumph when the silvery white banner broke across her chest. Behind the leveled binoculars, Bianca Coltrane's eyes narrowed, and she pushed her full lips together.

"*. . . finishing with a time of . . .*"

"Who, the heck, cares?" Bianca turned in her seat, aimed the binoculars at the hard running figure in the gold-and-white jacket. "AJ." She would have known him anywhere. Around her, the cheering crowd was on its feet and waving flags, sweaters, and anything else they could find. Bianca stood, too, training her binoculars on the track. AJ was running full force when he reached Marlea. "What kind of silly victory dance is that?" Bianca muttered, struggling to dial up the magnification on her field glasses. "She ought to be ashamed of herself."

"You know her?" A big-eyed woman in a baggy tennis sweater looked hopefully up at Bianca, begging her to say yes.

Bianca took her time looking down at the woman. *It's bad enough that I had to leave my apartment today to drive all the way up here to witness this spectacle, and now you want me to act like I'm glad to be here? If I didn't need to know what was going on, I would be . . . I would be doing something more useful than this!*

Bianca didn't bother to utter a word, but when she looked down, her eyes held fire enough to singe the pudgy woman's red hair, and she moved a few steps away before resuming her cheer.

Bianca raised her binoculars again.

On the field, AJ whooped, jumped a fence, and made straight for Marlea. Yelling his name, she leapt for him, landing with her legs wrapped tightly around his hips and her arms threaded around his shoulders. Her face pressed against his, and she might have been crying. "No dignity," Bianca frowned, sitting hard.

Reaching under her seat, Bianca pulled out the leather binocular case and carefully repacked them. "I'll return them to the store on my way home." She tucked the case under her arm and stood to edge her way along the row of seats to the aisle. Gritting her teeth, she picked her way down the steep stairs and headed for the exit, all the time debating her next move.

She stopped talking to herself out loud when a pair of tall beer-bellied strangers offered to show her a good time. Keeping her thoughts to herself, she bared her teeth at them, then hastened from the stadium. *She's a winner now, and she's got a hold on him; their bond will be stronger than ever. But I can't let that get in my way. I saw him first, he loved me first, and he's still mine. That means that I'll have to shatter this relationship irreparably if I'm going to break AJ away from her.*

So what will it really take to drive them apart? If it were just AJ, it would be all about trust. Clearly, that little hot-footed ragamuffin is going nowhere. Bianca thought hard. According to all the gossip she had heard, and she had heard plenty from her little clique of Atlanta-based spies,

Marlea Kellogg would have cut off her whole foot before she would betray AJ.

She's a woman in love; even Ray Charles could have seen that. Bianca had a sharp mental flash of Marlea's face when AJ showed up on the field, and it made her head hurt. Marlea's was the face of a woman in deep and unshakable love.

Well, her love might be unshakable—for now, but . . . where there's a will, there's a way.

It's hard to believe that she still trusts him so completely after his trip to New York. Then it dawned on her. *He didn't tell her about New York!* Bianca almost skipped across the parking lot's asphalt. Her stiletto-heeled sandals were hurting her feet when she finally found her rental car and slid behind the wheel, but she couldn't have cared less. *Omission opens doors that hands can never touch.* Relieved, she slipped the sandals off and massaged her feet. *Where to begin?*

CHAPTER 28

Walking briskly in her new Payless flats, Bianca Coltrane stepped carefully around the loose gravel in the Wal-Mart parking lot and headed for her rental car. *And to think, I swore that once I got old enough to do better, I would never put anything this cheap on my body again.* She checked the plastic bag holding her red-soled Louboutin sandals and ignored the white-haired man waiting in the ancient gray Buick. *He's certainly got more time than he has money. He can wait for me to move.* Taking her time, she walked on. *At least my feet don't hurt.*

Jamming the key into the door, she looked around to see if anyone had noticed her. *No,* she decided, *they're all too busy scrambling for 'values.' Besides, no one I know would ever shop at a place like this.* She slid into the car seat, slamming the door behind her. *I can't believe it's come to this—discount shopping, and twice in one day. Ugh!*

But you do what you have to do to get where you have to go. Folding the credit slip into a pocket of her Coach bag, she thought of Taurean Odom. *Thank God he's still in love with me and hasn't yet cut off the credit cards he gave me. He's not all that bright, but at least he was generous during the time we were together, thank goodness. The Lord knows I don't know what I would do without my wallet crammed with his gold and platinum cards.*

Opening her wallet, she fingered the credit cards. They all bore her name, but there was no way she could have paid the bills. For now, she was using the MasterCard to pay off the Visa for utilities and transportation and clothes, and the American Express for paying rent and buying groceries. The airline cards were a part of her emergency reserve.

Damn that wretched Guilliame des Verriers. She cursed him for the twentieth time that day. *If he hadn't made such a tacky mess of my fall line and then bad-mouthed me to every other buyer in the country, I would be doing this strictly for love—not money.*

And even with that little cripple in the way, I do love, AJ—in my own way. I love the security he offers. She looked back at the big white-and-blue Wal-Mart sign. *With AJ, I'll never have to shop here again or clip another coupon. Besides that, I love that he's not mean, and that his kind of love focused on me as if I was the only woman in the world—kind of like a warm and soothing light. He made me . . . better, somehow.* Bianca remembered the feeling and judged it worth having again. *And keeping, maybe for the rest of my life. I could be faithful to him, if I had to.* She thought about it. *Or at the least, I could avoid getting caught the next time.*

She shoved her purse to the passenger-side, and took the folded newspaper from the seat. "Now where did it say the competitors were staying?"

Rereading the article, Bianca finally found what she was looking for. "The Hilton Inn West," she read.

Pulling a pen from her bag, she circled it. "I can't just go walking up in there without a plan. How do I get to her?"

A minivan pulled into the parking slot next to her, and a denim-clad blonde woman climbed out. Bianca fumbled with her door and finally managed to lock it. The blonde slung an oversized tote onto her shoulder and bent at the waist to peer into Bianca's window. Seeing Bianca clearly, her full lips formed a surprised 'O', then she smiled apologetically. She mimed rolling the window down.

Cautious, Bianca lowered the glass just a bit.

"Honey, I am so sorry to startle you. It's just that your car looks like the one a friend of mine drives." She looked sweetly sorry and laced her fingers in front of her. "I said something to her that I shouldn't have, and since she was coming over here, I thought I would catch her off-guard and apologize."

"How sweet," Bianca said. *And I should care, because . . .*

"Not really," the woman demurred. "She's not that good of a friend, more of an annoyance, really. I just don't want to have to deal with any of this later on. I'll say what I need to say, and it'll shut her up, get her out of my way, and I can get on with life." She fingered her blonde tresses. "I guess that makes me sound a little hard-hearted, doesn't it?"

"Not at all," Bianca smiled. "I think it's kind of smart." *And it could work for me, too.*

The woman suddenly straightened. "There she is. I have to go." She gave Bianca's door a pat. "Sorry again. Bye."

"Bye." Bianca savored the cool air flowing into the Stratus through the open window. Suddenly, things were clear. She dug into the Coach bag and found her cellphone. It took less than a minute to get what she needed from information.

~◦◦◦~

Only twenty seconds over my best time, Marlea exalted, pulling the new DreenScape dress from her closet. Holding the dress to her body, she danced across the carpet. *Great time, and I get to celebrate the win with AJ.* She stopped in front of the mirror. *I cannot believe that I'm about to put this beautiful dress on for a man.* She moved her hips and enjoyed the swish of silk chiffon against her terry robe.

The jangle of the telephone drew her away from the mirror. *Must be AJ, and I'm not nearly ready.* She hooked the dress hanger over the door on her way to the phone. "Hello?" she was breathless, but he always left her that way.

"Congratulations," a sultry female voice offered. "I had a chance to see you run today, and you were absolutely inspiring."

"Thank you." Marlea tried to remember where she had heard the voice before. *A reporter?* No, that didn't feel right.

"We may have gotten off on the wrong foot, and I would like the chance to make things right between us."

"You would?"

"Absolutely." The voice seemed to catch. "Oh, my goodness, I'm so sorry. You don't know who this is, do you?"

"No, I don't." Marlea was prepared to hang up, but she was curious. "Who are you?"

Laughing lightly, the caller finally said, "This is Bianca Coltrane, and I really do want you to know how happy I am for you." When Marlea was silent on the other end of the line, Bianca unctuously tried to flatter her into conversation. "It was a beautiful race."

"Thank you."

"I don't blame you for being short with me, after the way I behaved when we met at the reception. I was under duress, but that wasn't your fault. I hope you'll accept my apology."

"Sure . . ."

"If you've got a few minutes, I brought a little token along—something to celebrate your victory, and I'd like to deliver it." Sure that the other woman was falling for her ruse, Bianca tried to breathe normally. "If that's all right?"

"Sure," Marlea finally agreed. "I'm in suite 1028."

"Okay." Bianca shifted the gift shop bouquet she held and looked at the room number she had noted on her newspaper. The room number was never in doubt, it was just a matter of getting through the door. "I'll see you in a few minutes."

Maybe I should just make her hand whatever it is through the door, Marlea was thinking, vividly remembering her painful encounter with Bianca. *Women like that don't give up easily.*

She quickly pulled on jeans and a tee shirt. *Facing her will be bad enough. I should at least not be standing here in a robe when she shows up.* She was still looking for shoes when she heard the knock.

Shoving her feet into running shoes, Marlea opened the door.

"Hi." Standing nearly six feet tall in high-heeled, ankle-wrapped sandals, her body obviously tight in all the right places, Bianca moved her head to swing soft, honey-gold hair over her shoulders. "You gonna invite me in?"

"Sure," Marlea stepped aside and allowed Bianca to enter her room. Closing the door, Marlea couldn't help feeling that the other woman was sucking all the air out of her space.

"These are for you." Bianca held out the bouquet of colorful flowers. "Congratulations."

"Thanks." Accepting the flowers, Marlea wondered why Bianca hadn't had them delivered. And why weren't they in a vase? *This is some kind of a trick.* She folded back the green florist's paper and fingered the petals of a sunflower. It was real. "They're very pretty," she said.

"I hoped you'd like them." Bianca draped herself onto the rose-colored velveteen love seat.

"You said you saw me run today." Flowers in her lap, Marlea sat in the chair across from Bianca. "How did that happen? Do you live near here?"

"Not far." Cascade Center was only three hours away from Manhattan. "I saw your name on the list of competitors and thought that maybe, after our last encounter, I owed you a little moral support. Do you mind?"

"No, not at all." Marlea said, touching the flowers again.

"It's good that you didn't have to face the competition all alone. I thought I saw AJ in the crowd."

She's smooth. Marlea felt her skin crawl. "Yes, he was there."

"Well," Bianca smiled beautifully. "Is he coming here? I would love to see him again."

"We're going to dinner. He should be here any minute now."

"How nice."

Marlea was about to ask Bianca to leave when she heard the knock at her door. She glanced at the clock.

AJ.

Eyes on the other woman and acutely aware that she couldn't be trusted, Marlea went to the door and pulled it open. He couldn't have looked any better. Neat gray slacks paired with a dark cashmere jacket and a striped, open-necked shirt attested to the care he had taken in dressing. *For me.* Marlea's heart took a little leap.

"Silk." Leaning into the open door, AJ put his arm around Marlea's waist and drew her to him for a kiss. "Is that what you're planning on wearing?"

"No." She stepped back and pointed. "I have a guest, AJ."

His eyes widened and then narrowed when he saw her. "Bianca? What are you doing here?"

"What kind of greeting is that?" she pouted. "AJ, you know I always see you when you're in New York." Her movement slow and deliberate, Bianca shifted slightly on the love seat. Long legs crossed at the knee, she smiled, raised an elegant brow, and spread her arms. Her low chuckle said that no further explanation was necessary.

Marlea cocked her head. "You always see her when you're in New York?"

"Why wouldn't he? I almost married him."

"AJ?" Ignoring the anger flooding AJ's face, Marlea pressed. "You didn't tell me you saw her when you were in New York."

"There was nothing to tell."

Bianca made a sucking sound and looked up at the ceiling.

"AJ?" He stared daggers at a blithely unconcerned Bianca. "You know, you promised me the truth. You promised me no drama," Marlea reminded him. "You promised me no drama, and that woman is drama in designer pumps."

"Have you forgotten the last time you were in New York, AJ?" Bianca taunted. "Do you think you would remember if I took off my clothes again?"

Marlea's lips parted and the pain in her eyes was more than AJ could stand. He took a step toward her, his hand extended. "Marlea . . ."

"What, AJ? What are you going to say to me, and why should I trust it? Is it true?"

"Marlea, I don't know what to say."

"Say that it's not true, AJ. Say that you didn't see her the last time you were in New York. Say that she didn't take her clothes off for you. Say something to make me believe you."

"It wasn't like that, Marlea."

"What was it like, AJ? And if it was so innocent, why didn't you say something to me?"

"Marlea, Bianca's twisted . . ."

"She has a point, AJ." Steeped in satisfaction, Bianca crossed her long legs and arranged herself more seductively on the velveteen love seat.

"Bianca."

Her name on AJ's lips sounded flat and bereft of emotion, but still more than Marlea could take. "What kind of fool do I look like to you, AJ? I wasn't smart enough to see the player in you, but I'm not entirely stupid, even if I did trust every word you said to me."

"And now here you are," Bianca said softly.

"Bianca, could you shut the hell up?" AJ said, standing between the two women. "Marlea, I don't want her. What do I look like to you?"

"You look like someone with no interest in a whore, and I understand that, 'cause I'm not interested in whores either, AJ."

"Marlea . . ."

Her raised hand and tightly drawn face stopped him. "This is my room, and neither of you are welcome here. You both need to go."

Bianca had the grace to follow AJ and then flinch when Marlea slammed the door behind them.

"Possessive, isn't she?" Bianca sniped.

"Why did you try to make it sound like something happened between us?"

"It might have. Besides, you were the one who didn't tell her, and it's not my fault if her imagination got the better of her." Looking into AJ's furious eyes, she smiled slyly. "Besides, I would cheat on her with me, if I were you. Better still, I would marry me and keep her on the side—if that's what you want. She's low maintenance, no threat."

AJ paced in agitation. "You know what? I . . . I'm not even sure why she let you through her door."

"AJ, please. I told you before that I was tired of you playing the innocent victim. You know she let me in for the same reason you always do—to see what would happen."

He blew hard air. "With you, I always know what'll happen."

Dismissive, Bianca flexed her fingers. "It's the man in you that does it. It's always the same with men. I figured that out a long time ago. You know, now that I think of it, it was the first time I showered with a man. There I was, all set to be in love, and brother was looking good and saying all the right things. It should have been romantic, but just before we stepped out of the water, I looked down at my nails. They were filthy: dirt and oil, all kinds of gunk under them.

"He caught me looking and turned up his nose when he saw what I was looking at. 'Ugh,' he said. 'You sure are dirty.' But it never occurred to him that I hadn't touched myself, only him. Turned out later that he was as dirty on the inside as he was on the outside, and he only wanted to be with me to see what would happen."

"That's a sad story, Bianca, but I don't have a role in it."

"Maybe not that one, AJ. But think of it as an illustration of sorts. You're kind of like him. You look at her, and all you can see is what you want to see—a chance to be noble." She shrugged. "Okay, maybe she's got some kind of party trick she can do with what's left of her foot, and the sex is . . . exotic. But you really are like him. You're taking what you want from her because you want to see what happens, and then afterwards, you'll be blameless because you did the right thing."

"You're talking crazy. I don't have it like that with her." He paced again. "You wouldn't understand."

"Whatever." Bianca planted a hand on his chest to stop him. "Where's your room, AJ? Let me remind you of what I have to offer."

"I'm about sick of you, Bianca." Gripping her wrist, AJ moved her hand. "There's a name for the kind of woman you are, and you're counting on my being too kind to use it. Marlea was right; you're a whore, but you're not my whore."

Her fingers curled over his, and she drew their joined hands to her lips. "AJ, you don't mean that. You can't."

"I mean everything I've said to you." Pulling his hand free, AJ frowned. "I'm not going to stand out here and trade insults with you, Bianca. But while I have your attention, let me break it down for you: I know you're having money problems, but we don't have the kind of relationship that would allow me to step in any further. You haven't earned any brownie points with me, and I'm not in the market for what you're selling."

"You know?" Her suddenly savage eyes raked his tall figure. "You arrogant son of a bitch. You put me through all this, and you knew? You could have saved me from this humiliation, and you didn't? When did you know?"

"When you forged my signature to sell the condo."

Bianca's mouth opened and closed as she gulped air.

"Capital City Bank called when you emptied the account there, too. They wanted me to know that your forgery was a federal offense because you used a wire transfer over state lines."

Disbelief forced her to take a step back. "You pressed charges against me?"

"I don't want to see you in jail, Bianca, but I do want you out of my life."

"I don't have to take this from you, AJ," she said, tossing her hair back. "I have friends, true friends that I can turn to."

"Yeah, you probably do. But I'm not going to discuss it any further. You need to go on to wherever you were headed before you came here. I have something else to do."

The Coach bag hung heavily in her hand, but she had to ask. Lifting her chin and posing bravely, she faced AJ's back. "Have you told anyone else about this?" Her voice quivered almost as much as her lips.

He turned slowly, the expression on his face unreadable. "Not yet, but I could give Taurean a call. He might prefer to hear it from me instead of someone from the credit-card companies. What do you think?"

Bianca's eyes fastened on her feet, and her lips folded into a tired, defeated line. When she looked at AJ again, she was resigned. "So it's finished, then?"

"It's finished. I made Marlea a promise, and it doesn't include you."

On her side of the door, Marlea pressed her eye to the peephole. She could see AJ's back, and Bianca's face. First sure, then bitter, and finally crushed, emotions rushed across the woman's finely defined features. Marlea could see the ex-lovers clearly, but hearing was harder. But she did hear AJ's final words, and she lost the battle with her tears.

I made Marlea a promise, and it doesn't include you.

"I guess that promise came with an expiration date."

There was a tap at her door. "Silk . . ."

Shaking her head and choked by anger, Marlea backed away from the door. "Don't call me that. You don't have the right any more."

"Silk, come on, please open the door . . ."

Going back to the door, Marlea took another look at him. She put her back to the door and wished she couldn't hear him. When he called to her again, her knees failed and she slid to the floor, weeping for what was lost.

CHAPTER 29

Martha Baldwin's glare was heavy with unspoken threat. "Boy, you done messed up now. That girl is in there packing her bags. She's moving back to Marietta. What did you do?"

"It's more like what I didn't do." AJ dropped the Vuitton tote at the housekeeper's feet and kept moving. Not to be outdone, she stepped over the tote and followed him.

"What's that supposed to mean? She leaves here with you and Rissa and Dench. Y'all call back here screaming that she did so well in her race. Next thing I know, a lone cab comes screechin' up to the door, and she tears through here talking about going home. Do you know it's danged near one in the morning? What kind of fool-ishness is going on up in here?"

Outside Marlea's door, AJ stopped and faced Martha. "Tell you what, I'll let you know when I know."

"Don't you take that tone with me, boy." She wiped her hands on her robe, then pointed a sharp finger at him. "Whatever your problem is with her, it's not with me. I live in this house, too, and whatever affects y'all, affects me. You love that girl enough to walk through fire for her, and yet you're out of this house, out of this city for two days, and look at the mess!" The wagging finger was joined by four others, forming a fist, which she didn't hesitate to shake at him. "Whatever you did wrong, you get in there and fix it!"

Martha huffed and started back down the long, moon-dappled hall. She stopped briefly and looked back at AJ. "I'm not playing with you, boy. Git through that door and do what you have to do." She flapped her arms at him. "Git!"

Behind, Rissa and Dench came running.

"Are they here?" Rissa lowered her voice and stopped running when Martha raised a finger to her lips. "They are here?" Her hand on his arm slowed Dench when Martha nodded.

"So what was the rush? Why did they leave us?" Dench whispered to Rissa. She gave him a look that made him wish he had kept the question to himself.

"They left before us," Rissa tried to explain when Martha Baldwin crossed her arms across her chest. "We wouldn't have known if we hadn't spotted AJ running from the hotel. We thought Marlea was with him, so we followed."

"Yeah," Dench nodded. "Good thing Delta has about a gazillion flights to and from New York."

Rissa heaved a sigh. "We saw AJ jump in a cab and heard him tell the driver to head for the airport. He went to Kennedy. Not thinking, we went to Newark."

"And got here just in time for the fireworks," Martha finished, shoving her hands into the pockets of her robe.

Rissa looked confused. "Why is he standing at Marlea's door like that? We all flew back to Atlanta as though something earth-shattering was going on here, and he's standing there." Cupping her hands around her mouth, she asked, "Why!"

"Shush!" Martha hissed, waving her arms. "Back up. Leave him alone." She turned to Rissa and Dench. "You two come on in the kitchen with me." When they were slow to move, she waved her hands again, shooing them down the hall. "He made the mess; let him clean it up."

Knowing the bait that would draw Rissa away from the door, Martha smiled. "Come on in the kitchen," she said, "I'll tell you all about it."

Still, Rissa was reluctant to move.

"It was a real mess before you got here."

"He made a mess? Oooh . . ." Pulling Dench along, Rissa walked toward the kitchen. "What happened? What did we miss?"

AJ was grateful for the small reprieve, but it didn't last long. "Silk?" He tapped at the door and was rewarded with the sound of slamming drawers. "Silk . . . Marlea, it's AJ. Could you open the door? I think we should talk."

More slamming, a closet door this time.

"Marlea?" He knocked at the door again, harder this time. "Marlea, open the door, please."

The slamming stopped and AJ waited. Just as he raised his hand to knock again, the door jerked open. Marlea stood in the doorway, her eyes darkly furious.

Her usual ponytail had come undone in her frenzied packing. The clip hung low, freeing her thick hair to form a halo around her head and shoulders. A dark smudge arched across one cheek, and the remains of her lipstick stained her lips. She had pulled her cotton sweater off and knotted it at her waist. She stood barefoot and glaring.

"I thought we should talk," AJ began, letting his hand fall to his side.

"Great. Your house, your rules." Stepping back, she let the door fall open. When he entered the room, she stayed by the door, standing in the shadow. "What do you think is left to say, AJ?"

He looked at the bed they had shared. "Why did you run away, Silk?"

"Don't call me that, and I didn't run." Moving out of the shadow, Marlea returned to the box she had been packing. Shoving a handful of books into the box, she refused to look at him. "What did you need me for, AJ? A witness?" She flattened the books, then grabbed two more. "Whatever you did with Bianca is your business. You're grown; you get to have business. It's okay. I just took what I thought we had way too seriously. Maybe it's because I've been alone for so long. Hell, you save up all that want and need for a lifetime, and any man starts to look good. I guess you're just lucky I didn't rape you or something."

"What did you think we had, Marlea?"

Wordlessly, she raised a hand and shook her head.

"And you think I would risk that by playing around with Bianca?" AJ sat on the edge of the bed and covered his face with his hand. "Marlea, I didn't say anything about seeing her because there was nothing to tell. I was in New York on business; you knew that. I did what I had to do, then got in after a long day and planned nothing more than talking to you, dinner, and a good night's sleep. I ordered room service . . ."

"And they delivered her on a silver platter. Nice hotel." Marlea ripped a length of packing tape off the roll and sealed the box.

"Close, but not quite. I was in the shower when they delivered dinner, and she walked in with the waiter. She was there when I talked to you, and now you're hurt. I understand that."

"You don't understand anything, and my being 'hurt' doesn't have anything to do with it. You talked to me with her in your room, and you didn't say a word." Marlea stopped folding the flattened cardboard to form a new box and looked at him.

"Wait a minute. It's almost two in the morning. Where did you get boxes from?"

"Not that it's your business, but I kept them when my stuff was moved here. I never planned to stay where I wasn't wanted, AJ, and it seems I've overstayed my welcome." She slapped tape across the bottom of the box.

"Silk . . . Marlea, you're wanted here." Standing, his arms opened wide, entreating. "I wish I could explain Bianca."

"I wish you could, too, but you can't." Marlea ignored his arms and refused to let the tears fall. "You waited too long, AJ. You let her tell me what you should have."

"And if I had?"

Marlea sniffed hard enough to make her head hurt. "I wouldn't have liked it. I would have had questions, but I would have at least had to respect you for respecting me enough to be honest with me."

"You're right," AJ said simply. "I should have said something, but would you have believed me? Especially when I told you that I didn't sleep with her, no matter what she implied when she talked to you."

"Okay, you say you didn't sleep with her—fine." Knowing that she was losing the battle with her tears, Marlea tried to answer around the lump in her throat. "Does it matter?"

"It does to me." Moving his head to see her face more clearly, AJ's eyes probed. "Do you believe me?"

"I don't know, AJ, probably not." Dropping her tape, finding a reason to hide her face long enough to brush away the errant tears, Marlea bent and took her time retrieving it. "Hell, if I had been a man, I would have slept with her. No, to tell the truth, if I were a different kind of woman, I might have slept with her."

"Well, I didn't."

Her accusing eyes were bright with unshed tears, saying what her lips didn't, and she tore another strip of tape from the roll.

AJ smoothed a hand over the bed's comforter. "You remember when you first moved in here? I wasn't all that sure you even liked me, let alone trusted me. A time or two there, I thought I would have to hog-tie you. Yet, you stayed and we made progress together. I liked that, Marlea. I liked working with you. When we got closer, I liked what we had together, and I can't believe it's so easy for you to pack it away in those boxes of yours."

She hung her head low and mumbled something.

"What?"

"I said, I liked it, too."

"Then why are you leaving?"

"Because I feel like I have to." Marlea pushed at her box before looking at AJ. "You know, Bianca once told me that you needed a pet, that it was no wonder that you took me on. She said that you'd always had a soft spot for the underdog." Marlea could almost hear Bianca's voice as she repeated the words. "She said that it must be hard to be treated like a pet by a man I could never have. She figured it would be nice for you to have a pet, even if it couldn't perform." Marlea pressed her fisted hand to her chest. "That's what she said to me, AJ. Then I find out you didn't think enough of me to tell me that she was in your room."

"You never told me that."

"I didn't think I had to. It was humiliating enough to hear it from her, and you wanted me to repeat it to you? How would that have changed where we are right now?"

"You're right, I guess. Telling me that would have only made me think a little less of Bianca than I already did."

Marlea flipped the top flap of her box a time or two, then closed her fingers around it.

"Look, Marlea, the thing Bianca wants with me is all about money, and I'm better than that. I deserve better than that. She's a manipulator, and you got caught in one of her schemes. Maybe I should be used to it, though. Back when we were together, it was all about, *give me, get me, buy me,* and *me, me.* What she wants with me now is to pay her bills and finance her business." His broad shoulders lifted and fell. "It's always about pulling strings. That's all it ever was and ever will be with her."

"And I guess I'm different."

"If you're not, you've fooled the hell out of me."

Lines creased Marlea's forehead. "What is that supposed to mean?"

"It means that the reason I care about you is that you're the kind of woman I can imagine children and a family with. Man, I can even see us collecting Social Security together."

"That's a touching picture, AJ, but my trust . . ." She shook her head. "I don't know . . ."

"I'm just puttin' it out there, just so you know." AJ lifted his hands, placating and trying to keep hope alive. "How about this, in the meantime? Don't leave. I know how much the 400 means to you. Will you at least stay and trust me enough to train with me?"

"I don't know if that's such a good idea."

"It's a great idea. We already know that Libby won't be here to work with you, and you know that the record from Athens came in under 52 seconds. At your best, you were pulling it at 40:33, and now you're missing two toes. You really want that gold, it's going to take some work to get there."

"And you think I can't do it without you?" Marlea's head came high and she squared her shoulders.

"No, it's not that. I just know that you *can* win it with me. You need a coach."

"I'll get by. I'll get a dog, like Gail Devers."

"Gail doesn't run the 400, and she's got all her toes." AJ grinned, standing. "Tell you what, you said that running into me is what got you here. Well, I'll make you a deal. I'll race you for it. You win, I'll buy the dog and still stand on the sidelines to cheer you on."

Marlea's eyes narrowed. "If I lose?"

"Then you've got a coach and you won't need the dog. I'll train you, and I'll still cheer you every step of the way."

"Fine. I'll race you." Needing something to do with her hands, she picked up the open box and held it in front of her protectively. "But I'm not losing."

"That's what you say now." AJ stepped close enough to feel the heat from her body. "Just remember, I matched your speed when I had bad knees and you had all your toes."

"You don't have to match me, you have to beat me. It's not the same thing." Jamming a hand against one hip, Marlea held the box against her other hip and frowned up at him. "And that's not what concerns me."

"What concerns you?"

"I can get a coach anywhere, but not a man I trust."

"And you still want to know if I'm that man?"

"Yeah."

"Then that means I still have half a chance, Marlea, and I'm willing to take it. What do I have to do to convince you that I deserve the other half? I don't know what to do."

"I don't either, AJ."

"One step at a time, then." He took the box from her and set it on the floor. "You'd better get some rest, and I'll see you for breakfast. Eight o'clock okay for you?"

"Fine. After that, you can watch my back when I leave you in my dust."

"It's a good lookin' back, but you'll have to let me know what you think of mine after I pass you," AJ said, leaving the room and closing the door behind him.

———

Marlea could hear his soft steps on the marble flooring as she stood staring at the door, wondering.

It's his house. I couldn't have very well told him not to come in. Eyes on her boxes, she felt the press of tears again. *I shouldn't have let him in. I should have told him not to come in. I should have . . .* Her shoulders heaved. *I should have gone straight to my place. At least in Marietta, I wouldn't have had to talk to him about Bianca—even if he is finally telling me his side of the story.*

But why did he wait so long? It felt so bad, her sitting there and rubbing it in my face. Her knowing something about 'my' man, something that I didn't know. Her knowing something about him that he should have told me.

Pressing her palms hard together, Marlea exhaled against them. *He said he didn't sleep with her. He said he didn't love her.*

It wasn't working. Pushing her last box aside, she walked over to the bed and stood looking down at it, remembering the last time she shared it with AJ. *There wasn't even a hint of Bianca between us then. But what was it Libby used to say? 'Never say never.' Ain't that the truth. I told myself that I would never run the 400 again, and here I am. I honestly believed that I would never doubt AJ—look where that's got me.*

She looked at the bed again and backed away. Putting her hand out, she found the cushioned chintz armchair and sat. Draping her long legs over the arm of the chair, she pulled a sweatshirt from the chair back and huddled beneath it. Strangely cold, she looked at her reflection in the window across from her. *I look awfully lonely without AJ,* she thought, pulling at the sweatshirt. *Might as well get used to it.*

———◆———

"Uh-huh." He looked over his shoulder. "Dench? Set us off."

Dench ran his tongue over his teeth and stepped back from the path. No use in getting run over. Raising his arms, he brought his cupped hands to his lips. "On your marks . . ."

Looking as grimly determined as she did, AJ mirrored Marlea's movements at their start, then changed his mind. She was using the modified stance preferred by Paralympians. He elected the traditional. Dropping low, knuckles resting in dust, he looked up at her. "You belong to me," he murmured through gritted teeth.

"Not in this life." She dropped her head, refusing to look at him.

"Get set . . ."

I let her outrun me and I lose her forever. AJ felt the drops of cold sweat break across his forehead. *Never gonna happen.*

"Go!"

Pushing off, feeling his heart lurch, AJ tasted challenge and swallowed it whole. Ignoring the tiny electrical jolt in his knee, he let his long legs find full stride, muscles in his thighs working with hydraulic precision. At his side, Marlea's feet pounded a flawless path, and AJ let his breathing drown out the sound. *Never let her see you sweat, dude.* Good advice, he judged, laying into the speed that was his nature.

Finding his rhythm, he could hear her steps. The pace had a distinctive rhythm, one foot slightly heavier than the other. Never good at shorter distances, Marlea had no time to worry about it—she was working too hard. He could tell by her breathing.

Her hot-fired body pushed, fighting for an edge, but it wasn't enough as he passed her. AJ crossed the electronic sensor planted at the end of the course five long steps ahead of Marlea. The sensor screamed success and AJ thanked God. *Seconds. I beat her by seconds.*

"Ahh, you did it, dude. You did it!" Dench whooped, doing a victory dance that only he could explain before running toward the finish line.

Marlea's breath pulled tight through her nose and rushed out past her open lips as she slowed. Her mouth felt dry and her lips were parched, but her legs felt like rubber. *I don't think I've ever run that hard. Where did he find the speed?*

Finished, she stood panting and blowing in front of AJ. "You won."

"Yep," he agreed, holding his face straight. "Fair and square."

"It'll never happen again."

"No, it won't, 'cause now you've got a coach."

CHAPTER 30

Watching from the corner of her eye, Martha Baldwin nudged Rissa, then motioned with her head. Careful not to stop what she was doing, Rissa kept her head low and dabbed at the spot on the lapel of her suit with a damp cloth. Sneaky but determined, the women kept their eyes on Marlea.

"Morning." Dressed for training, she slunk past, not really noticing the women. Dumping herself into a chair, she reached for the paper and idly flipped the pages.

What? Rissa mouthed, dabbing faster.

Martha shrugged. *Might as well see what's up with her.* Picking up the coffeepot and a cup, Martha ambled over to the table. One eye on Marlea, she poured carefully. "How about some breakfast?" she offered, breaking the silence, but not the tension.

"Pancakes," Marlea said, turning the newspaper page.

Martha's brows rose and she looked back at Rissa, who stopped dabbing and started rubbing instead. Turning back to Marlea, the housekeeper set the coffeepot on the table. "I'm sorry, what did you say?"

"Pancakes."

Martha's mouth opened, then closed. Planting a hand on one solid hip, she looked down at Marlea. "I must not have heard you right. I could have sworn you said 'pancakes.'"

"I did." Marlea said, not bothering to look up.

Forgetting all about the spot on her lapel, Rissa moved close and leaned on the stone counter, her eyes zipping from one woman to the other. When she saw Martha tuck her tongue into her cheek and place a hand on her other hip, she wondered if Marlea had any idea how much trouble she was about to step in. When Marlea finally lowered the paper and stared up at the housekeeper, Rissa knew that she didn't have a clue.

Running her thumb along the band of her apron, Martha took a long, slow breath. "You're in training, and you think you're going to eat pancakes at my table? You haven't eaten pancakes for as long as you've been here, and suddenly, today, you want pancakes?"

Taking a white linen napkin from the tabletop, Marlea spread it neatly across her lap. "You make them for him, you can make them for me." She pushed her plate toward the older woman. "Pancakes."

Rissa cringed. Rude as that was, Marlea had nerve, if nothing else. But Martha had standards, and she never had been one to be trifled with.

"Wait a minute, Miss Missy, let me tell you something. You don't talk to me no any kind of way—that's number one. Number two, you're in training, and you're going to eat like you're in training, like it or not." Taking a step toward Marlea, Martha seemed to be struggling for control. Her face was stony, her posture unyielding. She took a deep breath, and Rissa knew she was counting to ten. She had seen her do it with AJ over dinner the night before. "Steppin' up in here, acting like you've got a right to say anything that crosses your little mind, and talking about you want to eat pancakes for breakfast, two weeks before final trials—it's not gonna happen. You know AJ won't like it . . ."

"AJ can kiss my round brown butt." Marlea held out her plate. "Pancakes."

"Oh, you are still trying to work a nerve up in here this morning? He might like that, kissing your butt, but I'm not trying to hear it, and I'm not the one for you to be playing with. Did you hit your head in the night? The way you've been acting lately . . . and now you're in here trying to throw away everything you ever wanted with both hands. It don't make no damned sense . . ."

Oooh, Rissa held her breath. *Marlea made her say 'damn'. . .*

Marlea's eyes flashed misery, then defiance. "It's not your business." She stood and collected her plate. Determined, she marched past Martha and a wide-eyed Rissa, heading for the warm pancakes waiting on the side of the griddle.

"Look at you." Martha shook her head and her finger. "The hell it's not my business. You and AJ have had everybody around here walking on eggshells since you got back from New York."

Marlea flipped three pancakes and a pair of link sausages onto her plate. She took a fourth pancake when she saw Martha's face. "I can go home."

Martha's laugh was a dismissive bark. "No, you can't. If you could, you would already be gone. As it is, you can't leave him, and he can't let you try. Y'all are pitiful."

"I am not pitiful." Marlea slathered butter on the pancakes and then hacked at them with her knife and fork. "I'm not pitiful," she insisted.

"Must be a new word for it, then. Last I heard, this," she said, tracking Marlea with a disdainful finger, "was called pitiful. You know you can't eat pancakes and run. Whatever happened in New York shoulda stayed in New York."

Marlea's hands tightened on her knife and fork; her eyes were trained on her plate. "It's not your business . . ." She seemed to want to say more, but her voice trailed off when she heard approaching steps.

Dressed in navy running shorts and a creamy white shirt, AJ walked into the kitchen and leaned against the granite-topped counter. Getting out of the line of fire, Rissa grabbed her briefcase and headed for the door.

Obviously preoccupied, AJ's eyes were steady as he poured juice, downing it in a single swallow. "You ready?"

Marlea stuffed a chunk of syrup-drenched pancakes into her mouth. "I'm eating."

"Outside. Ten minutes." He left the kitchen.

Marlea stopped chewing. She couldn't swallow.

"You sure do know how to complicate things," Martha observed.

Trying not to choke, Marlea forced herself to swallow what was already in her mouth. "I don't know what you mean."

"Yes, you do," Martha said. "Play stupid if you want to, but you know what you want and you know what you need, and you don't have a clue what to do about it, now do you? Well, you didn't ask, but I'm gonna tell you. You need to get over your little snit and go after that man. He's a big part of the solution, and you'd better figure out a way to let him know it before you let your pride cheat both of you. That's all I have to say on the subject."

"Oh, don't stop now."

"Aanh!" Clearly at the end of her patience, Martha dismissed Marlea with a wave of her hand.

Rissa scooted through the door just ahead of Marlea. She had her cellphone out by the time she slipped behind the wheel of her car, and Dench answered before she made it through the gates. "Baby, you are not going to believe it. Let me tell you what just happened . . ."

———— ≈≈≈ ————

Marlea stood, snatching her napkin as it slid from her lap. There wasn't a whole lot more to say, and she stalked from the kitchen.

Arguing with Martha Baldwin left a bad taste in her mouth. *I don't know why she chose today to step all up in my business. It was bad enough to come across that damned wedding announcement.* Marlea ignored the urge to stomp her feet and fall out like a two-year-old. *Why did I have to go flipping through the paper today and find a wedding announcement for Dr. Parker Reynolds and what's-her-name? Was it, Desireé?*

There she was in the engagement picture, smiling for all she was worth, announcing a wedding timed with his release from jail, and anticipating happily ever after. And what am I doing? Arguing with somebody about pancakes!

Passing the laundry room, exiting through the side door, Marlea pushed Parker Reynolds's upcoming nuptials from her mind, and tried not to remember the first time she had come through the same door with AJ, or the times since that first time. *Maybe this ought to be the last time . . .*

AJ would be good and mad at me if I walked through this door, down the drive, and just kept on walking. She thought about it for a moment and felt the hurt place in her soul swell again. *No use picking at the hurt, trying to work around it. If Bianca's little stunt didn't kill what we had, I guess I've let it die of attrition by now.*

Days of virtual silence, passing each other without so much as the brush of hands, avoiding each other, even for meals, had taken its toll.

I miss him, and for all the good it's done, I still love him. I just don't know what to say, or how to bridge this gap between us. Besides, he's already mad at me, anyway. Now I'm supposed to meet him to train, even though the last few sessions have been really bad.

She would have given almost anything not to have to admit to herself how bad they had been, filled with falls and false starts—little mistakes that showed she wasn't paying attention. And it was wearing on AJ, too. *Yesterday, he yelled at me for not concentrating. How does he expect me to concentrate when he's yelling at me? Besides, I've been running most of my life, it's not like he created me.*

He's just taking his frustrations out on me, and I haven't made things easy for him. He's not the only one missing sex and the closeness we once shared, but at least I don't spend hours and hours in the gym trying to pump iron and then tell myself it takes the place of what I really want.

No, instead, I've been holed up with a stack of Rissa's romance novels, reading and wishing I was one of those rescued heroines. If it hadn't been for Bianca . . . what? What would have been different if not for her? When it's not right, there has to be more wrong than 'the other woman,' right?

So what else is wrong with AJ? With what we had? Why can't I find a way to tell him, to show him, that I forgive him? He says he didn't sleep with her, and I've thought about it. Father, forgive me, but I've thought of almost nothing else. She almost heard Martha Baldwin's voice in the gentle rustle of foliage as she passed. *I believe him. I don't honestly believe he could have come back here the way he did, that he could hold me the way he did, that he could call me . . .*

Silk.

For a second, she could hear his voice, feel his touch, and she hungered for more.

Sense memory, that's all that is. Me missing him. And she felt the tender ache in her soul echo like a repeating dream. She surprised herself by clinging to it.

Jealousy and pride, she admitted, *Mrs. Baldwin was right. I've pretty much let them dig me into my own private hell, and then I took AJ along for the ride. She's right. I am pitiful.* Turning, walking backward, Marlea looked back at the house. *I'm gonna owe her an apology—a big one.*

Turning again, Marlea swiped at a holly bush with the napkin she still held. *What was I thinking, dragging this thing with me? I'm tempted to toss it, but it would be just my luck that Mrs. Baldwin counts the napkins and would miss this one.* She stuffed it in her pocket.

But what about AJ? What do I say to him to fix this? Reaching down to the bush, she pulled several of its crisp, prickly leaves free. Crushing them between her fingers, she kept walking. *What can I say to let him know that I believe him, that I haven't given up on . . . us?*

What do I say to him so that he doesn't give up on me? It's not like I've given him much of anything to hope for lately. I really haven't been cooperating during our last few training sessions. With little effort, she could hear herself complaining: *Why do we have to do gym and two runs a day? It's only 400 meters. It's not like I'm a long-distance runner. I could understand it if I was going to run a marathon; twenty-six miles takes a lot more preparation . . .*

Marlea let her feet drag her along the hillside path leading to the 400-meter run AJ had laid for her training. Sitting on a massive gray boulder, he was waiting when she got there.

"About time."

"Yeah, yeah. I'm here now."

"You still need to warm up."

She looked at him and prayed for words. None came. He stood in a shaft of golden sunlight and her hungry eyes moved over him—broad shoulders, tight-muscled hips, and the long arms and legs she had missed in the night. "I'm warm enough." *What an understatement.* "Let's just do this."

"Marlea, if you don't really want to do this . . ."

"What?" She let her arms fall to her sides, palms up. "Now you want to pick a fight?"

"*I'm* picking a fight?" Walking in a small circle, he shook his head. "I don't even know why I'm trying."

"Like I'm not?" Marlea put on her determined face. "AJ, I've never stopped trying. I've put in all kinds of effort and . . ."

"And you still don't believe me, do you?" Her expression wasn't working on him. "You still don't trust me, and now you're willing to throw away everything because of it. Damn it, Marlea, I love you. Stop trying to punish me. I've done everything I know how to convince you that Bianca means less than nothing to me. You don't want to hear that from me, fine. You want gold? You want the 400? I'm here to help you get it, and that's still not good enough. What do you want from me?"

"I want . . ." *to say what I have to say and not look or sound like a fool in the process. I want things to be like they were before. I want you to know that I couldn't do any of this without you behind me. I want you to believe in me as much as I believe in you. I want* . . . Her cheeks flushed and she had to talk around the growing lump in her throat. "I want you to race me again."

"No." AJ threw up his hands.

"No? Why?" Marlea's mouth opened and closed. *Mrs. Baldwin was right* . . . "You have to."

"No, I don't have to." AJ turned his back and paced a few steps away. Turning back, he shook his head. "No, I'm not doing it. That's like pulling petals off a daisy. 'She loves me, she loves me not.' She'll race me, she'll race me not . . . What would it prove, anyway?"

"Scared?"

"No, I'm not scared."

"Then race me." Marlea moved to the starting line and kicked the button triggering the motion-detecting clock. "How 'bout it?" she beckoned to him. When he held his place, she cocked her head, challenge in her eyes. "You gonna run or not?"

"Fine. We run." He moved to stand beside her. "Who's going to . . ."

"Go!" she shouted and took off.

"What the hell?" Unable to ignore challenge, even if she was going to cheat, his foot hit the ground five steps behind her. Working hard to narrow the gap, AJ dropped his head to concentrate, his arms and legs pumping, but he skidded to a stop just beyond the 100-meter marker. He was alone on the measured track.

"What the hell? Where is she?" She never passed him. He turned, looking back the way he had come, and she was nowhere near him. Instead, Marlea sat in the middle of her lane, waving a white napkin. Walking back toward her, breathing hard, hands on his hips, AJ was confused. "What in the hell?"

"I changed my mind," she said, when he stopped in front of her.

"Changed your mind about what?" He looked down at her. "A napkin? What, you want more pancakes?"

"No." She waved the napkin, swaying it from side to side. "This is my white flag."

"A white flag is for surrender. What are you trying to surrender now?" His eyes narrowing, he looked at her suspiciously. "Is this some kind of game, Marlea? Are you trying to tell me that you've changed your mind about running? That you don't want to run the 400 anymore? 'Cause if you are . . .'"

Okay, now this is taking a bad turn. "Could you help me up?" She offered her hand.

AJ shook his head and stepped back from her. "No. You got down there by yourself, you can get up by yourself."

"Nasty attitude," Marlea huffed, pushing to her feet, grateful that he hadn't walked away—yet. "AJ, I wanted to talk to you about this. It's, 'just a symbol, a declaration of faith.' Isn't that what you called it when you came to my hospital room?"

"I don't know what you're talking about." He looked at his watch and then into her face.

There's still a chance, Marlea thought. *He hasn't walked away from me.* "Yes, you do, AJ. Remember when you came to see me in the hospital? You wanted to convince me that therapy was in my best interest?"

"And you weren't having it."

"I was wrong then, and I'm wrong now. I'm apologizing." Marlea moved to match his step as he turned and walked away from her. Blocking his path, she looked up at him and hoped. "AJ, I was wrong. And I was mean about it." Watching him watch her, Marlea was tempted to look down at her shirtfront, sure that he could see her heart jumping in her chest. "I should have known where to place my trust. I should have known that a woman who meant me no good from the first time we met couldn't be trusted. I should have known to trust you to be who you are." She lifted the napkin again. "I'm declaring my faith in you, AJ. Okay?"

"No, it's not okay." Reaching out, his hand brushing hers, he took the little white cloth. He looked at it for seconds that felt like hours. When it fell from his hand, he stared at it on the ground. "I'm not sure what I did to make it so easy for you not to trust me."

"Mostly you were just who you are, and that was scary for me—new and scary. There's never been a man like you in my life before. Gorgeous and smart, caring and available, and then she was there. Bianca. And I knew what you once shared with her, and I didn't want her to have a part of you that meant so much to me, and . . . and I guess I didn't see myself as whole enough to deserve you. It wasn't about you; it was about me and the limits I couldn't take myself past." She took a deep breath and tried to still the quiver in her lips. "And I'm sorry."

"Marlea, none of what we have is about Bianca, unless you look at her as the one who showed me what I don't want in a woman."

She refused to ask a question she already knew the answer to.

"Marlea, you and me, we've got trust between us. You and me, we have things to laugh about, we have things to talk about. We have things that anchor us to each other. I thought that was enough."

"You said have, that we have each other." Almost afraid to ask, she squinted up at him. "Is it still there for you, AJ? It is for me, and I couldn't lose it if I had to."

"Marlea . . ." Something tender and as rich as hot expresso rushed through his eyes, drenching her. "I told you; I feel anchored to you, like I'm never lost as long as we're together. I don't ever want you to lose faith in me or wonder if your trust is well-placed in me."

"How about we both promise not to ever forget that?"

"You're silly, you know that?" AJ smiled, and Marlea felt herself breathe.

"I may be silly." She took a step toward him and tapped his chest with her finger. "But silly as I am, you like it."

"Okay, you got me. Yeah, I like it." AJ closed one hand over her finger and his other arm encircled her waist, pulling her close. "One last thing, though. What about this training?"

"I'm as committed to my training as I am to you." She raised her right hand. "No more slacking off, no more half-stepping. I'm there; totally committed."

Satisfied, AJ stood wider and pulled her closer, taking her weight and lifting her from the ground. "Good. Are we fixed, now?"

"We are, if you admit that you're as silly as I am."

"You mean 'cause I didn't say anything about seeing Bianca in New York?" He pulled back to see himself reflected in Marlea's eyes. "Yeah, that was pretty silly, now that I look back at it."

"Then I guess that fixes us, except for one thing . . ."

"What?" AJ studied her eyes and found no answer. "I already admitted . . ."

"My name." Her legs climbed his to lock around his hips. "I want to hear you say it."

"Marlea . . ."

"No, not that one. You know." Pressing her hips to his, Marlea drew her arms tighter around his neck, bringing AJ's face closer. "Say my name," she whispered nuzzling close, finding the sweet corner of his mouth. "Say my name."

"Silk." The soft breeze of a gentle Georgia fall day rustled the leaves on the trees, but Marlea heard him against her lips. "Silk," AJ whispered, slipping a hand beneath her shirt. "Silk . . ."

CHAPTER 31

Atlanta

"Ten minutes, ladies."

"Yeah, yeah, yeah," Rissa promised, pushing Libby past the muscular woman in the red, white, and blue U.S. Track and Field Association jacket. "We're going to run right in, deliver a message from her coach, and be out of here."

"For real," Libby agreed, slipping through the double doors of the locker room.

"Well, now that we're in here, where is she?" Turning in a circle in the massive Phillips Arena locker room, Rissa tried to orient herself. All around her, more than a hundred women in various stages of dress and undress seemed to be in constant shouting motion.

A frustrated trainer carrying an armload of braces and wraps pushed past without saying anything. Rissa made a face at the woman's back. "Apparently, the opportunity to perform for the USTAF is a big deal."

Libby looked at Rissa as if she had just discovered that the woman was from the moon. "You bet your sweet butt it's a big deal. These women are the best in the country. Some of em, like Marlea, are damned near the best in the world—even with their challenges. Did you know that the recent International Paralympic records are this close," she pressed her fingers close together, "to the non-disabled records? It's all about the training and the heart these athletes have. Why, they got more heart than . . ."

"Uh-huh. Anyway, do you see her?" Rissa shouted to Libby.

Looking helpless, the little black-haired woman stood on her toes and gave the room a quick once-over. She shrugged. "I don't see anybody I know in here," she yelled back.

"'We've only got ten minutes, and we have to find her." Jamming her hand into her leather tote bag, Rissa pulled out her cellphone. She scrolled for the number and hit 'send' when she found it. "I am not about to waste that little bit of time."

Marlea answered on the second ring.

"Where the heck are you, girl? Me an' Libby are just standing here turning in circles, looking for you." Rissa listened, then pointed. "Uh-huh, yeah. We're coming." Grabbing Libby's arm, she led her across the room. In red sports bra and panties, Marlea was standing on a bench, her head barely visible over the head and shoulders of a thin woman with twisted braids.

Jerking free of Rissa's hold, Libby threw herself at Marlea just as she stepped down from the bench. "I'm so glad to see you, ooh, and I'm so proud of you that I could just burst."

"Don't burst. We're all proud of her, Libby." Eyes tightly shut, Rissa wrapped her arms around Marlea and Libby.

"And I appreciate it." Marlea worked herself out of the tangle and reached for her navy-trimmed singlet.

"So many women here . . . we had no idea it would be so hard to find you."

"And would you believe I actually ran into someone I know? Another runner, Kendra Asaou. She's an amputee, too. I met her in New York."

"Oh, Lord," Rissa rolled her eyes. "Not New York . . ."

"Ignore her," Libby gushed, "USTAF Invitational, who'd have thought it?" She shoved Marlea's bag to the floor and plopped down on the bench. "It's a Paralympic preliminary and you're here—by invitation, girl."

Marlea pulled her shorts from her bag and stepped into them.

"You don't have to say anything, but you're not fooling me, I know how proud you have to be. This is the closest you've ever come to keeping that promise you made to your mother." Libby sighed and hugged herself. "You're headed for gold today, and I just know she's with you. But Marlea, she can't be any prouder of you than I am, 'cause girl, I knew you back when."

Marlea passed her hand over her face and had to look quickly to the ceiling. "You're going to keep on until you make me cry, Libby."

"Oh, hell no." Rissa used her hip to urge Libby to move over on the bench. "There will be no crying up in here today. You and my brother have had to work too hard to come this far, and I don't want him blaming me for making you cry and miss out on your shining moment. You are bringing gold up out of here today, one way or another."

"Amen to that," Libby crowed, nudging Rissa.

The meeting of their eyes and the brightly smug expression they shared was brief, but Marlea caught it. "Why are you testifying? Like you know something?"

"Know something?" Libby puffed, ignoring the look Rissa sent her way. "Something, like what?"

"Like you're keeping a secret from me, is what."

"I don't know what you're talking about."

"You said that too fast." Marlea pressed her back to the gray metal locker and carefully raised her leg. Pointing her toe, she slipped on her sock, watching Libby all the while. "So what's the secret?"

"I don't know any secret. Nobody in here has a secret. Right, Rissa?"

"Not that I know of. Oh, Dench is here." Obviously the wrong person to ask, Rissa dropped her eyes and fidgeted with her tote. "He wanted me to tell you that he's proud of you, too."

"That's really nice." Marlea pulled at her other sock and watched.

Trying to look innocent, Rissa let her eyes move around her. At her side, a long jumper checked her prosthesis, then carefully fastened it into place under the watchful eye of another woman, presumably her trainer. "This whole thing is pretty prestigious, isn't it?" she finally said, looking back at Marlea.

Libby slipped her hands beneath her hips and looked at the floor. "Connie and Jeanette are in the stands with Hal. You know how hard it is to get my husband to come out to these things, but he said he wouldn't have missed you in this for anything in the world."

Now, they're both babbling . . . Something is really up. Rissa couldn't keep a secret if her life depended on it. Marlea eyed her.

Feeling the pressure, Rissa's eyes jittered, then fell to the floor. Then, to her horror, her mouth opened and words fell out. She couldn't look at Marlea, but she couldn't stop talking, either. "Not to make you nervous, or put you on the spot or anything, but the parents' group from the Runyon School bought a block of tickets, and just about every kid in the school is out there ready to cheer for you."

That's the big news? A little disappointed, and certain that Rissa was somehow managing to hold back, Marlea crossed her arms and waited. It didn't work, but Rissa babbled on.

"You know, as a role model, you really are standing strong for those kids. You've made an indelible mark on all their lives, you know? They think woman and they speak of you. They think triumph and they think of you. They think indomitable and they think of you . . ."

Marlea gave up. "No pressure there, right? I'm glad the kids are here, but did AJ send you guys in here to cheer me up or scare me to death?"

"Mostly he wanted us to remind you of how proud he is of you."

"And how much he loves you," Libby chimed in.

"Oh, and balance," Rissa recalled. "He said to remember to stay centered in your lane and to stay balanced."

"You know, you two are carrying messages like your names are Western and Union." *And I still don't know what secrets you're keeping.*

"Time! Please clear the locker room. Competitors only in the locker room."

Jumping to her feet, grateful for the announcement, Rissa snagged Libby's arm, towing her along. "We gotta go."

"Well, go on and take your little secret with you." Marlea gave it a final shot and got nothing for her effort.

"Whatever." Rissa and Libby backed toward the end of the aisle, heading for the door. "Just know that we love you, and we want you to run faster than ever before."

"See you at the finish line," Libby yelled as she disappeared from sight.

"Yeah, see you." Marlea waved at the spot where her friends had stood, then bent to pull her shoe from her bag and wondered—but she didn't have a clue. *Guess I had better hurry up and cross that finish line if I'm ever going to know what they're hiding.*

———

"Dude, you got us sitting right on the track, almost." Dench looked around the arena, approving the seats. "Big as Phillips Arena is, we're close enough to feel the breeze when they go by. We're going to have a real nice view of Marlea when she stands up on that podium to accept her gold medal . . . just as soon as she wins."

"That was the plan," AJ grinned, pulling off his jacket.

"You know he wanted to see his best girl when she wins, and so did we," Connie giggled from the row behind them. She squeezed AJ's shoulder and then unfurled a large hand-lettered banner and held it just high enough for him to read it. "See? Jeanette and I plan to be moral support. Besides, we heard about what you've got in your pocket."

"Connie!" Jeanette nudged her and Connie shook it off.

"We've come this far with you two, and we deserve to know how it ends. And you know we want to see her face." She giggled harder when Jeanette pinched her arm.

"Since she brought it up, what about the *rest* of the plan?" Dench asked, watching Connie and Jeanette roll and secure their banner. "You ready for that?"

"Yeah, I'm ready. Don't worry, man. I got this." AJ was grateful for the interruption caused by the man in the blue jacket. Trying to reach his seat on AJ's left, the man had to wait at the end of the row for Dench and AJ to stand.

"AJ? Well, how about that?" the man laughed, offering his hand. "Small world." Adrian Kessler seemed delighted with the turn of his luck. "I got assigned to cover this women's invitational event today. I got here at the last minute, looked at my ticket, and they had me sitting way up there with the families of a couple of the athletes. Then I got a call from *Atlanta Sports and Fitness* asking me to try to get some pictures. Their chief photographer is tied up in traffic on I-285 or something."

"Good thing I had my camera and access. So I jumped up and ran down here, and lo and behold, I get to sit next to you and get your take on the races." Kessler dropped into his seat and pulled a small tape recorder from an inside pocket, all in the same motion. "Did you see the earlier races? What did you think?" Watching the former footballer's face, the swarthy reporter grinned suddenly, flashing white teeth. "Better still, got any predictions on the 400-meter run?"

"Dude, you already know he's got Kellogg to win in record time," Dench shouted at the reporter, leaning across AJ.

"Marlea's gonna dust her," AJ agreed.

"I've got to disagree with you on that one. I admit she's a beautiful woman and a talented athlete, but . . ." AJ's calm ruffled the reporter.

"You asked. I'm just sayin'," AJ drawled.

"Your girl's got all that speed, but she's running against that hot kid from the University of South Carolina." Kessler's fingers dipped into a pocket to pull out a small pad and a pen. "They're both foot amputees and fast as greased lightning, even though Kellogg's almost twice Connor's age."

"Not gonna be a problem."

"You sound pretty certain." Kessler scribbled on his pad. "Can I quote you on that? It'll save me the effort of tracking you down later."

"Yeah, you can quote me," AJ nodded, stretching his long legs.

Kessler's pen tapped the pad. "Are you sure about that? There are five other runners in the 400 and four of them are good, but not great. That really leaves only one to beat, and Kellogg's what, almost thirty-three? She's got to outrun Elise Connor, and Connor's only nineteen." Kessler looked down the field, focusing on the athletes and their warm-ups. "The math is not on Kellogg's side."

"You didn't write it down when I told you." Smiling, AJ's thumb stroked his cheek. "Marlea is a smart, seasoned runner with a hell of a lot of heart, and she's gonna give that kid a lesson in how to run the 400. A fast lesson." He tapped the reporter's notepad. "Did you get that?"

"She can't run forever."

"But she can run today."

Sly as a jackal, Adrian smiled, electric light from the track painting his sculpted features. "Would you put money on it?"

AJ reached for his wallet. "How much you willing to lose?"

"Whoa, man." Kessler raised a hand and shook his head, eyes on the bills AJ was fingering. "I'm not a big baller like you; I ain't got it like that."

Dench looked confused. "You're working on this story; should you be making *any* kind of bet?"

"There's no conflict of interest here. She's not *my* runner," Kessler said. "I just think that nineteen goes a whole lot faster than thirty-three—toes not withstanding." He turned back to face AJ. "Let's make this a working man's bet."

"If you're not sure, then you had better make it something you can afford." AJ's lazy smile was confident.

Concentrating and already figuring the odds, Kessler looked down at the field, then back at AJ. "Let's make it five hundred on the race, and a fifty a second, over five."

"Done." AJ gripped the reporter's hand firmly, sealing the wager. Settling back in his seat, he turned back to Kessler and said, "You do know I don't plan to take a check, right?"

Dench raised his binoculars and scanned the field of female athletes on the track. He kept his prediction to himself, but he honestly thought the reporter looked worried.

CHAPTER 32

Sizing up the competition, Marlea jogged from foot to foot, trying to shake the tension out of her shoulders and legs. Elise Connor pranced by, dreadlocks swinging and tight gold shorts cutting into the perfect curve of her sculpted, black-skinned buttocks. She moved with the grace of a gazelle. Marlea thought she heard someone behind her say something about Reebok or some other big company offering to sponsor her.

Must be nice, Marlea thought, recalling what she knew of her. Connor was a sophomore at the University of South Carolina in Columbia. She known for taking chances. The word on the running circuit was that taking chances was how she had lost her toes; trying to hitch a ride at the back of a city bus on a skateboard at twelve, she had fallen and her foot had been crushed.

She had taken to running in high school, possibly as a way of making up for what other kids teased her about, or maybe it was just to impress a boy. *But she didn't give up*, Marlea thought. *She kept going, and now she's a tough, hard-running competitor. She started out running the 200 and the 4-by-4, but she switched to the 400 for the same reason I did.*

Hand on the stadium wall, and drawing a leg up to grasp her ankle, Marlea stretched her quads and watched

Connor high-step her way back down the sidelines. The nineteen-year-old's body moved like a machine, and she looked like a world-beater. Two of the other 400 competitors, Betty Graves from NC State and Lauren Thomas from California, put their heads together. Graves looked nervous. She jammed her thumb into the armhole of her North Carolina blue singlet and pulled at it. Thomas kept shaking her head. Pointing from Elise to Marlea, the pair talked furiously, something like fear growing in their eyes.

Connor is psyching them out, Marlea realized. *I heard she was good at that, but that crap is not going to work on me—not today. I raced her a month ago in Denver and I beat her, and I've trained more since. I'm going to beat her again.*

Beginning a slow jog, trying to warm cold muscles, Marlea took an easy turn along the side lane. Concentrating on her stride, she looked up when she heard her name.

"Hey, Ms. Kellogg! Over here!"

Jogging toward the sound, she was thrilled to see rows and rows of children and adults dressed in the red and gold colors of the Runyon School. Big, square-shaped, multicolored signs bore her name and words of encouragement. Raising both arms in happy salute, she ran toward her loyal fans.

"Watch out!"

She heard the shouted warning in the very second that her foot found a forgotten hurdle brace. Caught in a hellish moment of fated disaster, her ankle rolled and her body pitched forward. Pain surged through her foot and ankle, and she looked up at the children in the stands, her mind locked on a single thought: *Not again!*

"No!" She saw the word form on small faces.

"No!" She heard someone scream in the crowd.

"Not again," she swore, as she fell, landing hard on her hands and knees. Elise Connor's face bobbed in the sea of faces for an instant. No condolence or consolation showed on her smooth young features, but Marlea saw the fire in her eyes. Sure that her cause was won, the corners of her mouth lifted.

Digging her fingers and toes into the synthetic track surface, Marlea's heart lurched at the ragged fire that ripped through her shocked body. *Not like this.* She tried not to give in to the wash of despair. *I don't mind being outrun, outclassed, but not like this. I can't lose like this . . .* Trying to catch her breath, she felt more than saw Libby and the USTAF officials rushing to surround her.

"Looks like she's out of it," Kessler gloated in the stands.

"You don't know her," AJ said, standing. "Just make sure you have my money," he advised, heading for the exit.

"Yeah," Dench seconded, rising to follow his friend. "Make sure."

"Yeah, what they said," Connie and Jeanette added, hurrying after the men.

The nurses stopped for ice, but Libby was already there and kneeling at Marlea's side when AJ pushed through the throng around her. Rolling onto her side,

Marlea gasped, pulled her leg in toward her chest, and hugged it desperately. AJ looked at her face and swallowed hard. Her eyes squeezed shut, the lashes stitched with unshed tears. He knew that look, had worn it himself. She was hurt.

Pushing closer, he dropped to one knee at her side. "Silk?" His palm pressed her clammy forehead. "How bad is it?"

Her lashes fluttered and she sniffed, but her eyes were bright when she looked at him. "How is it that I find you next to me every time I fall?"

"Just lucky, I guess." His hand moved to her cheek and he couldn't help smiling.

Squatting, Libby and a USTAF doctor moved in on Marlea, and air hissed past her lips when Libby touched her ankle. Experienced fingers probing, she looked at the doctor and shrugged. Not liking the shrug, AJ moved his own hand to Marlea's ankle. Tense fingers pressed, questioning the injury.

"Doesn't seem like a break," he said to a solemn-faced Libby.

"No, but a bad sprain can be as bad as a break, or worse."

AJ's fingers moved again and Marlea moaned.

"Look, sir," the doctor tried to shoulder past AJ. "We don't want to call security on you. Why don't you go back to the stands and let the professionals handle this." It wasn't a question, but an order. AJ's jaw tightened, and the doctor shrank away from what he saw in the big man's face. Not ready to relinquish his authority, he studied AJ's stern features, then recognition dawned. "I know you. You're Yarborough, aren't you? AJ Yarborough, the football player, right?"

"Yeah. I'm also a degreed and licensed physical therapist, and her trainer."

A close look at the big man's eyes was enough. Hearing his words, the doctor moved back. AJ slipped his fingers beneath Marlea's sock and pressed, looking for heat and swelling. She bit her lip and held her breath. He didn't like it at all. "Silk, you've got a sprain here. It's not the worst one you've ever had, but I don't think you want to run on it."

"Dude, what about your bet?" Dench flinched when AJ's eyes singed him.

"What bet?" Marlea wanted to know.

"He bet that writer, Adrian Kessler, that you would take this race." Dench flinched again when AJ gave him another withering glare.

"You made a bet?" Still lying on the ground, Marlea hugged her leg and suddenly grinned. "On me?"

"Big mouth," AJ muttered. "Dench and Rissa are made for each other."

"You had that much faith in me, huh?" Marlea pushed herself up on her elbows. "How much did you bet?"

Dench opened his mouth, but closed it quickly when he caught the warning in AJ's eyes.

"Look, Silk, you're the one who promised me that I could always have faith in you, so when he put it out there, what else could I do? I put my money on you."

Elise Connor capered past, watching from the comer of her eye. Propped on an elbow, Marlea sat a little higher and made a decision. "Libby, have you got tape or Ace bandages?"

"Right here." Jeanette scooted around Connie and Dench, pulling the elastic bandages from her windbreaker. Breaking the cellophane wrappings, she pulled the clips free and offered the bandages to AJ.

"I'm ready." When he hesitated, Marlea shook her foot and grimaced. "Are you going to wrap my ankle, or do I have to do it myself?"

"I've got you, Silk." He took the wrappings from Jeanette and waited for Libby to remove Marlea's sock and shoe. "The swelling hasn't begun yet . . ."

"Good, let's make sure that it doesn't," Marlea smiled. "Make the wrappings tight, I won't be in them long."

"I have this for you, too." Connie popped past AJ with a bit of string in her hand. "A little kid gave it to me on the way down here. It was one of your children, right? She said it was for luck. I think you need some luck right about now. Hold out your arm."

Marlea extended her arm obediently and waited for Connie to twist the red-and-gold braided yarn bracelet into place. The small talisman seemed to work instantly. "Thanks, Connie." Fingering the yarn bracelet, Marlea squared her shoulders. "Know what, AJ? Your faith and your bet are safe—I'm about to blow the dust off this track."

Helped up from the ground, Marlea managed to stand on her own. AJ looked ready to rush in and carry her off the field, but she motioned everyone to stand back. The first two steps she took were cautious but stable, and the people around her released a collective sigh of relief.

Encouraged, Marlea shifted her weight from foot to foot, then put a bit of bounce into it. Stunning pain arched through her foot and lanced into her ankle, making her stomach cramp abruptly. Her knee came perilously close to buckling. AJ's arm was there. She caught it and leaned, for a moment, catching her breath.

"*. . . 400 meters. Runners for the 400-meter event . . .*"

Marlea and AJ both turned toward the track. "That's my event. It's time."

"You don't have to do this," he whispered, holding her tighter.

"Oh, yes, I do," she whispered back, pushing free. She took two steps away from him, then stepped back. "But I would like it a lot if you were there when I cross the finish line."

AJ's lips touched hers. "I'll be there."

"Good," she kissed him back.

He pushed a hand into his jacket pocket. "Silk, before you go, I just want to . . ."

"I'll be right back; wait for me." She gave his arm a light pat. "Don't go too far away, and don't blink, 'cause this won't take a minute."

AJ watched her limp toward the staging area. Shoving his hands into his pockets, he felt for the small, square box and wished he could run for her.

Dench draped an arm around his friend's shoulders. "Whatcha gonna do?"'

"Only thing I can do. I'm gonna watch her run and be there when she finishes."

———◦∾◦———

Walking, exhaling slowly, Marlea counted eight beats, then sucked in another big breath and let it course through her long lean frame. *I'm here for a reason,* she reminded herself. *I've been on my way to this place all my life. I finish this race, and I can look forward to the Paralympic Masters competition in San Sebastian and a place on the team.* Her stomach fluttered at the thought of returning to Spain, and she clamped down on it. *San Sebastian is not Barcelona.* She ignored the harsh flash of pain in her ankle. *Phillips Arena is going to see my best today—whatever it takes.*

Heading for her lane, Marlea's fingers twisted the yarn bracelet as she concentrated on what it would feel like to release the power and run.

"I saw you fall." The voice was soft and Southern, its insinuation gentle. "It must have really hurt. Are you sure you can run on that ankle? I mean, nobody would blame you if you sat this one out."

"I'm fine, thanks." Marlea smiled at Elise Connor. *The kid might as well pull in her claws and save that fake sympathy for someone else. I've dealt with bigger cats than her and survived.* Sliding her hands over her sleek head, Marlea walked to her assigned area. Ponytail intact, she tried to focus, to recall Libby's mind/body routine.

Pulling her thoughts away from AJ and Elise Connor to focus on the race took some effort, but Marlea managed to find the number four slot without incident. "Number four," she whispered to herself. "That's really got to be my lucky number." It seemed that her best races were run in the number four lane.

Hands on her hips, she walked to the start and took a deep breath. Looking at the women lining up with her, she thanked God for second chances. Kicking her toes along the synthetic track, Marlea wiped her hands against her shorts and then pressed them against her thighs. She smiled at the women in her field. *Good luck to all of you,* Marlea thought, *but I'm taking this one. This is my race.*

"Runners, take your mark . . ."

Shaking off anything that had nothing to do with the run, Marlea coiled her body into starting position. At her side, one of the women began a low-voiced, droning prayer. Pressing her heel against the block, Marlea dropped her head and offered her own silent prayer.

"Get set . . ."

Breathe . . . She pulled deep and listened, tuning into the energy of her internal rhythms.

". . . Go!"

Her face tightened and her arms pumped when she heard the crack of the starter's pistol. The first strike of Marlea's foot against the track ignited the speed in her soul. With no thought for anything but the run, she picked up her pace and grinned into Elise Connor's fierce eyes. Even at the start, she was fighting to stay even and praying to pass.

Somewhere in a world beyond the track, Marlea heard the crowd. The muted roar launched her, sucking the breath from her lungs and the ground from beneath her feet. She knew that if she tried, she would be able to smell fear and yearning oozing from the pores of the other running women, and it meant nothing—even when the ripping crackle of grief in her ankle went hot, then cold and numb, as she outran the pain.

At her side, Elise Connor bared her teeth and strained with effort.

Not today, sweetie! Marlea dug deeper and pulled on resolve and twenty years of passion and craving. *It's only 400 meters to gold.* Driving hard, her chest burned and threatened to burst at 300 meters, but she could see the goal. *Breathe!* When Elise fell steps behind, with less than ten meters to go, Marlea could almost feet the push of time and the other woman's desire against her hot skin.

In the stands, binoculars found the number four runner and held. In spite of the injury, her head was high, her shoulders level, and her hips tight. Marlea's strides stayed long and even, the rhythm setting her ponytail swinging. Her high kick and unbound speed carried her across the finish line ahead of the other runners. Arms high, her head fell back as she finished. Her throat was tight with triumph when the silvery white banner broke across her chest.

"Damn," Adrian Kessler swore from behind his leveled binoculars. "Hell of a run. He said she was fast, but I know that was a record." Lowering the field glasses, he was glad that Elise Connor was in the field. Finishing seconds behind Marlea, she was going to save him a few hundred dollars. "I'm going to have to say something nice about her in my article."

". . . Finishing with a time of . . ."

Marlea's feet, trained for more years than she could count, slowed, but continued to run, as adrenaline ebbed low through her hot-fired body. Her mouth felt dry, and her breath pulled tight through her nose and rushed out past her open lips.

"Silk!" Eluding a line of gray-shirted security guards, AJ bolted over the chain link fence surrounding the track. Shouting her name, he ran toward her.

Flying into his arms, Marlea clung to him, screaming, "Thank you, AJ! Thank you, thank you, thank you!"

"You're welcome, but for what?"

"Your promise, don't you remember? You once promised me that I would dance with you, and I did. Now I'm running." She buried her face in his neck and her warm tears tracked his throat.

"Hey!" Screams, shouts, and swarming people fell on Marlea and AJ like a heavy net. "The time, did you hear the time?" Libby was closest, and frantic. Slapping at Marlea's sweaty leg, she seemed desperate to separate her from AJ, or to at least get her feet back on the ground. "Did you hear them? Did you hear it?"

"Hear what?"

"Your time," Libby screeched, jumping up and down.

Suddenly aware of what she must look like, Marlea reluctantly slid from AJ's embrace. His arm still draped her shoulders as she faced Libby. Reaching up, she found his hand and laced her fingers through his. People cavorted and danced around the field, but she couldn't distinguish a single word. A few feet away, Elise Connor looked ready to chew nails as she brushed off the consoling hand of her coach.

"I didn't hear it, Libby." Marlea's fingers tightened on AJ's. "What was it?"

"It . . . was . . . 48:20! That means gold, baby! Pure gold!"

The arena spun as Marlea's knees gave out and only AJ's strong arms saved her from crashing to the ground. Libby crowed like a Bantam rooster and went into her version of the Harlem Shake. Dench and Rissa found the event worthy of a celebratory kiss. Recovery took almost a full minute as Marlea took in everything around her.

When AJ's hand moved against her shoulder, she looked up at him. "This has got to feel good. You're going to get to stand on that podium and take gold. You're part of the U.S team now. Everything you ever wanted."

"Not quite everything, AJ. Will you be there with me?"

"Didn't I promise you that I would be?" AJ looked up to see Adrian Kessler walking among the group of reporters headed across the field, and he steered Marlea away from them.

"Yes, you did." Marlea nodded, looking down at their feet as they walked away. Funny, but she had forgotten all about her ankle. "And of course, you always keep your promises."

"And I'm going to keep this one, too. Right with you is exactly where I'm going to be, come hell or high water."

"There are some places where not even coaches are allowed to be."

"How about husbands?"

Surprised, Marlea's mouth dropped. "Whose husband are you talking about?" She stopped walking and her eyes followed the hand AJ pulled from his pocket.

"How about yours? If you'll have me."

"Have you?" Recognizing the small blue velvet jeweler's box for what it was, she answered her own question and his. "And a ring, too? Oh, yes." She blinked up at him, then had to laugh. "Rissa managed to keep *this* a secret? I can't believe it; you must have threatened her with death!"

"Something like that," AJ drawled.

"Whatever it took, it's worth it." Folding her hand into AJ's, Marlea laughed again. "I've got to admit, when you tripped me at the Peachtree Road Race, when you walked into that hospital room . . . I knew you had changed my life, but man, I never saw this coming. Falling for you is the best thing that ever happened to me, AJ."

"Me, too, Silk. Me, too."

Holding out her hand and letting him slide the gold band onto the third finger of her left hand, she could have sworn she felt its warmth and promise surge through her heart. When he leaned close to kiss her, she whispered, "I guess this means that I now officially have everything I ever wanted."

EPILOGUE

Eighteen Months Later

Rissa turned the band on her finger to a more comfortable place. She wasn't used to wearing it yet, but the eight carats glittered in the sun, and she knew she would grow more than comfortable with it.

Angling herself against the sun, she leaned on the knees of the man behind her and adjusted the sight on her binoculars until she could pick out the couple on the dirt track. She found them easily, and smiled. They looked good together—like a match made in heaven. It was obvious when they turned simultaneously and looked at each other and then focused on the distance together. They were matched and mated.

Oh, sure. You could call it a Kodak moment—the two of them caught in the sun and sharing a mutual glow of perfection—if you had a limited vocabulary and only a bit of imagination. But Marissa Yarborough Traylor had words for it.

My brother and his wife, just the way they were always meant to be.

Rissa tightened the focus on the binoculars again. At trackside, Marlea held her side, a stopwatch balanced on her belly. Facing into the wind, she screamed at the running kid to pick up his kick. AJ cupped his hands around his mouth and joined her yelling.

Enjoying the sight from her place in the stands, Rissa jumped when AJ turned suddenly, his image leaping through the magnifying lenses.

"What did he say?"

Rissa lowered the binoculars and listened. Stunned, she let the heavy binoculars fall to her breast and looked back at her new husband. "Dench, baby, he said, time . . . It's *time!*"

"What's happening?" Dench pulled the strapped binoculars and Rissa to him.

Arms flailing, struggling not to follow the strap around her neck when he stood, Rissa tugged the binoculars back from him. "Baby, you know she's pregnant; well, her water has just broken. Looks like that honeymoon baby is on the way!" Tangled between the bleacher seats, Dench pulled Rissa to her feet, and they rushed from the stands.

On the field, a richly pregnant Marlea was already waddling toward AJ's jeep. Solicitous and frantic, he hurried behind her.

Jogging from the stands, not wanting to miss anything, Rissa swatted at her silly man as she managed to pull her cellphone from her pocket. Still running, she hit speed dial and was rewarded by a brief ring, followed by a warm greeting. "Mom? Have you got film in that old camera of yours?"

"Sure and again, good morning to you, too," her mother said. "You know I always keep film and flash around for . . . why?"

"You know how you always wanted a picture of that first grandchild? Well, you're about to get one of the best shots of your life! But you've got to hurry, 'cause we're headed straight to the hospital."

Her mother screamed and Rissa laughed. "Don't worry, Mom. AJ's driving. Marlea's not running—this time."

From *The Atlanta Journal-Constitution*:

USTAF and International Paralympic 400-meter gold medal winner Marlea Kellogg and husband, recent NFL Hall of Fame inductee AJ Yarborough, have been named to the President's Council On Fitness. The couple designed and will head the Southeastern region of Project ABLE, a pilot program designed to support "other-abled" athletes in sport, fitness, and wellness careers.

Project ABLE, based in Atlanta, will combine the efforts of Morehouse Medical School, Georgia State University, Emory University, Georgia Technical Institute, the National Football League, and the United States Track and Field Association. A long-time dream of Kellogg and Yarborough, both career athletes, Project ABLE will provide housing, training, support activities, and funding for athletes.

Parents of a healthy and active two-year-old son, Jabari, and ten-month-old daughter, Nia, Kellogg and Yarborough lead very busy lives. A special education teacher for the Runyon School, Kellogg continues to actively support USTAFA and Paralympic-sanctioned events. Yarborough operates a successful physical therapy practice and participates in ongoing NFL-sponsored youth programs.

Yarborough says that Project ABLE is a challenge, destined to make dreams come true.

"But if you have a dream," Kellogg adds, "you have to be willing to run for it."

AUTHOR'S NOTE

Dear Readers,

Thank you more than words can say for your ongoing support of my work and your faith in the stories I love to tell. This one was a long time coming but it was a labor of love and I hope you found it worth the wait. Marlea and AJ have rested in my heart and mind for quite a while and I hope you've enjoyed sharing the workout these two give to the adventure of love.

Life is not always easy and, as Marlea would be quick to tell you, it certainly doesn't always go the way we've planned. On the other hand, AJ would tell you that one of the best things in life is the chance to change and grow.

I'm wishing you well, and hope that the reading blesses you as much as the writing does me.

Gail McFarland
P.O. Box 56782
Atlanta, GA 30343
The_fitwryter@Yahoo.Com
Visit my website: "http://fitwryter.tripod.com

ABOUT THE AUTHOR

Gail McFarland was born and raised in Cleveland, Ohio. She attended Cleveland State University where she was psychology major with a special ed. Minor. She is a certified aerobics and American Red Cross CPR/AED/First Aid Instructor. Her hobbies include reading writing, yoga, Pilates, swimming, cycling, and enjoying far too many of Atlanta's wonderful restaurants. She works in wellness/fitness as an Activities and Program Director and she also teaches aerobics. She now lives in Atlanta, Georgia and loves it!

Coming in June from Genesis Press:

Africa Fine's *Looking for Lily*

CHAPTER 1

"Cleveland is home, Ernestine."

The first thing I noticed when I walked into the tall, narrow house was the smell. It was the scent of the discarded past: yellowed photographs, thirty-year-old furniture and White Shoulders perfume, which no one born this side of 1960 wears. Aunt Gillian has lived here forever, my entire life and longer. My childhood and adolescence were spent in this echoing house in East Cleveland, with its ancient hard candies set in rust-colored ceramic bowls on the coffee table and its cream-colored furniture that was not meant to be sat upon. I set down the boxes I carried and waited for my friend Jack to bring in the rest. We were packing up Aunt Gillian's things and saying good-bye to an era.

Aunt Gillian raised me after my parents died when I was just six months old. She never thought twice about adopting her sister's child, but I have to say that neither of us was ever quite what the other wanted. While the mothers of my classmates all had jobs or were going to night school to get their degrees, Aunt Gillian worked nights and took care of me during the day. She believed it would take her undivided attention to mold me into her image.

"Ernestine, you have to stop climbing trees and playing ball with those boys. A lady doesn't do those things," she would say.

At eight years old, I already knew two things for sure: I hated my name, and I didn't want to be a lady.

"Call me Tina."

My aunt put her hands on her hips and shook her head.

"Your mother named you Ernestine, and that is what I will call you."

Even then, I realized that I could never win a verbal argument with her. Subversion was the only way to get my way. So I agreed to wear the frilly dresses to school. Once I arrived, I went straight to the bathroom to change into the jeans and t-shirt I smuggled in my backpack. I spent all of recess playing kickball with the boys. And I demanded that all my teachers and friends call me Tina.

I remember coming home from elementary school to find my aunt engrossed in the details of cooking something I would refuse to eat. I may have been the youngest vegetarian in the history of Cleveland. A PBS documentary on slaughterhouses, watched with secret relish, made me pity the poor pigs whose carcasses populated our dinner plates. Around that same time, I noticed the hives and throat-swelling that visited me whenever I ate fish. I told my fifth-grade teacher, who thought I might be allergic to seafood. She suggested I see a doctor, but Aunt Gillian scoffed at this notion.

"All that allergy business is just a way for you to get out of eating the perfectly good food I cook for you."

The next night, she berated me until I gave in and ate a piece of cod. I don't remember whether she apologized after I swelled up with hives the size of golf balls, but I think she felt bad for me afterwards. She didn't think she was *wrong*, of course. She contends to this day that there is no such thing as a food allergy. She had been a nurse before I was born, so you'd think she would have believed the physical evidence of my allergies. Even science couldn't disabuse Aunt Gillian of her convictions.

Throughout my childhood, she cooked elaborate, gourmet-quality meals that were flawless in both presentation and nutritional value. Her meals always had names that made them sound appealing. It was never just pasta; instead, we had linguine with shrimp and lemon oil. Instead of baked chicken, we ate chicken vesuvio. Once, I looked in one of her cookbooks and requested home-baked macaroni and cheese, with almond blueberry popovers for dessert. She said it was too fattening and instead set a plate of iceberg with summer tomatoes in front of me.

I refused to eat what she cooked because I was a vegetarian, because I was allergic, because I was spiteful. It depended on the day.

"You spend more time pushing your food around than eating," she said one night. "You'd think you'd be as thin as a stick."

I shrugged my chubby shoulders. I was already in the early stages of what would become a life-long struggle with obesity. I might have starved to death if it wasn't for the Twinkies and Moon Pies I shoveled into my mouth just before falling asleep each night. Not to mention the taco boats and Starburst candy I bought in the school cafeteria after I'd sold my lunch to a girl named Gretchen, who liked turkey on whole wheat, hold the cheese, hold the mayo.

Aunt Gillian had no first-hand knowledge of Gretchen, taco boats and Moon Pies, but she knew something was up. At the dinner table, we were in silent agreement: I was in no danger of starvation.

But her days of cooking were long gone. When Aunt Gillian turned sixty, she announced that she was old enough to let other people do the cooking, although I had not asked about this particular topic. Now she was almost seventy, and I hadn't lived in Cleveland since I left for college. I was settled in South Florida, far enough away so my aunt couldn't run my life, but also too far for me to help her. The older she got, the more guilt I felt, but she wouldn't let me arrange for household help. Instead, she paid local girls to run to the store for her to buy toiletries and pick up her takeout dinners. She told me that I was not to worry about her, that she had taken care of herself all her life and she didn't intend to stop any time soon. When I came from West Palm Beach to visit her two or three times a year, I took her out to dinner but I never stayed in my old room. I couldn't face the reminders of childhood, and my aunt didn't seem to mind me staying at hotels. When I visited her at home, she would rush me out of the house before I could take in the peeling paint that the on the walls and the cobwebs in the corners.

This year, I had rescheduled my spring visit to Cleveland to attend a conference. As an associate professor of English at Mizner University, I was obligated to present papers at conferences, and this was not one I could skip. So I came to see Aunt Gillian after the spring semester, at the end of May.

My aunt was expecting me, but I wasn't expecting what I saw when I got there. I was going to use my key, but the front door was already unlocked and ajar. I found her sitting on the living room floor, dazed and disoriented, surrounded by four or five people I had never seen before. Although the air conditioning was going full blast, the air in the house was moist and still. Summer had come early to Ohio, and by late May there had already been several ninety-degree days. The day I found Aunt Gillian on the floor—the last day, as it turned out, that she spent on her own—was another scorcher. The air was hazy with impending rain showers, and it was only eleven o'clock in the morning.

I had expected a relaxed day spent catching up with my aunt. Although we had never seen eye to eye on what was most important to us both, I was looking forward to seeing her. I was single, often alone, with my career and Jack as mild comforts. I wondered if I'd ever have a husband and children of my own, and I wanted to feel a family connection, even if it was with Aunt Gillian.

But when I arrived at her house, the ambulance had already been called, and my day—my life—was about to change.

The people standing around, who identified themselves as neighbors, told me that Aunt Gillian had blacked out and fallen. Later, I wished I had asked more questions —questions like who they were and why they were all just standing around her instead of helping. I rushed over to her and said a small prayer, thanking God or fate or whatever it was that sent me to her house on this day.

I found out later at Holy Cross Hospital that it wasn't first the time she had fallen. My aunt was, at best, taciturn. At worst, she was completely withholding. She didn't like to talk about herself or the past. It wasn't just that she didn't like it. She refused to do it, no matter how many questions I asked, no matter how much I claimed it was my right to know. She insisted on looking forward, not backward, and she never seemed to consider the damage that her secrecy could do.

So it wasn't a surprise to me that I didn't know about her falls. She was the most independent, self-sufficient person I had ever known. If she had boyfriends, I never knew about them. Her women friends were acquaintances rather than confidantes, which made sense, since Aunt Gillian confided nothing. She didn't seem to need anyone. Not even me, and we were each other's only family.

But at the hospital, painkillers loosened her tongue. She admitted that she had been blacking out and falling often, and by the tired tone of her voice I could tell that she had come to terms with the fact that she could no longer maintain her total independence. It was a bitter admission from a woman who'd prided herself on self-sufficiency for so many years. But she was also smart, and she knew that the next fall might result in something way worse than a bruised shoulder and a damaged ego.

"I know I can't live on my own anymore," she said in a small voice. She had been sleeping since we arrived at the hospital and I was sitting next to her bed, watching and waiting, preparing myself for a fight that never happened. I never thought she would agree to leave her home, the house she had lived in since she was little more than a teenager. I never thought she would welcome my interference in her life because she never had before. After years of pushing away my concerns, she now looked happy to see me. Thank God for Percocet.

"Where do you want to go, Aunt Gillian? What do you want to do?"

She turned and looked out the window, where I could see Lake Erie far to the west. The hospital was the best in the city, offering everything a patient could want except the guarantee of health. The walls were painted in pastels and every corner was clean, but the smell of bleach and Lysol were constant reminders of illness. Aunt Gillian was quite well off, having lived many years on her salary as a nurse. After retiring from nursing, she made savvy investments using money whose source was always a mystery to me. That and Social Security made her economically comfortable.

"I don't want to be any trouble," she said. "I'm sure I can hire someone to come to the house once in a while."

I pictured those neighbors who'd been in her house when I arrived. Who would check up on her? I lived hundreds of miles away. What if she fell again, or worse? I knew it was my responsibility to figure out a solution. The only one that seemed viable was also the one that was the most difficult.

"You'll come live with me," I said, my voice firm even though I hadn't even thought the whole thing through in any rational way.

"In Florida?"

She looked at me, doubtful. She had only been to Florida once, last Christmas, and she had complained most of the time. She'd lived in Cleveland since 1956, and I'd never once heard her talk of moving. To me, Cleveland was the worst of what America had to offer: de facto segregation, a bad economy, racial strife and a staid Midwestern attitude. No Rock and Roll Hall of Fame, sports arena or lake cruise was going to make me see Cleveland as a great place to be.

There was a generational disconnect as well. For Aunt Gillian, home was created by circumstance, by responsibility, by convenience. You didn't worry about whether home made you happy. She scoffed at such ideas.

"Home just is. You don't choose it," she always said.

I knew other older people who seemed to think the same way. They lived their lives in places they didn't love, just because. They never considered moving to try to find someplace better. People my age seemed to believe that home was indeed a choice, and one that needed to be made without consideration of obligation. I would never live somewhere just because I had ended up there by accident. When I told this to Aunt Gillian, she frowned.

"When you have a family to care for, you can't think only of yourself."

When I was a teenager, it seemed to me that thinking of herself is how Aunt Gillian had always operated, but I knew better than to ever say that her.

To Aunt Gillian, who'd followed her ex-husband here from Howard University, Cleveland was more home than her native Baltimore. She'd spent most of her life here. I had spent most of my life trying to get away.

"Maybe you could move back home."

There was a long pause after she said this. We both took time to digest how difficult it was for her to ask this of me. Aunt Gillian had never asked me anything in her life. She demanded, cajoled, threatened. To now be in a position to *ask* showed me just how serious the situation was.

I shook my head. "I have a good position teaching at the university, and faculty positions are not easy to come by, not in this economy." And I hate Cleveland, I wanted to add but didn't.

"Cleveland is home, Ernestine."

Aunt Gillian had never been one to give up on an argument, especially not one as important as this. She was still the only person who ever called me Ernestine.

But she was weak, and her voice shook when she spoke.

It hit me then. Aunt Gillian was getting old.

Our discussion continued for a few days, during which my arguments grew stronger and hers weakened. I realized that she wanted to come to Florida, but it was impossible for her to say so. Her pride, while wounded, wouldn't allow it.

On her third day in the hospital, she was due to be released. Her doctor was the one who gave us the means to make the final decision.

"Mrs. Jones, your head is fine and you were lucky not to break anything. But I don't want you living alone anymore. It's not safe."

I was sitting in a chair by the window as he spoke, looking out at the gray skies, watching the heat make waves in the air above the pavement, wishing I were back in Florida. I looked over at my aunt. Her shoulders slumped.

She didn't answer the doctor, just nodded. He looked at me for a moment, and then smiled as he turned to leave.

"I'm sure your niece will take excellent care of you, Mrs. Jones. You're very lucky."

I almost laughed. This was the first time Aunt Gillian had ever been told she was lucky to have me.

"What about my house?" she asked after the doctor left.

"We'll close it up for now and decide what to do about it later."

"I don't want to be any trouble," she said, still proud. "I can take care of myself, no matter what that doctor says."

I shook my head. "Of course it's no trouble. We're family."

Here I was a week later, standing in Aunt Gillian's house, ready to clear out her things in preparation for her move to Florida. In my more forgiving moments I looked up to my aunt, who, all on her own, had supported herself—and then me—after her ex-husband, Jeremiah, left her years before I was born. When I was feeling loving, I saw toughness in her, instead of a mean spirit. And I could sometimes see humor in the biting jokes about my weight and my hair. I tended to take things too personally. On nights when sleep was elusive, I saw fragility in my aunt's insistence on independence. Now that she needed me, I couldn't walk away.

Jack, who volunteered to fly to Cleveland to help us pack up, did not think moving Aunt Gillian into my house was a good idea.

"You don't want to put her in an assisted-living facility?" he had asked when I called him to tell him that my aunt was moving to Florida. I'd just relayed all that had happened, and he asked patient questions.

"A nursing home." I said this as if the idea had never occurred to me, although it had over the past few days. I tried, but I couldn't picture myself taking Aunt Gillian to a *facility*.

"It'll work out," I told him.

There was long pause.

"You could convert the downstairs office into a bedroom for her so she doesn't have to climb the stairs," he said. I could hear the smile in his voice, and I knew what that smile meant. It meant that he would help me even though he was sure I was doing the wrong thing.

"As long as you do the converting."

But I already knew that he would help, even do most of the work. Jack and I had known each other for five years, and I had grown to depend on him. The role fit him—he was a caretaker, a problem-solver. Although my life seemed pretty together on the outside, I had a lot of problems that needed to be solved. Struggles with weight, concerns about my teaching career, worries that I would never have a family of my own, a man of my own to take care of me the way Jack did. When we first met, I thought Jack might be that person. I hoped he would be that person. But things never worked out between us, whether it was because of my own insecurities or his lack of interest. I only admitted to myself, on nights when I was feeling especially lonely, that I still had feelings for Jack. But I was convinced that he saw me as just a friend, so I pretended to feel the same.

On nights when I was feeling cynical and bitter, I thought that I was just another project for Jack. Engineers live to fix things, to build things up, to make them better. Why wouldn't the same apply to people? Maybe I was broken.

2008 Reprint Mass Market Titles
January

Cautious Heart
Cheris F. Hodges
ISBN-13: 978-1-58571-301-1
ISBN-10: 1-58571-301-5
$6.99

Suddenly You
Crystal Hubbard
ISBN-13: 978-1-58571-302-8
ISBN-10: 1-58571-302-3
$6.99

February

Passion
T. T. Henderson
ISBN-13: 978-1-58571-303-5
ISBN-10: 1-58571-303-1
$6.99

Whispers in the Sand
LaFlorya Gauthier
ISBN-13: 978-1-58571-304-2
ISBN-10: 1-58571-304-x
$6.99

March

Life Is Never As It Seems
J. J. Michael
ISBN-13: 978-1-58571-305-9
ISBN-10: 1-58571-305-8
$6.99

Beyond the Rapture
Beverly Clark
ISBN-13: 978-1-58571-306-6
ISBN-10: 1-58571-306-6
$6.99

April

A Heart's Awakening
Veronica Parker
ISBN-13: 978-1-58571-307-3
ISBN-10: 1-58571-307-4
$6.99

Breeze
Robin Lynette Hampton
ISBN-13: 978-1-58571-308-0
ISBN-10: 1-58571-308-2
$6.99

May

I'll Be Your Shelter
Giselle Carmichael
ISBN-13: 978-1-58571-309-7
ISBN-10: 1-58571-309-0
$6.99

Careless Whispers
Rochelle Alers
ISBN-13: 978-1-58571-310-3
ISBN-10: 1-58571-310-4
$6.99

June

Sin
Crystal Rhodes
ISBN-13: 978-1-58571-311-0
ISBN-10: 1-58571-311-2
$6.99

Dark Storm Rising
Chinelu Moore
ISBN-13: 978-1-58571-312-7
ISBN-10: I-58571-312-0
$6.99

2008 Reprint Mass Market Titles (continued)

July

Object of His Desire
A.C. Arthur
ISBN-13: 978-1-58571-313-4
ISBN-10: 1-58571-313-9
$6.99

Angel's Paradise
Janice Angelique
ISBN-13: 978-1-58571-314-1
ISBN-10: 1-58571-314-7
$6.99

August

Unbreak My Heart
Dar Tomlinson
ISBN-13: 978-1-58571-315-8
ISBN-10: 1-58571-315-5
$6.99

All I Ask
Barbara Keaton
ISBN-13: 978-1-58571-316-5
ISBN-10: 1-58571-316-3
$6.99

September

Icie
Pamela Leigh Starr
ISBN-13: 978-1-58571-275-5
ISBN-10: 1-58571-275-2
$6.99

At Last
Lisa Riley
ISBN-13: 978-1-58571-276-2
ISBN-10: 1-58571-276-0
$6.99

October

Everlastin' Love
Gay G. Gunn
ISBN-13: 978-1-58571-277-9
ISBN-10: 1-58571-277-9
$6.99

Three Wishes
Seressia Glass
ISBN-13: 978-1-58571-278-6
ISBN-10: 1-58571-278-7
$6.99

November

Yesterday Is Gone
Beverly Clark
ISBN-13: 978-1-58571-279-3
ISBN-10: 1-58571-279-5
$6.99

Again My Love
Kayla Perrin
ISBN-13: 978-1-58571-280-9
ISBN-10: 1-58571-280-9
$6.99

December

Office Policy
A.C. Arthur
ISBN-13: 978-1-58571-281-6
ISBN-10: 1-58571-281-7
$6.99

Rendezvous With Fate
Jeanne Sumerix
ISBN-13: 978-1-58571-283-3
ISBN-10: 1-58571-283-3
$6.99

2008 New Mass Market Titles

January

Where I Want To Be
Maryam Diaab
ISBN-13: 978-1-58571-268-7
ISBN-10: 1-58571-268-X
$6.99

Never Say Never
Michele Cameron
ISBN-13: 978-1-58571-269-4
ISBN-10: 1-58571-269-8
$6.99

February

Stolen Memories
Michele Sudler
ISBN-13: 978-1-58571-270-0
ISBN-10: 1-58571-270-1
$6.99

Dawn's Harbor
Kymberly Hunt
ISBN-13: 978-1-58571-271-7
ISBN-10: 1-58571-271-X
$6.99

March

Undying Love
Renee Alexis
ISBN-13: 978-1-58571-272-4
ISBN-10: 1-58571-272-8
$6.99

Blame It On Paradise
Crystal Hubbard
ISBN-13: 978-1-58571-273-1
ISBN-10: 1-58571-273-6
$6.99

April

When A Man Loves A Woman
La Connie Taylor-Jones
ISBN-13: 978-1-58571-274-8
ISBN-10: 1-58571-274-4
$6.99

Choices
Tammy Williams
ISBN-13: 978-1-58571-300-4
ISBN-10: 1-58571-300-7
$6.99

May

Dream Runner
Gail McFarland
ISBN-13: 978-1-58571-317-2
ISBN-10: 1-58571-317-1
$6.99

Southern Fried Standards
S.R. Maddox
ISBN-13: 978-1-58571-318-9
ISBN-10: 1-58571-318-X
$6.99

June

Looking for Lily
Africa Fine
ISBN-13: 978-1-58571-319-6
ISBN-10: 1-58571-319-8
$6.99

Bliss, Inc.
Chamein Canton
ISBN-13: 978-1-58571-325-7
ISBN-10: 1-58571-325-2
$6.99

2008 New Mass Market Titles (continued)

July

Love's Secrets
Yolanda McVey
ISBN-13: 978-1-58571-321-9
ISBN-10: 1-58571-321-X
$6.99

Things Forbidden
Maryam Diaab
ISBN-13: 978-1-58571-327-1
ISBN-10: 1-58571-327-9
$6.99

August

Storm
Pamela Leigh Starr
ISBN-13: 978-1-58571-323-3
ISBN-10: 1-58571-323-6
$6.99

Passion's Furies
AlTonya Washington
ISBN-13: 978-1-58571-324-0
ISBN-10: 1-58571-324-4
$6.99

September

Three Doors Down
Michele Sudler
ISBN-13: 978-1-58571-332-5
ISBN-10: 1-58571-332-5
$6.99

Mr Fix-It
Crystal Hubbard
ISBN-13: 978-1-58571-326-4
ISBN-10: 1-58571-326-0
$6.99

October

Moments of Clarity
Michele Cameron
ISBN-13: 978-1-58571-330-1
ISBN-10: 1-58571-330-9
$6.99

Lady Preacher
K.T. Richey
ISBN-13: 978-1-58571-333-2
ISBN-10: 1-58571-333-3
$6.99

November

This Life Isn't Perfect Holla
Sandra Foy
ISBN: 978-1-58571-331-8
ISBN-10: 1-58571-331-7
$6.99

Promises Made
Bernice Layton
ISBN-13: 978-1-58571-334-9
ISBN-10: 1-58571-334-1
$6.99

December

A Voice Behind Thunder
Carrie Elizabeth Greene
ISBN-13: 978-1-58571-329-5
ISBN-10: 1-58571-329-5
$6.99

The More Things Change
Chamein Canton
ISBN-13: 978-1-58571-328-8
ISBN-10: 1-58571-328-7
$6.99

Other Genesis Press, Inc. Titles

A Dangerous Deception	J.M. Jeffries	$8.95
A Dangerous Love	J.M. Jeffries	$8.95
A Dangerous Obsession	J.M. Jeffries	$8.95
A Drummer's Beat to Mend	Kei Swanson	$9.95
A Happy Life	Charlotte Harris	$9.95
A Heart's Awakening	Veronica Parker	$9.95
A Lark on the Wing	Phyliss Hamilton	$9.95
A Love of Her Own	Cheris F. Hodges	$9.95
A Love to Cherish	Beverly Clark	$8.95
A Risk of Rain	Dar Tomlinson	$8.95
A Taste of Temptation	Reneé Alexis	$9.95
A Twist of Fate	Beverly Clark	$8.95
A Will to Love	Angie Daniels	$9.95
Acquisitions	Kimberley White	$8.95
Across	Carol Payne	$12.95
After the Vows	Leslie Esdaile	$10.95
(Summer Anthology)	T.T. Henderson	
	Jacqueline Thomas	
Again My Love	Kayla Perrin	$10.95
Against the Wind	Gwynne Forster	$8.95
All I Ask	Barbara Keaton	$8.95
Always You	Crystal Hubbard	$6.99
Ambrosia	T.T. Henderson	$8.95
An Unfinished Love Affair	Barbara Keaton	$8.95
And Then Came You	Dorothy Elizabeth Love	$8.95
Angel's Paradise	Janice Angelique	$9.95
At Last	Lisa G. Riley	$8.95
Best of Friends	Natalie Dunbar	$8.95
Beyond the Rapture	Beverly Clark	$9.95

Other Genesis Press, Inc. Titles (continued)

Blaze	Barbara Keaton	$9.95
Blood Lust	J. M. Jeffries	$9.95
Blood Seduction	J.M. Jeffries	$9.95
Bodyguard	Andrea Jackson	$9.95
Boss of Me	Diana Nyad	$8.95
Bound by Love	Beverly Clark	$8.95
Breeze	Robin Hampton Allen	$10.95
Broken	Dar Tomlinson	$24.95
By Design	Barbara Keaton	$8.95
Cajun Heat	Charlene Berry	$8.95
Careless Whispers	Rochelle Alers	$8.95
Cats & Other Tales	Marilyn Wagner	$8.95
Caught in a Trap	Andre Michelle	$8.95
Caught Up In the Rapture	Lisa G. Riley	$9.95
Cautious Heart	Cheris F Hodges	$8.95
Chances	Pamela Leigh Starr	$8.95
Cherish the Flame	Beverly Clark	$8.95
Class Reunion	Irma Jenkins/ John Brown	$12.95
Code Name: Diva	J.M. Jeffries	$9.95
Conquering Dr. Wexler's Heart	Kimberley White	$9.95
Corporate Seduction	A.C. Arthur	$9.95
Crossing Paths, Tempting Memories	Dorothy Elizabeth Love	$9.95
Crush	Crystal Hubbard	$9.95
Cypress Whisperings	Phyllis Hamilton	$8.95
Dark Embrace	Crystal Wilson Harris	$8.95
Dark Storm Rising	Chinelu Moore	$10.95

Other Genesis Press, Inc. Titles (continued)

Daughter of the Wind	Joan Xian	$8.95
Deadly Sacrifice	Jack Kean	$22.95
Designer Passion	Dar Tomlinson	$8.95
	Diana Richeaux	
Do Over	Celya Bowers	$9.95
Dreamtective	Liz Swados	$5.95
Ebony Angel	Deatri King-Bey	$9.95
Ebony Butterfly II	Delilah Dawson	$14.95
Echoes of Yesterday	Beverly Clark	$9.95
Eden's Garden	Elizabeth Rose	$8.95
Eve's Prescription	Edwina Martin Arnold	$8.95
Everlastin' Love	Gay G. Gunn	$8.95
Everlasting Moments	Dorothy Elizabeth Love	$8.95
Everything and More	Sinclair Lebeau	$8.95
Everything but Love	Natalie Dunbar	$8.95
Falling	Natalie Dunbar	$9.95
Fate	Pamela Leigh Starr	$8.95
Finding Isabella	A.J. Garrotto	$8.95
Forbidden Quest	Dar Tomlinson	$10.95
Forever Love	Wanda Y. Thomas	$8.95
From the Ashes	Kathleen Suzanne	$8.95
	Jeanne Sumerix	
Gentle Yearning	Rochelle Alers	$10.95
Glory of Love	Sinclair LeBeau	$10.95
Go Gentle into that Good Night	Malcom Boyd	$12.95
Goldengroove	Mary Beth Craft	$16.95
Groove, Bang, and Jive	Steve Cannon	$8.99
Hand in Glove	Andrea Jackson	$9.95

Other Genesis Press, Inc. Titles (continued)

Hard to Love	Kimberley White	$9.95
Hart & Soul	Angie Daniels	$8.95
Heart of the Phoenix	A.C. Arthur	$9.95
Heartbeat	Stephanie Bedwell-Grime	$8.95
Hearts Remember	M. Loui Quezada	$8.95
Hidden Memories	Robin Allen	$10.95
Higher Ground	Leah Latimer	$19.95
Hitler, the War, and the Pope	Ronald Rychlak	$26.95
How to Write a Romance	Kathryn Falk	$18.95
I Married a Reclining Chair	Lisa M. Fuhs	$8.95
I'll Be Your Shelter	Giselle Carmichael	$8.95
I'll Paint a Sun	A.J. Garrotto	$9.95
Icie	Pamela Leigh Starr	$8.95
Illusions	Pamela Leigh Starr	$8.95
Indigo After Dark Vol. I	Nia Dixon/Angelique	$10.95
Indigo After Dark Vol. II	Dolores Bundy/ Cole Riley	$10.95
Indigo After Dark Vol. III	Montana Blue/ Coco Morena	$10.95
Indigo After Dark Vol. IV	Cassandra Colt/	$14.95
Indigo After Dark Vol. V	Delilah Dawson	$14.95
Indiscretions	Donna Hill	$8.95
Intentional Mistakes	Michele Sudler	$9.95
Interlude	Donna Hill	$8.95
Intimate Intentions	Angie Daniels	$8.95
It's Not Over Yet	J.J. Michael	$9.95
Jolie's Surrender	Edwina Martin-Arnold	$8.95
Kiss or Keep	Debra Phillips	$8.95
Lace	Giselle Carmichael	$9.95

Other Genesis Press, Inc. Titles (continued)

Other Genesis Press, Inc. Titles (continued)

Other Genesis Press, Inc. Titles (continued)

Revelations	Cheris F. Hodges	$8.95
Rivers of the Soul	Leslie Esdaile	$8.95
Rocky Mountain Romance	Kathleen Suzanne	$8.95
Rooms of the Heart	Donna Hill	$8.95
Rough on Rats and Tough on Cats	Chris Parker	$12.95
Secret Library Vol. 1	Nina Sheridan	$18.95
Secret Library Vol. 2	Cassandra Colt	$8.95
Secret Thunder	Annetta P. Lee	$9.95
Shades of Brown	Denise Becker	$8.95
Shades of Desire	Monica White	$8.95
Shadows in the Moonlight	Jeanne Sumerix	$8.95
Sin	Crystal Rhodes	$8.95
Small Whispers	Annetta P. Lee	$6.99
So Amazing	Sinclair LeBeau	$8.95
Somebody's Someone	Sinclair LeBeau	$8.95
Someone to Love	Alicia Wiggins	$8.95
Song in the Park	Martin Brant	$15.95
Soul Eyes	Wayne L. Wilson	$12.95
Soul to Soul	Donna Hill	$8.95
Southern Comfort	J.M. Jeffries	$8.95
Still the Storm	Sharon Robinson	$8.95
Still Waters Run Deep	Leslie Esdaile	$8.95
Stolen Kisses	Dominiqua Douglas	$9.95
Stories to Excite You	Anna Forrest/Divine	$14.95
Subtle Secrets	Wanda Y. Thomas	$8.95
Suddenly You	Crystal Hubbard	$9.95
Sweet Repercussions	Kimberley White	$9.95
Sweet Sensations	Gwendolyn Bolton	$9.95

Other Genesis Press, Inc. Titles (continued)

Sweet Tomorrows	Kimberly White	$8.95
Taken by You	Dorothy Elizabeth Love	$9.95
Tattooed Tears	T. T. Henderson	$8.95
The Color Line	Lizzette Grayson Carter	$9.95
The Color of Trouble	Dyanne Davis	$8.95
The Disappearance of Allison Jones	Kayla Perrin	$5.95
The Fires Within	Beverly Clark	$9.95
The Foursome	Celya Bowers	$6.99
The Honey Dipper's Legacy	Pannell-Allen	$14.95
The Joker's Love Tune	Sidney Rickman	$15.95
The Little Pretender	Barbara Cartland	$10.95
The Love We Had	Natalie Dunbar	$8.95
The Man Who Could Fly	Bob & Milana Beamon	$18.95
The Missing Link	Charlyne Dickerson	$8.95
The Mission	Pamela Leigh Starr	$6.99
The Perfect Frame	Beverly Clark	$9.95
The Price of Love	Sinclair LeBeau	$8.95
The Smoking Life	Ilene Barth	$29.95
The Words of the Pitcher	Kei Swanson	$8.95
Three Wishes	Seressia Glass	$8.95
Ties That Bind	Kathleen Suzanne	$8.95
Tiger Woods	Libby Hughes	$5.95
Time is of the Essence	Angie Daniels	$9.95
Timeless Devotion	Bella McFarland	$9.95
Tomorrow's Promise	Leslie Esdaile	$8.95
Truly Inseparable	Wanda Y. Thomas	$8.95
Two Sides to Every Story	Dyanne Davis	$9.95
Unbreak My Heart	Dar Tomlinson	$8.95

Other Genesis Press, Inc. Titles (continued)

ESCAPE WITH INDIGO !!!!

Join Indigo Book Club©
It's simple, easy and secure.

Sign up and receive the new
releases
every month + Free shipping
and
20% off the cover price.

Go online to www.genesis-
press.com and click on Bookclub
or
call 1-888-INDIGO-1

Order Form

Mail to: Genesis Press, Inc.
P.O. Box 101
Columbus, MS 39703

Name _____
Address _____
City/State _____ Zip _____
Telephone _____

Ship to (if different from above)
Name _____
Address _____
City/State _____ Zip _____
Telephone _____

Credit Card Information
Credit Card # _____ ☐ Visa   ☐ Mastercard
Expiration Date (mm/yy) _____ ☐ AmEx   ☐ Discover

Qty.	Author	Title	Price	Total

Use this order form, or call 1-888-INDIGO-1	**Total for books** _____ **Shipping and handling:** $5 first two books, $1 each additional book _____ **Total S & H** _____ **Total amount enclosed** _____ *Mississippi residents add 7% sales tax*